SHARP MINDS

"Have a seat, monsieur," snapped Arianna, indicating the lone stool at one end of the steel-scarred length of maple. She set aside the fillet blade and took up a paring knife. "While I peel and dice the carrots."

"No amanita mushrooms?" he said softly.

The reference to the deadly poisonous species took her aback. *Good God, did the man actually have a sense of humor?*

Arianna grunted in reply. "Zees may be a joke to you, sir, but it eez my reputation at stake."

"Not to speak of your life."

She felt herself blanch, but remained silent.

Perching a hip on the stool, Saybrook watched her scoop up a handful of the vegetables and begin trimming off the tops. "You have the hands of an artist, Monsieur Alphonse," he remarked, shifting his gaze to the heavy steel blades and graters arrayed around him and then back again. "One would not expect such fine-boned fingers to wield the tools of your trade with quite so much skill."

Her throat seized and Arianna didn't dare try to speak, fearing a feminine squeak would give her away. At this distance, the darkness of his eyes appeared due to the telltale dilation of his pupils—Mr. De Quincy clearly imbibed a goodly amount of laudanum to ease his pain. But apparently the drug had not dulled the sharpness of his wits.

She must not make the mistake of underestimating him. She had made too many errors already.

SWEET
REVENGE

A LADY ARIANNA REGENCY MYSTERY

ANDREA PENROSE

AN OBSIDIAN MYSTERY

OBSIDIAN
Published by New American Library, a division of
Penguin Group (USA) Inc., 375 Hudson Street,
New York, New York 10014, USA

Penguin Group (Canada), 90 Eglinton Avenue East, Suite 700, Toronto,
Ontario M4P 2Y3, Canada (a division of Pearson Penguin Canada Inc.)
Penguin Books Ltd., 80 Strand, London WC2R 0RL, England
Penguin Ireland, 25 St. Stephen's Green, Dublin 2,
Ireland (a division of Penguin Books Ltd.)
Penguin Group (Australia), 250 Camberwell Road, Camberwell, Victoria 3124,
Australia (a division of Pearson Australia Group Pty. Ltd.)
Penguin Books India Pvt. Ltd., 11 Community Centre, Panchsheel Park,
New Delhi - 110 017, India
Penguin Group (NZ), 67 Apollo Drive, Rosedale, North Shore 0632,
New Zealand (a division of Pearson New Zealand Ltd.)
Penguin Books (South Africa) (Pty.) Ltd., 24 Sturdee Avenue,
Rosebank, Johannesburg 2196, South Africa

Penguin Books Ltd., Registered Offices:
80 Strand, London WC2R 0RL, England

First published by Obsidian, an imprint of New American Library,
a division of Penguin Group (USA) Inc.

First Printing, April 2011
10 9 8 7 6 5 4 3 2 1

for John R. Ettinger
Saybrook rules!

ACKNOWLEDGMENTS

A book is much like one of Lady Arianna's delectable chocolate confections—it requires the perfect ingredients, much chopping and stirring, followed by carefully calibrated heat to emerge from the oven with just the right crunch and texture.

Several "chefs" have added their expertise to my own efforts and I wish to raise a cooking spoon in salute!

Gail Fortune, my agent extraordinaire, deserves much credit for helping me concoct the mixture of chocolate and mystery. I'm incredibly "fortunate" to be working with such an amazing talent. . . .

John R. Ettinger, a dear friend and brilliant intellect (honestly, who else would admit to having a "favorite" mathematician!), was kind enough to spend hours giving me a crash course in basic economic theory. Any errors in logic are the fault of the chardonnay and my own feeble brain. . . .

Sandy Harding, my wonderful editor, offered much sage advice in polishing the final manuscript, and patiently helped me untangle myself from various plot twists.

To all of you, I am profoundly grateful.

"Sweet is revenge—especially to women. . . ."

—George Gordon Byron
DON JUAN (CANTO I, ST. 124)

1

From the chocolate notebooks of Dona Maria Castellano

How fascinating! I recently discovered an old Spanish missionary's journal in a Madrid bookstore and found a number of references to chocolate among his writings. According to him, ancient Aztec legend has it that the cacao tree was brought to Earth by their god Quetzalcoatl, who descended from heaven on the beam of a morning star after stealing the precious plant from paradise. No wonder that the spicy beverage made from its beans was called the Drink of the Emperor. It is said that this xocoatl or chocolatl was so revered that it was served in golden goblets that were thrown away after one use. . . .

Rum Truffles

⅔ cup heavy cream
8 ounces 60% dark chocolate
2½ tablespoons dark rum
¼ teaspoon fresh lime juice
3 tablespoons unsweetened cocoa powder

1. Heat cream in saucepan on medium heat until steaming. Remove from heat and add dark chocolate, stirring until melted. When mixture cools to

room temperature, add rum and lime juice. Refrigerate until firmly chilled.

2. Form 1-inch balls from the chilled mixture using a melon baller, teaspoon, or your hands. Roll in unsweetened cocoa powder.

3. Store in airtight container between layers of waxed paper.

The scent of burnt sugar swirled in the air, its sweetness melting with the darker spice of cacao and cinnamon. Candles flickered, the tiny tongues of flame licking out as the footman set the plate on the dining table.

"Ahhhh." The gentleman leaned down and inhaled deeply, his fleshy face wreathing in a sybaritic smile. "Why, my dear Catherine, it smells . . . good enough to eat."

Laughter greeted the bon mot.

"Oh, indeed it is, poppet. I've had my chef create it specially for you." The heavily rouged lady by his side parted her lips, just enough to show a peek of teeth. "And only you."

"How delicious." Plumes of pale smoke floated up toward the painted ceiling and slowly dissolved in the shadows. His lazy, lidded gaze slid past the glittering silver candelabra and took in the empty place settings of the other half dozen guests. "And what, may I ask, is it?"

"Chocolate."

"Chocolate," he echoed, sounding a little puzzled. "But—"

"*Edible* chocolate," explained Catherine. "A new innovation, fresh from Paris. Where, as you know, the French have refined sumptuous indulgence to an art form in itself." She lowered her voice to a sultry murmur. "Aren't you tempted to try it?"

All eyes fixed hungrily on the unusual confection. Soft mounds of Chantilly cream ringed the porcelain plate, accentuating the dark, decadent richness of the thick wafers arranged at its center. Ranging in hue from *café au lait* to burnished ebony, they rose up from a pool of port-soaked cherries.

"I must warn you, though," she teased. "Chocolate is said to stimulate the appetite for other pleasures." Her lashes fluttered. "But perhaps you are already sated after such a rich meal."

"One can never have enough pleasure," replied the gentleman as he plucked the top piece from its buttery perch and popped it into his mouth.

A collective sigh sounded from the others as he gave a blissful little moan, squeezed his eyes shut . . .

And promptly pitched face-first into sticky sweetness.

There was a moment of dead silence, followed by a slow, slurping shudder that sent a spray of ruby-red drops and pink-tinged cream over the pristine tablecloth.

"Good God, send for a physician!" screamed one of the guests. "The Prince Regent has been poisoned!"

2

From the chocolate notebooks of Dona Maria Castellano

Chocolate was served during religious rites and celebrations. It was often mixed with such flavorings as vanilla, cinnamon, allspice, chiles, hueinacaztli—a spicy flower from the custard apple tree—and anchiote, which turns the mouth a bright red! The Aztecs also believed that the dried beans of the cacao tree possessed strong medicinal properties. Indeed, warriors were issued cacao wafers to fortify their strength for long marches and the rigors of battle—a fact that Sandro will undoubtedly find of great interest. I, too, have remarked on the nourishing benefits of hot, sweetened chocolate....

Spiced Hot Chocolate

8 cups milk
¼ cup achiote seeds
12 blanched almonds
12 toasted and skinned hazelnuts
2–3 Mexican vanilla beans, split lengthwise, seeds scraped out
¼ ounce dried rosa de Castillo (rosebuds)
2 3-inch canela (soft Ceylon cinnamon sticks)

1 tablespoon aniseeds
2 whole dried serrano chiles
8 ounces 70% dark chocolate
sugar to taste

1. In a heavy saucepan, heat milk with anchiote seeds over medium heat. Bring to low boil, stirring constantly. Reduce heat to low and let steep for 10 minutes, until milk is brightly colored with the anchiote.
2. Grind almond and hazelnuts together to the consistency of fine breadcrumbs. Set aside.
3. Strain out achiote seeds from milk and return milk to saucepan. Add the ground nuts, along with the vanilla beans and rosebuds, cinnamon, aniseeds, and chiles. Bring to low boil. Reduce heat and simmer for 10 minutes. Remove from heat.
4. Stir in chocolate. Taste for sweetness, and add sugar to taste. Strain through a fine mesh strainer.
5. Transfer chocolate to tall, narrow pot and whisk vigorously with a *molinillo* (wooden chocolate mill) or handheld immersion blender. It adds a wonderful frothy head. Serve immediately.

❧

Steam rose from the boiling water, enveloping the stove in a cloud of moist, tropical heat.

"Hell." A hand shot out and shoved the kettle off the hob.

Cleaning up after such a feast would likely take another few hours, thought the chef irritably. But that was the price—or was it penance?—for choosing to work alone. A baleful glance lingered for a moment on the kitchen's worktable, the dirty dishes and pots yet another reminder that the aristocratic asses upstairs were gluttons for decadent foods.

More, always more—their hunger seemed insatiable. But it wasn't as if their appetites for sumptuous pleasures came as any great surprise to Arianna Hadley. Contempt curled the corners of her mouth. Indeed, she had counted on it.

Turning away from the puddles of melted butter and clotted cream, she wiped her hands and carefully collected the scraps of paper containing her recipes. The edges were yellowing, the spidery script had faded to the color of weak tea, and yet she could not quite bring herself to copy them onto fresh sheets of foolscap. They were like old friends—her only friends, if truth be told—and together they had traveled. . . .

Her hands clenched, crackling the papers. Not that she cared to dwell on the sordid details. They were, after all, too numerous to count.

She closed her eyes for an instant. For as far back as she could remember, life had been one never-ending journey. Jamaica, St. Kitts, Barbados, Martinique, along with all the specks of Caribbean coral and rock too small to have a name. Foam-flecked, rum-drenched hell-holes awash in rutting pirates and saucy whores. And from there across the ocean to the glittering bastion of civilized society.

Ah, yes. Here in London the scurvy scum and sluts were swathed in fancy silks and elegant manners. Fine-cut jewels and satin smiles. All thin veneers that hid a black-hearted core of corruption.

Tracing a finger over a water-stained page, Arianna felt the faint grit of salt and wondered whether it was residue from the ocean voyage or one of the rare moments when she had allowed a weak-willed tear. Of late, she had disciplined herself to be tougher. Harder. But as the steam wafted over the sticky pots, stirring a sudden, haunting hint of island spices, she blinked and the words blurred. Light and dark, spinning into a vortex of jumbled memories.

Fire. Smoke. The lush scent of sweetness licking up from the flames.

"Breathe deeply, ma petite.*" Her voice lush with the lilt of the tropics, the mulatto cook leaned closer to the cop-*

per cauldron. "Drink in its essence." She sprinkled a grating of cinnamon, a pinch of anchiote over the roasting nibs. "Watch carefully, Arianna. Like life itself, the cacao is even better with a bit of spice, but the mix must be just right. Let me show you. . . ."

Dark as ebony, Oribe's hands fluttered through the tendril of steam. "Theobroma cacao—food of the gods," she murmured. "Now we must wait for just the right moment to douse the flames. Remember—its magic cannot be rushed." From a smaller pot, the cook poured a measure of hot milk into a ceramic cup. Adding a spoonful of ground beans, thickened with sugar, she whipped the concoction to a foaming froth with her molinillo. *"But patience will be rewarded. Drink this—"*

Then the image of the old servant dissolved, and Arianna found herself staring into the shadows.

Shadows. She remembered shifting shapes of menacing black, and the rumblings of thunder from a fast-approaching storm. Dancing to the drumming of the wind against the shutters, a tendril of smoke had swirled up from the lone candle, casting a trail of twisted patterns over a bloodstained sheet.

"Drink this, Papa." She was holding a glass of cheap rum to her father's trembling lips. *"A physician will be here soon with laudanum to help ease the pain,"* she lied, knowing full well that not a soul would come rushing to help two penniless vagabonds.

"I would rather have a sip of your special chocolate, my dear." He tried to smile, despite the jagged knife wound gouged between his ribs.

So much blood, so much blood. Cursing the stinking wharfside alleys and the shabby tavern room, she pressed her palm to the scarlet-soaked handkerchief, trying to staunch the flow.

"I—I shall always savor the sweet memory of you," he went on in a whisper. *"I . . ."* A groan gurgled deep in his throat. *"God in heaven, forgive me for being such a wretched parent. And for sinking you in such a sordid life."*

"You are not to blame! You were falsely accused."

"Yes, I was—I swear it," he rasped. *"But . . . it doesn't matter. Not for me."* He coughed. *"But you—you deserve better. . . ."*

"Never mind that. You deserve justice, Papa. Tell me who did this to you."

"I . . ." But there was no answer, only a spasm of his icy fingers and then a silence louder than the wailing wind.

Arianna shifted on her stool, recalled back to the present by the clatter of footsteps on the stairs. Her skin was sheened in sweat and yet she was chilled to the bone.

"Chef! Chef!" Fists pounded on the closed door. "Monsieur Alphonse, open up! Something terrible has happened!"

Smoothing at the ends of her false mustache, Arianna quickly tucked the papers into her smock and rose.

Perhaps it was too late for justice. Perhaps all that mattered now was vengeance.

"Indeed?" Lord Percival Grentham's expression remained impassive. A senior government minister in Whitehall's War Office, he was in charge of security for London, which included keeping watch over the royal family. And with the King lingering in the netherworld of madness and his grown children mired in one scandal after another, it was a task designed to test his legendary sangfroid.

Grentham's assistant nervously cleared his throat. "But he's going to survive, milord," he added hastily. "A physician happened to be treating a patient next door and was summoned in time to purge the poison from the Prince's stomach."

"More's the pity," snapped Grentham's military attaché, who was standing by his superior's desk, arranging the daily surveillance reports. "Bloody hell, if Prinny can't control his prodigious appetites, he could at least have the decency to fall victim in his own establishment."

The assistant didn't dare respond.

Leaning back in his chair, Grentham tapped his elegant fingertips together and stared out the bank of windows overlooking the parade ground. Rain pelted against the misted glass, turning the vast expanse of gravel to a blur of watery gray. Beyond it, the bare trees in St. James's Park jutted up through the fog, dark and menacing, like the jagged teeth of some ancient dragon.

"How long until he can be moved from Lady Spencer's town house?" he asked slowly.

"Er . . ." The assistant consulted the sheaf of papers in his hands. "Another two or three days."

"Bloody, *bloody* hell," swore the attaché. "If word of this reaches the newspapers—"

"Thank you, Major Crandall." The tapping ceased—as did all other sounds in the room. Turning to his assistant, Grentham continued with his inquiries. "I take it that the other guests have been sworn to absolute secrecy, Jenkins?"

"Yes, milord. And they've all promised to be silent as the grave."

"Excellent," he replied mildly. "Oh, and do remind them that they had better be, else their carcasses will be rotting on a transport ship bound for the Antipodes."

"Y-yes, milord." The young man was new to the job and hadn't yet dared ask what had become of his predecessor. Rumors of Grentham's ruthlessness were rife throughout the halls of the Horse Guards building, and it was whispered that even the Prime Minister feared to provoke his ire.

Taking up his pen, Grentham jotted several lines on a fresh sheet of foolscap. "Do we know for certain what poison was used?"

"Not as yet, sir. The physician says it is difficult to discern, on account of the, er . . . substance that the Prince ingested." The young man paused, looking uncertain of whether to go on.

"Well, do you intend to keep me in suspense all afternoon?" asked Grentham softly. "Or is this meant to be an amusing little guessing game, seeing as I have nothing else to do with my time?"

"N-n-o, sir." The assistant gave another glance at his notes. "It was . . . chocolate."

"Chocolate?" repeated Crandall incredulously. "If this is your idea of a joke, Jenkins—"

"It's n-no joke, sir, it's the God-honest truth." Jenkins held out a piece of paper with a suspicious-looking stain streaked across its bottom. "You may see for yourself."

Grentham waved away the offending document with a flick of his wrist. "I am a trifle confused, Jenkins," he murmured. "I thought you said Prinny *ate* the stuff, not *drank* it."

"He did, sir. It says here in the physician's report that the Prince Regent collapsed after eating a disk of solid sweetened chocolate." Seeking to forestall another acerbic attack, he quickly went on. "Apparently the confection is a recent culinary creation, developed in France. It is said to be very popular in Paris."

"Chacun à son goût," said Grentham under his breath.

"Sir?"

"Never mind. Go on—anything else of interest in the report?"

"Well, milord, the man does mention the possibility that the Prince might have sickened from overindulgence, and not from any toxin." Jenkins swallowed hard. "But the Prince's private physician questions whether chocolate in this new, solid form might have naturally occurring poisonous properties."

Grentham thought for a moment. "So in fact, we don't have a clue as to whether this was an attempt on the reigning sovereign's life, or merely another example of his appetite for pleasure getting him in trouble."

Looking unhappy, Jenkins nodded. His superior was known as a man who preferred to view the world in black and white. An infinite range of grays merely muddied the subject—which did not bode well for whoever presented the ill-formed picture.

"I should be tempted to let him stew in his own juices . . . ," began the Major, but a sharp look from Grentham speared him to silence.

The minister fingered one of the leather document cases piled on his desk. "Given the current situation, it is imperative—*imperative*—that we ascertain whether foul play was involved. What with the upcoming arrival of the Allied delegation and our troubles with the upstart Americans, the death of the Prince Regent could be catastrophic for the interests of England."

The assistant instinctively backed into the shadows of the dark oak filing cabinets, though he had a feeling that the basilisk stare of his superior could see straight through to the deepest coal-black pit of hell.

"And so," he mused, "however unpleasant a task, we must extract the truth from this sticky mess."

Jenkins gave a sickly smile, unsure whether the minister had just attempted a witticism.

"The question is, who among our operatives is best equipped to handle such an investigation?" Grentham pursed his lips. "Any suggestions?"

The Major quickly shot a look at Jenkins.

"Well, milord, I . . . I . . ."

"Spit it out, man," ordered the Major. "We haven't got all day."

Sweat beaded on the assistant's brow, though his throat remained bone-dry. "I was just going to say, perhaps one of our Peninsular allies might prove u-u-useful. Seeing as it was the Spanish who brought cacao to Europe from the New World, it would seem logical that they would be the most knowledgeable on the subject."

Grentham looked thoughtful.

The Major's gaze narrowed to a crafty squint. "Yes, I was just going to say that I think it an excellent idea to look outside our own circle of intelligence officers," he said quickly. "They are all personally acquainted with the Prince, and we wouldn't want any question of impartiality to color the conclusion of the investigation. I mean, sir, if anything were to . . ." He let his voice trail off.

Grentham flashed a semblance of a smile. "Good God, I may actually have a body or two around me with a brain." Setting down his pen, he contemplated his well-manicured hand for a bit before slowly buffing his nails on his other sleeve.

Swoosh, swoosh, swoosh. The sound was soft as a raptor's wing-beat, as the bird homed in on its kill.

"Send a messenger to Lord Charles Mellon. Tell him that I wish to see him as soon as possible."

Arianna added a spoonful of sugar to her morning coffee and slathered a scone with butter. *The condemned ought to eat a heartier meal,* she thought sardonically as she broke off a morsel of the still-warm pastry and let it crumble between her fingers.

If Luck was indeed a Lady, the traitorous bitch had a perverse sense of humor.

Biting back a grim smile, Arianna had to admit the irony of the situation. After all her meticulous plotting and carefully calculated moves, one unfortunate little slip had wreaked havoc with her plans.

The best-laid schemes of mice and men go often askew, and leave us nothing but grief and pain. . . . Her father, who had carried a love of poetry—and precious little else—with him from England to Jamaica, had enjoyed reading Robert Burns to her on the rare evenings when he wasn't sunk too deep in his cups. Arianna had cherished those times together, curled in the comforting shelter of his arms.

She sucked in her breath, her lungs suddenly filled with the memory of his scent—an earthy mix of tobacco, leather, and citrus-spiced sandalwood.

Oh, Papa, she thought, expelling a slow sigh. So brilliant, yet so naïve. Scandal had stripped him of all his rightful honor, forcing him to survive on his wits. But even his enemies admitted that Richard Hadley, the Earl of Morse, was a charming dreamer. Like fine brandy, his mellifluous laugh was smoothly seductive, making even the most grandiose schemes seem plausible. The earl was so convincing that over the years he had come to believe his own lies.

Blood must run true, mused Arianna, for it seemed that she had inherited his gift for deception.

Raising a defiant finger, she traced the burnt-cork stippling that darkened her jaw. A short stint with a theater troupe in Barbados had taught her the art of disguise. *Paint and glue. False hair and feather padding.* With the right touch, a skillful hand could alter one's appearance beyond recognition. It helped that most people were easy to fool. They saw only what they expected to see and rarely noticed what lay beneath the surface.

"Mr. Alphonse!" The shout cut through the quiet of the kitchen. "Captain Mercer will see you. Now!"

"Oui, oui, I am coming," she called. Thank god her voice was naturally husky—a slight roughening of the edges was all it required to mimic a masculine growl.

Making no effort to hurry, Arianna paused to make one last check of her reflection in one of the hanging pots. She would have preferred to be interrogated here in the kitchen, where she was master of her own little Underworld. The light was kept deliberately murky, while the crowded racks of cookware and herbs created added distraction. However, if there was one thing she had learned over the years of fending for herself, it was how to improvise.

"Step lively," snapped the guard, punctuating the command with a rap of his pistol against the door. Though dressed as a footman, there was no mistaking his military bearing. "The likes o' you ought not keep your betters waiting."

She took her time mounting the stairs.

"Bloody frog," he muttered, shoving the gun barrel between her shoulder blades to hurry her up the last few treads.

The guard escorted her into the breakfast room, where a big, beefy army officer sat perfectly centered on the far side of the dark mahogany table. All the other seating had been cleared away, save for a single straight-back chair set directly opposite him. It looked rather forlorn in the wide stretch of empty space.

"Sit down," he barked.

For an instant, Arianna debated whether to remain on her feet. Goading him to anger might distract him from his intended line of questioning. But she quickly decided against the strategy. However cleverly padded, her body was best not put on prominent display.

"Merci," she mumbled, slouching down in her seat. It was only then that she noticed a second figure standing by the bank of mullioned windows. He, too, was dressed in scarlet regimentals, but the color blended neatly into thick damask draperies of the same hue. The slanted shadows and angled sunlight made his features hard to discern. It was his carefully groomed side whiskers that caught her attention. Sparks seemed to dance through the ginger hair as if it were on fire.

"Well, what have you to say to defend yourself, Mr. Alphonse?" went on the officer seated at the table.

Shifting her gaze to the papers piled in front of the pompous prig, Arianna replied with exaggerated surprise, "Am I being accused of something, *mon General*?"

"Oh, so you think yourself a clever little bastard, eh, to make light of an assassination attempt on the Prince Regent of England?" The captain, whose rank was clearly denoted by the stripes on his sleeve, thinned his lips. "I promise that you will soon comprehend it is no laughing matter."

"Non, iz not amusing. Not in ze least," she agreed, deliberately drawing out her French accent. "Iz *grave*, very *grave*."

The captain glared, uncertain as to whether he was being played for a fool. Snapping open a leather-bound ledger, he scanned over several pages of notes before speaking again. "I have sworn statements that you were the only one working in the kitchen the night the Prince was poisoned. Is that true?"

"Ça dépend—that depends," answered Arianna calmly. "The servants who carried the dishes up to the dining room were in and out all evening." She paused. "I'm

sure you have been told that the supper was a lengthy affair, with numerous courses."

"Did you see anyone tampering with the food?" he asked quickly.

"Non."

"Nor anyone lingering below stairs?" It was the officer by the window who asked the question.

"Non," replied Arianna, not looking his way. While her first response had been the truth, this one was a lie. She *had* seen someone, but she had no intention of sharing that information with the Crown.

Shoving back his chair, the captain rose abruptly, setting off a jangle of metal. Arianna watched the flutter of ribbons and braid as the gaudy bits of gilded brass and enameled silver stilled against his chest. *Did the man have any notion how ridiculous he looked, strutting about in his peacock finery?* His martial scowl was belied by the fleshiness of his hands as he braced them on the polished wood. They looked soft as dough.

A bread soldier, thought Arianna. A staff flunky. Put him in a real fight and a butter knife would cut through him in one swift slice. As for the other one, he looked to be made of sterner stuff. She guessed that he was the man in command.

"Mr. Alphonse!" Raising his voice to a near shout, the captain leaned in and angled his chin to a menacing tilt. "Did you try to murder the Prince Regent?"

Arianna ducked her head to hide a smile. *Conceited coxcomb—I've been bullied by far more intimidating men than you.*

"If you answer me honestly, it will go a lot easier for you," he went on. "Otherwise future interrogations could become quite unpleasant." His mouth twitched into a nasty smile. "For you, that is."

"I have told you ze truth. I did not poison the Prince," she said. "If you don't believe me, why don't you search the kitchen?"

The draperies stirred, echoing a low laugh. "What do you think my men are doing as we speak?" The officer there moved to stand in front of the windows. Limned in the morning light, his silhouette was naught but a stark dark shape against the panes of glass—save for the halo of ginger fire.

"I have nothing to fear," she answered calmly. The bag containing her disguises was well hidden beneath a pantry floorboard, with the weight and odor of the onion barrel discouraging too close an inspection of the dark corner. "I am innocent of any attack on your Prince."

The captain replied with a vulgar oath.

"Am I under arrest?" asked Arianna, deciding it was to her advantage to end the interview as soon as possible. She had overheard two of the guards discussing their orders earlier, and was aware that Whitehall was sending another interrogator later in the day. She would save her strength for that confrontation.

"Not yet, you stinking little piece of—"

"Leave us for a moment, Captain Mercer." The other officer cut off his cohort with a clipped command.

The captain snapped a salute. "Have a pleasant chat with the Major, Froggy," he muttered under his breath.

The Major's boots clicked over the parquet floor, echoing the sound of the door falling shut. Approaching the captain's vacated chair, he picked up a penknife from the table and slowly began cleaning his nails.

Snick. Snick. Snick. The faint scrapings were meant to put her on edge, thought Arianna as she watched the flash of slivered steel. Like her, the Major understood the importance of theatrics.

The noise ceased.

Bowing her head, she remained silent.

"I think you are lying to us, Mr. Alphonse," he said in a deceptively mild tone.

She lifted her shoulders in a Gallic shrug. "What can I say? Iz hard to offer proof for an act that I haven't committed."

"Oh, I don't expect you to speak right now. I am perfectly happy to let you stew a little longer about your fate." He stroked at his side whiskers, and his fingers came away with a trace of Macassar oil on their tips. "You see, I expect you to die. But if you give us the information we want, the process will be a good deal less painful for you."

Arianna kept her expression impassive.

"What's the matter, cat got your tongue?"

"Arguing with you would only be a waste of breath," she murmured. "Am I excused? The household expects to eat at noon."

"Go." He placed the blade atop the captain's sheaf of notes. "But be assured, you haven't heard the last from me."

3

From the chocolate notebooks of Dona Maria Castellano

The cacao tree was a symbol not only of health but of wealth. A prized commodity, the beans were used as currency by Aztecs. The missionary mentions seeing a local document that listed some of the trading values—a tomato cost one cacao bean, an avocado cost three beans, and a turkey hen cost 100 beans. . . . The next few pages of his journal show some sketches of various drinking vessels for cacao. Oh, how I should like to find one of the ceremonial cups, made from a hollow gourd, that were used to serve the army its elixir. It would make a special gift for Sandro, and perhaps keep him safe. . . .

Chocolate Stout Cake

1 stick (½ cup) unsalted butter, plus 2 melted tablespoons
½ cup stout, such as Mackeson or Guinness (pour stout slowly into measuring cup; do not measure foam)
½ cup packed soft pitted prunes (6 ounces), chopped
3½ ounces fine-quality bittersweet chocolate (not unsweetened or extra-bitter), chopped
1¼ cups all-purpose flour
¼ teaspoon baking soda

¼ teaspoon salt
2 large eggs
1 cup packed dark brown sugar
1 teaspoon vanilla

1. Put oven rack in middle position and preheat
   oven to 350°F. Lightly brush 6-cup Bundt pan or
   8-by-3-inch ovenproof ring mold with half the
   melted butter and chill 2 minutes. Then butter again
   and chill while making batter.
2. Bring stout to a boil in a small saucepan and add
   prunes. Remove from heat and let stand until most
   of liquid is absorbed.
3. Meanwhile, melt chocolate and remaining stick
   butter together in a small heavy saucepan over
   low heat, stirring constantly. Sift together flour,
   baking soda, and salt into a bowl.
4. Beat together eggs, brown sugar, and vanilla in a
   large bowl with an electric mixer at high speed until thick, about 2 minutes. Add chocolate mixture
   and beat until just combined. Reduce speed to low
   and add flour mixture, mixing until just combined.
   Stir in prune mixture until combined well. Spoon
   batter into pan and bake until a wooden skewer
   inserted into middle of cake comes out clean, 40
   to 45 minutes.
5. Cool cake in mold on a rack 10 minutes, then invert
   onto rack to cool completely, at least 30 minutes.

❧

"Thank you for coming to see me, Lord Saybrook."
Grentham didn't look up from the document he
was reading. "I trust that the request did not inconvenience you."

Without waiting for an invitation, Alessandro Henry
George De Quincy, the fifth Earl of Saybrook, shifted his
cane and sat down in the chair facing the desk. "Not at
all. I am always at the beck and call of the government."

Grentham dipped his pen in ink and wrote a lengthy notation in the paper's margin before setting his work aside. "How kind." Narrowing his gunmetal-gray eyes, he subjected Saybrook to a lengthy scrutiny.

The earl stared back, seemingly unconcerned that he looked like he had just crawled out of the deepest, darkest corner of hell. His long black hair was neatly combed and his face freshly shaven, but no brush or razor could disguise the ravages that pain and narcotics had wrought on his body. Sallow skin stretched over bones sharp as sabers, bruised shadows accentuated his hollow cheeks, and his clothes hung loosely on his lanky frame.

Grentham, on the other hand, was immaculately attired in a charcoal coat of superfine wool, which set off the starched folds of his snowy cravat to perfection.

"But now that we have met," the minister went on, "I cannot help but wonder whether your trip here was a waste of both your time and mine."

"My uncle has explained the task at hand," replied Saybrook, matching the other man's sardonic tone. "If I did not feel myself up to its rigors, I should not have bothered coming here." After allowing a fraction of a pause, he added, "One of the first lessons I learned as an army intelligence officer was that appearances can often be deceiving."

Grentham's nostrils flared for an instant, but he covered his displeasure with a bland smile. "So, you think that you are capable of rising to the occasion, Lord Saybrook?" Again the gunmetal gaze raked over the earl's legs. "Despite your infirmity?"

"I assure you, sir, my infirmity does not affect my performance."

The minister folded his well-tended hands on his blotter. "And yet, according to the surgeon's report on you, the French saber cut perilously close to your manhood. I wonder . . ."

Saybrook maintained a mask of indifference. "Do you anticipate that the job will entail swiving one of the witnesses?" He paused for a fraction. "Or buggering the cook?"

"Are you fond of boys, Lord Saybrook?" countered Grentham.

"Not *unnaturally* so," he answered.

"And women?"

"Why do you ask?"

"Let us just say that I am curious," replied the minister.

"And let us just say that I am not inclined to satisfy your curiosity."

"You are very clever, Lord Saybrook. But cleverness can sometimes lead a man into trouble."

"So can stupidity." Appearing to tire of the cat-and-mouse word games, Saybrook regripped his cane. "If you wish to speak about the assignment, let us do so. Otherwise, I will return to my town house. You have obviously read a thorough dossier on me, so I imagine you have already decided whether you think me fit for the job."

"A written report can tell only so much about a man," replied the minister. "I prefer to judge for myself before making a final decision."

Saybrook started to rise.

"Please sit, Lord Saybrook." Papers shuffled. "I've been told that you are—for lack of a better term—an expert in chocolate. Might I inquire how you came to be so?" An edge of sarcasm crept into his voice. "Assuming that I am not offending your delicate sensibilities with my questions."

"My Spanish grandmother passed on her knowledge to me," replied Saybrook. "In Andalusia, she was renowned for her healing skills, as well as her cooking talents."

"Cooking," repeated Grentham as he plucked a page from his notes and reread it. "Your grandmother was a countess—is that not correct?"

"Yes. But in Spain, highborn ladies have a different notion of what is—and isn't—beneath their station. Cuisine is not menial labor—it is an art. As is healing," said the earl. "She was interested in the medicinal properties of many foods and plants, including *Theobroma cacao*."

The minister frowned.

"The Latin name for the tree that yields cacao beans," he explained. "I studied botany at Oxford before joining the army."

"A strange combination."

"Not as strange as you might think," said Saybrook. "The ancient Aztec soldiers used chocolate as a stimulant—"

"I am not interested in a scientific lecture," snapped Grentham. "What I want to know is this—in your learned opinion, could chocolate in and of itself have poisoned the Prince Regent?"

"No," replied Saybrook without hesitation. "If, perchance, the Prince had an intolerance to the cacao fruit, he would have suffered an adverse reaction from drinking a beverage made from the beans. And according to my uncle, Prinny has enjoyed his morning chocolate for years."

"True," mused the minister. "So, who would you consider the prime suspect?"

"I do not yet know enough about the case to form an opinion."

"Well, we don't have a great deal of time to ponder the question, Lord Saybrook." Grentham steepled his well-tended fingers. "I assume Mr. Mellon has explained the situation."

The earl inclined his head a fraction. "Next month, a secret delegation of our Eastern allies is due to arrive in London for talks on how to end this interminable war. Napoleon's counteroffensive in Spain may be losing ground, but he has rebuilt the army shattered by the retreat from Russia into a formidable force and has taken personal command of the troops. Once again he is marching east, looking to crush any resistance to his domination of the Continent. It's critical that England coordinates its efforts with those of Tsar Alexander, the Austrians, the Swedes, and the Prussians. However—"

"However, the death of our nominal ruler would throw the alliance into disarray," interrupted Grentham. "The result could be catastrophic."

"An English breakfast might soon consist of *oeufs aux champignons* and *café au lait*," observed Saybrook.

The minister fixed him with a frigid stare. "There is likely an assassin on the loose, and rather than make clever quips about cuisine, I expect you to apprehend him before the Allied delegation arrives in England."

"Assuming I agree to take the assignment," reminded Saybrook softly.

Grentham's expression remained impassive, but clearly he was unused to having anyone refuse to bow to his authority. "Let me phrase it differently, Lord Saybrook. It would be a great service to the government if you could help us apprehend the miscreant, and assure the Prime Minister that the threat has been eliminated," he said with syrupy sweetness. "For a man of your reputed talents, it should prove a simple task. Your expertise in chocolate should allow you to quickly identify the poison tainting the wafers. From there you have only to ascertain who had access to the kitchen." He gave a dismissive wave. "And *voilà*."

"You seem rather certain that the case won't be a hard nut to crack."

"The cook is the logical suspect, but we need to know if he has any coconspirators. I am sure if you apply some heat to the fellow, you will get some quick answers."

"Do you want a confession?" asked Saybrook. "Or do your want the truth? For in my experience, torture elicits naught but what the prisoner thinks his tormentor wishes to hear."

"Torture is such an unpleasant word. I prefer to call it persuasion." Grentham's lip curled ever so slightly. "Surely, Lord Saybrook, you would agree that to be an effective investigator, one must be persuasive."

"Among other things," answered Saybrook. "But should

I undertake this assignment, I would have to have *carte blanche* from you to handle it as I see fit. There is an old adage about too many cooks spoiling the broth."

"That could be a recipe for disaster."

"You'll just have to trust my skills in the kitchen."

Grentham considered the request for several long moments before giving a curt nod. "Very well. It is in the best interest of the government to have an independent investigator handle the matter. The military men assigned to my department are too close to the Prince Regent. I would not want it said that their judgment was clouded by personal feelings."

He tugged on a small cord beneath his desk, and within seconds a young man opened the office door.

"Milord?"

"Ask Major Crandall to join us, Jenkins," said the minister. Without another word to Saybrook, he turned away and began flipping through a stack of papers set on the far corner of his desk.

"Sir!" The Major marched in and clicked his heels. "You wished to see me?"

"You will be in charge of briefing Lord Saybrook on the facts that have been gathered so far concerning the poisoning of the Prince Regent. Give him the background information on the other guests present that evening, on Lady Spencer's staff—anything he wants."

"Shall I call a carriage and escort His Lordship to Lady Spencer's town house?"

Grentham answered with a thin-lipped smile. "That is entirely up to him. He demanded complete autonomy in this case, and given the circumstance, I felt I had no choice but to agree."

Crandall shot Saybrook a look that left little doubt where his loyalties lay.

"You will soon discover, Crandall, that Lord Saybrook is a very unusual fellow." The smile turned a touch malicious. "For one thing, he likes cooking, and— Oh, forgive me. I neglected to ask if you also enjoy embroidery."

"Alas, no," responded Saybrook politely. "The only sliver of sharpened steel I've ever wielded is a saber—Oh, and a stiletto." He tapped a finger to his chin. "Come to think of it, though, I did embroider a rather distinctive design on a man's chest once. It was the words 'COWARDLY CUR' spelled out in large capital letters. Seeing as he liked to rough up women before forcing himself on them, I thought it only sporting to give the weaker sex fair warning."

He and Grentham locked eyes. Neither one blinked.

It was Crandall who broke the tense silence with a cough. "Will that be all, milord?"

"Yes, yes." A drawer clicked open. "On your way out, ask Jenkins to bring me the file on the Swedish ambassador's brothel visits."

"This way, Lord Saybrook," growled Crandall.

Slipping out from the stairwell, Arianna hurried down the dimly lit corridor and eased open the door to her employer's study. Lady Spencer was upstairs entertaining the Prince Regent as he dined on his midday meal, and despite the strict restrictions on the royal appetite, the interlude ought to last at least another hour. *In and out.* With the servants gathered for their own repast, the chances of being caught seemed slim.

It was worth the risk, she decided. At any moment the military might return to begin holding her balls to the fire—metaphorically speaking. When it came to that, she had an idea of how to escape the heat, but she would hate to flee empty-handed.

Hearing the crunch of gravel, Arianna ducked behind the draperies and watched as a guard dressed as a gardener marched past the window.

Bloody hell. With disguises and deceptions running rampant, the situation bordered on pure farce. Her father, whose favorite Shakespeare play was *As You Like It*, would have roared with laughter at seeing his daughter tweak the noses of the authorities by playing a modern-day Rosalind. Her mouth gave an involuntary twitch. *Aye, and it would be even more amusing were my life not dangling by a thread.*

Reminded of the danger in dallying, Arianna quickly crossed to the Chinoise escritoire set in the far corner of the room. Like its owner, the striking piece was designed to draw the eye. The exotic bamboo legs, twined with sinuous serpents, gleamed with gilded gold. In bold contrast, the ebony-trimmed drawers and writing surface were lacquered in a deep shade of vermilion.

The color of blood, thought Arianna, riffling through the sheets of scented stationery that lay in careless disarray beside the crystal inkwell. Finding them all blank, she moved on to the row of drawers, whose contents proved to be just as uninteresting.

Moving on, she found only stubs of sealing wax and a vial of musky perfume in the last compartment.

Damn. There *must* be something. Her employer's reputation for pursuing profligate pleasure was the reason she had spent weeks of manipulation to gain a position here.

The pigeonholes were stuffed with various bills, most of them unpaid for some time, judging by the shrill tone of the shopkeepers. As she sorted through them, Arianna mentally reviewed what she knew about the mistress of the house. A buxom blond widow of moderate means, Lady Spencer was no stranger to dalliances with rich men. The Prince Regent was her latest paramour, and by all accounts, the affair had started six months ago, when the two of them had met during a weeklong party at the Prince's Royal Pavilion in Brighton.

Finished with the bills, Arianna paused, taking a moment to study the decorative strip of paneling above the drawers. Reopening the center one, she pulled it out all the way and slid her hand into the opening, feeling for any ridge or groove hidden at the back.

There were other, darker rumors, too. Whispered hints about Lady Spencer's involvement with men far more debauched than Prinny. It was said that she had been introduced to the Royal Rake by several of his cronies from the Carlton House set, men who sought to use the royal connection for—

Snick. The paneling sprung open, revealing two hidden compartments.

The first one held a sheaf of folded letters tied with a length of red velvet. *Billet-doux*, by the look of them. Arianna thumbed through them, pausing over several from the same gentleman. After a slight hesitation, she slipped one of them into her sleeve before retying the ribbon and returning all the others to their original position.

The second one contained an assortment of keys. Buried amid the jumble of wrought iron and silvery steel was a small drawstring pouch made of tan chamois. Inside were a handful of identical reddish gold medallions engraved with an image and several lines of ornate script. Arianna tucked one in her pocket before returning the rest to the little bag.

Intrigued by what she had found so far, Arianna spent a moment longer exploring the depths of the hidden compartment. Sure enough, there was something else there—her fingers brushed over a slim pasteboard folder wedged against the grained wood. She fished it out and found it contained a sheaf of papers covered with mathematical equations. The top sheets appeared yellowed with age, while the ones beneath them seemed—

Suddenly aware of the rustle of heavy silk in the corridor, Arianna hesitated, but curiosity won out over caution. No doubt it would prove useless, but the idea that Lady Spencer had a hidden interest in something besides men was too tantalizing to ignore.

Stuffing the folder beneath her stomach padding, she quickly tidied up the telltale signs of her snooping, then spun away and took up a position by the marble mantelpiece.

"Why, Monsieur Alphonse, what a surprise to see you in the light of day!" Lady Spencer paused in the doorway to smooth out her skirts. "Like a mushroom, you seem to favor dark places."

"Alors," replied Arianna, casually replacing the Sevres snuffbox that she had been examining. "Seeing as our little world has been turned topsy-turvy, I thought I had better come up and fetch the week's menus. You have not yet sent me your list—or have you lost your appetite for my cooking?"

Lady Spencer smiled, showing off a set of dimples. Arianna could understand the widow's appeal to the pleasure-loving Prince Regent. Everything about her had an earthy lushness, from her bulging bosom and rounded hips to her throaty purr, which oozed sensuality. As she moved closer, the air thickened with the honeyed scent of lilacs.

"No, monsieur. I vow, I cannot imagine life without your *gateaux aux chocolat.*" Fanning her cheeks, she gave Arianna a wink. "Are you sure I can't seduce the recipe out of you?"

For a moment, Arianna wondered how Lady Spencer would react if she were allowed to uncover the shocking truth . . . and then promptly decided that the Prince's mistress might not be as horrified as she should be.

"Quite sure, *madame,*" growled Arianna, retreating a step at the unwelcome thought of being invited to make up a royal ménage à trois.

"What a pity. I adore plump men."

"Not when they haven't a feather to fly with, *madame.*" Arianna folded her arms across her goose-down stomach. "I couldn't afford you." *In more ways than one.*

"True," agreed Lady Spencer, a note of regret shading her voice. "But you have a rather . . . unique charm."

Choking back the insane urge to laugh, Arianna dipped into a formal bow. "The supper menu, *madame*?"

"Ah, yes. Supper." Lady Spencer licked her lower lip. "Something simple, Monsieur Alphonse. After all you have been through lately, I don't want to put you through any further trouble."

The carriage wheels spun through a sharp turn, the iron rims jolting over the cobblestones as the driver urged the team to a quicker pace. Saybrook and his escort had exchanged few words since the earl had agreed that a visit to Lady Spencer's town house should be the first order of business. However, the Major's displeasure was eloquent in his body language. He was sitting pressed against the far panels, creating as much space as possible between them. As if fearing that Saybrook's friction with Grentham might rub off on him.

"Tell me," asked the earl slowly. "Why wasn't the cook placed under arrest right away? Your superior seems sure he is the culprit."

"As I've tried to explain, we did not wish to draw any undue attention to the incident," answered Crandall with a martyred sigh. "Lord Grentham wishes to handle the interrogations discreetly, so for the moment, no one will be taken into official custody. But be assured, the entire household staff is under strict orders not to leave the premises."

"You are not afraid that he might escape?"

"Let him try. Naturally, we have men watching the place to ensure that no one slips away." The Major smoothed a thumb over his mustache. "Personally, I should not be surprised if he attempted to flee. There is something very havey-cavey about the fellow."

"How so?" inquired Saybrook.

"To begin with, he is French."

"So are most of the chefs who serve the *ton*," he observed.

"I wouldn't know," replied Crandall stiffly.

The rest of the ride proceeded in rigid silence.

Saybrook stepped down awkwardly from the carriage, his cane catching in the iron rung of the bottom step.

The Major watched the earl's stumbling with an ill-concealed smirk. "If you will follow me, Lord Saybrook, I shall show you the way to—"

"Actually, that won't be necessary."

The smirk slid from Crandall's face.

"I prefer to conduct my inquiries alone. In my experience, people are more apt to speak freely when they aren't surrounded by strangers."

"I don't think that's a good idea," argued the Major.

"Perhaps not. However, you heard Lord Grentham—he has given me the authority to do as I see fit." He held out his hand. "I shall keep the files on the staff and the guests, if you please."

Crandall passed over the document case, although he looked none too happy about it.

"Thank you for your briefing. If I have any other questions, I know where to find you."

An angry flush of red mottled the Major's cheeks at the unexpected dismissal. "Would you care to keep the carriage?" he asked through gritted teeth.

"No, I would rather you take it." Saybrook glanced up and down the quiet street. "As you so kindly pointed out, the less attention we draw to the place, the better."

Turning on his heel, Crandall stalked back to the waiting vehicle.

In response to several sharp raps of the knocker, the heavy oak-paneled front door opened a crack, and a pair of wary eyes fixed the earl with a basilisk stare. "If you are soliciting money for a wounded war veterans' fund, we cannot help you, sirrah. The lady of the house cannot be disturbed."

"I'm not here about money," said Saybrook, smiling slightly as he shrugged his bony shoulders. "As for Lady Spencer, I'm afraid that I'll have to trespass on her hospitality," he added. "I've come from Whitehall."

The butler stepped back and allowed him to enter the town house. "If you would wait in the drawing room, sir . . ." A wave of a white-gloved hand indicated a pleasant, light-filled room to his right. "I will fetch Her Ladyship."

Saybrook shuffled over the brightly colored carpet, eyeing the jade dragons on the mantel and bright silk pillows embroidered with unicorns nestled on the window seat. Next to it, a pair of faux-gold monkeys danced atop a brass tea chest.

"Do you like my menagerie, sir?"

Saybrook turned from his study of an alabaster lion. "You have collected quite a kingdom of wild animals," he answered slowly. "Including the King of the Jungle."

Her laugh was low and sultry, making her sound as if she had just tumbled out of bed. "Thank God that someone from Whitehall actually has a sense of humor. You cannot imagine how tedious that stiff-rumped Major Crandall has been this last week, glowering at me and my staff like we were a vile plague about to infect his private parts."

Saybrook nodded gravely, though a tiny twitch did seem to play at the corners of his mouth. "I confess that I am also included on his list of noxious diseases."

"I'm delighted to hear it," she said cheerfully. "May I offer you some refreshment—tea, sherry, or something stronger—so that we may toast to the prospect of his phallus falling off in the near future?"

"Thank you, but no. Though I do second your sentiment."

She smiled.

"As you can guess, this is not a purely social call, Lady Spencer."

Sighing, she brushed an errant curl off her cheek. "Oh, very well. I suppose that you, too, have a barrage of questions you wish to fire at me, Mr. . . ."

"I'm Saybrook," he said softly. "The—"

"The new earl?" exclaimed Lady Spencer.

His nod drew another peal of laughter. "How delicious—that is, once we put some meat on your bones." She winked. "I would recommend my chef, who really does create the most divine delicacies, but I daresay you might not find the suggestion a tasty one, given the circumstances."

"I appreciate the offer, but perhaps some other time," he answered. "For now, I will settle for having a few words with the man."

Lady Spencer's gaze lingered for an instant on his cane. "Please make yourself comfortable on the sofa,

Lord Saybrook. I shall send someone to fetch Chef from his quarters."

"No need," replied Saybrook, though a sudden spasm of his leg seemed to say otherwise. "I would, in fact, prefer to go to him."

"Unfortunately, that will entail a trip down a rather steep set of stairs, sir. You see, Chef resides in a small room off the kitchen."

"Indeed? It's a bit odd that he would choose to live with the likes of the boot boy or coal monkey."

"Oh, he doesn't permit anyone else to live downstairs with him." Seeing Saybrook arch a brow, she explained, "He's a trifle eccentric—or perhaps temperamental is a better word. But then, most great artists are."

"Ah."

"Truly he is—an artist, that is," she assured him. "I do hope you haven't come to arrest him. Even the Prince expressed hope that Monsieur Alphonse doesn't end up on the chopping block. Prinny is very fond of the man's *boeuf en croûte* and *crème brûlée*." Her lips twitched. "And, *entre nous*, he is heartily sick of the beef tea and broths that Whitehall insists on sending."

"England does not employ the guillotine, Lady Spencer," the earl replied dryly. "If your Cook is innocent, he has nothing to fear from me."

"Chef," she corrected. "He is very particular about all the little details." Her skirts fluttering with a silky swoosh, she turned for the door. "Come this, way, sir."

4

From the chocolate notebooks of Dona Maria Castellano

Legend has it that Quetzalcoatl, the god of civilization and learning, was banished from Earth for bringing the gift of chocolate to mankind. The Aztecs believed that he would one day return in glory—and when Hernan Cortez and his fleet of galleons sailed over the horizon in 1519, he was thought to be the ancient god. Alas, poor Montezuma! Though it is recorded that he drank fifty cups of chocolate a day, his magical military elixir proved no match for the Spanish guns and horses. Cortez plundered Tenochtitlan and carried back a wealth of treasures to Spain, including gold, silver, and cacao. . . .

Guatemalan Cacao-Chile Balls

3 ounces (about ²⁄₃ cup) cacao nibs
3 ounces (about 1 cup) piquin chiles
1 1-inch stick soft Ceylon cinnamon, coarsely chopped
½ teaspoon allspice berries
1 teaspoon salt
1 teaspoon Spanish smoked paprika

1. Heat griddle or medium cast-iron skillet over medium heat. Add cacao nibs and dry-roast for

2 minutes, until fragrant, stirring constantly with wooden spoon. Turn into separate container and set aside.

2. Add chiles, cinnamon, and allspice berries to the griddle and roast the same way, stirring, for 2 minutes. Scrape into electric spice mill or coffee grinder with salt and paprika and grind to a fine powder.

3. Combine spice mixture and roasted cacao nibs in a mini food processor and process into a sticky paste, 3–4 minutes, stopping to scrape down sides of bowl. Turn onto a work surface and shape into 12 small balls. Let sit until thoroughly dried.

4. Store in tightly sealed jar. When ready to use, grate over any dish to add a piquant seasoning.

*T*hump, thump, thump. The sound of the graceless descent gave Arianna ample warning that her bailiwick was about to be invaded.

Sure enough, several moments later a man appeared in the doorway of the kitchen. He was tall and broad-shouldered, though at present his big body was slightly hunched in pain. Taking in the cane and the awkward shift of his weight, she guessed that his stiff left leg was its source.

She looked up. His face might once have been called handsome, but its chiseled planes had sharpened to the point of gauntness. Black lashes framed eyes dark as volcanic ash. Yet as his gaze met hers, she was almost certain that she saw a burnt-gold spark smoldering in their depths.

She had expected another soldier. Instead they had sent . . . Satan incarnate.

No need to let my imagination run wild, she chided herself. Not when an all too real Hell was already erupting around her.

Shaking off her flight of fancy, Arianna quickly slipped into her role of aggrieved Frenchman.

"*Sacre bleu*, not another attack on my integrity," she muttered, cutting an angry little swish through the air with her fillet blade. "I am fast losing my taste for London. It is clear zat my talents are not appreciated here."

"I shall try not to take up too much of your time with my questions," said the intruder, his ash-black eyes following the flight of her hands.

"Hmmph!" Scowling, she waved him on. "Come, if you wish to talk, you will have to do it while I prepare ze stew for supper, Monsieur . . ."

Who the devil was he?

"De Quincy," he answered. After a fraction of a pause, he added, "Or Saybrook, if that comes easier to your tongue."

"Given a preference, sir, the only word I would be saying is *adieu*," she shot back.

"Unfortunately, that is not possible quite yet. But as I said, I will endeavor to keep our talk brief." Strangely enough, his gaze remained focused on her hands. "And to the point."

Her grip tightened on the hilt. "Ze household must eat, *n'est-ce pas*, Monsieur De Quincy?"

"But of course," murmured Saybrook.

Arianna led the way to a massive worktable set in the center of the space. "Have a seat, monsieur," snapped Arianna, indicating the lone stool at one end of the steel-scarred length of maple. She set aside the fillet blade and took up a paring knife. "While I peel and dice the carrots."

"No amanita mushrooms?" he said softly.

The reference to the deadly poisonous species took her aback. *Good God, did the man actually have a sense of humor?*

Arianna grunted in reply. "Zees may be a joke to you, sir, but it eez my reputation at stake."

"Not to speak of your life."

She felt herself blanch, but remained silent.

Perching a hip on the stool, Saybrook watched her scoop up a handful of the vegetables and begin trimming off the tops. "You have the hands of an artist, Monsieur Alphonse," he remarked, shifting his gaze to the heavy steel blades and graters arrayed around him and then back again. "One would not expect those fine-boned fingers to wield the tools of your trade with quite so much skill."

Her throat seized and Arianna didn't dare try to speak, fearing a feminine squeak would give her away. At this distance, the darkness of his eyes appeared due to the telltale dilation of his pupils—Mr. De Quincy clearly imbibed a goodly amount of laudanum to ease his pain. But apparently the drug had not dulled the sharpness of his wits.

She must not make the mistake of underestimating him. She had made too many errors already.

Willing herself to remain calm, Arianna took up a butcher's knife. *Chop, chop, chop.* The familiar rhythm steadied her nerves, and in a matter of seconds, the carrots were reduced to a pile of uniform slices.

"If Prinny had been gutted and quartered instead of poisoned, you would be an even more obvious suspect," he added conversationally.

"Does that mean that you have come to arrest me for attempted murder?" she demanded.

Instead of answering, he asked, "Have you always been interested in cooking?"

She lifted her shoulders. "From an early age I had to learn how to fend for myself, and at times I had to be creative in order to keep from starving. I discovered that I had a knack for working with food, and I find it interesting." A sweep of the blade pushed the vegetable aside. "But you—you look like one of zose monkish men who subsist on bread and water—and ze thrill of hunting down dangerous criminals and eliminating them from society."

"I've been recovering from an injury," he answered brusquely.

Had she touched a sore spot? If so, Mr. De Quincy was quick to cover his discomfort. "As it happens," he went on calmly, "I do have an interest in cuisine. And from what I have heard, you are very good at what you do."

Another shrug.

"Did you learn your art in France? I am trying to place your accent. . . ."

"*Non*, in ze islands of the Caribbean," she growled. A head of garlic, finely diced, joined the carrots in a large copper pot. "Martinique, Guadeloupe, St. Barthelemy. Then I drifted to Jamaica for a time." Arianna reached for a bowl of small white onions. "Do you require references?" she added with a sarcastic laugh.

"Not at present," replied Saybrook politely. "So, what brought you to London?"

"I was bored and wished to expand my horizons."

His dark brow notched up a fraction.

"Zhis is a city of great wealth and opportunity," she went on. "People hunger for fine things, and I saw a chance to profit from it."

"A very pragmatic assessment, Monsieur Alphonse," murmured Saybrook.

"Unlike you fancy Ingleeze gentlemen, I did not grow up in a cosseted world of pampered privilege. I had to survive on my own wits, so yes, I am pragmatic. Is zat a crime in this country?"

"Not that I am aware of." Saybrook shifted slightly, and Arianna guessed that he was trying to ease the pressure on his injured leg. "What makes you think I am a gentleman?"

"Your coat is tailored by Weston. He only caters to a wealthy, titled clientele."

"You have a discerning eye, Monsieur Alphonse."

"Cooking requires one to pay attention to the small details."

Saybrook remained silent as he watched her pluck a bouquet of fresh herbs from the overhanging rack and methodically mince a handful of the leaves.

"Rosemary." Saybrook sniffed the air. "As well as thyme and savory."

She looked up in surprise.

"I spent time in my grandmother's kitchen when I was a boy."

"You are an odd agent of the government—a member of the upper class who chooses to get his hands dirty"—the chopping grew louder—"with desperate criminals, like *moi*."

"Perhaps, like you, I am bored," said Saybrook pleasantly. "By the by, *are* you a desperate criminal?"

"Ha! You don't care about ze answer." She flashed him a sardonic smile. "All you and your government care about is making an arrest. *Voilà*—the problem is solved, and be damned with the inconvenience of ze truth. *N'est pas?*"

Saybrook turned slightly, a pensive look shading his profile. The window draperies were drawn almost shut, and in the low light, shadows danced over the taut skin and harsh bones. The air was growing heavy with the warmth of the simmering pots on the stove, and Arianna saw a beading of sweat break out on his forehead.

Hell, what madness had possessed Whitehall to send a cadaver to confront her? Or was the government playing some diabolical game with her? Perhaps in some hideous twist of logic they had poisoned the man in order to confront her with her own supposed crime. . . .

Don't panic, she told herself. The idea was insane . . . and yet, the man looked on the verge of dropping dead on the spot. Which would only lay another sin at her feet.

"Are you ill, sir?"

His lids flew open.

"You look pale. Here, have a morsel of my chocolate." Arianna shoved a plate toward him. "It works wonders at reviving both body and spirit—assuming you are brave enough to try it." A bitter laugh. "But of course, I may simply be seeking yet another victim for my poison."

"Thank you." Saybrook took a small chunk of the nut-brown confection. "I confess, I have been very curious to sample chocolate in an edible form. The Aztecs issued wafers of solid chocolate to their soldiers on long marches. It was believed to increase stamina."

"How—how is it that an Ingleeze gentleman knows about such things?" asked Arianna. She was usually very good about reading a person's strengths and weaknesses. But Mr. De Quincy was proving difficult to decipher. He was too . . . unpredictable. A strange mix of odd angles and unexpected contrasts. Now that she had had a chance to study him more closely, she saw that his eyes were not as black as she had first supposed. They were more of a toffee-gold amber, sparking the unsettling feeling of being trapped like a fly in their depths.

Arianna shifted uncomfortably, angry at herself for letting him put her off balance.

"Most men of your rank are indolent idlers, interested in nothing but superficial pleasures."

"Perhaps I am not quite what I seem." Placing the morsel of chocolate in his mouth, Saybrook let it dissolve on his tongue. "How interesting. You've flavored the cacao with vanilla, sugar, cinnamon, and a touch of nutmeg."

An agent from Whitehall with an expertise in cooking? She ducked her head, trying to mask her confusion by peeling away the greased wrapping from a slab of beef.

"I recently came across an old Spanish recipe for a similar combination," continued Saybrook. "However, I have not yet had a chance to try it."

Arianna knew she shouldn't bite, but curiosity overcame caution. "A recipe?" she echoed. "For chocolate?"

The crackling of the wrapping paper faded as her ears filled with a far more soothing sound.

"Cooking is a metaphor for life, ma petite. You must be bold, and use your imagination," whispered her old cook's voice. In her mind's eye she could see gnarled brown hands

spinning the molinillo faster and faster to froth the steaming milk and cacao. "Never cease to be curious. Never be afraid to experiment. That is the recipe for feeling alive."

A sweet memory—ah, but Oribe had been wise beyond words.

Shaking off the reverie, she added, "Considering your official duties, you have very strange interests, Mr. De Quincy."

"True." Saybrook's mouth softened into a faint smile. "I inherited them from my late grandmother. Chocolate was her passion. She scoured the antiquities shops of Madrid and Barcelona, looking for manuscripts and diaries from the New World. She left me several notebooks filled with the recipes and legends she collected."

"What a treat it would be to read them," mused Arianna.

"Perhaps you'll have a chance." He made a wry face. "I have been working on translating them into English, with the hope of finding an interested publisher."

"Unlikely," she scoffed. "They are far more interested in horrid novels, with fainting heroines, talking swords, and dastardly villains."

"Stranger things have happened," he replied with an enigmatic look. His gaze lingered on her face, and then suddenly cut down to the chopping board, where she was slicing the beef into small pieces for the stew.

Arianna felt a strange prickling, like dagger points dancing down her spine.

Dangerous. Though she had hardened herself to emotion, she felt a clench of fear squeeze the air from her lungs. There was something deceptively dangerous about the man. She had the feeling that despite his mild manner he was ruthlessly probing her defenses, looking to deliver the *coup de grâce*.

She closed her eyes for an instant, trying to master her momentary weakness. But when she opened them, she saw that Saybrook had taken up one of her paring knives and was testing the edge of its blade against his thumb.

"Could I convince you to give me the recipe for your chocolate wafers?" he asked.

"Non." Arianna edged a step into the shadows. "I don't share my secrets, sir."

Perhaps it was merely a quirk of light, but Saybrook's lidded gaze seemed to sharpen. "Is there a reason you work in such darkness, monsieur?" he asked abruptly. "I would have thought that a man so conscious of detail as you are would prefer a brighter room."

A serving spoon clattered to the floor. "I—I worked aboard ships, and have become used to it."

He suddenly shifted the knife to his other hand. And then—

And then it cut through the air, a quicksilver streak against the gloom.

Dear God, the man was mad!

"Monsieur!" Arianna tried to parry the blow, but Saybrook, anticipating the move, slid his blade up and under her guard. The sharp point sliced through her linen smock and sunk smack into the middle of her belly.

"Ummph!" Her jaw went slack as she stared down at the quivering steel.

He drew in a sharp breath and held absolutely still, watching, waiting ...

Slowly, a snowy white feather spilled from the slash, then another.

Saybrook jerked the knife free and with a quick flick of his wrist knocked the toque from her head. A slice severed the ribbon tied around the tightly wound mass of curls.

Recovering from her initial shock, Arianna let fly with a dockyard curse. "You bloody bastard," she added, sliding hard to her left. Lifting her own weapon in a quick feint, she whipped it down in an angry arc.

Saybrook pivoted just in the nick of time, causing the blade to brush over his trousers.

Damn the man. Arianna used a few more moves from her arsenal of filthy tricks, yet he managed to elude the stabs aimed at his injured leg. She was good with a knife. But so was he.

A flurry of wild slashes drove him back several steps. Steel rang against steel as he parried her blows. Regaining his balance, he countered with a series of probing jabs. He handled his weapon with expert ease—it was clear that he wasn't trying to draw blood, merely to disarm her. Which somehow made her temper flare. Did he think he could toy with her, simply because she was a woman?

Steady, steady. Reminding herself that fighting a *mano a mano* battle was foolhardy, she edged closer to the curtained window. Saybrook shifted his stance to match her movement, opening up an angle to an iron-banded door, a tradesmen's entrance, set to the left of the mullioned glass.

Arianna drew a quick breath and darted forward.

With a spinning lunge, he moved to block her path. His boot came up, lashing a well-aimed kick that buckled her knee. As she stumbled, he flicked a chop with the flat of his hand, sending her weapon flying across the room.

"Damn you to hell!" she spat out, rubbing at her bruised leg and then at her wrist. Dropping the French accent, she added a perfectly irate English curse.

"I've been there and back," replied Saybrook calmly, watching a few more downy fluffs seep from the gaping wound in her padded middle. "But be assured, mademoiselle, that I'm not going anywhere until I get some answers from you. And nor are you."

She shot him a daggered look.

"No need to stare like that. I'm well aware that you would like to cut out my liver and make it into pâté. However, having left a small chunk of myself on the battlefields of Spain, I would prefer to keep the rest of my body intact."

"I—I was not really trying to hurt you," she muttered. "I was simply—"

"Trying to escape," he finished for her. "I don't really blame you for trying. But I cannot permit that to happen."

She looked away, expelling a sigh. "How did you know?"

"Like you, I try to be observant, and pay attention to the small details. You are good—very good—but there are certain subtle ways in which a woman is different from a man."

Her mouth formed a mocking curl. "How *very* clever of you to have noticed, Mr. De Quincy."

"Your hands, for one thing," he went on pleasantly, ignoring her sarcasm. "By the by, how did you learn the art of disguise?"

"I had a friend in a theater troupe in Barbados. It seemed a useful skill to know." She hugged her arms to her chest. "Though binding your breasts is cursedly uncomfortable. So is walking around with a wool stocking stuffed in your crotch."

"I shall take your word for it," replied Saybrook dryly.

She twitched a grudging smile. "You are a *very* odd man, Mr. De Quincy."

"That is rather the pot calling the kettle black, Miss . . . or is it Missus?"

"Miss." Her chin rose a fraction. "Smith."

"Smith," repeated Saybrook. "Ah, I should have guessed."

She merely shrugged. "Speaking of taking my word, sir, I'll have you know that I had nothing to do with poisoning the Prince Regent."

"I hope, for your sake, that is true." Reaching over with his knife, he speared a morsel of chocolate from the worktable and lifted the blade to his lips. "It would be a great pity if your sweet secrets went with you to the grave."

"I know it looks rather suspicious, sir, but I can explain my masquerade," said Arianna. "However, it has no relevance to your investigation. . . ." She paused.

"I'm afraid I must judge that for myself," responded Saybrook.

"It's a rather lengthy story."

"Nonetheless, I must insist on hearing it," he said.

"What if I were to tell you that I possess information that could help lead you to the real culprit?" she countered.

"Then I should suggest it would be greatly to your benefit to share it with me."

Her jaw tightened. "Not without getting something in return from you."

"You are hardly in a position to bargain," pointed out Saybrook. Shifting his weight, he began to massage his thigh. "Might we sit down and negotiate over a plate of your special chocolate," he suggested. "I am willing to listen—" His voice cut off abruptly.

Arianna followed his gaze and caught sight of a shape—more of a shadow—through the light-colored weave of the window draperies. It moved again, a blur of dark against the coarse linen.

"What—"

Reacting at the same split second, Saybrook grabbed her and flung her to the floor, just as one of the glass panes exploded and a bullet whizzed overhead.

5

From the chocolate notebooks of Dona Maria Castellano

Intrigued by the missionary's journal, I have begun to search for other old papers documenting the first reactions to cacao here in Spain. So far, the earliest mention I have found occurs in 1544, when a delegation of Dominican friars returned from Guatemala and presented Prince Philip with a pot of hot, frothed chocolate. His reaction is not recorded, but I have learned that the Spanish found the Aztec preparation too bitter and spicy for their taste, and so began adding sugar from the cane plantations in the Caribbean islands, along with old-world spices like pepper instead of chiles. . . .

Cacao Shortbread

1 cup (2 sticks) unsalted butter, softened
2/3 cup confectioner's sugar
2 teaspoons pure vanilla extract
2 cups all-purpose flour
1/4 cup Dutch-processed cocoa powder
1/2 teaspoon salt

1. Preheat oven to 350°F.

2. Using an electric mixer, beat butter and sugar until creamy, about 2 minutes.
3. Add vanilla and beat well.
4 Mix in flour, cocoa, and salt on low speed until just combined. Form dough into disk, wrap in plastic, and chill for at least 2 hours.
5. Roll dough between 2 sheets of wax paper to a ¼-inch-thick rectangle. Use a sharp knife to cut shortbread into 2-inch squares.
6. Place squares on baking sheet 1 inch apart and prick tops with fork. Bake 15–18 minutes. Cool completely on wire rack.

With the sound of the gunshot still echoing in her ears, Arianna crabbed toward the side door.

"Stay down," barked Saybrook, seeing her push up to her hands and knees.

A plume of smoke wafted in through the gaping hole, and with it the acrid tang of burnt powder. Arianna gagged, the smell triggering another rush of memories. *Blood. Screams. Death.* Kingston was a notoriously violent port of call, and escaping the clutches of a slave ship captain had sparked a horrifying brawl.

Arianna's pulse kicked up a notch, and as she pressed a palm to the wainscoting, she could feel her heart pounding against her ribs. No matter which way she turned, the Grim Reaper seemed intent on shadowing her steps.

Get hold of yourself, Arianna, she thought with an inward grimace. However, the warning was unnecessary. Already her instinct for survival had taken charge and her mind was racing to assess her options.

A quick glance showed that Saybrook had crawled to the door and was lifting the iron latch.

It released with a soft *snick*.

At the same instant, a force outside slammed into the door, flinging it open. A man burst in, the smoking pistol still grasped in one hand. With the other, he raised a second weapon, its hammer already cocked, and took dead aim at her.

A mirthless laugh welled up in her throat as she stared into the unblinking eye of the gun barrel. Of all the damnable ironies—she had survived on her own in some of the most brutal hellholes on earth, only to stick her spoon in the wall in a nondescript London kitchen.

Oh, Papa, I'm so sorry for failing—

Out of the corner of her eye, she saw Saybrook lunge with his knife, and the blade, still sticky with chocolate, cut across the assailant's sleeve.

The pistol fired, echoing her scream.

Dazed and half deafened by the explosion, Arianna fell back against the wall. Through the haze of smoke, she saw a cloud of feathers floating in the air, but as her hands flew to her stomach, she found that only her padding had suffered a mortal wound. Save for a nick on her cheek from a shard of glass, the rest of her was unscathed.

"Buggering bastard." The assailant cursed and slammed the butt of the spent weapon into Saybrook's ribs, knocking him back against the worktable.

Biting back a grunt of pain, Saybrook threw himself sideways, narrowly avoiding a vicious smash aimed at his head. The tabletop shivered, and a pewter tray crashed to the stone tiles, along with a basket of cutlery.

A kick caught him flush on his injured leg, and Arianna saw his face contort in pain. "Duck!" she cried, casting a look at the spent pistol just out of arm's reach. If the fight shifted just slightly, she would have a chance. . . .

Saybrook's hands clenched and somehow his fingers closed around his cane. Blocking a punch, he countered by ramming the silver knob into his assailant's groin.

The man dropped to his knees with a strangled snarl. "You're a dead man," he rasped, sweeping up a big-bladed butcher's knife from the floor. His voice was further muffled by the black silk mask covering his whole head. There was a slit for his mouth and two rough-cut holes for his eyes, which blazed with a malevolent gleam. "You and that nosy little she-bitch will soon be feeding the fish in the Thames."

The slim ebony stick wasn't much of a match for the length of murderous steel. Saybrook shuffled back, darting a sidelong look at the cleavers hanging at the far end of the overhead rack. Arianna saw it, too—another step or two would bring them within his reach.

"De Quincy!" she warned.

The assailant had scrambled to his feet, and with a roar of rage launched into a head-on charge.

Bracing himself, Saybrook managed to block the first stab. He held the advantage in height, but the other man was built like a bull, with thick limbs and slabs of solid muscle. The blade flashed again, slicing the cane in two.

"The next one will sever your jugular."

Saybrook ducked the slash and spun around, raking the jagged wood across the man's knuckles.

Blood welled up from the furrow, but the assailant kept hold of his weapon. Its steel danced through the air, sleek and sinuous as a snake ready to strike.

Anticipating the blow, Saybrook quickly dodged to his left, but his leg, weakened by the struggle, was slow to react. The knife cut through his trousers, scoring a gash in his thigh.

Arianna bit back a cry.

The momentum of the attack sent both of them sprawling to the floor. Saybrook landed awkwardly, his head hitting hard against the stone tiles. The other man fell on top of him, flailing, cursing, kicking.

The blood pounding in her ears, Arianna watched with a strangely detached sense of calm. *It was over.* Saybrook was trying to fight off the attack, but it looked as though his strength was ebbing fast. In another moment, she, too, would be dead.

With a savage snarl, the assailant reared up. His upraised arm hovered for a heartbeat in the hazy shadows. . . .

Thwock. Steel stabbing into flesh made a sickening sound.

Then, as if in slow motion, the blade fell harmlessly from the man's lifeless fingers and his body toppled forward, landing heavily atop Saybrook's sprawled form. The impact appeared to rouse him from his momentary stupor. Twisting out from beneath the limp limbs, he eyed the hilt of a carving knife protruding from the man's back and expelled a ragged breath.

"Thank you," he croaked, slowly levering to his feet.

"*De rien,*" muttered Arianna, wiping her red-stained fingers on the remains of her smock. "You saved my life earlier. Now we are even."

She quirked a sardonic smile, but realized her hands were shaking uncontrollably. Clasping them to her mutilated belly, she slanted a look at the lifeless body. "Oh, *merde.*" Her words were barely a whisper. "Now I am really in the suds."

Saybrook bent down and pressed a finger to the man's throat. "The fellow is dead," he confirmed after several long moments.

Arianna blinked. "I . . . You . . . you are hurt," she said, eyeing his slashed trousers, the fringes of charcoal wool now black with blood.

"Just a scratch," he replied. Sitting back on his haunches, he slowly peeled the mask from the corpse's face.

"*Merde,*" she muttered again, echoing her earlier epithet. It seemed exactly the right word to sum up her sentiments.

"Do you recognize him?" he asked.

Arianna nodded grimly.

"So do I." But before he could elaborate, the hurried thump of boots upstairs warned that all hell was about to break loose.

How long had it been since the first shot? A few minutes at most, she calculated.

"Bolt the door," he suddenly ordered.

Arianna hesitated.

"*Quickly*, goddamn it!" He rushed to the window and checked the back garden. Seemingly satisfied, he turned. "Then hide in the pantry. Don't make a sound."

At the moment, he seemed like the lesser of two evils, so she decided to do as she was told.

Tucking the mask in his pocket, Saybrook hurriedly retrieved the pistols and dropped them close by the body. Gritting his teeth, he yanked the knife from the dead man's back and rolled the body over. "God forgive me," he muttered, cutting several quick jabs into the fast-cooling flesh before lodging the blade between two ribs.

What was he doing? she wondered, casting a sidelong glance at the macabre scene.

After reordering a few of the other fallen objects, Saybrook rose awkwardly to his feet.

"Open up! Open up!" A fist pounded on the kitchen entrance, rattling the locked latch.

"I'm coming!" Glancing down at his bloodied trousers, Saybrook gave a wry grimace. "I won't have to exaggerate my own ineptitude," he added under his breath.

Shooting back the bolt, he flung the door open. "Don't just stand there," he snarled at the four guards who were staring in bewilderment at the carnage. "The chef has escaped. I tried to stop him but the damned fellow is as skilled as a butcher. You and you"—he jabbed a finger at the two closest men—"go after him. He fled through the garden. But have a care—he's armed and dangerous."

As the pair headed off in pursuit, Saybrook quickly turned to the remaining men.

Crouched in the darkness, Arianna listened to his orders, growing more mystified by the moment. He was saving her from the wolves. *But why?*

Through a crack in the door, she saw Saybrook grab the nearest man by the arm. "I want you to carry a message to Mr. Basil Henning, at number six Queen Street—and do it with all haste," he barked. "Tell him that Lord Saybrook needs to see him immediately, but say nothing of what has happened. You are to wait and escort him back here. Understood?"

"Yes, milord!"

Milord? She frowned, feeling even more disoriented.

Saybrook waved the man on his way, and then addressed the last man. "And you are to remain with the Prince Regent. Lock yourself in his chamber, draw the curtains, and admit no one until I come and tell you otherwise." He paused for a fraction. "Is that clear?"

The man snapped a salute.

"Go!" he ordered.

Drawing a deep breath, Saybrook waited for several long moments before approaching the pantry. He opened the door a touch more but did not enter. "I assume you have female clothing hidden in your room."

"Yes," answered Arianna in an equally low voice.

"Get dressed. And pack up any traces of your disguises," he said curtly. "Be quick about it. When the moment comes, we will have to move fast. In the meantime, stay quiet as a church mouse."

Arianna didn't waste any time with questions. Gliding past him with quick, silent steps, she slipped into the shadows of the bedchamber.

"Who the devil are you?" he growled.

"I could ask the same of you, sir."

He made a face. "A far more pressing question for both of us, Miss Smith, is why Major Crandall, late of the Horse Guards and Lord Grentham's senior staff, is lying dead on the kitchen floor."

6

From the chocolate notebooks of Dona Maria Castellano

Oh, how I had to laugh when I found another old journal in which the writer debated whether it was Columbus or Cortez who brought the first cacao beans to Europe. My research leads me to agree with his conclusions that Columbus had little interest in chocolate. But a far more delicious discovery was that English pirates who preyed on the Spanish treasure fleets sailing from the New World once burned an entire cargo of cacao beans, thinking they were sheep turds! Sandro will find that story greatly amusing. . . .

Mini Brownie Cupcakes

4 sticks unsalted butter, cut into pieces
8 ounces unsweetened chocolate, chopped
1¾ cups all-purpose flour
½ cup unsweetened cocoa powder (preferably Dutch-processed)
½ teaspoon salt
3¾ cups granulated sugar
8 large eggs
vegetable-oil cooking spray
confectioner's sugar (optional)

1. Preheat oven to 350°F and line 2 mini-muffin tins with liners. Spray liners with cooking spray.
2. Melt butter and chocolate in a 4-quart heavy pot over moderately low heat, stirring until smooth. Whisk together flour, cocoa, and salt. Remove pan from heat and whisk in granulated sugar. Add eggs, 1 at a time, whisking after each addition until incorporated, and stir in flour mixture just until blended.
3. Spoon batter into muffin liners, filling cups to top, and bake in middle of oven 25 to 30 minutes, or until a tester comes out with crumbs adhering. Cool 5 minutes in tins and turn out onto racks. Repeat with remaining batter.
4. Dust with confectioner's sugar if desired.

"**T**his way—and quickly, damn it." Wrapping his long fingers around her arm, Saybrook shoved her past the upturned corpse. "You moved fast as a snake earlier."

Arianna tore her gaze from the slashed shirt linen and pooled patterns of viscous red. Bile rose in her throat but she forced down her momentary nausea with an acid retort. "For which you should be bloody thankful."

"I'll compose a suitably sentimental ode to your audacity later." He inched the door open a fraction and made a rapid survey of the garden. "Let's go."

Ungrateful wretch.

Saybrook stumbled on the uneven gravel but quickly steadied his stride and cut through a narrow gap in the ornamental plantings. Despite the labored hitch of his gait, he moved with surprising speed. Arianna found herself hurrying to keep pace.

Hugging close to the leafy shadows of the ivy-twined wall, he led the way to the side gate, which gave access to an alleyway.

"Left leads past the mews and out to Welbeck

Street," she murmured as he ventured a peek through the wrought iron bars. Her first day of employment, she had scouted out the area, making a mental note of how to disappear in a hurry. "Right goes straight to Wigmore Street. It's shorter, but there's usually more traffic."

"Which means a greater likelihood of finding a hackney," he said, more to himself than to her. "We'll chance it." He shifted his weight, leaning a shoulder to the painted metal. His coat covered the rent in his trousers, but she saw that the wool was growing wet and sticking to his knee.

"Your leg—"

"Sod my leg," growled Saybrook. "You ought to be far more concerned about your neck."

She bit back a sharp reply. His face was deathly pale, accentuating the Stygian shadows beneath his hooded eyes.

The gate creaked, and in another moment they were turning the corner.

"Aren't you afraid that we'll attract attention?" demanded Arianna. His hand was still clamped like a manacle around her arm. To emphasize her point, she gave a small shake of her canvas satchel. "You are limping, and ladies aren't often seen carrying such bags."

Saybrook reached around and plucked it from her grasp.

"Don't be an arse," she protested in a low voice. "You're having trouble enough hauling your own carcass to the next crossing. What I meant was, I would draw less notice on my own."

"Arse?" His grip tightened. "I was an arse to accept this . . . this . . ."

This what? Arianna waited for him to finish, but he merely sucked in a breath and looked up and down the street.

"If any of the guards spot us," he added, after hailing a hackney, "I shall say that I saw you walking past the house and wish to detain you as a possible witness."

"I still say that you should let me go ahead on my

own," she pressed. "We can choose a place to meet up later."

He answered with a curt, mirthless laugh. "I may be an arse, but I'm not an idiot," he added. "Though given my earlier incompetence, I can hardly blame you for thinking me a bumbling fool."

Whatever else he was, Mr. De Quincy was no fool, thought Arianna. She had merely hoped to catch him off guard.

"It was worth a try," she replied coolly.

"You'll have to do better," said Saybrook, helping her none too gently into the hired carriage. He climbed in after her and collapsed in an inelegant sprawl beside her.

She could feel heat emanating from his body. *Fever? Anger? Or some dark, drug-deranged emotion that she could not name?* It bothered her that she was having such a difficult time figuring him out. Men were, in her experience, primitive creatures, ruled by three basic lusts—power, money, and sex. That made them rather simple to understand.

And manipulate.

But Mr. De Quincy was proving an exception to the rule. Which made him dangerous.

Slanting a look through the grimy glass panes, Arianna reminded herself that she had survived for years by outwitting men who posed a far greater threat than her captor. It should be easy to escape his clutches—she would just have to pick the right moment. One twist, one lunge, and she could surely outrun him, leaving her free to pursue her own quarry.

Let De Quincy chase his own specters. All she cared about was the ghosts from her father's past. Step by step, she was coming closer to the truth. So close she could almost taste it.

Sweet, sweet revenge.

"Turn here!" Rapping his knuckles on the trap, Saybrook called out a few more commands.

As Arianna watched the buildings roll by, she forced herself to quell the flutter of unease in her belly. *Where was he taking her?* At present, he seemed reluctant to turn her over to the authorities.

But that could change in the blink of an eye.

She had better seize her chance to run, and soon.

The wheels clattered to a halt on the cobblestones, and once again Arianna let herself be hustled down an alleyway and through a garden gate. The terraced grounds were far fancier than Lady Spencer's haphazard layout. Formal hedges of trimmed yew flanked pristine paths of white gravel, their precise symmetry blurred by a profusion of colorful flowers.

"Where are we?" she asked abruptly.

Saybrook brushed by a trellis of climbing roses, stirring a sudden, overpowering sweetness in the air. For an instant, she was dizzy, disoriented. The lush floral fragrance seemed so insanely at odds with the metallic smell of death still lingering in her nostrils. *Silk and steel.* Seeing the swirl of soft pinks darken to deep red, she choked down a burble of hysterical laughter.

Don't panic, she chided herself. Not when she could still salvage victory from the jaws of defeat.

Shaking off the strange light-headedness, Arianna tried to concentrate on memorizing the layout of the gardens. There was a second gate ahead, just past a small storage shed discreetly hidden from the main house by a screen of holly trees. The door was partly open, revealing sacks of manure and an assortment of terra-cotta pots—

Without warning, Saybrook whirled and shoved her inside.

"Sorry." The click of the padlock punctuated the apology. "I need to arrange things inside the main house."

"Bloody bastard," she hissed, thumping her fists against the oak planks.

"I suggest you remain silent, Miss Smith. You're a good deal more comfortable in there than in one of the Horse Guards interrogation chambers."

His reply only fueled her frustration. Kicking at the clay shards underfoot, she muttered several words in Creole under her breath.

"Look, you ungrateful wench, I've put my neck on the chopping block for you," he snapped. "The least you can do is refrain from insulting my manhood."

Arianna clenched her teeth.

"And in case you are wondering, all the sharp implements are kept elsewhere. So resign yourself to spending the next little while inside. If you'll notice, I tossed your valise inside with you, so you are not entirely stripped of creature comforts."

"It's dark in here," she muttered, squinting at the thin slivers of light coming in through the cracks. "And it stinks of *merde*."

"I seem to recall that you prefer the dark," said Saybrook. "As for the odor, would you prefer the smell of death?"

"How long do you plan to keep me confined in this cesspool?"

"Hard to say," he replied. "In the meantime, there's a small potting bench built into the back wall. "I suggest that you sit quietly and contemplate the error of your ways."

She ground out another oath.

"Rather than spend your time cursing me to the devil, you might want to think about this—it was *you*, not *me*, who Major Crandall was trying to kill. Would you really rather take your chances on the streets of London, with no idea of who else might be hunting for you?"

I can take care of myself. The words were on the tip of her tongue but she held them back.

"Ah, I had a feeling your oh so clever brain would grasp the logic in that." She heard him move away. "I'll return as soon as I can."

Logic. Arianna felt her way to the back of the shed and found a sliver of space on the rough planks. Curling up against the stone-cold clay pots, she tried to still her spinning thoughts and focus on making sense of the last few days. It seemed that in hunting down her own quarry, she had unwittingly stepped into a nest of vipers. Slithering serpents with bared fangs, coiled to strike. She drew her knees to her chest, aware of the prickling of gooseflesh along her arms.

So close, so close, and then she had turned careless in her last few steps. The question was, would their bite prove fatal?

Lord Concord and Lord Hamilton.

She had crossed an ocean to pursue those two cold-blooded reptiles. It had been a shock to learn from Lady Spencer that Hamilton had broken his neck six months ago during a drunken carriage race from London to Brighton. But that still left Concord, and she had always considered him to be the more dangerous of the two.

That he might be dangerous enough to dare an attack on the Prince Regent added an unexpected twist.

And suddenly her quest seemed tied in a Gordian knot.

Arianna thought of the three items she had taken from Lady Spencer's desk. For now, they were her only tangible clues to cutting through the secrets surrounding her father's death.

Revenge. Redemption. For years, those twin desires had driven her onward. But in her heart, she also wanted to know the truth.

Saybrook shifted in his seat, his boots scuffing softly over the minister's Turkey carpet. "And so, after a quick check of the surroundings showed no sign of the chef," he explained, "I thought it best to leave the pursuit to the guards and returned to the town house, in order to arrange for the body to be taken away." A pause. "I assumed you would want me to dispose of the problem quickly and discreetly."

"How very thorough of you," said Grentham, his expression remaining inscrutable.

"I try to be," replied Saybrook blandly.

The minister tapped his fingers on the three sheets of paper that Saybrook had handed over. "Tell me again precisely what happened."

"The details are spelled out in my report." Another pause. "Milord."

"Nonetheless, I should like to hear you recount them again," said Grentham softly. "Assuming you haven't suffered too great a shock."

Saybrook carefully repeated the sequence of events, omitting any mention of the chef's transformation from "he" to "she."

"Two shots, you say." Grentham fixed him with a long look. "And yet Major Crandall was accorded to be a crack shot. I wonder how two bullets managed to go so badly astray?"

He shrugged. "I couldn't really say, sir. In the heat of battle, strange things happen."

"Strange things happen," repeated the minister softly.

Saybrook sat in steadfast silence.

"I can't help but wonder . . ." Grentham smoothed the creased papers, and then slid them into a dossier. "Have you any idea as to why Crandall would try to kill the Frenchman while you were interrogating him?"

"No."

"And you wouldn't care to hazard a guess?"

"I don't care for parlor games," replied Saybrook. "If you wish to hear people engage in idle speculation, I am sure you have plenty of lackeys outside your door who will be only too happy to oblige you."

"You're a good deal more facile with your tongue than you are with a weapon, Lord Saybrook." The minister leaned back in his chair. "I put you in charge of this investigation and what do I have to show for it? Within less than half a day, the Prince's assassin has escaped, my military attaché is dead, and you—you're barely able to crawl through my door with a few pathetic pieces of paper." A slow, mocking clap of applause echoed off the sherry-colored paneling. "Bravo, sir. Bravo."

Saybrook's only reaction was to continue contemplating the top of his cane. This one was fashioned with a polished steel knob and a heavy bezel that rotated to release a stiletto hidden within the stout oaken shaft.

A hush fell over the room, save for the ticking of a tall case clock in the corner. A full minute passed before Grentham added, "I am waiting with bated breath to see how you will extract yourself from this steaming pile of *merde*."

"Then I had better be on my way, before the evidence grows too cold to be of any use."

Grentham waited until the earl had his hand on the latch before replying, "Yes, I would hurry if I were you. But I would also tread very carefully. For be assured that if you make one more mistake, you'll find yourself buried so deep in trouble that you'll wish yourself dead."

A ghost of a smile greeted the minister's words. "If you are trying to frighten me, you'll have to come up with a better threat than that."

Metal rasped against metal, jarring Arianna from a troubled half sleep.

"How kind of you to remember your prisoner," she mumbled, rising from the bench and brushing the cobwebs from her hair. As the door swung open, she saw that the gardens were darkening with twilight shadows. No wonder her stomach was growling in protest. She hadn't eaten since morning.

"I—," she began, only to be cut off by a curt order.

"This way." Taking her arm, Saybrook turned off the gravel path and cut across the grass.

Arianna bristled, hating her loss of control. But after a sidelong glance at her captor, she held back further sarcasm. His skin was drawn taut over the bones of his face, and with fatigue hazing his gaze, he looked on the verge of collapse.

Time enough later to argue against Fate. For now, she tried to concentrate on making a mental note of her surroundings.

Tall, well-pruned plantings, set in a symmetrical pattern. . . . Leaves slapped softly against her cheeks, and through the hide-and-seek flickers of light and dark, she had only a fleeting impression of the imposing town house just beyond the privet hedge. *A tiered terrace . . . classical colonnading . . . tall Palladian windows framed in pale Portland stone . . .*

She stumbled, suddenly feeling disoriented. The place exuded an aura of power and privilege. Which made absolutely no sense ... unless he was playing some devious mental game to break down her defenses.

"In here."

Stiffening her resolve, Arianna steadied her step.

They passed through a stone-floored scullery and down a long corridor. Saybrook paused to light a branch of candles, the flare of flames illuminating a stretch of burnished mahogany wainscoting and gilt-framed paintings.

Reflected in the glint of his amber gaze, the browns and gold began to dance in a whirling dervish blur.

Where the devil am I?

He opened a paneled door set into the wall and stepped aside. "After you, Miss Smith. Have a care. The stairs are rather steep."

At the top landing, they exited into yet another corridor and passed through a set of carved double doors. "In here, if you please." Saybrook indicated the second door on the right.

Arianna stepped into a large bedchamber tastefully furnished in shades of taupe and cream.

"I imagine you're hungry. I've ordered up a hot supper."

She unwound her shawl and draped it over the dressing table chair. The rich brocade and burled walnut wood had an understated elegance that bespoke money. Heaps of money.

"I'm not being put on bread and water until I confess?"

"I think you will find Bianca's cooking palatable," he replied. "Please make yourself comfortable. If you would like, I'll have a bath sent up after your meal."

Her skin began to itch at the prospect of scrubbing away the filth of the day. "Thank you." Arianna was grateful, but it nettled her pride to have to admit it. She glanced around, noting the locked window latches and heavy oak door, and couldn't keep from adding, "However gilded, it appears that this is a cage. I take it that I am to be held as a prisoner here?"

Saybrook raised a brow. "Would you rather be in Newgate? The cells there are damp, dirty, and infested with lice that would eat you alive."

"I suppose this is a preferable alternative." She took a seat on the edge of the massive four-poster bed, feeling even more out of place as her work-roughened knuckles brushed against the eiderdown coverlet. "Assuming I don't expire from boredom."

"There is a library at the far end of the corridor. Feel free to choose a book to occupy your mind. But be advised that the main doorway will be locked, and the servants have strict orders that you are not allowed to leave." Saybrook let the words linger as he carefully lit a branch of candles. "And in case you are wondering, they are quite loyal to the owner of this place, so don't bother trying to bribe them."

Arianna gave a bitter laugh. "Unfortunately I have nothing to barter, save myself."

He turned away and gestured at the massive armoire. "Feel free to place your belongings in there. If you are in need of anything else, you may ring for a maid and she will attend to it."

The opulence was overwhelming. Everything about the house—the look, the feel, and even the smell—exuded refinement. *Delicate colors, feathery silks, the sweetness of lavender.* Arianna blinked back the sting of long-ago memories, refusing to be intimidated. Be damned if the Polite World considered her naught but a verminous insect. She would show them that an insect's bite was cause for alarm.

"Where am I?" she demanded.

Saybrook didn't answer.

"Bloody hell, Mr. De Quincy, I think I'm entitled to some answers."

That drew a gruff laugh. "So do I, Miss Smith," he replied as he drew the door shut. "So do I."

7

From the chocolate notebooks of Dona Maria Castellano

Having discovered so many interesting facts in my missionary's journal has led me to explore other Church records, and I have just learned some new information. In 1569, chocolate became widely popular in Catholic countries because Pope Pius V ruled that drinking the beverage did not break the fast, and so it could be taken as nourishment on Holy Days. However, I doubt such news will be of any interest to Sandro. He shows little reverence for organized religion....

Spanish Hot Chocolate

2 cups milk
2 ounces sweet chocolate
½ teaspoon cinnamon
2 beaten egg yolks

1. Stir the milk with the chocolate and the cinnamon over low heat until the chocolate dissolves.
2. Add the egg yolks and beat the mixture until it becomes thick, taking care not to boil.
3. Serve in coffee mug.

❧

"**S**o that, in a nutshell, is what happened, Uncle." Saybrook paused just long enough to chuff a mirthless laugh. "Thank you for drawing me back into the King's service." Raising his glass, he cocked a salute. "For God and country. Huzzah."

Stealing closer to the library door, Arianna crouched down and eased it open a touch wider. Minutes earlier, the sound of footsteps and the low murmur of masculine voices in the corridor had drawn her attention from the book she had borrowed. Her curiosity piqued, she had given them time to settle in before following along.

The room was unlit, save a single argent lamp set on the sideboard next to a tray of crystal decanters. Appearing as stark silhouettes against the pale marble of the hearth, the two men were seated facing each other, their dark leather armchairs drawn close to the banked fire.

"I considered it my duty to pass on Grentham's request," said the earl's companion.

De Quincy's uncle? Arianna craned her neck for a better look. In contrast to her captor's angular features and coal-black hair, the other man had a smooth patrician profile and silvery curls cut short in the latest *à la Brutus* style. His clothing was elegant and exquisitely tailored as well, the folds precise, the lines faultless.

Saybrook quaffed a long swallow of his drink and muttered something under his breath.

Damn. Arianna inched forward, straining to hear.

"But now that you have recounted the day's events, I'm convinced that I should counsel you to wash your hands of the matter," continued the other man.

There was a sliver of silence, save for the faint hiss of the burning wick.

"Oh, well done," said Saybrook softly. "Holding out a temptation, and then taking it away is a very effective strategy. But then, the highly respected Right Honorable Mr. Mellon is known for his persuasive powers." To

Arianna, his voice sounded slightly slurred. "Tell me, did Whitehall ask you to make sure that I wouldn't crawl away with my tail between my legs?"

Mellon's face tightened and his mouth went white at the corners. "I shall assume it was the drug speaking, not you, and so will forgive that remark. However, if you dare insult my integrity again, I will thrash you to a pulp—wounded leg be damned."

After draining the last bit of liquid from his glass, Saybrook pressed it to his brow. "Christ, forgive me. That was a rotten thing to imply."

"Yes, it was," growled Mellon. "As if I would throw my brother's son to the proverbial wolves."

"You would become the next earl if anything were to happen to me," he pointed out. But as his uncle started to sputter anew, he held up a hand. "Cry *pax*. In Spain, one had to have a certain sense of gallows humor to survive with a modicum of sanity."

Arianna could scarcely believe her ears. The dark-as-the-devil specter was an *earl*? She hadn't paid any heed when he offered a second name, but she realized now that it must have been his title. *Another slip on my part.* She couldn't afford to miss such details. All too often they could mean the difference between life and death.

Mellon exhaled a long breath, interrupting her mental monologue and drawing her gaze to his face. "Well, seeing as you escaped slaughter in the wilds of the Guadarrama Mountains, I should hate to see you come to grief here in the heart of civilized London." His tone was light, but beneath the conciliatory smile he looked troubled.

Setting aside his empty glass, Saybrook gingerly shifted his outstretched leg. A spasm of pain pinched at his mouth, but he quickly covered it with a cynical grimace. "Death isn't overly discriminating as to place or time, Uncle." He smoothed out a wrinkle in his trousers. They were, noted Arianna, a new pair, fashioned out of dove gray superfine. "Just why do you advise me against remaining in charge of Whitehall's investigation?"

"Because I don't trust Grentham farther than I can spit. By all accounts, he's a devious, duplicitous bastard," replied Mellon. "There's no question that he's extremely effective as head of security, but he's also scheming, manipulative—and utterly ruthless when it serves his purpose."

"He would hardly be any good at his job if he weren't," observed Saybrook dryly.

"I suppose that's true." Mellon rubbed at his jaw. "But I have been thinking . . . there might well be another reason, aside from your military intelligence experience and your knowledge of chocolate, that Grentham is anxious to have you handle the investigation of this case."

"Ah, yes." Saybrook's eyes fell half closed.

Probably due to the drowsying effects of the narcotic he had added to his wine, thought Arianna.

"Having a half-blood Spaniard in charge provides a convenient scapegoat if things go awry," the earl went on. "It would be oh so easy to call my loyalties into question."

Interesting. She held herself very still, intent on not missing a single word. The more she knew about her captor, the better her chances of outwitting him.

"I fear so," admitted Mellon. "Not that anyone in his right mind could question your commitment to your country. Good God, you're a decorated war hero who served as an officer of army intelligence in the most brutal campaign of the Peninsular War." He rose and went to pour himself another brandy. "Not to speak of holding one of the most distinguished titles of the realm."

"Some people consider that a sacrilege, rather than a mark in my favor." Saybrook made a face. "Oh, yes, I've heard the murmurs—What a pity that the august earldom of Saybrook has fallen to an olive-skinned foreigner."

Saybrook, she repeated to herself, trying to recall whether Lady Spencer and her dissolute friends had ever mentioned the name. But nothing came to mind.

"And while you are up, you may bring me another

glass of port. With a generous splash from the vial beside it, if you please."

Mellon frowned but did as he was asked. "The blood you spilled on the battlefield of Salamanca flows back to William the Conqueror."

"All the more reason that many sticklers of the *ton* resent me." He took a sip of the laudanum-laced spirits. "But never mind that. There is an old adage—sticks and stones may break my bones, but words can never hurt me."

"With Grentham, I would not be so sure," said Mellon. "He wields them with all the skill of a Death's Head Hussar."

"Thank you for the warning, but I am familiar with the shadowy underworld in which he moves," replied Saybrook. "Lies and innuendo. Deception and duplicity."

Oh, yes, thought Arianna. *I'm familiar with that world, too, milord.*

Lifting the cut crystal glass to the candle, he spun it in his fingers. "Grentham may wish to maneuver me like a pawn on his chessboard, but he won't find it quite so easy to control my every move."

"You might not find it quite so simple to slip free from his iron-fisted control," said his uncle.

"Perhaps not." A hint of humor seemed to creep into the earl's voice. "But as you pointed out when you first came to me with this proposal, maybe I need a challenge to rekindle a spark of life."

"Just as long as you don't end up being burned to a crisp." Mellon grimaced. "Speaking of which, how is your leg? You said you suffered a fresh wound?"

"Naught but a scratch," replied Saybrook. "Henning stitched it up for me. He's quite clever with a needle, a skill that I trust he will put to good use on the late Major Crandall. Grentham has not yet sent round one of his lackeys to take a look at the corpse, but I daresay he will."

"Do you trust this fellow?" asked his uncle in a near whisper.

"With my life," responded Saybrook without hesitation. "Henning and I fought together during Wellington's campaign to push Massena out of Portugal, as well as the attack on Ciudad Rodrigo." Despite the low light, Arianna saw his body tense and a sheen of sweat lick across his brow. "A man shows his true mettle when he's plunged into the very deepest pits of hell. There's no comrade I would rather have watching my arse."

"Just so long as he doesn't stick a knife in your back. Grentham has ways of convincing a fellow to betray his friends."

"I'm confident that my luck in dodging sharpened steel will hold." He gestured at his thigh. "Don't forget, you are the one who admonished me to crawl out of my cave of self-pity and stand on my feet again."

"So I did. And while I don't regret the spirit of my words, I fear that I was wrong in suggesting you get involved in this sordid mess." Shadows hid his expression as Mellon shook his head. "This is too dangerous, Sandro. There is something havey-cavey going on here. Ask yourself, why did Crandall try to kill the Cook? If they wanted him—or her—dead, they had only to arrest her and do the deed quietly somewhere in the depths of Newgate."

"Yes," mused Saybrook. "I agree. It makes no sense."

"All the more reason to distance yourself," pressed Mellon. "Turn the woman over to Grentham and be done with it."

Arianna shot an involuntary glance down the darkened corridor. How many guards did he have posted beyond the door? And were they armed? Her skill at picking locks was quite good, but dexterous hands—and quick feet—would be no match for loaded pistols.

Looking back, she saw Saybrook press his fingertips to his temples and begin a slow massaging. "Good God, you can imagine what they'll do to her, knowing she stabbed the Major."

Mellon stared into his brandy.

"She did it to save my life. I can hardly in good conscience hand her over to suffer for my own ineptitude."

His uncle's lips thinned. "What the devil is your alternative?"

There was a long silence. "I haven't decided," he admitted. "I will think about it tonight. And in the morning, I will have another talk with Miss Smith. Perhaps she will be more forthcoming after sleeping on the fact that right now she's the most hunted criminal in England."

"I wouldn't count on it. From what you described, I'd say the woman has brass balls."

A chuckle rumbled in Saybrook's throat. "Actually, brass is far too soft a metal. I would say that her *cojones* are made of Toledo steel."

"It's nothing to laugh about." Mellon rose. "Try to get some rest yourself, Sandro. You look like hell."

Lost in thought, Arianna was slow to react.

"I'll see myself out," he added, seeing the earl awkwardly lever to his feet.

"I'm not so crippled that I can't walk you to the door, Uncle," muttered Saybrook.

Gathering her skirts, Arianna spun around and, after gauging the distance to her room, ran for the closest door.

The closing thud of the oak doors was echoed by the sharp metallic snick of a key turning in the lock. Arianna held her breath, waiting for the sound of the earl's shuffling steps to recede. Surely he would lose no time in returning to the library. She had seen the hungry look in his eye as he had glanced at the sideboard. Pain must be gnawing at his leg—

He stopped, mere inches away from her hiding place, and in the stifling silence she could hear the soft whisper of wool as he shifted his stance.

"You can come out now."

Arianna slipped out of the linen closet. "Whatever else is ailing you, it appears there is nothing wrong with your ears," she muttered.

"Nor with yours," he replied. "I assume you heard everything."

She nodded.

Saybrook closed his eyes for an instant as a spasm of pain pinched at his mouth. Arianna felt a clench of guilt—then quickly shook it off.

Sympathy was a weakness she couldn't afford.

Averting her gaze, she reminded herself to remain detached. *Don't allow it to get personal.* The earl was just another obstacle blocking her road to redemption.

Or was it the path to perdition? She had been traveling for so long that perhaps she could no longer discern the difference.

"Come along," he finally said. "We may as well have a talk now."

"It can wait until morning, if you wish," replied Arianna. "You look to be dead on your feet. And I daresay your uncle would have no qualms about handing me over to the government if you shuffle off this mortal coil."

"Are you intending to sleep?" he demanded.

"No," she admitted.

"Nerves still on edge? It's a common reaction after the heat of battle. A drink can help dull the memory." He turned away. "I intend to have another glass of port before I retire. . . ."

Liberally doused with opium, no doubt.

"Whether you choose to join me is entirely up to you."

After a slight hesitation, she followed along. Why refuse when the drug might further weaken his defenses?

"Sherry?" His voice was muffled by the clink of the crystal.

"I would prefer brandy, assuming it's a decent vintage."

"It is." More sharp-edged sounds seemed to betray an unsteady hand. Yet somehow he managed to cross the carpet without spilling a drop.

"Thank you," she said, accepting her drink. Eyeing the viscous, garnet-colored liquid in his glass, she said, "Did you pick up your dependence on opium in the Peninsula?"

Saybrook settled himself and propped his leg up on the hassock before answering. "You know a good deal more about me than I know about you."

She took a sip of her brandy. "You're right. It's superb."

"That's not quite sporting," he went on, ignoring her comment.

Arianna shrugged. "I don't believe in playing by the rules. Especially as they have been made by gentlemen—highborn hypocrites whose notion of honor is conveniently twisted to suit their own games."

"True."

She had expected an earl to take umbrage at the unflattering assessment, so his concession took her somewhat by surprise. *Damn.* Her intention was to push him off balance, not loose her own equilibrium. Lifting her glass to her lips, she let the burn of the brandy steady her thoughts.

"You have an impressive collection of books here," she said, trying another way to goad him into a temper. "I took your advice and came here earlier to find some reading material." Lowering her lashes, she added, "I happened to see your grandmother's journals on your desk."

Saybrook darted a glance to the shadowed interior and frowned.

"I hope you don't mind that I borrowed them?"

"Would it bother you if I do?"

"Not really."

He let out a low bark of laughter. "In that, at least, you are honest."

"They contain some interesting material." "Fascinating" was more the word, but she was careful to mask her enthusiasm. "Dona Maria Castellano appears to have been a singular lady."

"Yes," he said tightly. "She was."

Had she succeeded in striking a sore point? Arianna probed a little deeper. "I take it she's no longer alive?"

"No." The reply was clipped.

"Was her death recent?"

The question stirred an odd gleam in his eyes. The amber hue seemed to brighten, as if a tiny flame had sparked to life somewhere in their depths. "Why do you ask?"

She curled a lock of her loosened hair around her finger. "Just curious."

Saybrook rose and limped back to the sideboard.

"You know, there are better ways of controlling pain than to make your body a slave to opium," she said without looking around.

"Thank you for your concern," he replied, his voice dripping with sarcasm.

"Your grandmother would be tossing in her grave if she could see you now."

A bottle slammed down, rattling the silver tray. "Enough, Miss Smith. I'm in no mood for your needling."

"You saved my life, so I'm simply trying to return the favor." She gestured at the vial of laudanum. "That drug will end up killing you."

"We're even," he said curtly.

"Not really." Arianna wasn't sure why she was pursuing the matter. *Let him cross over the River Styx if that's what he wants.* Still, she found herself saying, "You've held off turning me over to Whitehall, which would mean a certain death. So the scales are tipped in your favor."

He returned to his chair—empty-handed, she noted. "And you appear to be doing your damnedest to make me change the balance."

At that, Arianna smiled. "True," she said, echoing his earlier comment. "But actually, I'd rather you hold off until I have a chance to finish reading Dona Maria's chocolate notes."

"Delicious, aren't they? Especially for someone interested in nuances of cuisine." He steepled his fingers. "A temporary truce might be negotiated. Assuming you are willing to offer something in return."

She took a long swallow. "I didn't poison the Prince, for I imagine that is your first question."

"An astute guess, Miss Smith. Yes, it makes sense to start there." He tapped his fingertips together. "If you didn't do it, who else might have had the opportunity?"

Arianna meditated on the question for several moments, trying to decide just how much to reveal. She would have to feed him a few tidbits—he was too sharp to be fobbed off with nothing.

"The guests had gathered early that evening, and Lady Spencer made no secret of the fact that I was preparing a special delicacy for His Royal Highness," she replied carefully. "One of the ladies—I don't know her name—did come to the kitchen and ask what it was, but I chased her away. For reasons that should be obvious, I did not encourage anyone to enter my bailiwick."

"The persona of temperamental chef helped disguise your secret," he mused.

She nodded. "My impression was that she merely wanted to tease the Prince with hints of what was coming."

"What about the kitchen help? Could one of the girls who helped you prepare the meal have slipped some substance into the chocolate?"

She shook her head. "As you saw, Lady Spencer isn't plump in the pocket. One of the reasons she valued me was that I didn't complain about working alone. As for the footmen who served the guests, I handed them the platters at the door."

Tipping back his head, Saybrook stared up at the ornate plaster ceiling, apparently lost in contemplation of the carved rosettes. As the silence stretched on for what felt like an age, she began to fidget.

"Feel free to refill your glass," he murmured, answering her unspoken question of whether he had fallen asleep with his eyes open.

As Arianna rose, he added, "You've stated that no one entered the kitchen while you were there. But did you perchance leave it untended at any time during the evening?"

Truth or lies? She watched the swirling pattern of the

thick Turkey carpet ripple beneath her stocking-clad toes. Could she slide by with a fib?

She looked up to find him watching her intently. "I was gone for a short while."

"Why?"

"The reason is not relevant to your investigation, Mr. De Quincy—or, should I say, Lord Saybrook?"

"Call me whatever you wish. I'm not a stickler for propriety," he replied. "However, as to the other matter, I'm afraid that I shall be the judge of that."

Her jaw tightened. "All you need to know is that I was absent for maybe a quarter hour. In returning, I did see two of the gentlemen guests in the back corridor, near the door to the scullery. One I did not see well enough to recognize, but the other was Lord Concord."

"You know his name?" It was half question, half statement.

"Yes," she replied, but did not elaborate.

"Hmm." Saybrook ran a hand over his thigh, kneading his palm against the injured flesh. A shock of his shoulder-length hair had fallen over his face, making it impossible to see his expression.

"You know, it would make things a good deal easier if you would tell me why you were working for Lady Spencer," he said, easing back in his chair. "It doesn't make sense, for a number of reasons. To begin with, you claim to have come to London in order to make a profit from its riches—and yet you sold yourself quite cheaply. A chef of your skills could have commanded far more money, not to speak of more comfortable working conditions."

"It's not my business to make things easier for you, Lord Saybrook. I overheard enough to know that your reasons for undertaking this investigation have nothing to do with me or my motivations."

"Save when it comes to keeping your neck off the chopping block."

"Why do you care about me?" challenged Arianna.

"I don't, per se. I care about the principle of justice,

even when it means defending a willful wench hell-bent on self-destruction."

The set-down brought a faint rush of heat to her cheeks. "You are one to talk," she countered. "And speaking of withholding information, Lord Saybrook, I heard you tell your uncle that man who attacked us was Major Crandall, a top aide to the Minister of State Security. Why was an officer of the Horse Guards trying to kill me? *And* you?"

The earl responded with a sardonic smile. "The reason is not relevant to your concerns. I am not at liberty to reveal any more than that."

A chill snaked down her spine. Cupping her hands around her glass, Arianna wished that she could draw a touch of warmth from the amber spirits.

"Touché," she murmured, unable to muster a sharper retort.

"I would prefer not to always be at daggers drawn with you." Saybrook sighed as he ran a hand through his unruly hair. "Too bloody dangerous."

The movement caused a momentary flicker of lamplight to play over his face. If anything, the bruised shadows under his eyes seemed to have grown deeper. Darker. He looked tired, and most of all, frustrated.

Not that she blamed him.

Swearing under his breath, the earl rose and made his way to the sideboard. It was only then that Arianna realized how badly his hands were shaking.

Her eyes narrowed. "If you are truly so concerned about solving this case, I'll repeat what I said earlier— you ought not dose yourself with that vile drug. For now it might dull the pain, but it's also dulling your senses, and creating a pernicious dependence that will eventually rot your mind."

"Thank you," he snapped, after returning to his seat. "In one subject, at least, you are a veritable font of information."

Coals crackled in the banked fire, sending up a spurt of sparks.

"There are other ways to deal with pain. I have some knowledge of healing arts. I can give your cook a list of the ingredients, and if you allow me in your kitchen I'll show her how to brew it."

He made a face.

"Stubborn arse," she muttered.

A glint of amusement lit for an instant in his eyes. "That's rather like the pot calling the kettle black."

She repressed an answering smile. "We seem compelled to thrust and parry tonight. Perhaps we ought to withdraw from the fray and lick our wounds."

Saybrook set aside the drug untasted, and levered out of his chair. "Right. Let us both get some sleep. Perhaps in the morning we can come together with a fresh perspective and negotiate a meeting of minds."

Sleep? The idea seemed impossible. Her body was heavy with fatigue, as if it had seeped into the very marrow of her bones, and yet Arianna felt too restless to seek the comfort of the splendid bed. Cupping the glass of brandy that she had carried from the library, she moved to the diamond-paned window and stood staring out through the misted glass. The blackness of night was far preferable to the vivid images imprinted in her mind's eye.

Out of the frying pan and into the fire. She had heard the expression often enough, but it took on new meaning when one's own flesh was hovering a hairsbreadth from the flames.

The liquor began to burn her throat—or perhaps it was only the sudden memory of black powder smoke, sharp and sour as it mingled with her scream. Setting aside the glass, Arianna turned abruptly and went to the armoire, where the contents of her valise sat folded on a single shelf. She had not called the maid to unpack her meager belongings. Her secrets were fast being stripped away, making it imperative to keep those she still had hidden for as long as possible.

Taking the pasteboard folder from inside the frayed

pair of men's breeches, Arianna carried it to the dressing table and drew the candle closer. Shadows danced over the age-worn top page, making the spidery writing even more difficult to make out. She wasn't quite sure what had impelled her to add the papers she had stolen from Lady Spencer's desk to her hastily collected jumble of clothing and face paints.

An intuitive flight of fancy?

No, more likely an utter waste of effort, she thought wryly.

It was the numbers. They intrigued her.

They always had.

Tracing a finger over the first equation, Arianna was reminded of her father and the idyllic games they had played throughout her childhood.

What's seven times twelve, divided by four, poppet?

"Twenty-one, Papa," she whispered, blinking away the sting of salt against her lids. There was something wonderfully pure about numbers and the abstract concepts they created. They were not intrinsically good or evil—they simply . . . were.

Arianna turned the first page, and then the second, and the third, losing herself in the intricacy of the equations. *Intriguing.* She wasn't quite sure what they meant, but following the progression of logic had provided a welcome diversion from her own tangled emotions.

Oddly enough, numbers had always been a source of solace. She had come to think of them as friends, playmates for a lonely childhood that helped keep the pinch of poverty at bay. That her father had encouraged the games, and had taken great pleasure at her skills, only added to the allure. The connection—the time together working out mathematical puzzles—was the one thing that could keep him from seeking escape in a bottle. He had tried to stay lucid for his nightly games.

But those precious moments had become rarer and rarer, and as she got older, Arianna had become desperate to keep him from drowning in drink. The games turned into arguments. Bitter ones at times. . . .

Snapping the pasteboard covers shut, she rose and returned the folder to its hiding place. As the candle sputtered and died, throwing the room into darkness, she found her glass and quickly swallowed the last splash of amber spirits.

Don't stir up painful memories of the past, she chided herself.

To survive, she must focus all her thoughts on the problems of the present.

8

From the chocolate notebooks of Dona Maria Castellano

We Spaniards were quick to make our own variations on the New World preparations of chocolate. Instead of frothing the drink by pouring it back and forth between two cups, as was the Aztec method, we created the molinillo, a type of wooden whisk that is submersed in the hot liquid and spun between the palms. It creates a lovely frothy foam, and I remember how Sandro loved to watch me in the kitchen, his tiny hands mimicking the rhythm of the whirling wood. . . .

Mexican Chocolate Cookies

1 cup all-purpose flour
½ cup plus 1 tablespoon unsweetened Dutch-processed cocoa powder
¼ teaspoon baking soda
¼ teaspoon salt
½ cup plus 1 tablespoon brown sugar
½ cup plus 1 tablespoon granulated sugar
3 tablespoons sweet butter, slightly softened
3 tablespoons stick margarine
½ teaspoon ground cinnamon

generous pinch of ground black pepper
1 teaspoon vanilla
1 egg white

1. Combine the flour, cocoa, baking soda, and salt in a medium bowl. Mix thoroughly with a whisk. Set aside.
2. Combine the sugars in a small bowl.
3. In a medium mixing bowl, beat butter and margarine until creamy. Add sugar mixture, cinnamon, pepper, and vanilla. Beat on high speed for about one minute. Beat in egg white. Stop the mixer.
4. Add the flour mixture. Beat on low speed just until incorporated.
5. Gather the dough together with your hands and form it into a neat 9-to-10-inch log. Wrap in waxed paper. Fold or twist ends of paper without pinching or flattening the log. Chill at least 45 minutes, or until needed.
6. Place oven racks in the upper and lower third of the oven and preheat to 350°F. Line cookie sheets with parchment paper or aluminum foil.
7. Use a sharp knife to slice rounds of chilled dough ¼ inch thick. Place 1 inch apart on prepared baking sheets. Bake 12 to 14 minutes. Rotate baking sheets from top to bottom and front to back about halfway through. Use a metal spatula to transfer cookies to a wire rack to cool.

It must have been the brandy, for despite feeling sure that Morpheus would not be her bedfellow, Arianna was drawn out of a deep sleep by a discreet knock on the door.

Sitting up, she winced as a blade of sunlight cut across her face. No rest for the wicked, she thought wryly, squinting through the diamond-paned windows. She usually rose with the dawn, but the previous day must have ...

The previous day.

Squeezing her eyes shut, Arianna pressed her palms to her brow. Was this living, breathing nightmare really less than twenty-four hours old? *Burnt powder. Twisted screams. Spattered blood. The smell of death.* A churning vortex of spinning, swirling memories stirred a sudden nausea.

No, no, no, it was hunger that had her feeling light-headed, not fear.

"Signorita?" The knock came again.

"Sí." Throwing back the covers, Arianna reached for her wrapper. The maid had brought her nightclothes the previous evening, gorgeous silken garments that slid over the skin like a whisper of tropical air. And certainly far more costly than any clothing she had ever possessed, she reflected, catching sight of herself in the cheval glass.

Dear God, in such borrowed finery, I actually look like a real lady.

A wink of light. A mere illusion. From her father she had learned how easily perceptions could be manipulated.

Turning abruptly, Arianna called, "Come in," then added in Spanish, *"Pase, por favor."*

The door nudged open and a middle-aged woman entered, carrying a silver tray nearly as wide as her own ample girth. It was loaded with food, the aroma of fresh-baked rolls and fried York ham mingling with the sugared scent of steaming hot chocolate.

Despite her earlier queasiness, Arianna suddenly felt ravenous. "Thank you—*Gracias*," she said as the woman set it down on a small table by the windows.

"De nada." After carefully arranging a fork and knife atop a starched white napkin, the woman gestured for Arianna to sit.

Pausing only to pick up a folded sheet of paper from the dressing table, she hurried to comply. A full cup was already waiting, and as the first swallow swirled down her throat, she let out a little sigh.

"Ambrosial," she murmured, savoring the rich taste of the cacao mingling with hot and sweet spices.

"Good?" asked woman in tentative English, her dark eyes watchful.

"Very good," replied Arianna. "Cinnamon, anchiote, vanilla . . ." She took another sip. "And some spice I can't quite place."

The woman tapped a finger to a tiny dish beside the chocolate pot and mimed a sprinkling motion. *"Nuez moscada."*

"Ah. Nutmeg."

Nodding, the woman turned to leave, but Arianna placed a hand on her arm. "A moment, *por favor.*" Handing over a recipe that she had scribbled out earlier, Arianna managed, through a mixture of English, Spanish, and hand language, to communicate what she wanted.

The woman's solemn expression gave way to a tiny smile. *"Sí, sí.* I understand, *signorita.* I will take this to Bianca."

"Tell your cook that if she doesn't have the ingredients in her pantries, they are all easily obtainable in London," said Arianna. "I will be happy to come down to the kitchen if she has any questions."

Tucking the paper in her apron, the woman bobbed her head and hurried away.

"A lost cause," she muttered to herself. "But then, who am I to talk?" Her stomach growled in answer. "Right—let the condemned eat a hearty meal."

After the first few bites, Arianna felt her mood brighten. The warmth of the chocolate, the dappling of the sun, the twittering of birds . . . a new day, and with it, she must look at her situation with a new perspective.

During the night, she had already decided on a change of plan. Her first impulse had been to escape, but on further reflection that seemed a bad choice. Flee now, and she would likely never get another chance at revenge.

Revenge. Her knife hovered for a moment over the plate. Strangely enough, she hadn't yet decided what she wanted. Was it to coax a confession from him and then slide a blade between his ribs? Or somehow see him brought to justice for his crime?

Either way, what mattered was that when the time came, Concord would know that a Hadley had not allowed the truth to die along with her father. *But to do that, I must get close.* The trouble was, the earl had seen her as a woman, and whatever his other faults, he was not a man who would be fooled twice by any disguise.

No, if she wanted to pursue her quarry, she would have to improvise. And after careful consideration, a plan had started to take shape. . . .

Another tap on the oak interrupted her thoughts, but this time it was Saybrook, not a servant, who entered.

"I see you have broken your fast." His expression conveyed an edge of irony as he surveyed the heaping platters.

"There is more than enough to share," said Arianna.

The earl pulled up a chair. A night had done little to improve his appearance. He had shaved, and brushed his long locks into some semblance of order, but the burnished blackness only accentuated the sickly pallor of his gaunt face.

Bloody hell, she hoped he wasn't about to expire. She needed him alive, at least for a little longer.

"I'm not hungry," he murmured.

"No wonder you look like you should be knocking on death's door, not mine." Arianna forked a piece of pineapple onto her plate. "By the by, isn't it highly improper for you to be visiting me in my bedchamber? My reputation would be in tatters if word got out." She met his grim gaze and grinned. "As would yours, milord."

"I think we can dispense with formalities, Miss Smith," said Saybrook dryly. "Our secret should be safe enough. For now, that is. However—"

"However, we must decide how to deal with this situation," she interrupted. "I agree, sir. I have been thinking . . . and I have a proposition."

The earl crossed one booted foot over the other. "Indeed?"

"Yes, and I shall cut to the chase, sir," said Arianna, deciding that coyness was a waste of time. "You need me. I have seen and heard certain things at Lady Spencer's establishment that may be of utmost importance in unraveling your mystery. So I'll help you—but only on certain conditions."

"Which are?"

"I'll tell you all I know, and I'll help you pursue certain leads—as to how is a detail that I will get to in a moment."

His face remained expressionless.

"But in return," she went on, "you must allow me the freedom to follow up on my own concerns. I assure you, they do not conflict with yours." Arianna paused for a fraction, giving him time to digest what she had said. "That is my offer. Take it or leave it."

"But you won't reveal what those concerns of yours are?"

She shook her head.

"You don't trust me?"

"Good God, no," she replied. "I've learned not to trust *anyone*." She slanted a challenging look at him. "Why should I? You aren't going to claim that you trust me, are you?"

"Good God, no," he said with a sardonic smile.

"There, you see," she said. "We are capable of establishing a certain level of honesty with each other. Within such a framework, we could be of use to each other."

"Perhaps." Saybrook folded his arms across his chest. "But since you are asking me to hang my cods over the fire, so to speak, I would appreciate a little more assurance that they will not end up burned to a crisp."

She swallowed a bite of creamed kippers before replying, "That's a fair request." Pouring herself another cup of chocolate she added a grating of nutmeg. "By the by, your cook is not half bad. Cilantro and guindilla verde peppers add a piquant flavor to the shirred eggs."

"I will pass on your compliments," he said. "But much as I enjoy discussing cuisine, I would prefer that we stick to the subject.

"Very well." Arianna buttered a thick slice of toast,

and then added a dollop of strawberry preserves. "Lady Spencer liked to talk, and I encouraged it. I would prepare a serving of my special hot chocolate on most afternoons, along with a plate of her favorite almond pastries. And while she ate and drank, I asked questions about her circle of friends."

"Why?"

"I've told you, my reasons are not relevant to your interests, Lord Saybrook."

He grunted. "Go on."

"So I learned a good many details about the Prince Regent and his current circle of fellow carousers. Suffice it to say, they are a depraved group, but Lord Concord and several of his friends in particular seem to be the leaders in a variety of vices. Lady S hinted that they are members of a secret society. I had to add a little rum to her chocolate in order to loosen her tongue, but I got her to admit that they made mention of the Hellfire Club on more than one occasion. And that she herself had participated in their rites."

Saybrook straightened slightly in his chair.

She didn't miss the subtle tensing of his body. "I see that's got your attention, eh? Yes, well, given its long and sordid history, Lord Dashwood's creation is likely the hotbed of all sorts of illicit activities."

"Most of which are prurient sexual practices, not murder," pointed out the earl.

"What about the dark rumors of rape and human sacrifice?"

He lifted a brow. "That was years ago. The truth is, the club is said to have died out long ago."

"That does not mean it hasn't been resurrected by a new group of devils," she countered.

Saybrook tapped his fingertips together. "You seem awfully knowledgeable on this esoteric bit of history."

"I have my reasons," she murmured.

"Yes, yes, I know—which naturally you have no intention of sharing with me."

"Naturally." Taking up a fresh cup, she switched from

chocolate to coffee. "You ought to ask for a slightly darker roast," she remarked, taking a moment to sniff the aroma. "These beans are from the Blue Mountains of Jamaica, and the extra heat would caramelize the natural sweetness."

"For a slender woman, you seem to consume a great deal of food."

"No doubt I shall grow quite fat in my old age. But for now, I consider eating one of life's little pleasures."

"You know, Miss Smith, you ought to be more concerned with your neck than your stomach," growled Saybrook.

"Irritable this morning, aren't you? No wonder, seeing as you've probably put nothing in your own breadbox, save for opium."

"I prefer a quiet, contemplative start to the day, and this constant verbal fencing is beginning to stick in my craw." He rose abruptly, cursing as his leg buckled slightly. "I shall leave you to your meal, seeing as you seem to be taking such great delight in it." His mouth thinned to a grim line. "Let us hope it is not your last."

Arianna carefully put down her fork. "Does my appetite offend you?" she asked.

"No, it's your bloody closemouthed stubbornness," he replied through gritted teeth. "If I were you, I would be a tad more anxious to help me find the real culprit. Until I do, you remain the prime suspect."

"I *am* trying to help," she retorted. "Shall I draw up a diagram, milord?" Her knife sketched several lines in the air. "The Prince connects to his coterie of fellow reprobates. These men are linked to a secret club . . . I should think it would all be very obvious."

"Perhaps *too* obvious."

"Please sit down, Lord Saybrook. You are clearly in great discomfort."

"That is because you, Miss Smith, are a royal pain in the arse."

She laughed. "I've been called far worse."

"I don't doubt it." The earl sat. "In another moment, it will be *me* blistering your maidenly ears."

"Why, sir, you actually possess a sense of humor."

He grimaced. "Rarely at this hour in the morning."

"I may have something that will help improve your disposition. . . ."

As if in answer to her thoughts, the woman from earlier reappeared. This time, she was carrying naught but a tall glass filled with a pale green liquid and a plate with several nut-brown wafers.

"*Buenos días*, Elena," began the earl, only to be cut off by a rapid-fire volley of Spanish.

His brows pinched together as he looked from the woman to Arianna and then back again. "What the devil . . .," he muttered, trying to ward off the libation being thrust at him.

"*Dio Madre*, drink it," snapped Arianna. "It's a draught for pain," she explained. "As a child, I was cared for by a local *quimboiseur* in the Caribbean. Like your grandmother, she was an expert in the healing arts, though some called her a witch."

"You expect me to swallow this . . . this black-magic potion?"

"It's far better than that dark drug that is rotting your innards," she countered. "But, of course, the choice is yours."

Elena wagged a thick finger and added her own admonition.

"Women," muttered Saybrook. But after a slight hesitation, he drained the glass and handed it back to Elena, who graced him with a beatific smile. "There. Satisfied, Miss Smith?"

Arianna cut off a tiny slice of fruit. "It's to my benefit that you stay alive a while longer." She looked at Elena and raised three fingers. "Thrice a day, and it's best taken with food." To the earl, she added, "Your appetite will quickly return, once you start weaning yourself from the opium. You will also find that the draught lessens the effects of withdrawal."

Still smiling, Elena placed the plate of wafers on the table and withdrew from the room.

"You don't waste any time in turning a household up-side down, Miss Smith," grumbled Saybrook.

"Look, I thought you were anxious to solve this case," retorted Arianna. "From what I overheard last night, time seems to be of the essence."

He fingered the small silver fob on his watch chain. "You ought not have eavesdropped on my private conversations."

"Yes, well, see how useful a woman with no shred of decency can be to you?" she countered. "I doubt that there are *any* rules that I'm not willing to break in order to get what I want." The soft splash of coffee punctuated her words. "And trust me, milord, there are things I can do to wheedle information out of the suspects that you, for all your military skills, can't." She fluttered her lashes. "If you grasp my meaning."

He stared at her, unblinking. "An interesting argument, Miss Smith. But for all your fancy verbal footwork, you still haven't explained just how you intend to put theory into practice."

"I was just getting to that." Arianna pushed back from the table with a contented sigh. "Ahhhh, that was delicious," she said, savoring the pleasant warmth radiating through her body. She had gone hungry often enough not to take it for granted. "I think much better on a full stomach."

"Then you ought to be a veritable genius," said Saybrook, eyeing her empty plate.

She responded by pouring the last bit of hot chocolate and nudging the cup his way. "While you are still snappish as a starved mastiff. Finish this while I talk."

He looked about to argue, then picked up the drink and took a small sip. "Now kindly continue, before I swoon from suspense."

Arianna smoothed at a fold in her wrapper. "I think we both agree that the person responsible for poisoning the Prince was either me or one of the guests at Lady Spencer's party, correct?"

The earl gave a tiny nod.

"Let's assume I'm telling the truth, so that would mean our remaining suspects are all ladies and gentlemen who move in the highest circle of Society." She didn't bother to ask for his affirmation. "Which means that for me to get close to them—close enough to learn their most intimate secrets—I will need to be accepted as one of their own."

Saybrook appeared to be more interested in the carved acanthus leaf ceiling molding than her words.

Ignoring his wandering gaze, she forged on. "How, you may ask, do I intend to do that? Well, the answer is ingeniously simple. Your uncle—the Right Honorable Mr. Mellon—"

"I'm acquainted with my relative's name," he murmured, which showed that he was listening after all.

"I'm aware that Mr. Mellon is a highly respected member of the *ton*, a paragon of virtue, a pattern card of propriety. So, if he were to introduce a distant female relative into Society, she would be welcomed without question. Embraced, as it were, with open arms."

That seemed to get his attention.

"Especially if word went out that she was a very wealthy widow. Men are attracted to money, all the more so when it is attached to a lady who is not a skittish virgin. And I know enough about the most likely suspect to offer just the right enticements so that he will be drawn to me—or, rather, my persona—like a moth to a flame."

When Saybrook didn't react right away, she asked, "So, what do you say?"

"I would say," he replied slowly, "you have a mind that rivals that of Machiavelli."

"I'll take that as a compliment."

"I'm not sure it was meant as one." He blew out his breath. "Clearly you are clever. And wily."

"Which are just the sort of qualities you need to catch a cunning criminal. Fight fire with fire."

"Yes, but that brings us back to the matter of trust. How do I know you won't run off and leave me in the lurch?"

"That is a chance you will have to take," she said. "But be assured that I have my own reasons for wishing to see this through. The fact that we have common goals should put your mind at ease." Seeing his frown, she quickly added, "And after all, it's not like you have much to lose. At the moment, you have no real leads, no real suspects."

"Save for you," he reminded her.

Arianna waved it off with an impatient huff. "You'll only waste your precious time pursuing that idea, sir." She paused for a moment. "By the by, why is time of the essence in tracking down the culprit?"

It was his turn to evade a question. "The reason is not relevant to your interests, Miss Smith."

Confident that she would find a way to worm the truth out of him if they joined forces, Arianna let it pass with a shrug. "Fair enough. So let's return to my proposal, Lord Saybrook. Surely you see that the positives far outweigh the negatives."

He fingered his chin, and she could tell he was giving it serious thought.

"Come, you have to admit that there is no reason it won't work. Chef Alphonse simply disappears, as befits a canny murderer. I, in turn, make an entrance into Society as a relative of Mr. Mellon and his family, which is all very proper and according to protocol."

"There are a number of rather important details, such as a fashionable wardrobe and a respectable residence. To be credible you cannot exist as a will-o'-the-wisp."

"True, but all of these things can be easily worked out." Arianna feigned a casual shrug. *Money, bloody money.* The cursed stuff—or lack of it—had controlled so much of her life. And now was no exception. Her plan depended on how much of his own the earl was willing to part with.

"You've plenty of blunt," she went on. "Surely you won't mind spending a bit to drape yourself in the glory of catching the Prince's poisoner. I'm sure His Royal Highness will reward you handsomely."

His eyes narrowed. "I'm not looking for another medal, Miss Smith. Or money."

"Ah, yes. Noble principle." Perhaps it was a mistake to mock him, but she couldn't keep the sarcasm out of her voice. "Well, not everyone can afford to have such integrity, Lord Saybrook. Most of us are willing to sell ourselves quite cheaply."

"But not you, Miss Smith," he responded, matching her tone. "What you are suggesting will cost me a pretty penny. A fancy wardrobe . . . a lady's maid . . . a residence and retainers." His brow rose a notch. "While we're at it, shall we add in a matched pair of winged unicorns to fly your spun-sugar carriage to the moon?"

"Not necessary. I told you, sir, I'm not going anywhere until we solve this case."

"We?" He chuffed out a harsh breath. "What makes you think you can carry off this charade? It's one thing to skulk around a darkened kitchen disguised as a rough-mannered man. But to parade as a gently bred lady under the glittering lights of a Mayfair ballroom will take more than *cojones.* . . ." He let his words trail off.

"I know more about your world than you might imagine." Vague memories stirred, like the flutter of gossamer silk in a summer breeze. *Candlelight and music. Champagne popping and couples dancing. The dulcet tones of her mother's laughter rising up to her hiding place at the top of the marble staircase.*

Strange, but it suddenly felt as if a flock of butterflies were beating their wings against her ribs.

Clearing her throat, she summoned from somewhere deep within herself the cultured tones of an English aristocrat. "I promise you, Lord Saybrook, I am quite capable of playing the role of a respectable female."

She looked up to find the earl's eyes boring into her. "Who are you?" he mused. "Not that I expect an answer."

Arianna brushed off the odd sensation. "My past isn't important," she said softly. "All that should concern you is what I can do for you in the next little while."

Saybrook rose and went to stand by the windows. Backlit by the morning sun, he appeared as a stark sliver of black, all sharp angles and impenetrable shadows.

"Not a soul is aware of my presence in London," she added. "Indeed, most people aren't even aware that I still exist. Which should count as yet another point in favor of my plan."

"Yes, it's doubtful Grentham knows anything about you," conceded the earl. He turned abruptly. "He would have pounced by now."

She could sense that he was wavering. As a distraction, she pointed to the plate of chocolate wafers that Elena had brought in. "You might as well begin your healing regimen right away. If you are to be of any use, you need to build up your strength."

He ran a finger over the glossy dark discs. "I thought you didn't share your secrets."

"Seeing as you shared your grandmother's journals—"

"Unwillingly, I might add."

"Be that as it may, I thought it only fair to reciprocate."

"Yet you've taken great pains to tell me you have no principles," pointed out Saybrook. "Isn't that a contradiction?"

"No doubt. I also told you I don't feel compelled to abide by any rules. You will have to get used to my mercurial habits."

Arianna could almost see his mind working. *Lies and flatteries, deceptions and betrayals.* The earl was wondering whether he was being set up. Ensnared in a silken web.

He rubbed at his injured leg. "We've spent a lot of time discussing the Prince's poisoner, but have you forgotten about Major Crandall? Why he wanted you dead is just as great a mystery?"

"Yes, it is." Arianna gave a small smile of triumph. "You solve that one while I apply myself to the other. Assuming, of course, that you accept the terms of my offer."

"You drive a hard bargain."

"Does that intimidate you, Lord Saybrook?"

The challenge seemed to spark a new light in the depth of his eyes. There was, she reminded herself, a luminous intelligence there, though the opium had made it difficult to discern.

Cat and mouse. They would both be playing a dangerous game, each determined to be the predator and not the prey.

His mouth curled up at the corners. "Oh, be assured that I am tougher than I look."

She felt her mouth go a little dry. "As am I, sir."

Saybrook acknowledged the assertion with a small nod.

"So, do we have a deal?" asked Arianna.

"I will likely regret it, but yes, we have a deal, Miss Smith." Picking up a piece of the chocolate, he broke off a sliver and popped it into his mouth. "Now get dressed. We must move quickly if we have any hope of making this work."

9

From the chocolate notebooks of Dona Maria Castellano

Ha! I have made another scientific discovery! In 1570, chocolate was being used as a medicine in Spain. Francisco Hernandez, the royal physician to King Philip II, believed that it was beneficial, and prescribed it to reduce fevers and relieve discomfort in hot weather. I have my doubts about the effectiveness of such treatments, but I applaud his intelligence in realizing the healthful benefits of chocolate....

Salted Chocolate Caramels

2 cups heavy cream
10½ ounces fine-quality bittersweet chocolate (no more than 60% cacao if marked), finely chopped
1¾ cups sugar
½ cup light corn syrup
¼ cup water
¼ teaspoon salt
3 tablespoons unsalted butter, cut into tablespoon pieces
2 teaspoons flaky sea salt, such as Maldon
vegetable oil for greasing

1. Line bottom and sides of an 8-inch straight-sided

square metal baking pan with 2 long sheets of crisscrossed parchment.

2. Bring cream just to a boil in a 1- to 1½-quart heavy saucepan over moderately high heat, then reduce heat to low and add chocolate. Let stand 1 minute, then stir until chocolate is completely melted. Remove from heat.

3. Bring sugar, corn syrup, water, and salt to a boil in a 5- to 6-quart heavy pot over moderate heat, stirring until sugar is dissolved. Boil, uncovered, without stirring but gently swirling pan occasionally, until sugar is deep golden, about 10 minutes. Tilt pan and carefully pour in chocolate mixture (mixture will bubble and steam vigorously). Continue to boil over moderate heat, stirring frequently, until mixture registers 255°F on thermometer, about 15 minutes.

4. Add butter, stirring until completely melted, then immediately pour into lined baking pan (do not scrape any caramel clinging to bottom or side of saucepan). Let caramel stand 10 minutes; then sprinkle evenly with sea salt. Cool completely in pan on a rack, about 2 hours.

5. Carefully invert caramel onto a clean, dry cutting board, then peel off parchment. Turn caramel salt side up. Lightly oil blade of a large, heavy knife and cut into 1-inch squares.

The next few days passed in a blur. Modistes, milliners, parasols, corsets . . . the list of shops to visit and things to order seemed endless. As did the long sessions with Lord Mellon and his wife, reviewing proper etiquette and the hierarchy of Polite Society.

Like any savage place, London had its own laws of the jungle.

Arianna saw nothing of Saybrook. After discreetly delivering her to his uncle's residence and recruiting him as a reluctant ally, the earl had disappeared. Mellon was far too well-mannered to express his true feelings, but worry was writ plain on his patrician face. Did he wonder whether he was harboring a murderer in his home? Or were his fears all for the consequences his nephew would suffer if this deceit of Whitehall became known.

They would, she guessed, be dire.

Well, the earl would have to look out for himself. As for carrying out her own part of the plan, she didn't intend to fail.

By the end of the interlude, even Mellon had been forced to concede that she learned her lessons well. Perhaps, thought Arianna sardonically, she had absorbed the essence of aristocratic bearing from her mother's milk. She remembered Lady Anne as an ethereal beauty, surrounded by an air of absolute tranquility. *The calm before the storm.* Her father's life had gone to pieces upon her death, no longer held together by his wife's serene good sense.

Ashes to ashes. But justice could rise, like a phoenix from the burnt-out coals.

Justice. In an odd sort of way, she and the earl did have something in common, though they might define the concept in very different ways.

So, she had worked diligently during the day, and spent long hours at night plotting, planning her strategy. Lord Concord—his depravities and desires were well known to her, thanks to the loose tongue of Lady Spencer. And she planned to use that knowledge as a weapon. The swoosh of a fan, the flutter of lashes . . . blades and bullets were not the only way to slay an enemy.

As Arianna ran her hand over the fancy gowns hanging in the armoire, feeling the seductive softness of the costly silks and satins, the intricate patterns of the exquisite beading and lace, her flesh began to prickle in anticipation. The act of sliding into a new persona was by now so familiar that it felt like donning a second skin. *Disguise and deception*. She had been hiding her true self for so long, she wondered whether it existed anymore.

Her fingers clenched. It didn't matter. She had waited for what felt like a lifetime to assume this role.

Let the play begin.

Gemstones sparkled in the blaze of the torchieres flanking the front door, looking like brilliant bits of colored fire against the swirl of dark velvet cloaks and black overcoats. The evening was cool, but the heat inside the crowded entrance hall was already cloying. Lush perfumes and spicy colognes mingled with the sweet scent of the roses, thickening the air so that every little breath was a tickling caress against bare skin.

Arianna quickly adjusted her shawl to cover the pebbling of gooseflesh on her arms.

She looked around, careful to mask her reaction to the sights, the sounds, the smells of her first London ball with an expression of regal indifference. No one must guess she was not at home in the splendor of Mayfair's mansions. She was now one of them, she reminded herself.

A lady of indolent leisure. Rich. Bored. Craving a taste of excitement.

Her own emotions had no place here. All her actions must be calculated to attract, entice a certain sort of gentleman.

"Abandon hope, all ye who enter here," said Saybrook in a sardonic murmur, while his uncle and aunt were drawn aside to greet some old friends.

"Is that meant to put me at ease?" she asked under her breath.

"God, no, simply an observation. I can't imagine anything putting your nerves on edge. Certainly not a gathering of rich, overfed aristocrats."

She laughed. "You, at least, appear the better for taking some nourishment. I trust that Bianca and Elena have been feeding you chocolate."

His mouth quirked. "Stuffing me like a pig."

"There's an old adage about casting pearls before swine." She noted that his evening clothes seemed close to fitting his lanky frame.

"Ah, you flatter me, Lady Wolcott," he murmured. Arianna had chosen her mother's middle name to use as her *nom de guerre*. "Though allow me to point out that most people will take such frankness amiss."

"I know what is expected of me," answered Arianna in a low whisper. "I shall not disappoint."

She could feel the curious stares as the earl handed her cloak to one of the porters. Her gown, fashioned from shimmering sea-green watered silk, was expertly cut to accentuate every subtle feminine curve.

"A lovely creation, madam," murmured Saybrook. "Your taste is exquisite."

"And expensive," she replied. "I hope you are a *very* rich man, milord."

He inclined his head a fraction. "I am. But be advised that I expect my investment to pay off."

The note of cool detachment nettled for an instant, but Arianna was quickly distracted by the arrival of Lord Concord, who came in with several other gentlemen.

As he turned to converse with his friends, she had a chance to study him under the bright light of the crystal chandelier.

Robert Mappleton, the Right Honorable Lord Concord, was a decade younger than her father—which put his age at forty-four—and had inherited the barony only recently. Those facts, and a good many other details about his background, she had committed to heart. Until now, however, she had caught only fleeting glances of his face.

Arianna could see why many women found him attractive. He possessed fleshy good looks that were just beginning to show the effects of his dissolute lifestyle. His dark hair was thick, with just a touch of silver showing at the temples, and his smile radiated a certain self-confident hauteur.

She angled her body, just enough to catch his eye, and then turned away. Let him wonder who she was.

"Quite a crush, is it not?" Saybrook surveyed the snaking line of guests winding their way up the curved stairway. "That is, by the by, the highest accolade for any evening entertainment."

Mellon and his wife rejoined them. "Shall we go up?" he inquired tightly.

"After you, Uncle," replied Saybrook, offering Arianna his arm.

The vast stretch of black and white marble floor tiles were barely visible beneath the sea of ruffled silks and polished evening pumps. The effect was still impressive, as was the pristine painted woodwork and the high, arched ceiling decorated with an Italianate fresco of cavorting cherubs.

She blinked, feeling a bit blinded by all the rich trappings of the haute monde.

A lady's light laugh sounded nearby, the dulcet tone blending with the masculine murmurs and the muted clink of crystal.

Privilege, power, pedigree. Wealth had a language of its own.

Her eyes once again found Lord Concord.

"If you are ready, Lady Wolcott, I think we ought to follow my uncle's suggestion and go meet our hostess."

Saybrook's words roused her from her study. "Yes, of course."

The stairs were still crowded. She felt the brush of wool against her bare arms and heard whispers stir behind her back. Their comments had drawn attention. People were curious about the new face in their midst.

Excellent.

Fluttering her fan, Arianna ventured a peek at the people below. Concord was leaning on the newel post, his head upturned, his gaze on her.

Better and better.

As they made the last turn to the upper floor, the light from the massive chandelier seemed to take on an even more glittering intensity. Mellon was waiting for them, and as his wife slipped away to greet a group of her friends, he held out a gloved hand. "I shall take our lovely relative to greet Lady Battell," he announced. "And then we will have the first dance before turning her over to you, Sandro."

The earl stepped aside with alacrity. "But of course. I will meet up with you later."

Arianna had no chance to see where he slipped off to, as she was immediately swallowed into a swirl of silken greetings. Names, faces, titles—she concentrated on keeping them all straight. Everyone, it seemed, was anxious to make her acquaintance.

"That seemed to go well," she murmured as Mellon finally was able to lead her on to the dance floor.

"Yes." The earl's uncle kept a dutiful smile pasted on his face, but no warmth reached his eyes.

"I know how little you like this, sir," she said. "But I'm not your nephew's enemy. I'm not going to stab him in the back."

"So you say." His jaw tightened. "Have you truly any idea of what a dirty, dangerous game you are playing?"

"I'm not afraid," answered Arianna.

"Well, you should be," whispered Mellon. "As should my nephew."

She wasn't sure how to answer, so they danced the rest of the quadrille in silence, their feet moving mechanically in time with the music.

"Your uncle dislikes me," she said, as the earl claimed her hand.

"He tends to be protective," answered Saybrook.

"Your grandmother's journal also expressed worry over you," she blurted out. "Why?"

"I was at war, Lady Wolcott. Naturally she was worried."

Despite the noise and the crowd, Arianna was suddenly aware of being very alone. No one gave a damn whether she lived or died. Even when her father was alive, he had shown little paternal responsibility. *Ev-*

ery man for himself was the unspoken credo. She had learned at an early age to fend for herself.

"Naturally," she replied coolly. "So who watched over you in the army? Do your fancy English regiments hire mother hens to keep watch over the precious chicks?"

The shadow of his lashes hid his eyes. "Have a care where you tread, Lady Wolcott," he said softly.

Arianna felt his shoe pinch against her toe.

"The dance," he chided. "Pay attention to the dance. If you wish people to believe you are who you say you are, you can't afford the tiniest slip."

"Thank you for the warning," she muttered.

"Call it a caution." He spun through an intricate turn. "I see that Lord Concord is here. I assume you wish to strike up an acquaintance."

"Correct," she said through her teeth.

"I know one of his companions. I'll introduce you when this sets ends."

"A Mr. Needham has claimed my hand for the next dance."

Saybrook's mouth curled to a semblance of a smile. "Prerogative of rank. I shall inform him that I want you to meet some of my friends."

"And your wish is my command?"

"So it will seem to him."

An oblique answer. Which was just as well. Having to work with anyone chafed. She didn't rub along well with figures of authority.

"My uncle and aunt will be leaving shortly—and by the by, we can trust that Eleanor has made certain that every gossip in Town is now aware that you are a very rich widow."

"Lucky me," she murmured.

"Yes, well, you'll have every fortune hunter sniffing around your skirts. But I imagine you won't have any trouble fending them off."

"Just get me close to Lord Concord, sir."

"As I said, that will be no problem." His face betrayed no hint of concern. Indeed, he looked almost anxious to feed her to the wolves. "Signal me when you are ready to leave. I will take you back to my uncle's town house in my carriage."

It was on the tip of her tongue to tell him that wasn't necessary. But it was. The rules of propriety must be maintained for now.

"Come," he said, as the trill of the violins died away. "Now that the erstwhile chef has spent a bagful of my blunt making herself look good enough to eat, let us see if Concord will bite."

"You are new to Town, Lady Wolcott?" asked Sir Philip Gavin as Saybrook excused himself from the group.

"Yes." Arianna flashed a smile at the three men, letting it linger just a little on Concord. "It's been ages since I've visited. I am so looking forward to enjoying myself."

Gavin looked at her intently, and then his mouth twitched—a little hungrily, she thought.

Encouraged, she leaned in a little, allowing them all a better look at her décolletage. "Is it very naughty to admit that I take pleasure in a party? My late husband preferred a quiet life in the country. We would occasionally journey to Harrowgate to take the waters. But the society there was very . . . dull."

"It's only natural for a lovely lady to prefer a more stimulating environment than the wilds of Yorkshire," replied Concord with a hint of a grin. "I assure you London is far more fun."

"Oh, I am delighted to hear you say so." Tapping her fan to his shoulder, Arianna asked, "Would you be so kind as to ask the waiter for a glass of champagne, sir?" She lowered her voice to a conspiratorial whisper. "I much prefer bubbly to ratafia punch."

"Vile stuff, ratafia," agreed Gavin. Neither he nor the honorable Mr. John Tipton had been present on the night of the Prince's poisoning. However, Lady Spencer had frequently mentioned them as being part of Prinny's inner circle of friends, whom the newspapers had dubbed the Carleton House carousers.

"Have you ever tried brandy?" asked Tipton, after exchanging a look with Concord.

She giggled. "Yes, but on the sly. It was strictly forbidden by my late husband."

"I bet that made it taste even sweeter, eh?" said Concord slowly.

"Yes." This time her laugh was a little throatier. "But I daresay I shouldn't admit it."

"Oh, we understand what you mean, Lady Wolcott," assured Gavin.

Arianna took a swallow of her champagne, wondering if she was appearing *too* eager. She didn't think so. According to Lady Spencer, young widows—preferably rich ones—were just the sort of females favored by men like Concord and his cronies. They had the relative freedom and independence to do as they pleased, provided they were discreet about it.

Besides, she had no choice but to flagrantly flaunt her availability. Time, as delineated by Saybrook, did not allow for a more subtle approach.

Driaining her glass she held it out for a refill. "Oh, how lovely to discover myself among such amiable gentlemen."

Their smiles put her in mind of a pack of feral dogs eyeing a fresh bone.

"You know, we are holding a party the day after the morrow. It promises to be quite amusing. The thing is . . ." Concord fingered his watch fob. "Some of the guests do not move in quite the exalted circle of Society as your relatives. Would that be a problem?"

"My distant relatives," stressed Arianna. "La, I am not a green girl, and they are not my guardians. They were kind enough to invite me to stay with them while they introduce me into the *ton*. But I intend to lease my own residence as soon as my man of affairs locates a suitable property." Her fan swooshed back and forth, stirring a tickle of cool air. "To be honest, they are nice, but . . ." She mouthed the word "dull."

"Ah. Dull is decidedly boring." A speculative gleam

lit in Concord's eye. "But what of the earl? He appears to be your escort here tonight."

Concord was, of course, aware that Saybrook was investigating the Prince's poisoning, so she quickly moved to distance herself from him. Any hint of an alliance and all her plans would be for naught.

"I did not wish to offend my cousin Mellon. But the truth is, I find Lord Saybrook worse than dull—I find him forbidding." She slanted a look across the ballroom to where he was standing in the shadows of the colonnading and feigned a shudder. "Look how he stands so solemn and silent. He reminds me of a monk from the Spanish Inquisition."

"Lud, you are right." Tipton made a face. "Dark, disapproving—he should have stayed in the god-benighted Peninsula, where he belonged."

"I know him from my club, but I cannot say we are friends," mused Gavin. "Indeed, I was greatly surprised that he chose to introduce you to us."

Arianna was ready with an answer. "I asked him to." She looked around quickly then lowered her voice a notch. "You three are the only *interesting* men in the room."

"Clearly you have a very discerning eye," joked Gavin.

Concord, she noted, had fixed her with an appraising stare. Taking care to appear unaware of his scrutiny, she playfully touched the cluster of fancy fobs dangling from Tipton's watch chain. "What pretty baubles. Have you others dangling somewhere else on your person?"

Tipton swallowed a snort while Gavin leered.

As for Concord, he hesitated, and then the corners of his mouth turned ever so slightly upward.

Arianna slowly released her pent-up breath.

"As I mentioned, we will all be going on to a more intimate party after the Bushnell soiree on Thursday," he said softly. "If you are free, perhaps you would like to join us?"

"I should like that, sir." She lowered her lashes. "Very much."

"You won't bring the Holy Terror along, will you?" said Tipton.

"Good God, no."

Tipton winked at his friends. "Excellent. We don't want to be punished for any sins we might commit, heh, heh, heh."

Arianna gave them a coy look. "*Are* we going to sin?"

"Oh, maybe just a little," replied Tipton. "So yes, it's best you don't bring Saybrook."

"Then again, maybe the earl is not incorruptible." Concord's gaze turned lidded. "I have heard that he is addicted to opium."

"Is he?" she responded, widening her eyes.

Concord gave a slight shrug. "It's said he nearly lost a leg to a French saber while fighting Soult's cavalry on the Peninsula."

Interesting. But any musing on the earl's history would have to wait until later.

"Perhaps that explains his strange mood swings," she said, making a moue of distaste. "One moment he is pleasant. The next he is, well . . . I fear that he is a little unstable." A tremulous sigh. "I do hope I am in no danger riding home in his carriage tonight."

"I'm sure you are quite safe, Lady Wolcott," assured Gavin. "The earl is odd, but I don't think he poses any threat."

Unlike me, she thought with an inward smile.

"Thank you, that is reassuring." Satisfied that she had titillated Concord's interest enough for the evening, Arianna decided it was time to withdraw. Casting another glance at the far end of the room, she sighed. "I had better return to him now, before he grows too restless."

The three of them responded with the requisite bows and polite murmurs.

Concord's voice was the last to fade away. "Until later, Lady Wolcott."

Yes, until later.

*   *   *

"I must warn you—your character has been savaged," said Arianna over the clatter of the carriage wheels. "Perhaps beyond repair."

"I daresay that I shall survive." Saybrook flicked a mote of dust from his sleeve. "Did you have any luck with Concord?"

"Yes."

He waited for her to go on. When she didn't, he prompted, "And?"

"And you need not concern yourself, milord. I have the matter well in hand."

The soft leather of the seat suddenly shivered against her spine as he turned and braced a palm against the squabs. "You have laid down a numbers of rules, madam. Now it is my turn," said Saybrook. "You are free to hurl epithets and insults—it matters naught what you think of me personally. But make no mistake, when it comes to this investigation, I am in command."

"I'm not used to taking orders."

"Nonetheless, you're going to do as I say," he replied softly.

Lifting her chin in deliberate defiance, she replied, "And if I don't?"

A plume of smoke from the oil lamp swirled in the low light, and for a moment it hung between them, obscuring his face. Then it curled upward, revealing a scimitar smile.

He was amused? Arianna wasn't sure how to react. She still found the earl a conundrum, a puzzle whose parts didn't quite fit together.

"Use your very vivid imagination," he drawled.

The remark should have sparked her to even greater anger, but for some reason she found herself smiling, too. "You are flirting with danger in making such a suggestion, Lord Saybrook. As you know, I can be very inventive."

"As can I, Lady Wolcott-Smith-Alphonse-Chocolat." He shifted and suddenly his silhouette seemed to loom larger in the flickering lamplight. "Don't cross swords with me on this. You won't win, but we would both be compelled to expend effort that would best be directed at defeating the enemy."

Put that way, her defiance did sound willfully childish.

"What do you want?" she asked warily.

"A daily report, with detailed information about your activities and what you have discovered. That means an accurate account of who you meet with and what is said."

"Including a menu of what I have for breakfast?"

"I will assume you fill your stomach, seeing as you claim to think better that way. And believe me, Madam whoever-you-are, you will need all your wits about you from now on." He leaned in a little closer, forcing her to meet his eyes. "Look, I am conducting my own investigations, and it could prove dangerous if we were to trip over each other's feet. Furthermore, I may see some clue that you don't."

Arianna swallowed a sarcastic retort. He was right, and she was pragmatic enough to admit it.

"Very well," she replied. "But I also have some demands of my own."

A tiny nod signaled that she should go on.

"I need the freedom of having my own residence. These men must perceive me as independent of you and your family as quickly as possible."

Saybrook considered the matter for a long moment before replying. "I'll arrange it. Along with a staff, of course."

"And a carriage," added Arianna, taking some small pleasure in seeing his mouth thin. "Am I putting a pinch in your purse, milord?"

"Does justice have a price?" he countered.

"Of course it does. The only real question is whether one is willing to pay it."

"You've a jaded view of life for someone so young," replied the earl slowly. "I wonder why."

"Why?" echoed Arianna. "Because I've seen enough

of human nature to know the difference between fairy tales and reality." She paused. "I trust you aren't going to insult my intelligence by trying to convince me that the world is filled with sweetness and light."

It may have been a quirk of the flame, but his eyes seemed to fill with shadows. "No, I'm not. But nor am I going to cede victory to bitterness and blackness so easily. Good can occasionally triumph over evil."

"Dear God, your grandmother must have read you a few too many bedtime tales of heroic knights slaying dragons." Her lip curled. "Or rescuing damsels in distress."

The barb didn't draw blood. He looked at her thoughtfully before asking, "And you, madam—what stories were read to you at night?"

Arianna felt her chest constrict. Looking away, she drew in a gulp of air, forcing her muscles to relax. "Let us not waste time indulging in childhood memories, Lord Saybrook." *Don't look back.* She had learned early on that to survive, one must focus on what lay ahead.

"We've still a number of practical matters to work out. You wish a daily report, and yet we can't be seen together. Committing any information to paper would be unwise—"

"Thank you for the primer on what won't work," interrupted the earl. "However, I am surprised that you, with your creative mind, are overlooking the obvious answer."

She frowned.

"Given your experience in appearing as a man, it should be simple for a street urchin to slip through the streets in the dark of night and enter my gardens."

"I shall likely be busy most nights," Arianna reminded him.

"Improvise, madam. It's something at which you excel." His voice held an undertone of amusement, but it quickly died away. "Make no mistake—we shall both need to be ready to react to the unexpected. Else we haven't a snowball's chance in hell of solving this case."

Hell. Arianna closed her eyes for an instant, recalling a ramshackle room . . . the shriek of the wind . . . her scarlet-stained hands. . . .

"Hell," she said aloud. "Like you, sir, I've been there and back, so I'm not afraid of doing whatever it takes to catch the real culprit."

"How fortuitous that we have met, madam." The earl eased his big body back against the seat. "For neither am I."

"Well, then, it should be interesting to see which one of us is most impervious to the devil's fire."

10

From the chocolate notebooks of Dona Maria Castellano

It seems that the Church continued to debate the use of chocolate. By the beginning of the seventeenth century there was a great debate on whether it should be considered a food or a drink. The distinction was important because of the many fast days. The richness of chocolate helped ease hunger pangs, so the stricter clergy frowned on its use. However, the Pope ruled that because it was taken in liquid form, it was permissible....

Fudgy Coffee Brownies

2 sticks (½ pound) unsalted butter
5 ounces unsweetened chocolate
2 tablespoons instant espresso powder
2 cups sugar
1 teaspoon pure vanilla extract
5 large eggs
1 cup all-purpose flour
1 tablespoon cinnamon
½ teaspoon salt

1. Preheat oven to 350°F with rack in middle. Butter and flour a 13-by-9-inch baking pan.

2. Melt butter and chocolate with espresso powder in a 3-quart heavy saucepan over low heat, whisking until smooth. Remove from heat and cool to lukewarm. Whisk in sugar and vanilla. Whisk in eggs 1 at a time until mixture is glossy and smooth.
3. Whisk together flour, cinnamon, and salt, then whisk into chocolate mixture.
4. Spread batter in pan and bake until a wooden pick inserted in center comes out with crumbs adhering, 25 to 30 minutes. Cool completely before cutting.

An elderly butler—even more elderly than the frail figure seated by the tall mullioned windows—led the earl into the sun-dappled morning room. "Your nephew, milady," he announced in a reedy voice. "Who assures me that you won't mind receiving a visit this early in the day."

"You are looking well, Aunt Constantina," murmured Saybrook, bending to plant a kiss on the lady's cheek.

"Hmmph. I wish I could say the same for you." The dowager Marchioness of Sterling set aside the newspaper and waved a frail finger at an armchair facing hers. Although her wrinkled skin was pale as aged parchment, and her auburn hair had faded to a silvery gray, the signs of encroaching age had not diminished her regal bearing. She still appeared a force to be reckoned with.

"Don't stand on ceremony with me, young man," she ordered. "Sit, before you fall on your *culo.*

"I wasn't aware that a lady of your rank would know such a vulgar word," said the earl, settling his aforementioned arse on the brocade pillows. "Much less say it aloud."

"I've accumulated a great deal of knowledge over my many years." She paused to ring for tea. "And see no reason not to express it."

"I was hoping as much."

Lady Sterling's pale gray eyes immediately looked more alert. "Does that mean your visit is not simply about making amends for your shocking neglect of your elderly great-aunt?"

"My *favorite* elderly great-aunt," amended Saybrook.

She gave a snort. "Your *only* elderly great-aunt."

"I did bring a little something to make up for my shameful neglect." He drew a small pasteboard box from his pocket.

"My taste runs to sapphires these days," quipped the dowager.

Leaning forward, he placed it in her lap. "I shall leave the jewels to your other suitors. I think you'll find these even more delicious."

The dowager opened the package and gingerly picked up a buttery brown cube dusted with cocoa powder. "Pray, what is it?"

"Chocolate. Go ahead—taste it."

Her brows rose a notch higher. "My dear boy, I wasn't born yesterday. If you wish to play puerile pranks on someone, please poison someone younger. My constitution is far too delicate to survive a mouthful of mud."

Saybrook laughed. "What fustian! You are hearty as a horse. And given your fondness for confections, you will be missing a rare treat if you refuse to be adventurous."

After a long look, she gave an experimental nibble. "Mmmm." The rest of the morsel disappeared in a flash and the purr turned into a sigh. "Edible chocolate! Lud, how divine. Is this something you discovered in your grandmother's journals?"

"The journals hold a number of fascinating secrets," he replied obliquely. "But speaking of stories . . ."

Lady Sterling popped another piece of chocolate into her mouth. "Very well, now that you have sweetened me up, you may go ahead and tell me the real reason for your visit."

"I am hoping that your memory is as sharp as your sense of humor, Aunt Constantina. For I need help in unearthing some information from the past." The earl shifted his outstretched leg. "You have always kept *au courant* with the gossip in Town. Do you recall an old scandal in which a gentleman of the *ton* was forced to emigrate to the West Indies?"

"More than a few," she replied dryly. "Jamaica and Barbados have long been popular spots for disposing of wayward sons. Can you be more specific?"

Saybrook made a face. "Not really. I would say we are talking about something that happened between ten and fifteen years ago, but that's merely a guess. The only thing I know for sure is that the gentleman involved had a young daughter who accompanied him to the islands."

"Hmmm." Looking pensive, the dowager fingered the rope of pearls resting at her bodice. "Why do you want to know?"

"I would rather you didn't ask."

"A romantic interest?" she pressed, looking hopeful.

He shook his head. "Sorry to disappoint you but it's nothing personal. I'm merely interested in solving a mystery, and if I could put a name to my conjecture, it would be extremely . . . useful."

"Let me think about it for a bit." A sigh, almost imperceptible, fluttered between them. "I can also pay a call on Lady Octavia Marquand. When it comes to peccadilloes of the peerage, she puts even my knowledge to blush."

"A frightening thought," observed Saybrook. He waited for the maid to place the tea tray on the table and leave the room before going on. "In all seriousness, Aunt Constantina, you must be absolutely discreet about making any inquiries. Not a soul must guess that you are trying to uncover information on a member of the *ton*."

Light winked off her spectacles. "Does this have anything to do with your military activities in the Peninsula?" She leaned forward. "Are you still a spy?"

"I'm simply an invalid, with far too much idle time on my hands," he replied.

A wisp of steam floated up as she filled two cups.

"And pigs have suddenly sprouted wings and can fly rings around the moon."

"Can they?" he replied without batting an eye. "Then perhaps the War Office ought to think of forming an aerial brigade to bombard Bonaparte's army as they march east. God knows, the Russian tsar could use some help from Above to keep the French from invading his country."

The dowager emitted a low snort. "A clever try, but diversionary tactics won't work on me, dear boy." She wagged a finger. "For heaven's sake, Sandro, I am very good at keeping a secret."

"If I didn't believe that, I wouldn't be here," he said quietly. "However, the less you know, the better."

"You mean to say it might be dangerous?" she demanded.

He stirred a lump of sugar into his tea. "Yes. So you must be very careful. God knows, I've enough on my conscience without drawing you into harm's way. But time is of the essence, so I must set aside my personal scruples."

"Don't worry about me, Sandro. I've a lifetime of experience in navigating through the shoals and crosscurrents of the *ton*," replied Lady Sterling. "I'm more concerned about you. The waters can be very treacherous for those who are unfamiliar with the shifting tides and hidden whirlpools."

"I'm a strong swimmer, Aunt Constantina."

"So are the sharks, Sandro. And they are quick to scent even a single drop of blood in the water."

"The warning is duly noted. Be assured that I will take great care to preserve what little I have left."

"See that you do." After a pointed look at his leg, she set down her beverage untasted. "Come back this evening. By that time I should have some answers for you."

Arianna opened the pasteboard folder that she had taken from Lady Spencer's desk and studied the topmost page. Then, pulling out a fresh sheet of paper from the escritoire drawer, she copied the equations and began working through their permutations.

Her father had loved the magic of mathematics, saying that it represented the essence of the universe. For him, numbers were gods.

Or devils. She sighed. No, it was only humans who embodied them with positive or negative forces. In and of themselves, they were purely functional, though to her, their limitless possibilities for combinations and complexities held a certain abstract beauty.

Looking back at her calculations, Arianna tapped the pencil to her chin. There was something familiar about the sequences, but she couldn't quite put her finger on it.

Tap, tap, tap.

However, further calculations would have to wait. A discreet knocking reminded her of an appointment with a modiste in Bond Street.

"Yes, I must swathe myself in fancy silks and satins," she muttered, reluctantly returning the papers to their hiding place. "For I've a far more pressing challenge to meet than the task of solving a mathematical conundrum."

"Here is the dossier you requested, milord."

Grentham made no move to open the folder. "And what, pray tell, ought I know about its contents, Jenkins?"

The young man cleared his throat. "Mr. Henning served as an army surgeon with the Third Regiment of Dragoons under Wellington in the Peninsula—as did Lord Saybrook. He resigned at the same time as the earl sold his commission on account of his injury, and both men returned to London on the same transport vessel." The shuffling of feet was muted by the thick Turkey carpet. "As for earlier background, Henning's father is an apothecary in Edinburgh, and is known for his outspoken views on social reform. His mother works at a local orphanage teaching the children to read and write."

"So we have a Scot who was suckled on idealism instead of whisky." A mirthless smile curled at the corners of Grentham's mouth. "Go on."

Jenkins rattled off a few more facts about the man's military service before moving on. "At present, Henning resides in a modest set of rooms at number six Queen Street and runs a clinic for wounded war veterans."

"Finances?" asked Grentham.

"Precarious at best, sir."

The minister squared the folder with the edge of his tooled blotter. "Any private patients?"

"One," replied the young man. "He seems to be Lord Saybrook's personal physician."

"Now why does that not surprise me?"

Jenkins did not venture an answer.

Rising, the minister moved to where a massive gilt-framed map of the city hung against the dark wood paneling. After studying a small section of snaking streets, he turned around. "Has Crandall's family claimed the body?"

"Y-yes, milord. Several days ago."

"Arrange for Peterson to have a look at it. I should like to have a second opinion."

"But, sir, the burial is scheduled for tomorrow in the family plot in Colchester."

"Then you had better move quickly. Otherwise you will be needing to dig up a crew of resurrection men to accompany Peterson."

"Yes, milord." His face turning pale as death, the young man scuttled for the door.

"And Jenkins . . ."

"Sir!"

"I want the information that I requested on the East India board of governors on my desk within the hour."

Jenkins bobbed a nod and disappeared before any other order could be issued.

His place was taken by a red-coated officer, who snapped to attention and saluted. "Lord Saybrook is here, milord."

"You may dispense with the parade ground theatrics, Colonel Saunders," growled Grentham. "Send him in."

The earl entered a few moments later and without invitation seated himself in the chair facing the minister's desk. That Grentham was still standing by the map seemed to make no impression.

"Seeing as you have made yourself comfortable, dare I hope that you have a lengthy report to make on how you have solved the case?" asked Grentham with exquisite politeness.

"Alas, no," replied Saybrook with equal formality.

The minister waited for further explanation, but Saybrook appeared engrossed in polishing a speck of dirt from the silver knob of his cane. Fixing the earl with a critical eye, he slowly circled around to his desk. "Perhaps your social engagements have distracted you from the assignment." His gaze lingered on the earl's face, which no longer looked like a death mask. The sharp-edged gauntness had softened and a touch of color had replaced the earlier stone-cold pallor. However, the improvements only seemed to elicit further sarcasm. "You seem to have regained an appetite for frivolous pleasure."

"Family obligations occasionally require that I appear in Society. If you are referring to Lady Wolcott's introduction into London Society, be assured that the duty did not interfere with my investigation."

"No?" Grentham lifted a well-groomed brow. "Then there must be some other compelling reason why you have made no progress in finding the Prince's poisoner."

"I didn't say that I had made no progress," murmured the earl. "You of all people ought not jump to conclusions, milord."

Grentham sucked in a silent breath. He took a moment to shift a folder from a desk drawer to the top of the stack on his blotter before replying, "The government is growing hungry for results, Lord Saybrook. And I am loath to keep serving up the same old excuses."

"I am well aware that my own head will end up on a platter if I fail," said the earl.

"That will be after your ballocks are fried in Spanish olive oil and offered to the cabinet ministers as *amuse-bouches*."

"I suggest that you season them with Andalusian rosemary and a sprinkling of Mediterranean sea salt. Otherwise they will taste a trifle bland."

Grentham thinned his lips. "You think it amusing to cross verbal swords with me? Be assured, it's no laughing matter—"

A knock on the door interrupted him.

"Yes, what is it, Jenkins?" called the minister.

"Sorry, milord, but you asked me to alert you as soon as the document for the Swedish minister was ready for your signature."

"Excuse me for a moment." Pivoting on his heel, Grentham left the room.

Saybrook shifted, then rose and flipped open the top folder on the desk. He quickly skimmed through several papers before closing the cover and returning it to the exact position as before.

Taking his seat, the earl resumed his position of studied nonchalance.

A moment later, Grentham came through the half-opened door and drew it shut behind him.

"Now, where were we, Lord Saybrook?"

"Discussing what spices to use on my ballocks when you serve them to the Prime Minister. However, I have been thinking—perhaps he would prefer them stewed, not fried."

"Let us not mince words," said Grentham slowly. "You may not care about having your already suspect reputation cut to shreds . . ." He paused for just a fraction. "But what of your half sister? Or, rather, your bastard sister, though the lovely young lady currently residing at Mrs. Martin's Academy for Ladies in Shropshire is registered as the legitimate offspring of some fictitious Spanish count—a highborn relative from the

Spanish side of your family, rather than your father's by-blow."

Saybrook's grip tightened on the shaft of his cane.

The minister did not miss the subtle gesture and a glint of malice sparked in his eyes. "Oh, yes, I know all about that, Lord Saybrook. Did you really think your private family peccadilloes would escape my notice?" Tracing a finger along the slim blade of his letter opener, he added, "Fifteen is an age of hope and dreams for a girl, is it not? The daughter of a Spanish noble, especially one with a family connection to the high and mighty Earl of Saybrook, can look forward to making a splendid match, and living a life of privilege here in England." The pause was perfectly timed. "But then again, the slightest stain on her name would ruin any hope of acceptance into the *ton*."

The earl's expression didn't alter. "Harm her in any way and you are a dead man," he said conversationally.

"You are in no position to be making threats," replied Grentham.

"Nor are you," countered Saybrook. "A good many people might be very curious to know more about the recent activities of dear, departed Major Crandall."

Grentham went very still.

"He was, after all, your senior military aide, and as such, your wish was his command."

"I confess that I, too, am very curious to hear where you are going with this."

"At the moment, I'm not far enough along on the trail to make an announcement on where it leads. However, I promise that you will be the first to know when I get there."

"I'm afraid you have lost me, Lord Saybrook."

"You—who know every twist and turn, every cesspool and hellhole in London?" A smile ghosted over Saybrook's lips. "I think not. Indeed, I'd be willing to wager you could find your way blindfolded through the scum and the dung, no matter how deep."

"How very poetic." Grentham perched a hip on the

corner of his desk. "But unlike you, I do not possess an artistic temperament. I prefer practical, pragmatic speech. So if you have an accusation to make, please do so."

"An accusation? Oh, I'm not quite as clumsy as you seem to think." Saybrook rose, and suddenly the slender length of ebony was a blur of black as it cut a series of feints through the air. "Swords—verbal or otherwise— are something I'm quite familiar with. A soldier never really loses touch with the art of war."

The silver ferrule stopped a scant half inch from Grentham's throat.

"You, no doubt, prefer a more cerebral weapon," continued the earl softly. "But there is a certain primitive pleasure in the feel of steel in your hand."

The minister slowly pushed the point away. "As you say, primitive. There are far less sweaty ways of destroying an enemy."

"Yet nothing is quite so supremely satisfying as going *mano a mano* with an opponent," replied Saybrook.

"Swordplay to rescue a damsel in distress? You've read too many romantic tales, Lord Saybrook," mocked Grentham. "Noble heroes are naught but a dribble of ink on paper."

"Then consider me a spawn of Satan. For if you ever threaten my sister again I shall follow you to the hottest hole in hell and slice off your cods," said the earl. "And then ram them down your gullet, uncooked and unspiced."

Grentham flicked a mote of dust from his lapel. "Would that you could show this much zeal in pursuing the fugitive chef."

Saybrook tucked the cane under his arm and walked to the door unaided. "I think we both know there are bigger fish to fry."

. . . I've found yet another reference from the early 1600s, recounting an incident when English privateers stopped a Spanish galleon loaded with cacao. This time, they

didn't burn the cargo, but dumped it into the ocean, once again thinking the beans were sheep turds! Oh, how I shall tease Sandro with this nugget of information—really, the Inglieze have no appreciation of fine food and wine. . . .

Arianna let out a low laugh as she looked up from Dona Maria's journal. The earl's Spanish grandmother had a deliciously sly sense of humor. No wonder his expression betrayed a hint of sadness when he spoke of her. From her writings, it was obvious that the contessa had been a remarkable lady.

Setting the book aside, she loosened the sash of her silk wrapper. It was late, and yet her nerves were still wound tight. She had spent the evening at a staid musicale, with card games and a midnight supper following the program of Italian opera arias. The singers had been mediocre, the punch weak, and the conversation boring. However, Mellon had insisted that she attend several respectable parties to establish some sort of credibility in Society.

But tomorrow night . . .

She rose and went to stand by the windows. The patter of a passing shower echoed against the panes. Pressing her palms to the glass, Arianna drew a deep breath and let the dampness seep through her skin. The chill took the edge off the frisson of fire twisting in her belly. The idea of getting close to Concord had her feeling both hot and cold. *So near and yet so far.* She had dreamed of revenge for so long. Yet now that it was in reach, her emotions were hard to untangle.

One step at a time, she told herself.

One step at a time.

Turning away, Arianna moved to the chest of drawers, where her newly purchased accessories lay neatly folded on lavender-scented paper. Lacey corsets, silk stockings, lawn cotton shifts soft and sheer as a dappling of sunlight. . . . Lud, she had never possessed such frilly, feminine things. They were luxuries, far too costly for a vagabond on the run.

Her fingers lingered on a curl of satin ribbon, its softness teasing against the callused tips. Then, swearing under her breath, Arianna thrust them beneath the pile of new clothing and found several of her old male garments. Pulling out the canvas smock, she fished a small pouch from a hidden pocket in the seam and carried it over to the bed.

A square of pale ivory paper and wink of fire-tinged gold fluttered in the candlelight as she shook the contents onto the counterpane. Picking up the medallion first, she held it closer to the light in order to study the engraving. She hadn't taken the time to scrutinize the items taken from Lady Spencer's desk drawers, but now that she was to meet with Concord, she couldn't afford to overlook any clue that might help bring her father's murderer to justice.

For it had been a premeditated murder, and not some random robbery. On that she was willing to bet her life.

Forcing her focus back from the past to the present, Arianna squinted at the curling script phrase on the medallion.

Fay çe que vouldras.

Her brow furrowed as she mentally translated the French into English.

Do as you please.

Unsure what to make of the words, Arianna replaced the medallion and the list back in the pouch and unfolded the letter. The message here was less cryptic. Lady Spencer had another paramour who was unhappy about her liaison with the Prince Regent. Did all of this—the murderous attacks, the violent death, the government panic—boil down to a simple matter of sex?

She tucked the paper away and put the pouch back in its hiding place. The earl ought to be told about the contents of the letter. It would save him from running in circles, chasing phantom conspirators. This was most likely not about international politics, but a personal grudge against a Prince who couldn't keep his pizzle inside his breeches.

However, sharing the information wasn't to her advantage.

Arianna looked around the elegant room and gave a sardonic grimace. Saybrook's goal was to end the investigation as soon as possible, while her role was simply to serve as a pawn—a pawn in a ruthless game where she was expendable. That he would not hesitate for a heartbeat to sacrifice her was a fact that she must never forget.

Kill or be killed. That was one of the cardinal rules of survival.

Indeed, it might be the *only* rule that mattered.

Because come hell or high water, she meant to survive long enough to taste the sweetness of revenge.

11

From the chocolate notebooks of Dona Maria Castellano

Senor Diego Martinez invited me to study some old books in his library, and in them I found the first mention that I've seen of chocolate in Italy! In 1606, Francesco d'Antonio Carlette, a merchant from Florence, submitted a report to Ferdinando de' Medici, the Grand Duke of Tuscany, on his world travels. In it, he includes a whole section on the New World and its trade in cacao. . . .

Chocolate Cookies with Gin-Soaked Raisins

½ cup golden raisins
⅓ cup gin
3 cups sifted confectioner's sugar (sift before measuring)
⅔ cup sifted unsweetened cocoa powder, preferably Dutch-processed (sift before measuring)
1 teaspoon instant espresso powder
2 tablespoons all-purpose flour (unsifted)
⅛ teaspoon salt
3 large egg whites
½ teaspoon vanilla
8 ounces pecans, toasted, cooled, and coarsely chopped

1. Combine raisins and gin in a cup and let stand at least 8 hours to macerate.
2. Preheat oven to 350°F. Butter and flour 2 large baking sheets, shaking off excess flour.
3. Mix confectioner's sugar, cocoa powder, espresso powder, flour, and salt with an electric mixer at low speed. Add egg whites and vanilla and continue mixing until smooth.
4. Drain raisins in a sieve, without pressing, then add raisins to dough with pecans. Stir until thoroughly mixed. (Dough will be thick and sticky.)
5. Working quickly, drop ¼ cup dough for each cookie onto a baking sheet, spacing cookies at least 3 inches apart, and gently pat down each mound to about ½ inch thick.
6. Bake cookies, 1 sheet at a time, in middle of oven, rotating sheet halfway through baking, for 15 to 17 minutes total, or until cookies appear cracked and centers are just set. Cool cookies on sheet 1 minute, then transfer carefully to a rack to cool completely.

Too unsettled to sleep quite yet, Arianna took up the candle and made her way down to the kitchen. Its worktables and well-stocked pantries were now familiar territory, for several days ago, on learning that Arianna was studying the chocolate notebooks belonging to the earl's grandmother, the cook had issued an invitation to help make up the week's supply of cacao for hot chocolate.

Apparently Arianna had passed the test, for she had been given carte blanche to make use of the space and supplies whenever she wished.

After adding fresh coals to the stove, she lit a lantern and gathered the ingredients she wanted. Spices and almonds, cream and butter, flour and sugar, a ball of cacao paste . . . after measuring out the exact amounts of several ingredients, she set the copper pot on the hob to heat.

As the gloom came alive with soothing sounds and

smells of cooking, she felt her tension melting away into the kitchen rhythms.

Lost in thought, Arianna wasn't aware of the approaching footsteps until the scrape of a boot on the mudroom floor jarred her from her work. Pulse pounding, she grabbed up the long-bladed chopping knife and whirled around from the worktable.

Framed in the doorway was a dark shape, a blur of black on black in the murky corridor.

Her throat seized, her hands clenched.

"A late supper?" The earl stepped out from the ominous shadows, his caped coat flapping around his shoulders.

The blade wavered as she expelled a sharp breath.

"Or is it breakfast?" added Saybrook, slipping out of his coat and shaking off the droplets of rain. He draped it over a stool and came forward into the pool of lantern light. In the flickering flame, he looked tired. Troubled.

Or perhaps pensive was more accurate. It was hard to say. She didn't know him well enough to recognize his moods.

"Neither," she replied.

"Well, it smells good enough to eat." He paused for a look at the simmering sugar, which was slowly caramelizing to a buttery shade of gold. "What are you making?"

Arianna pointed to the sheet of paper by the grater. "I copied one of your grandmother's recipes for a chocolate and almond confection. I was too restless to sleep, so I thought I would try it. I find cooking relaxing."

"Sounds delicious." He went to a tall cabinet by the larder and took down a bottle. She heard a soft splash, and when he returned he was cupping a rounded glass filled with a dark amber liquid.

"Spanish brandy," he said, catching her questioning look. "Simpler and sharper than the French style. But I'm not in the mood for complexity tonight."

She looked away from his shadowed face. "What are you doing here?"

"I don't need an invitation to enter my uncle's house. I am family, and welcome at any hour."

Family. For a fleeting moment Arianna found herself wondering what it would be like not to be always alone.

"What about you, Lady Wolcott?" His dark eyes seemed to pierce her private thoughts. "Or whoever you really are. You must have family somewhere."

"No." Arianna scooped up a handful of almonds and set them on the chopping block. "Not all of us are privileged enough to have loving relatives. I'm on my own in this world, naught but a nomad."

"Even a nomad has a family name, one that roots her to the past, whether she likes it or not."

"I have a family name," she shot back. "I told you, it's Smith."

"I think not."

"It's of no concern to me what you think, sir."

"I beg to differ, Lady"—there was a quiver of silence before he spoke the next words—"Arianna Hadley."

The blade slipped, nicking her finger. "I—I don't know what you are talking about," she stammered as a bead of blood welled up from the cut. In the low light, the color appeared more black than crimson.

Saybrook passed her his handkerchief. "To be more specific, Lady Arianna Hadley, the only child of Richard Hadley, the fourth Earl of Morse, who left England for Jamaica in '02. The rumors hint at some dark scandal. Would you care to illuminate it?"

Arianna answered with a low curse.

"I can easily find out all the details," he went on. "But it would save me time if you told me yourself."

"Why does it matter?" she demanded.

"I don't know that it does. However, experience has taught me that in any investigation, it's important to have all the facts at hand, no matter how irrelevant they may seem."

She heaved a harsh sigh and resumed chopping. "He was accused of cheating at cards. One of his so-called friends confronted him with the charge, and another bloody bastard corroborated it. My father was given a choice—leave the country or have the incident made public." The staccato sound of the blade hitting wood grew louder. "You know the aristocracy and their precious code of honor. Had he stayed, he would have been forced to put a bullet through his brain."

"Again, I ask why?"

"Why did they frame him?" Arianna lifted her shoulders. "How in Hades should I know? Perhaps they were bored, like so many indolent aristocrats. Or perhaps they resented that my father had a knack for winning." She caught his expression and quickly added, "And before you ask—no, he was *not* guilty of cheating!"

Saybrook said nothing.

Unwrapping the ball of cacao paste, she began to dice it into tiny pieces. *Thwock, thwock, thwonk.* The rhythmic rap helped calm her temper. "My father was very clever with numbers," she went on. "He had a system of counting—the cards, that is—which allowed him to work out patterns of probability. He said it gave him an edge in calculating the odds."

"A helpful skill for a gamester."

Arianna measured out some flour, then took the mixture of melted sugar and butter from the stove. "How many eggs?" she asked abruptly, after stirring in the chopped cacao paste.

Saybrook consulted the recipe. "Four. The yolks are to be separated and the whites whisked until they form soft peaks."

Before she could reach for the egg crate, he pulled it to him and deftly cracked them one by one.

"What the devil are you doing?" she demanded.

The wire whisk was already thrumming against the bowl. "I, too, find cooking relaxing," murmured the earl.

She chuffed a sigh. "Yet the last time we were together in the kitchen, someone ended up dead."

"Let's try to avoid any more bloodshed," he replied, casting a glance at her hand. "For now, at least."

"I'm innocent of any misdoing—save to be in the wrong place at the wrong time," she countered.

"So you keep telling me." He quickened his strokes. "By the by, this is just about ready."

Arianna added the chopped almonds to her mixture, then gently folded in the whipped egg whites. After spooning it into a pan, she placed it in the oven.

"And now?" asked Saybrook.

"We sit," she said, perching herself on one of the kitchen stools. "And wait. But you need not stay, sir. Obviously, you are not happy unless you are poking your nose into some dark, disgusting hole, in hopes of stirring up the muck."

"On the contrary, I take no pleasure in unearthing painful memories, Lady Arianna—"

"Lady Arianna," she interrupted bitterly. "I did not give you leave to use my given name, sir. There is no intimacy between us."

"None was intended," answered Saybrook mildly. "Perhaps you've forgotten the all the complex rules of aristocratic address. As the unmarried daughter of an earl, the proper form of address is Lady Arianna, not Lady Hadley. When you marry, you will take your husband's name, or title if he has one. I, on the other hand, am never called Lord Allessandro, but Lord Saybrook, or simply Saybrook—"

"Spare me the prosy lecture on Polite Society's asinine rules," she snapped.

"If you mean to be successful in your charade, you cannot afford to ignore them."

Arianna hesitated, and then heaved a reluctant sigh of surrender.

"Look, like it or not, we have both been sucked into a cesspool of troubles," pointed out the earl. "And if we wish to better our odds of emerging unscathed, it would behoove us to cooperate."

"Ha!" She let out a mocking laugh. "You have some nerve to talk of trust when you have been spending your efforts digging up dirt on me, rather than pursuing the real culprit."

"If you had been more forthcoming with me, I should not have had to waste my time."

"So far, I've had precious little offered to me in return."

Saybrook lifted a brow. "You've been swathed in expensive silks and satins, and introduced to the crème de la crème of Society. On the day after tomorrow you move into your own spacious town house, complete with a retinue of servants. So do forgive me if I fail to see how you have been left holding the short end of the stick."

"I was referring to information, sir," she said. "You aren't any more eager to share your secrets than I am."

He picked up a stray almond and absently popped it into his mouth. "It seems that past experience has taught both of us to be wary."

"Have you a fresh reason to fear?" she asked, not really expecting a serious answer.

"Perhaps." Saybrook gathered up a few more nuts and arranged them in a neat row before going on. "I paid a visit to my friend Henning earlier this evening, and learned that Lord Grentham is sending someone to have a look at Crandall's body—even it if means exhuming the corpse."

Arianna felt the color drain from her face. "Good God, how did your friend hear about that?"

"The minister is not the only one with a network of informers," answered the earl. "Henning provides a great service for those who could not otherwise afford medical treatment. In return they keep him informed of what is going on in Town."

Despite the warmth of the kitchen, a chill skated down her spine. "H-how will that affect us?" she asked—then quickly corrected herself. "I mean *me*. Will they guess it was murder?"

"Hard to say. Henning is very skilled with repairing flesh, and the body is, to put it delicately, losing its ability to tell a clear story." The earl appeared engrossed in reordering the almonds. "That people do not take kindly to having their graveyards despoiled by resurrectionists also works in our favor. Word has been sent. Grentham's man may not find his task an easy one."

The knot inside her belly relaxed somewhat. "Thank you."

Saybrook looked up through his lashes, the momentary spark of topaz mirroring the exact hue of the caramelized sugar. "There are some benefits of working together, Lady Arianna. When you are surrounded by danger, it is not a bad thing to have a comrade in arms watching your arse. Unless, of course, you have eyes in the back of your head."

Perhaps. Arianna acknowledged the observation with a slight nod. And yet, she thought cynically, in her experience when a man was watching her arse, it was not for altruistic reasons.

The earl let the silence stretch out a moment longer before adding, "But of course, you are certain that you can look out for yourself."

The aroma of the baking chocolate—sweet, seductive—wafted up from the oven. *Trust.* It was a tantalizing notion to lower her guard just a little, realized Arianna.

A flare of light illuminated his profile, and she saw more clearly the tiny lines of tension etched around his mouth. Something else was upsetting him. A sixth sense, a finely honed instinct of self-preservation, allowed her to pick up on a person's inner conflict. Weakness could often be turned into a weapon.

"Grentham did more than threaten to exhume the body, didn't he?" she asked.

Arianna couldn't quite describe it in words, but as Saybrook turned, his expression hardened. The change was subtle, but in that split second, his face became a mask that might well have been sculpted out of hard, cold stone.

"It's none of your concern, Lady Arianna."

"Did he threaten your family?" she prodded.

"Enough," he said softly.

"Or perhaps you have siblings?"

A faint ridge of color darkened his cheekbones. "You wish to initiate a conversation on family genealogy?" he asked. "By all means. That should prove a *very* interesting topic."

"Very well, let us not open Pandora's Box, as it were."

His response was a gruff growl. "God only knows what other secrets you are keeping locked away in a dark place."

"I had better check the cake," she said, turning abruptly and taking up a chamois cloth to protect her hand. "Overcooking will ruin it."

"And it would be a great pity to waste all our cooperative efforts," murmured Saybrook.

Arianna didn't reply. Setting the hot iron pan on a trivet, she nudged it to the center of the worktable and dipped a fork into its center. The tines came away with a slight coating of the batter.

"Not bad," she mused, taking a moment to taste the medley of spices. "But naturally, it must cool for a bit before any final judgment can be made."

"You are cruel and heartless, Lady Arianna."

"Yes," she agreed. "I am."

Saybrook rose and went to pour himself another brandy. He returned with a glass for her. *"À su salud."* The liquid swirl spun from pale gold to fiery bronze as he raised his drink in salute.

Arianna couldn't help but remark the odd twinkle in his eye. In spite of her resolve to remain at odds with him, she smiled. "Yes, I suppose we should toast to the fact that we are still alive."

"Ah, as the Roman emperors said—eat, drink, and be merry, for tomorrow you die." The earl quaffed a long swallow of the brandy. He seemed to be sinking into an even more strangely reflective mood. Or perhaps he was simply getting a little drunk. "Though I prefer the phrase *carpe diem*. It sounds so much more elegant."

"However you dress up the sentiment, the meaning remains the same. In truth, I think Thomas Hobbes said it best—the life of man is solitary, poor, nasty, brutish, and short."

"You have studied political philosophy?"

"No, Lord Saybrook, I have studied the everyday realities of life in the streets, not some fancy leather-bound book."

"The two are not always at odds with each other."

She slowly sipped her brandy while mulling over his meaning.

The earl, too, seemed lost in his own thoughts. It wasn't until his glass was empty that he spoke again. "I do not normally give in to my baser appetites, Lady Arianna, however, I find my willpower weakening in the face of that sinful-looking confection."

"I think we may go ahead and test it." Cutting two thin slices, she placed them on a plate and pushed it toward him. "You ought to have the first taste of your grandmother's recipe."

He broke off a small piece and took an experimental bite.

"Well?"

"Excellent. The flavor of the nuts is a nice complement to the smokiness of the *trinitario* beans." The earl took another morsel and chewed thoughtfully. "I'm also thinking that the addition of sultanas would make for an interesting contrast of textures. What is your opinion?"

She took a taste. "Hmmm ... yes, the softness of dried fruit would be a good counterpoint to the crunchiness of the almonds." Her tongue began to tingle. "Sweet and salty ... I like the combination. It's unexpected."

"Layers of complexity add interest to food," he murmured.

Arianna let the last of the chocolate melt in her mouth. She meant to remain distant, detached, but the seductive warmth of the brandy, the sugar, and the mellifluous sound of his voice nibbled away at her resolve.

"Does the phrase *Fay çe que vouldras* have any significance to you?" she suddenly said.

The earl's expression didn't change but she sensed that he was suddenly on full alert. "Why do you ask?"

She considered a lie, but then decided against it. "Sorry. I can't tell you that right now."

"You know, trust is an essential ingredient in any successful partnership."

"We are not partners," she pointed out.

"Yes, and your stubborn refusal to consider it is likely to land both of us in the fire." His fist suddenly smacked the table, rattling the dishes. "Damn it all, Lady Arianna, against all common sense, I have shown some faith in you."

True. Arianna stared down at her half-eaten cake. It was hard to swallow her misgivings. But she did need his help, so she decided that it wouldn't hurt to feed him a crumb or two.

"The morning after the Prince was poisoned, I decided to do a little snooping in Lady Spencer's study. I found a medallion hidden behind a false panel in her escritoire. It had those words engraved on it."

His jaw unclenched. "Thank you."

"Have you any idea what it might mean?" she asked.

"As a matter of fact, yes."

Arianna waited.

"But I need to make a few inquiries before I explain."

It was her turn to express outrage. "I should have known better than to think you would be fair—"

Saybrook touched a finger to her lips. "Must you always assume the worst?"

As if there was any other choice.

"Your anger is always so quick to boil over. As a chef, you should know that a judicious application of heat yields far better results."

"I don't need a cooking lesson," she muttered. "I know my way around a stove, milord."

"You are about to step out of the kitchen and into a world where the flames are far more dangerous."

Arianna's low laugh sent a ripple of lantern light dancing across the tabletop. "I've been to some hell-holes that would make the devil's hair curl, sir. Nothing in London can hold a candle to them."

"Don't bet on it," he growled.

They locked eyes, and the air seemed to echo with

the silent clash of steel on steel. Neither of them seemed willing to yield an inch.

And then, to her surprise, the earl suddenly sheathed his sword. "Christ Almighty, I suppose if I don't tell you something, you'll get yourself into trouble by charging in where angels should fear to tread."

"I'm no angel," she said, tentatively accepting the truce.

"True. If I had to compare you to any heavenly body, it would be one of the figures from ancient mythology—an Avenging Fury, or the Goddess of Revenge." Saybrook thought for a moment. "There must be one, though the name eludes me at the moment."

"Nemesis," she whispered. "It derives from the Greek word νέμειν, which means 'to give what is due.' Or, more simply, divine retribution."

"With you as the self-appointed Almighty?"

When she didn't answer, the earl slowly spun his empty glass through several rotations. "You made mention of the Hellfire Club that first morning at my uncle's town house."

"Yes, and you dismissed it as a harmless ghost story from the past."

"So I did. But that phrase you just recited, *Fay çe que vouldras*, was the motto of the original members." He hesitated, as if carefully choosing his next words. "For you see, those gentlemen considered themselves above any moral restraints."

"Do what you please," said Arianna.

"Just so." He took a deep breath. "As I told you then, the embers were said to have been stamped out long ago. However . . ."

"You think they may have come back to life?"

"I don't know," admitted Saybrook. "I will need to poke my nose into a few more deep, disgusting holes in order to answer that."

Recalling the flicker of the burnished gold, Arianna added, "I suppose I should also mention that there were a handful of the medallions. I took one of them with me."

"I would like to see it, if you don't mind."

"Very well." *In for a penny, in for a pound.* "I'll fetch it from my room."

She returned shortly and handed the medallion to him. As for the letter and the other items, she had decided to keep that information to herself. It was always wise to have bargaining chips in reserve.

Saybrook studied it for a long moment. "May I keep this for a while?"

She nodded.

His lashes lifted, yet his eyes remained shrouded in shadow. "In the meantime, bear in mind that men who consider themselves superior to ordinary mortals are very dangerous. You may think yourself tough as nails, Lady Arianna, but if they perceive you as a threat to their interests, these self-styled Lucifers won't hesitate for a heartbeat to hammer your coffin shut."

Her skin began to prickle. "You are beginning to sound like one of those gothic novels from the last century. Next you'll be telling me about deep, dark dungeons and underground torture chambers." She dismissed the idea with a sardonic smile. "Sorry, but I don't frighten easily."

"You should," he replied gruffly. "Even in your wildest dreams, I doubt you've imagined the real evil that man can do to his fellow beings."

Her mind was suddenly awash in a flood of memories—*the feel of blood, the taste of fear, the roar of fury, the look of lust....*

"It's late," she muttered, collecting the knives and plates. "And I'm tired."

The earl rose and draped his caped coat over his shoulders. "Let us both get some sleep. And don't forget, I'll expect a full report after the party."

"Or?" she couldn't help asking.

"Or not only will you have to answer to the Devil, Lady Arianna. You will have to answer to me."

12

From the chocolate notebooks of Dona Maria Castellano

As we all know, the Italians take the art of life very seriously. So it doesn't surprise me to learn that Francesco Redi, the personal physician to Cosimo III and one of the leading scientists of his day, spent time experimenting with the creation of decadent recipes for chocolate. Some of his concoctions included drinks perfumed with ambergris, musk, and jasmine. I don't think they would be to my taste....

Banana Chocolate Walnut Cake

2¼ cups all-purpose flour
1 teaspoon baking soda
½ teaspoon salt
1 stick unsalted butter, softened, plus 2 tablespoons, melted and cooled
1 cup sugar, divided
2 large eggs
1¼ cup mashed very ripe bananas (about 3 medium)
²/₃ cup plain whole-milk yogurt
1 teaspoon pure vanilla extract
1 (3½- to 4-ounce) bar 70% cacao bittersweet chocolate, coarsely chopped

1 cup walnuts, toasted, cooled, and coarsely chopped
½ teaspoon cinnamon

1. Preheat oven to 375°F with rack in middle. Butter a 9-inch-square cake pan.
2. Stir together flour, baking soda, and salt.
3. Beat together softened butter (1 stick) and ¾ cup sugar in a medium bowl with an electric mixer at medium speed until pale and fluffy, then beat in eggs 1 at a time until blended. Beat in bananas, yogurt, and vanilla (mixture will look curdled).
4. With mixer at low speed, add flour mixture and mix until just incorporated.
5. Toss together chocolate, nuts, cinnamon, melted butter, and remaining ¼ cup sugar in a small bowl. Spread half of banana batter in cake pan and sprinkle with half of chocolate mixture. Spread remaining batter evenly over filling and sprinkle remaining chocolate mixture on top.
6. Bake until cake is golden and a wooden pick inserted in center of cake comes out clean, 35 to 40 minutes. Cool cake in pan on a rack 30 minutes, then turn out onto rack and cool completely.

Propelled by the crescendoing music, the ladies around her whirled faster and faster, their laughter echoing the capering notes of the violins.

Closing her eyes for an instant, Arianna tried to bring her skeetering emotions under control. Now that the time for snaking off to Concord's party was drawing near, her heart was beating so loudly that it nearly drowned out the music.

"The waltz is exhilarating, is it not, Lady Wolcott?" remarked Sir Leete, dabbing a sleeve to his brow. His protruding belly and beet-red face seemed to signal that he rarely indulged in anything more strenuous than lifting a fork.

"Quite," replied Arianna, grateful that the dance excused the breathless hitch of her voice. Beads of sweat trickled beneath the laces of her corset, teasing a flare of fire to every tiny nerve ending.

"Might I fetch you a glass of ratafia punch?"

"Yes, thank you." She turned, angling her gaze across the crowded room. *One, two, three* . . . There, in the fourth arch of the colonnading, stood Concord and several of his friends. Catching her eye, he nodded ever so slightly, a signal so subtle that she would have missed it if she hadn't been expecting it.

A moment later, the men were gone, leaving naught but a smudge of shadows between the white marble columns.

Dark and light. Despite what she had said to Saybrook, Arianna felt a frisson of fear.

"May I take the liberty of inquiring as to how you are enjoying London, Lady Wolcott?"

A voice, uncomfortably close, jerked her thoughts back to the present moment.

"We were introduced at the Averills' soiree," continued the gentleman, who was now standing by her side. "Though I daresay you don't remember."

"Yes, of course I do," said Arianna, covering her flinch with a polite smile. He looked vaguely familiar.

"You are too kind—I imagine you've met far too many strangers to keep all the names straight," he murmured. "I am Lord Ashmun."

"Thank you for your inquiry, Lord Ashmun. I am enjoying the city and its activities immensely," she answered. *Now go away,* she added to herself.

"I can't help but wonder," he went on. "Are you perchance related to the Wolcotts from Somerset?"

"No," responded Arianna, hoping the curt reply would discourage any further questions.

Ashmun didn't take the hint. "No?" he echoed. "Then are you from farther north?"

Something in his tone stirred a sense of unease. "My husband's family is from Yorkshire, sir. The village is too small for anyone to recognize its name."

His hazel eyes narrowed, and his long nose seemed to quiver, like a bird dog looking to pick up a scent. "Oh, but having hunted in Yorkshire, I am very well acquainted with the countryside."

"I doubt you are familiar with this particular place." She looked away, anxious to escape further interrogation. "Ah, there is Lord Leete with my drink. If you will excuse me . . ."

To her dismay, Ashmun followed. "Might I have the pleasure of taking you in to supper, Lady Wolcott? I should very much like the chance to converse with you—I believe we may have . . . mutual acquaintances."

"I think you must have me confused with someone else," said Arianna coolly, though her insides were starting to clench in alarm.

He sidled closer. "I—"

"My apologies for the delay, Lady Wolcott!" exclaimed Leete. "There was quite a crowd around the punch bowl."

Arianna heaved an inward sigh of relief. "Thank you," she said, accepting the glass and quickly raising it to her lips.

"Our hostess is renowned for her lobster patties and creamed quail." Ashmun was proving relentless in his pursuit. "Allow me to escort you to a table."

"Tempting," she replied. "But the last week has been awfully fatiguing, so I'm going to take my leave early. Good evening, gentlemen." Before either of them could reply, she turned and took her leave from the ballroom.

It was foolish to let her imagination run wild, she reminded herself. Her nerves were on edge, that was all. Lord Ashmun was simply a nosy old man, not a specter of impending danger.

Still, try as she might, Arianna couldn't shake the feeling that she had seen him somewhere other than last week's soiree. Had he been a guest at one of Lady Spencer's parties? He didn't seem the type.

But appearances could be deceiving.

Reminded of her own charade, Arianna forced her thoughts to the coming encounter.

Turning up the hood of her cloak, she stepped out into the night shadows and hurried to her waiting carriage. She must hide her jitters, mask her doubts . . .

Play her role.

"How delightful that you decided to join us, Lady Wolcott," called Gavin as she entered the drawing room of Concord's town house. "May I offer you a welcoming libation?" Detaching himself from a group of men by the hearth, he glided over to greet her. "It's a unique concoction, a specialty of the house, if you will."

"How can I resist?" The ornate goblet, made of spangled Murano glass, was filled with a dark garnet-red liquid. "I trust that it's more potent than the watery punch that was served at the earlier party."

"Much," assured Gavin. "Can you guess at some of the ingredients?"

"Something *very* sweet," she answered with a throaty purr. "Whatever it is, I like it."

"Ah, I see you have a palette for pleasure," he said. "The ingredients come from the Caribbean tropics."

"A world which is unfamiliar to me," said Arianna. "But I am looking to expand my horizons."

"You have chosen a good place to start," said Gavin smoothly.

Before she could reply, a voice interrupted their tête-à-tête.

"Now, now, Gav, don't be a naughty boy and try to keep our new guest all to yourself."

Arianna didn't need to turn around to recognize the chiding laugh.

"Do introduce us."

"But of course, my sweet." Gavin pulled back a touch, allowing Lady Spencer to come closer. "Allow me to present Lady Wolcott, who has just arrived in Town from—"

"A dreadfully dull little town in Yorkshire." Arianna

lowered her gaze. A liberal application of kohl had altered the shape of her eyes and darkened her lashes. And as a false mustache had always disguised the shape of her mouth and chin, she had no reason to fear that the other lady might see shades of the fugitive Monsieur Alphonse in her face.

"Oh, I assure you that London is never, ever dull," said Lady Spencer. "Especially if you know the right people."

"I am counting on that," replied Arianna.

"I have a feeling we are going to become very good friends." Her erstwhile employer flashed a conspiratorial wink and looped an arm through hers. "Come, let me show you some of our host's Eastern art collection while we get better acquainted."

Better acquainted? Arianna repressed the urge to laugh.

Waving off Gavin's offer to accompany them, Lady Spencer pursed her carefully colored lips. "No, no, no, I must insist on having a private interlude with Lady Wolcott. It's only fair that she be warned about the dangers of consorting with rogues like you."

Gavin smiled, showing a brief flash of teeth.

"I hope I am not frightening you with such talk, my dear."

"Not at all," murmured Arianna, knowing exactly what words and tone would pique the other lady's interest. "After all, they say that danger adds a certain spice to life."

The reflection of the candle flames glittered off the gilt scrollwork of the wall sconces, tantalizing flickers of gold on gold. *A mere illusion,* Arianna reminded herself. And a reminder that here she was surrounded by gleaming lies.

"My diet has been bland for so long," added Arianna, "that I find myself craving something bold, something unexpected." She cocked her head. "That is, if you know what I mean."

"Oh, I understand you," assured Lady Spencer, drawing her into the oak-paneled corridor. "La, what a pity my cook has disappeared. You would have adored his creative confections."

"Disappeared?" she repeated, taking care to sound surprised. "You mean he left your employment?"

"Yes." Lady Spencer seemed to regret her slip of the tongue. "Rather abruptly. It was quite inconvenient. . . ." She looked away and pressed her palm to a door, which swung noiselessly open. "Come, I think you will find this interesting."

Two ornate brass candelabras, their curling arms made up of arched cobras, flanked an arrangement of display shelves and art on the far wall. "Lord Concord is a connoisseur of Indian art," said Lady Spencer, leading the way across the room. Flickers of light danced over carved wood and polished metal set with semiprecious stones. "His connections in the country allow him access to some very special treasures."

"Impressive," murmured Arianna, eyeing a series of black jade sculptures, which depicted men and women engaged in a variety of explicit—and exotic—sexual positions. "Imaginative."

"Yes, aren't they?" A sly smile spread across her companion's face. "It takes a special individual to appreciate imagination and creativity. Alas, most people are so . . . ordinary. Their minds are constrained by such rigid notions of morality."

"True," replied Arianna. Recalling some of the comments she had heard her erstwhile employer make on the subject, she carefully paraphrased the same sentiments. "They have little curiosity to experience all that life has to offer."

The smile stretched wider, and as Lady Spencer edged closer, the undulating candle flames made it appear as if the snakes had come alive. *Medusa.* Arianna quickly averted her eyes. According to ancient legend, any onlooker who dared to look directly at the gorgon's terrifying beauty would turn to stone.

"Oh, I see that you *do* understand, Lady Wolcott." A

whisper of breath teased against her cheek. "You know, we are very selective about whom we invite into our inner sanctum."

"I am honored." Lady Spencer was now a little too close for comfort. Under the guise of examining one of the woodcuts, Arianna slid a step to her left. "I look forward to learning more about the nuances of art from such experts."

She could sense that Lady Spencer was watching her intently. *Push and pull.* They were engaged in a complex dance of manipulation, and her companion must not guess at who was really seducing whom.

"Have we met before, Lady Wolcott?" asked Lady Spencer suddenly. "You look . . . familiar, though I can't quite place your face."

Arianna gave a little laugh. "I'm afraid that you must be confusing me with someone else."

A tiny frown furrowed Lady Spencer's brow, then just as quickly relaxed. "Oh, I daresay it's your eyes. They are the exact shade of green as those of the Marchioness of Quinley."

"Actually, I would say our guest's eyes are a darker, more complex hue." Lord Concord moved out of the shadow of the curio cabinet. "Like melted emeralds swirled with smoke."

"I am flattered that you noticed the color of my eyes, sir," said Arianna, fluttering her lashes.

He flicked a gesture at the erotic art. "I consider myself an expert on the human form, so I make it a point to study such nuances."

"Have you a specialty?" she murmured.

His laugh was low, like distant thunder. "Oh, the female body is a particular interest."

Rather than answer, Arianna turned her gaze back to the carved figures.

"My dear Catherine, why don't you return to the drawing room? I believe Hastings and his party will be arriving at any moment, and I don't trust Tipton or Gavin to make them feel welcome."

Lady Spencer drew in a breath, the light catching the flare of her nostrils. However, she quickly covered the look of annoyance with a dimpled smile. "Of course, Robert. I'm always happy to play mistress of the house for you." Sauntering off with a slow, provocative sway of her hips, she quit the room.

Leaving the door wide open, observed Arianna with inward amusement. Her former employer did not like being asked to play a secondary role in the proceedings, but was too shrewd to voice any open displeasure.

"Be careful of Cat. Beneath the soft purrs, she has very sharp claws." Concord had a very sensuous mouth, in contrast to the obsidian hardness of his eyes. There was a flat blackness there that reminded her of a cold-blooded reptile. "And often takes pleasure using them on other females."

All those chats over chocolate with Lady Spencer were now bearing fruit. Arianna knew that Concord and his friends were hunters at heart and liked the excitement of a chase. Lifting her chin, she fixed him with a challenging look. "She said much the same thing about you."

"Did she?" He opened a small box on the shelf and took out a slim cheroot. "Does that alarm you, Lady Wolcott?"

"Should it?" she countered.

"You intrigue me."

Arianna felt her chest tighten in anticipation. *Slowly, slowly,* she warned herself. One false move would ruin everything.

"Indeed?" she responded, keeping her voice cool.

"I look forward to—"

Before he could go on, an agitated call sounded from the corridor. "Damnation, Concord, I must have a word with you."

"I'm occupied at the moment," he answered.

"I don't care if you are swiving the Queen of Sheba, we need to talk!" A fair-haired gentleman of medium height hurried in, his bootheels beating a staccato tattoo on the parquet floor. His face was ruddy, but whether it was from anger or prolonged exposure to the sun was hard to discern.

"Calm yourself, Kellton," warned Concord. "As you see, I am entertaining guests."

"Let *them* wait," growled the other man. He gave Arianna a cursory look, then turned his attention back to Concord. "The devil take it, we had a deal."

"Let us not bore the lady with our personal business." The words were said softly but there was no mistaking the note of command. Flicking a bit of ash from the tip of his cheroot, Concord offered her an apologetic shrug. "If you will excuse me, I must take a moment to deal with a business matter."

"But of course."

"Feel free to stay here and admire the art for as long as you like. There are some books on the side table that you might also enjoy."

"Thank you," said Arianna. "I think I shall—stay here for a bit, that is." Taking up a thin volume bound in snakeskin, she perched herself on a settee upholstered in plum-colored velvet. "So please, don't trouble yourself about me."

"You've chosen the most interesting work," he observed with a lascivious wink. "I believe you'll be here for some time." Taking the other man's arm, Concord ushered him back the way he had come. "We'll discuss this in my study."

Arianna waited for several minutes, then tossed aside the book and hurried to the door. There were no wall sconces lit in this stretch of the corridor. Standing very still, she thought she could detect a faint buzz of voices from the right. In the opposite direction lay only deep shadows, heavy with silence.

And a fleeting whiff of smoke.

It was a risk, but she could always feign confusion and claim she had become disoriented in the darkness. . . .

The scent of spiced tobacco led her through an archway and down another passage. Up ahead, a narrow sliver of light at floor level alerted her to the presence of a door set in the paneling.

She pressed a palm to the polished oak. *Damn.* It was firmly shut and she didn't dare fiddle with the latch.

Looking around, she spotted a set of glass-paned doors leading out to the back garden. Easing the lock open, she slipped outside and picked her way through the shrubbery. As the evening was pleasant, the study windows might well be open to the evening breeze.

Had the gentlemen been conversing in normal tones, her efforts would have gone for naught. At that moment, however, Concord's visitor was expressing his displeasure in a near shout.

"Don't try to fob me off with some farrididdle, Concord! My source at Whitehall informs me that Grentham plans to exhume the body. What the devil is he looking for?"

The slight silence was amplified by the stillness of the garden. And then, "What body?"

The question triggered another explosion. "Damn you! Are you pretending not to know that the minister's top military lackey was stabbed to death by Lady Spencer's chef, who has so far eluded capture despite the princely ransom on his head?"

"Ah." The word was punctuated by another pause. "So you, too, have access to sensitive information within the department of security. I wasn't aware of that. The public announcement was that Crandall choked to death on a piece of beefsteak."

"Of course I have ears within Whitehall. Like you, I have my interests to protect." Concord's visitor sounded a little shaken. "I don't appreciate being played for a fool." Arianna shrunk back into the bushes as he approached the windows. "I take it you have the chef well hidden somewhere safe."

Arianna heard a desk drawer open and shut. "You need not concern yourself with the chef," said Concord. "It does not affect our arrangement."

"Bloody hell, our arrangement didn't include sticking a blade up Grentham's arse. I'm willing to take risks, but only reasonable ones, Concord. I've got a good mind to . . ."

"To what?"

She caught a quick glimpse of the man's face as he turned away from the leaded glass. Sweat sheened his skin. He was not only angry. He was frightened.

"To reconsider my position," he answered tightly.

"You're overreacting. Sit down and have a brandy." Concord's voice had smoothed to a mellow flow. "The incident at Làdy Spencer's had nothing to do with our arrangement."

Try as she might, Arianna could catch only fleeting words as the two men settled into the two armchairs by the hearth.

Blunt . . . sword blade . . . letters of exchange . . . Overend . . . Gurney . . .

As their tone dropped even lower, Arianna decided that there was little more to be learned, and the risk of discovery was growing too great. Retracing her steps, she made her way back to the room of erotic art. Something sinister was at play here—that Concord was involved in some sordid game for profit was no surprise. The question was how to unknot the serpentine tangle of lies and deception.

"Why, Lady Wolcott, surely you don't mean to deprive us of your company any longer." Gavin joined her, a fresh goblet of punch in each hand. "Can I entice you to return to the drawing room?"

"Of course," she murmured. "I should like nothing better."

Concord rejoined his guests shortly after her return, bringing with him several servants bearing a pair of ornate Indian water pipes that emitted a low gurgling along with a cloud of sweet smoke. The laughter grew more languid after that, and one or two couples withdrew into the shadowed alcoves.

Arianna managed to appear an eager participant in

the revelries, though much of her punch was discreetly dumped into the potted plants.

Despite his smiles, Concord seemed on edge. He made no move to renew his flirtations, and disappeared again after perhaps a half hour.

As it was now nearing dawn, she felt that she could take her leave without drawing any suspicion. Saybrook had, after all, demanded a report on the evening, and while she did not mean to dance to his tune, she had her own reasons for sharing what she had overheard.

Her carriage was waiting on the side street. A breeze ruffled through the ivy leaves on the garden walls, and aside from the *swish, swish, swish* of her skirts on the walkway, the creak of the harness leather mingled with the raspy snores of the drivers were the only other sounds.

Lost in thought, Arianna dropped her reticule in fumbling for the door latch. Swearing to herself, she turned to retrieve it from the cobblestones.

Damn.

As she crouched down, a movement in the shadows of the nearby linden tree caught her eye. A clatter of steps, and the figure darted into the alleyway, but not before the fleeing face was limned for an instant in the scudding moonlight.

Rising slowly, she felt a frown pinch her brow.

Why was Lord Ashmun lurking outside Concord's residence?

It was, she reflected, yet another question to which she had no answer.

13

From the chocolate notebooks of Dona Maria Castellano

Although there is some debate about how chocolate was introduced into France, I believe the credit most likely belongs to Anne of Austria, the daughter of King Philip III of Spain. My research has turned up evidence that she gave her husband an engagement present of chocolate, packaged inside an ornately decorated wooden chest. Whether it is true or not, it makes a very sweet story....

Coconut Chocolate Bites

¾ cup sweetened flaked coconut
¾ cup unsweetened dried coconut
¹/₃ cup sweetened condensed milk
3½ to 4 ounces fine-quality bittersweet chocolate
(preferably 70% cacao), finely chopped

1. Line bottom and 2 opposite sides of an 8-inch-square metal baking pan with a sheet of wax paper, leaving a 2-inch overhang on both sides.
2. Mix together flaked and dried coconut and condensed milk with your fingertips until combined

well, then firmly press into pan in an even layer with offset spatula. Chill, uncovered, 5 minutes.

3. Melt chocolate in a metal bowl set over a saucepan of barely simmering water or in top of a double boiler, stirring until smooth. Spread chocolate evenly over coconut layer with offset spatula and chill until firm, 5 to 7 minutes.

4. Lift confection onto a cutting board using overhang and halve confection with a sharp knife. Sandwich halves together, coconut sides in, to form an 8-by-4-inch rectangle, then discard wax paper. Cut rectangle into 32 (1-inch) squares. Arrange paper cups (if using) on a platter and fill with candies. Chill, covered, until ready to serve.

❧

"**A**nother dead body." Straightening from his examination, Basil Henning absently wiped his fingers with a frayed handkerchief. In the murky light of early morning, the library was dark as a crypt. "I dunna like the look of it, Sandro."

"Nor do I." Saybrook slowly circled the large pearwood desk, taking in every detail of the scene. The gentleman's corpse was seated in a rattan-backed chair, and he appeared to have expired just as he was beginning to write a note on the sheet of paper that lay on the blotter. The pen had slipped from his fingers, spattering ink over an illegible scrawl, but otherwise it was hard to tell that anything was amiss.

A closer look, however, revealed hands curled like claws and a grimace frozen on the bloodless lips.

"Do you think he died of natural causes?" asked the earl, once he had returned to his starting point.

"Hard to say." Henning ran a hand over his stubbled jaw. "I see no sign of foul play, but the coincidence of yet another death among the people you are investigating strikes me as awfully suspicious, laddie."

"Indeed," agreed the earl. He gave another long look at the body. "You could, of course, have a much better picture of what happened if you were to get a more thorough look."

The surgeon grunted. "Lock the door. Then help me get his coat and shirt off. It's a damnably tough job once *rigor mortis* has set in."

They worked in silence for several minutes, wrestling the garments from the rigid limbs.

"An interesting design," observed Saybrook, before setting the intricate stickpin atop the rumpled cravat.

"Looks to be a blood ruby," said Henning, not bothering to hide his disdain. "Such a bauble could feed a regiment of hungry men for a year."

"Few people are as altruistic as you are, Baz."

"Hmmph." A last hard tug pulled the shirt free. "Draw the draperies," said Henning as he lit the argent desk lamp and angled its light over the marble-white flesh. "And then tell me again how ye happened to be having a dawn appointment with a cadaver."

"I tracked down the gentleman in question at his club yesterday afternoon," began Saybrook. "And asked if I might have a chat with him about some recent bills of lading from the Madras trade route."

The surgeon's bushy brows rose in question.

"His Lordship is—or was—an under-governor with the East India Company, and oversaw trade from the southern part of the country," he explained.

"What in the name of God does that have to do with the Prince's poisoning and a dead military man from Whitehall?"

"I'm not sure," answered the earl. "But when I was in Grentham's office, he was called away for a few minutes and I happened to spot a file from the Madras office of the Company on his desk."

"Odd."

"Very." Their eyes met. "And yes, I'm thinking the same thing you are. The minister is far too clever to have left a sensitive document out in the open by mistake. I am assuming he wanted—nay, expected—me to see it. The question is why."

Henning rummaged in the canvas satchel by his side and withdrew a large magnifying glass, along with a blunt wooden probe. "Too many bleeding conundrums in this case, if ye ask my opinion." He lifted the man's lips away from his teeth and had a quick look at the traces of spittle. "Go on."

"Our friend here seemed on edge and claimed to have a pressing engagement that prevented his granting my request. He put off setting another time to talk until later in the week. But then, late last night, a note was delivered to my town house, requesting that I come by before first light, for he didn't wish for it to be known that we were meeting."

"I take it he didn't admit you himself."

"No," replied Saybrook. "The note told me to come in through the back entrance, which would be unlocked. I was directed to proceed up the stairs and come to the library."

From outside in the alleyway, the faint rattle of a coal cart sounded. "The household will soon be stirring to life," remarked Henning wryly. "Come around here and hold the light for me."

The earl took up a position by the corner of the desk and lifted the lamp. "See something?"

Henning bent lower, until his lens was nearly touching the thick peppering of hair on the dead man's chest. "Higher," he muttered, using the probe to part a tangle of coarse curls.

The oily flame illuminated a small round bruise, less than a quarter inch in circumference, just above his breastbone. In its center was a pinprick of darker purple.

"The fellow appears to have stuck himself with his fancy piece of jewelry," remarked Saybrook.

The surgeon canted the magnifying glass one way and then the other before replying. "Perhaps. But the contusion beneath the skin seems to indicate a tad more force was used than one would normally require for pushing a pin through linen. And as for its color . . ." He pursed his lips and shook his head after taking a closer look. "Hmmph."

"What—"

Henning waved him to silence. "We don't have long before the servants start to notice something is amiss." Setting aside the probe, he skimmed a hand down to the dead man's belly and palpated the now cold flesh. "Help me shift him, so that I can get a look at his back."

Together they tilted the corpse forward. Saybrook steadied the body, while Henning did a quick check. "Nothing of note here," he growled. Dropping to his knees, he lifted the man's trouser legs. "Or here." A pause. "He was out earlier this evening. There is mud on his shoes, and it's still wet."

The earl took a look. "I don't suppose there is any way to tell from where it came?"

Henning rolled his eyes. "Bloody hell, Sandro. Do you think me a magician?"

Saybrook's lips quirked. "As a matter of fact . . ."

A low snort, then the sound of scraping. "Hand me your handkerchief. I'll be damned if I'm going to dirty mine." After stuffing the folded silk into his satchel, Henning stood and shook the wrinkles from his canvas pants.

"If you have finished," murmured the earl, "we had best get him dressed before taking our leave."

"Right." Henning glanced at the desk, then gingerly picked up the stickpin and wrapped it in his own pocket square. "If ye dunna mind, I'd like to take a closer look at this."

"I was hoping you would."

Working quickly, they managed to get the corpse dressed in some semblance of normalcy and propped back in the chair. "Leave off the damned cravat," muttered Henning. "It's natural that he might have removed it while sitting down to work."

The earl nodded. "An observant eye will notice that there's nothing natural about this, but perhaps the physician who is summoned will not care to look too closely."

"Then you don't mean to report this yourself?"

"Not at present, Baz," replied Saybrook softly.

"Aye, I didn't think so." Henning picked up his bag. "In that case, we had better take our leave."

The taste of the steaming chocolate—strong, sweet, and hot—helped wake Arianna's sluggish senses. "Thank god for *Theobroma cacao*," she murmured. "The life of an indolent aristocrat is harder work than I thought."

Moving to the windows, she looked down on the back garden. The earl had chosen a charming town house for her on South Audley Street. She could almost imagine herself at home here, reading, cooking, relaxing. . . .

She spun around and set aside her empty cup. *Wishful thinking made one weak.* And she had made a vow to be strong.

A glance at the mantel clock showed that she had only slept for several hours since returning from the party. Saybrook could not complain if she took another interlude of rest before making her report. But in truth, she was anxious to tell him all that had happened during the evening.

Concord's late-night visitor added yet another shadowy figure to the specters of evil. It seemed that the baron had lost little time in finding a new crony in crime after Hamilton had stuck his spoon in the wall.

Fetching a bandbox from the top shelf of the armoire, Arianna drew out an assortment of ragged garments and a floppy wool cap, along with her bag of cosmetics and face paints. It was short work to transform herself into a street urchin. Satisfied with the results, she stepped away from the cheval glass, feeling a rush of anticipation at once again having the freedom to move unnoticed through the streets of London. She didn't envy highborn ladies, who couldn't twitch a skirt without someone watching that the gesture conformed to the rules of propriety.

Arianna shuddered, unable to imagine living such a constricting, confining life. She, at least, could choose her own path . . . even if it led to perdition.

Saybrook had assured her that the small staff he had assembled for her were utterly trustworthy, so she didn't worry about crossing through the pantries and exiting the house through the scullery door. It was a short walk to the earl's town house, where she went around to the tradesmen's entrance and was admitted by a dark-eyed maid who immediately escorted her to the kitchen.

Bianca greeted her with a broad smile and an offer of hot chocolate topped with whipped cream. "Too *magro*," she clucked. "Too thin."

"Thank you, but I would rather have coffee," said Arianna.

"I shall have the same," said Saybrook from the archway of the corridor. His hair was windblown and a stubbling of whiskers darkened his jaw.

"Magro, magro," repeated Bianca, fixing him with a critical squint.

"You may bring some buttered rolls and jam as well," he said, taking a seat at the worktable. "And perhaps some of your almond cakes. Our visitor has a very healthy appetite."

Arianna observed the smudged shadows under his eyes. He, too, appeared to have had little sleep. "Enjoying a night of revelries, milord?"

"Only if you count dancing with death a form of entertainment."

Her mouth went a little dry. "Good God, who? Does it have anything to do with us?"

"No one you would know," he answered. "As for the connection, I cannot say." He pressed his fingertips to his temples. "And before you take umbrage at that, it is because I don't know. I may have a better idea after Henning has a chance to examine the evidence that we removed from the body. At the moment it's unclear whether the deceased was murdered or died from natural causes."

She made a wry face. "I take it there were no knives."

"No knives." His expression, however, looked a bit odd.

"What?" she pressed.

He shook his head. "It's nothing, really. Henning sometimes has very strange notions."

Before Arianna could ask him to elaborate, the cook approached with the coffee and a platter of food. *"Buen apetito."*

Saybrook poured two cups and passed one to her. "What about your evening? Did you learn anything of note?"

"Other than the fact that Concord possesses a private collection of erotic art that would put a whore to blush?" Arianna paused for a sip of the steaming brew.

If the earl had any reaction, he hid it well.

"My discoveries may not have been as dramatic as yours, but I think you will find a few things very interesting." She went on to recount the details of her night, from Ashmun's probing, to Lady Spencer's veiled innuendos, building up to Concord's quarrel with the stranger. "And then, as I was climbing into my carriage," she went on, "I happened to see Ashmun hiding in the bushes. He must have followed me, but it's a mystery as to why."

Saybrook had listened without interruption. She waited for him to speak now, but instead he picked up a pastry and took a taste.

Arianna bit back a caustic comment. The earl had some nerve to criticize *her* eating habits.

"These are superb," he murmured, nudging the platter her way. "I was under the impression that you needed sustenance in order to think properly."

The scent of almonds tickled her nose. "And I was under the impression that you found my appetite offensive."

"Compromise is the essence of a good battle plan." He helped himself to a roll. "One would be a fool not to learn from one's allies."

She realized she was famished. "I've never thought you a fool, Lord Saybrook." Arianna broke off a buttery wedge and popped it into her mouth. "An ass, but never a fool."

He smiled and refilled her cup. "Now, tell me again about the argument."

"As I said, I could only hear bits and snatches. The stranger was agitated, and confronted Concord with Crandall's death and my disappearance. He seemed to feel that some deal had been broken."

Saybrook stared meditatively into his coffee. "Try to remember exactly what was said."

She thought for a moment. "The stranger assumed Concord was responsible for the Major's demise and asked if the chef had been smuggled out of the country. Concord didn't correct him, but merely said not to worry about the chef because it didn't affect their business arrangement."

The earl nodded for her to go on.

"But that only made the other man more angry—or rather, frightened. Grentham worried him, and he said he had a good mind to . . ." Arianna let her words trail off, just as the stranger had. "At that point they moved away to the hearth. I could only make out a word here and there."

"Which were?" he asked, still not looking up.

Arianna wished that she could answer with something more helpful. "Blunt . . . sword blade . . . Overend . . . Gurney," she said carefully. Seeing his brow furrow for an instant, she added, "Sorry. I did try. However, as nothing was making any sense to me, I decided to return to the drawing room. Concord joined us shortly afterward, but he seemed distracted and disappeared again. I left an hour or so before dawn, and that's when I saw Ashmun lurking in the shadows."

"Hmmm" was the only reply.

Reaching for the rest of the almond cake, she finished it in two quick bites, then dusted the crumbs from her fingertips. "Why, Bianca has added morsels of chocolate to the cake," she suddenly exclaimed, wondering how she had missed it on the first taste. "Brilliant."

"Yes, isn't it?" murmured Saybrook abstractly.

"Sorry I can't offer you more. Hell, a blunt sword blade isn't much of a clue." She made a wry face. "Perhaps they are trading in military supplies."

"An interesting thought." The earl began to drum his fingers on the knife-scarred maple. "A pity you didn't hear the fellow's name."

"Concord seemed loath to introduce us," she replied. "He didn't— No, wait. He did! Say his name, that is." Squeezing her eyes shut, Arianna replayed the encounter in her mind. "Cotter ... Calvin ... Kelling ..." Her lids flew open. "Kellton. It was Kellton."

The drumming stopped. "Describe him."

"Heavyset, medium height, fair hair with a bald spot at the crown," she answered. "His face was ruddy, as if he had spent time in the sun."

"Dio Madre," he muttered, his leg buckling slightly as his feet hit the floor.

"What?" cried Arianna, alarmed by the sudden shift into action.

"It appears, Lady Arianna, that you were one of the last people to see my corpse alive."

14

From the chocolate notebooks of Dona Maria Castellano

Sandro will be pleased to learn that chocolate finally arrived in England by the mid-seventeenth century. I find it interesting that coffee from the Middle East and tea from the Orient arrived around the same time. Chocolate was the most expensive of the three, but it still became popular, especially among the elite of London, despite the cost. Samuel Pepys, the great chronicler of his time, makes regular mention in his famous diaries of drinking chocolate. . . .

Chocolate Angel Food Cake

½ cup all-purpose flour
½ cup unsweetened cocoa powder, plus more for dusting
1½ cups sugar, divided
½ teaspoon salt, divided
12 large egg whites (1½ cups), at room temperature
30 minutes
1 tablespoon fresh lemon juice
1 teaspoon pure vanilla extract

1. Preheat oven to 350°F with rack in middle.

2. Sift together flour, cocoa powder, ¾ cup sugar, and ¼ teaspoon salt.

3. Beat egg whites with lemon juice, vanilla, and remaining ¼ teaspoon salt using an electric mixer on medium-high speed until they just hold soft peaks. With mixer on high speed, add remaining ¾ cup sugar in a slow stream and beat until whites hold stiff, glossy peaks, 3 to 5 minutes.

4. Sift flour mixture over whites and beat on low speed until just blended (folding in any unblended flour mixture by hand if necessary).

5. Spoon batter into ungreased tube pan and smooth top. Run a rubber spatula or long knife through batter to eliminate any large air bubbles.

6. Bake until a wooden pick inserted into middle of cake comes out clean, 40 to 45 minutes. Remove from oven and immediately invert pan. If pan has "legs," stand it on those. Otherwise, place pan over neck of a wine bottle. Cool cake completely, upside down, 1 to 1½ hours. Turn pan right side up. Run a knife around edge and center tube of pan. Lift cake, still on bottom of pan, then run a knife under bottom of cake to loosen. Invert to release cake from tube, then reinvert onto a plate. Dust lightly with cocoa powder.

7. Serve with vanilla yogurt or lightly sweetened whipped cream, and fresh berries.

"Good God, surely you don't think that *I* had anything to do with his death," exclaimed Arianna.

The earl didn't respond to her question. "This changes everything," he muttered, more to himself than to her. "I had better go inform Henning immediately."

He turned for the doorway . . . and nearly collided with a man rushing in from the stairwell.

"Auch, I was hoping to find you at home," said the

newcomer. He was nearly as gaunt as the earl, but stood a head shorter. The contrast didn't stop there. *Dark and Light.* In contrast to Saybrook's olive complexion and jet-black hair, the fellow had sandy locks, now liberally threaded with silver, and fair skin.

A Northern warrior, thought Arianna, spying the jagged scars sliced on his brow and cheek.

The heavy Scots burr confirmed the surmise. "Yer housekeeper said ye were engaged in a private meeting, but I assured her that ye wuddna mind the invasion."

Arianna saw him slant a sidelong glance her way.

"I take it this laddie is yer lady."

"Lady Arianna, allow me to introduce Basil Henning, former surgeon to the Third Regiment of His Majesty's Dragoons," said Saybrook. "Baz, this is indeed our master of disguise."

Lamplight winked off his spectacles as Henning subjected her to a lengthy stare. "Ye make a very fetching male, milady."

"Thank you," she murmured. "I think."

"You've saved me the bother of traipsing through St. Giles to find you," said Saybrook without further preamble. "I've some important news—"

"As do I, Sandro," interrupted the surgeon.

The two men locked gazes, and Arianna sensed that they did not need words to communicate.

"Very well, you first," said the earl, resuming his seat. "Would you like some coffee? Or chocolate?"

"I'd rather have good Highland malt, but as I know ye only have Spanish brandy, I'll settle for that." Heaving a sigh, Henning fetched the bottle and poured a generous splash of the spirits. "*Slainte Mhath,* milady."

"Baz," began Saybrook.

"A man must remember his manners," replied the surgeon before quaffing another long swallow. "Ahhh, now I feel a touch more civilized."

The earl said something under his breath that drew a hoot of laughter from his friend.

"Hold yer water, Sandro," said the surgeon, once his

amusement had died away. "After running me ragged all night, ye could at least have the courtesy to allow me a wee dram."

"*Baz*."

"Oh, very well." The impish grin gave way to a more sober expression. Drawing three small vials from his coat pocket, he carefully stood them in a tight row on the table. "Take a good look at these." The first appeared to contain a clear liquid, the second was colored a deep Prussian blue, and the third cadmium red.

"I take it we are not here to admire a new formula for watercolor pigment," said Saybrook dryly.

"No, not pigment." Henning placed another item on the table.

In the lamplight, it seemed to glow with an inner fire. . . .

"Don't touch it!"

Arianna jerked back her hand. "I wasn't about to steal it, Mr. Henning."

"Yer pardon, milady. But I didna want ye to prick yer finger."

"I'm not some delicate English rose. I don't wilt at a mere touch."

"Trust me, ye might shrivel up and die from that thorn," he growled. "I canna be sure that I've removed all the poison, so I would rather be safe than sorry."

Poison. For an instant, she felt a little light-headed. First the Prince, and now . . .

Saybrook frowned. "So you were right in your suspicions?"

"Aye," replied Henning. "The froth of his spittle and the clawing of his hands indicated an unnatural death, as did the color of the contusion on the victim's chest. That was the key clue. I suddenly recalled where I had read about a magenta aureole around the purple and green of a normal bruise—it's very distinctive and very rare. So I decided to make a few tests." He sat back with a look of grim satisfaction. "And you'll never guess what I discovered."

"I'm in no mood for playing parlor games, Baz," replied the earl. "Like Lady Arianna, I've had precious little sleep, so kindly get to the point."

"All right, all right." The surgeon looked a little hurt, but that quickly faded as he took a wad of crumpled notes from his coat. "Ye remember in Spain how we was reading that book on Alexander von Humboldt's discoveries in the New World?" He turned to Arianna. "Sandro studied botany at Oxford, so we often enjoyed studying scientific—"

"Baz, Lady Arianna is not interested in my educational history," interrupted the earl.

Strangely enough, Arianna realized that wasn't entirely true. *A scholar and a soldier?* He was an intriguing mix of contrasts and conundrums.

But this was hardly the time or place to sort them out.

Henning made a face. "You might at least let me crow a little about my cleverness."

"Go on, Mr. Henning," she said. "I'm anxious to hear about it."

"Thank you, Lady Arianna." He shuffled through his notes. "Getting back to von Humboldt—who was, by the by, a renowned scientific observer of the natural world—Sandro and I were reading his account of a trip through Brazil and Amazonia. While Sir Walter Raleigh and other early explorers had heard about certain indigenous toxins used by the native peoples, von Humboldt was the first European to observe its making."

Saybrook frowned. "Do you mean curare?"

The surgeon nodded. "It's an extremely lethal substance," he explained to Arianna. "But to be precise, the name is used for a variety of poisonous plant concoctions. However, the most common source is the bark of *Strychnos toxifera* mixed with *Chondrodendron tomentosum.*" He blotted his brow with his sleeve, which Arianna noted was already mottled with a number of dubious smudges.

It was a wonder, she thought, that he hadn't expired from his own experiments.

"Sometimes they add snake venom to the mix. Quite inventive, I must say," he went on. "But I digress. The usual method of preparation was to boil the bark scraping and other plant material in waters for several days, reducing it to a viscous paste. It's not dangerous if swallowed, but if introduced directly into the bloodstream by a prick or cut from a tainted object, death is swift and sure."

She felt herself pale.

"I must say, the effect is quite unique," he mused. "Last year, Sir Benjamin Brodie noted that during curare poisoning the heart continues to beat, even after breathing stops."

"I doubt that is any consolation for the victims," murmured the earl. "All of this is very interesting, Baz. But how can you be sure that it's curare on the stickpin?"

"I assumed that would be your first question." The surgeon allowed a tiny triumphant smile. "The subject intrigued me, so I had done some further reading on it after my return to London. Knowing what chemical compounds are in the barks used for curare, it was not all that difficult to do some specific tests." A *tap, tap* set the colored liquids inside the vials to swirling. "These reactions prove without a doubt what killed Kellton."

"I wouldn't presume to question your scientific skills," said the earl. "But unfortunately, that stirs up a whole new . . ."

As his words trailed off, he flicked a look at Arianna, and though the movement was subtle, she sensed immediately what was coming.

Damn the man.

Sure enough, the slight hesitation gave way to a brusque cough. "Lady Arianna, there's really no need for you to stay," he went on. "Why not go home and get some sleep. For the moment, there's nothing more you can do."

In other words, leave the thinking to the men.

She fisted her hands, feeling a surge of fury well up in her throat. "Ah, right. Females are only useful for cooking and cleaning. Oh, and swiving."

Henning blinked.

"I'd rather not argue with you," began Saybrook.

"I don't intend to argue." Arianna crossed her arms. "Nor do I intend to be sent off to bed like a helpless child."

"You misunderstand me—"

"Do I?" she challenged.

The earl's eyes narrowed. "Willfully."

The surgeon appeared to be following the argument with great interest. Setting down the vials, he leaned forward on his elbows, clearly awaiting the next exchange of words.

"And so," continued Saybrook. "Despite your refusal to see reason, I don't intend to let you be part of the discussion. It's too dangerous."

"How do you intend to stop me? Chain me up in some remote castle dungeon like the dastardly Spanish villain in that silly horrid novel by Mrs. Radcliffe?" Actually, Arianna had found the book quite entertaining, but that was beside the point.

"Ye mean *The Mysteries of Udolpho*?" asked Henning helpfully.

"Yes, that's the one," she said.

"Montoni was Italian," murmured Saybrook.

"Mea culpa," retorted Arianna.

"And that is Latin," he pointed out.

"You," she said slowly, "are an overeducated, aristocratic ass."

Henning stifled a snort.

"And you," countered Saybrook, "are a bloody thorn in my lordly posterior."

The surgeon decided to intervene. "Come, come, let us not war with each other. We have far more serious battles to fight." He looked at the earl. "There's no denying that the lady is already in the thick of things."

"Oh, bloody hell. I suppose I have little choice but to admit you into our confidences," said the earl grudgingly.

She watched the sooty shadow of the lamp flame dance across the grained wood. "You won't regret it."

His silence was eloquent in its skepticism.

"All right then, no more fiddle-faddle." The surgeon slapped his palms together. "Sandro, as you were about to say, Kellton's murder presents a whole new set of questions. Beginning with, what were he and Concord quarreling about?"

"There's that," agreed Saybrook. "As well as why Grentham all but asked me to read a file on his recent activities." His finger traced over the myriad knife scars in the tabletop. "And then there is the conundrum of why an East India Company under-governor was killed with a South American poison. The two concerns are worlds apart."

"And yet they have come together," mused Henning. "Of course, it could be coincidence."

Saybrook made a face. "How many people in London have access to curare?"

"Very few," conceded the surgeon.

"There has to be a connection. We simply need to see it."

"One other thing," added Henning. "The mud on his boots contained particles of hemp, pine tar, and crushed shells, as well as the type of clay that is common to the Thames riverbanks. So I would say it came from one of the dockyards around the Isle of Dogs. Not all that suspicious, given his position with the East India Company—save, of course, for the time of night."

Saybrook didn't reply.

Arianna searched her memory for any new observation that she could offer into the conversation. Nothing came to mind, save what she had already mentioned to the earl. "One would have expected this man Kellton to have been stabbed, seeing as he and Concord were arguing over blunt sword blades." She meant it half in jest, but after a moment's reflection, she added, "As I said before, do you think it possible they were involved in some shady dealings with military supplies to our army, or the troops of our allies?"

Henning looked at Saybrook and arched a graying

brow. "You did say that Whitehall is worried about any disruption of talks with the Russian and Prussian envoys next month."

"Very worried," agreed Saybrook. The planes of his face seemed to sharpen in the flickering lamplight. "That is, if we trust Grentham's explanation for bringing me into this investigation. That he may have other, ulterior motives is something we have to consider."

Arianna suddenly felt a little dizzy.

"Blunt . . . sword blades, blunt . . . sword blades," mused Henning aloud. "British India and Spanish America."

Saybrook sat, head bowed, unmoving. He looked as though he were carved out of obsidian, she thought. *Dark, impenetrable.*

A grunt of laughter from Henning drew her attention away from his profile. "Blunt . . . sword blades—hell, perhaps someone has resurrected the old South Sea Company of a century ago."

Beneath the rough-spun cotton shirt, Arianna felt a pebbling of gooseflesh shiver down her arms.

"Ye all right, milady?" asked the surgeon. "Ye look as if ye've seen a ghost."

I have, in a manner of speaking. But unwilling to reveal any reaction until she had time to compose her thoughts, Arianna shook her head. "I'm simply feeling a little fatigued, is all," she mumbled.

Henning made sympathetic sounds, but as the earl raised his gaze to meet hers, she sensed that he saw through the lie.

Looking away, she sought to deflect his scrutiny. "What do you mean, Mr. Henning?" she asked quickly.

He answered with a question of his own. "Are you familiar with the term 'blunt' as it is used in common cant, Lady Arianna?"

"It is slang for money, is it not?" she replied slowly.

"Correct. And do you know why?"

Though she knew the reason all too well, Arianna pretended to think for a moment. "I would imagine that it is because money dulls the edge of poverty."

"An excellent guess," said the surgeon. "However, the truth is, it's based on an actual person. Sir John Blunt was an entrepreneur from early in the last century."

The name caused a clench in her belly. Some men had patron saints, but her father had worshipped at the altar of the Almighty Sir John Blunt.

"For a time his name was synonymous with easy riches," went on Henning. "For you see, he offered people a simple way of amassing great wealth with little or no effort."

Oh, if only she had a penny for every time she had heard plans for such a scheme. "That sounds too good to be true," she said warily.

"It was," said the earl. "Have you read anything about the South Sea Bubble?"

She took care to answer obliquely. "Remember, I didn't attend your fancy schools, Lord Saybrook. I've not spent my life with my nose buried in some musty book."

"Perhaps your father made mention of it," he suggested. "Given his interest in gambling and numbers, it would seem likely."

Arianna shook her head, "If he did, I don't recall it."

His gaze lingered on her face for a long moment, leaving her skin feeling slightly scorched.

"It was a stock scheme," offered Henning. "Initially, the South Sea Company was created in 1711 by the Lord Treasurer Robert Harley as a way of funding the national debt, which was ballooning because of England's wars. It then put together a very sophisticated proposal for raising money, based on the government granting it exclusive trading rights in Spain's New World colonies. Now, dunna ask me to explain the fine points of finance, for such intricacies are far too complicated fer my simple brain. But basically, it involved a swap of private stock for government debt. . . ."

Arianna listened in mute dismay as he went on to explain the initial investment phases. She had heard it all before. And yet it still sounded reasonable. But then, the clever plans always did.

"A New World trading company should have proved enormously profitable on its own," said Arianna. Something was niggling at the edges of her consciousness, but she couldn't as yet put a finger on it.

"The actual trading became a minor concern," said Saybrook. He was watching her closely. "Once the majority of the public agreed to accept the initial offering of company stock in exchange for their government holdings, the main thrust of the South Sea governors was to drum up enthusiasm for the venture, in order to drive up the stock price."

"That's why the South Sea Company asked Sir John Blunt to join forces with them," explained the surgeon. "Blunt had made a name for himself promoting highly profitable lotteries for the government. He brought in the Sword Blade Bank as a new partner."

"An odd name for a bank," she mused. Her surprise was genuine. She couldn't recall her father ever mentioning such an entity.

"It began as a manufacturing company of—yes— sword blades crafted with smithing techniques brought to England by Huguenot refugees. The company failed, but Blunt, who was a mere scrivener at the time, put together a group of investors and turned it into a land bank, which granted mortgages, accepted deposits, and issued notes. In 1711, it won a lottery to raise two million pounds. Based on Blunt's success in selling the subscription, the bank then went on to become the financial arm of the South Sea Company."

"H-how do you know so much about all this, Mr. Henning?" asked Arianna, once the lengthy explanation was done.

The surgeon made a face. "Because my grandfather lost all of his blunt when the South Sea Bubble burst. Left him penniless. He had to sell his house, a lovely stone cottage with orchards and grazing lands, and find work in Edinburgh. My father was forced to take up a trade, rather than study at the university, as was always intended."

So hers was not the only life ruined by a desire for instant riches. *Oh, Papa.* How was it that he never really learned a thing from his beloved John Blunt?

Her face must have betrayed a hint of what she was thinking, because Henning gave a gruff grunt. "Those caught up in a dream never think it can turn into a nightmare, eh?"

Arianna tucked her hands into her lap, trying to evade the memory of the shrieking wind and trembling fingers sticky with blood. "What has a century-old scandal to do with these current crimes?" she asked in a small voice.

"A good question," answered the surgeon. He slanted Saybrook a questioning look. "Ye were rather good at solving conundrums for Wellington and his staff. Have ye got no ideas?"

Saybrook's mouth quirked up at the corners. "I don't have quite the freedom in London as I did in the Peninsula," he pointed out. "There I had resources to call on, and an idea of what mission I was trying to accomplish. While here I feel as if I am spinning in circles. It's unclear to me why, but I suspect that I've been put in motion for reasons that have little to do with uncovering the truth."

Arianna tried to squelch the tiny stirring of guilt in the pit of her stomach. Truth, she told herself, was all relative. Its definition depended on what one was seeking. And the Earl of Saybrook was looking for something far different than she was.

"Tell me again exactly what you overhead, Lady Arianna," said Saybrook. "Every word, precisely as you remember them."

She did as he asked.

Henning scratched at his chin. "Gurney. That's a litter fer carrying wounded men," he said helpfully. "So maybe this is about some sort of business with military supplies."

The earl nodded abstractly. "Given Kellton's position with the East India Company, it raises a number of questions. Nitrates, which are essential for gunpowder, come to us from the east—"

"Sir." She wasn't even aware that she had spoken until Saybrook turned around.

"Yes?"

"Forgive me for interrupting, but . . ."

He waited, dark and silent as a storm cloud hovering on the horizon.

"But before you go on, there is something that you ought to know. It may have no bearing on your investigation, but along with the medallion, I . . . I also took a letter from Lady Spencer's desk." She met his eyes. "And it so happens that it was from Kellton."

15

From the chocolate notebooks of Dona Maria Castellano

Like many of the most scrumptious flavorings for chocolate, praline—a sweetly crunchy almond concoction—was the result of a fortuitous kitchen accident in 1671. A bowl of almonds dropped into a pan of burnt sugar . . . in a panic, the last minute creation was served to the Duke of Plesslis-Praslin, a diplomat in the service of King Louis XIII of France, who adored it and gave the new dish his name. Today, praline is, of course, a very popular filling. I must remind Sandro to use Spanish Marcona almonds . . .

Chocolate Chipotle Shortbread

1 cup all-purpose flour
¼ cup unsweetened cocoa powder
½ teaspoon chipotle chile powder
½ teaspoon cinnamon
⅛ teaspoon salt
1 stick unsalted butter, softened
⅓ cup superfine granulated sugar

1. Preheat oven to 350°F with rack in middle.

2. Whisk together flour, cocoa powder, chile powder, cinnamon, and salt in a bowl.

3. Beat together butter and sugar with an electric mixer at medium speed until pale and fluffy. At low speed, mix in flour mixture until well blended. Divide dough in half and pat out into 2 (7-inch) rounds (¼ inch thick). Arrange rounds 2 inches apart on an ungreased baking sheet. Cut each round into 8 wedges (do not separate wedges). Prick all over with a fork.

4. Bake until dry to the touch, 16 to 18 minutes. Recut shortbread while hot, then cool on sheet (shortbread will crisp as it cools).

❧

"How kind of you to share that information with us," replied Saybrook with undisguised sarcasm.

"Sandro," chided Henning.

"Dare I inquire as to its contents?" he went on, ignoring his friend's warning. "Or is that too much to ask?"

"His Lordship has a right to be peeved," she said to the surgeon. "But until this moment, I honestly did not see what the letter had to do with his investigation."

"That is precisely the point of sharing information," he said through gritted teeth. "Though it may come as a rude surprise, Lady Arianna, you are not always in the best position to judge what is relevant and what is not."

"I am aware of that, sir. Just as I am aware of the fact that who I can and cannot trust is even more difficult to discern."

"I don't know what else I can do to prove that I'm not your enemy, Lady Arianna."

Nor do I. Like truth, trust was a hard concept to capture in words.

"Yes, well, instead of debating our philosophical differences, milord, wouldn't you rather hear about the letter," she retorted.

"Por favor," he muttered.

"It was mostly a passionate plea, bemoaning the loss of her favors in bed. I only took it because ... well, Lady Spencer was careful to choose influential lovers. Having a bargaining chip with such men sometimes proves useful." Arianna heard Henning add a splash of brandy to his glass. "As I said, I didn't think it relevant."

Saybrook released a pent-up breath.

"But in light of the present circumstances," she went on, "his pleas about betrayal may have a more sinister meaning."

"Before I comment on that, is there anything—*anything*—else you are holding back?"

Somehow, to give voice to the cryptic sheet of numbers and the folio of equations was to give them actual substance. *And why?* Her vague suspicions were absurd—absurd. To explain them would mean stripping away the last of her protective secrets.

"As far as I know, I possess no other information that may prove useful," she replied carefully.

The earl looked less than satisfied with her answer, but he let it pass. "You are sure that the letter is from Kellton?"

"His hand is very legible. The signature reads, *Your devoted servant Gideon Kellton.* I wouldn't imagine there are two rich men of that name."

Clasping his hands behind his back, he began to pace the length of the kitchen. For some moments, the scuff of leather on stone overwhelmed all other sounds. Then it suddenly stopped.

"It seems to me," he announced, "that it's time to get reacquainted with Lady Spencer."

"But—," she began, then hesitated.

The earl fixed her with a mocking look. "You think I don't qualify? I possess a title and wealth. As for my ability to meet her other requirements, I daresay I shall rise to the occasion."

Arianna felt herself flush. To cover her embarrassment, she quickly said, "And starting tonight, I shall heat up my efforts to cozy up to Concord. It's obvious that he and Lady Spencer are close. For what reason is something we need to find out."

"You mean that you will tumble willingly into his bed?" asked Saybrook quietly.

"Yes. If need be."

"No." It was barely more than a whisper, but there was no mistaking the note of command.

She opened her mouth to retort, but Henning hastily intervened.

"Lady Arianna, I think what Sandro meant is, we certainly don't expect you to, er, sacrifice your, er, virtue to ensnare these criminals."

A laugh, bitter as bile, welled up in her throat, but Arianna forced it into a sardonic smile. "Mr. Henning, I've had to fend for myself since I was fifteen years old, and the West Indies are far more primitive than the fancy streets of Mayfair. I assure you, my virtue is not an issue."

The surgeon looked uncomfortable, while Saybrook . . .

Arianna could not quite describe the earl's expression. His dark eyes had a trick of turning opaque and allowing nothing to penetrate their depths.

"All questions of morality aside, I would suggest we try to avoid that scenario," said Saybrook, his voice devoid of emotion. "It would place you in far too vulnerable a position. The smallest slip . . ." He shifted his injured leg. "We can assume that Concord is extremely dangerous and won't hesitate to kill if he feels threatened."

"You think Lady Spencer is any less dangerous for being a female?" she demanded.

Rather than reply, Saybrook turned his focus to another conundrum. "We cannot forget about Grentham, or how he fits into the puzzle."

"I wuddna be surprised to find he is the one trying to put all these filthy pieces together," growled Henning.

The earl seemed less certain. "I have heard that he is ruthless, but as far as I know, there are no rumors that he is corrupt."

"Power always corrupts," replied Henning darkly. "Besides, who else ordered a senior officer of the Blues to try to murder Lady Arianna, not to mention an under-governor of the East India Company?"

"I prefer to keep an open mind—"

A tenuous cough from the archway interrupted him. "Your pardon, milord." One of the earl's footmen held out a letter. "A messenger from Whitehall just delivered this. He said it was urgent."

"Speak of the devil." Cracking the seal, Saybrook skimmed over the contents and then looked up. "I am summoned for a meeting with the minister. As soon as possible."

"Kellton?" asked the surgeon.

"It doesn't say. But I would be surprised if he hasn't heard of the death."

"What do you plan on telling him?"

The earl shrugged. "That depends on how much he knows—or claims to know. Conversing with Lord Grentham is always a game of cat and mouse."

Anxious to think over what she had just heard in the privacy of her own house, Arianna took up her hat and pulled it low over her brow. "I had better go and try to catch a few hours' sleep before Lady Ravenell's ball tonight."

She half expected Saybrook to forbid her attendance. However, he made no response, save to reach for Henning's glass and quaff the last swallow of brandy.

"I'll take my leave as well." The surgeon gathered up his vials and placed them back in his bag. "I have patients to see."

Rather than follow him into the corridor, Arianna turned for the passageway leading to the back door.

To her surprise, the earl fell in step behind her instead of accompanying his friend. Arianna quickened her pace, hoping to slip away without any further exchange of words. She was tired, and in no mood for argument.

His hand, however, caught her sleeve, and pulled her around.

Arianna chuffed an impatient sigh. "Whatever you have to say, please make it quick."

"This will only take a moment."

Her heart began hammering against her ribs as he learned in closer.

"Be careful."

"W-what?"

"Be careful," repeated Saybrook. "I am not exaggerating when I say that the unknown enemy is diabolically dangerous. And utterly amoral. As you heard Henning say, curare is a particularly unpleasant death."

"Why should you care about me?" Arianna knew she sounded belligerent, but couldn't help it.

"For any number of reasons," he went on softly. "Because you have courage and strength. Because you have passion and intelligence." His fingertips brushed a lock of hair from her cheek. "But most of all, because you don't expect anyone to give a damn whether you live or die."

The sting of salt burned against her eyelids. At that instant, she almost hated him for making her feel this way. *Alone. Uncertain. Vulnerable.*

Wrenching free of his hold, Arianna braced a hand on the storage shelf. "Well, don't bother," she drawled with feigned nonchalance. "Caring, that is. It's not as if we are going to be friends for long."

Saybrook pulled back just a fraction, and she felt the heat of his body dissipate in the still air.

"True," he agreed amiably. "But I didn't delay you merely to discuss personal matters, Lady Arianna. My warning was simply a prelude to a request—I want you to keep Concord and his cronies occupied tonight."

"W-what do you mean?"

"I will also be attending Lady Ravenell's ball."

"But why?" blurted out Arianna.

"I wish to observe them for myself." There was a slight pause. "And then there is Lady Spencer to cultivate."

The thought of the earl and the widow together stirred a strange sensation in the pit of her stomach. "Yes, well, keep in mind that she is like one of those exotic plants that devours flesh-and-blood creatures that stray too close."

"Why should you care about me?" he asked, echoing her earlier challenge.

"I don't. That's another fundamental difference between us. I've long since learned that sentimental feelings are a waste of effort."

This time, when she turned, the earl made no move to stop her.

However, his last words swirled through the shadows, a taunting whisper just loud enough to be heard over the angry tattoo of her boots.

"Until this evening, Lady Arianna."

"Another corpse was brought to my attention early this morning, Lord Saybrook." Looking up from his desk, Grentham set aside the paper he had been reading and tapped his fingertips together. "I find it very disconcerting."

"Much as I hate to upset you further, I daresay more than one person expired in London over the course of the night," responded the earl. "Large cities are, by their nature, dangerous places. The government really ought to consider establishing a permanent professional force to police the streets."

The tapping stopped. "I shall pass your suggestion on to the proper department. However, I didn't summon you here to discuss the moral imperative of protecting the public."

"I didn't think so."

Grentham waited for him to go on, but Saybrook merely straightened his leg and began pinching specks of dust from his trousers.

"Have you any explanation, Lord Saybrook?" asked

the minister, after allowing the sartorial adjustment to go on for several moments. "For the dead body, that is, not the state of city crime."

"Should I?" asked the earl.

"A tall man with a limp was seen near the house of the deceased sometime just before dawn."

"Leg injuries are hardly uncommon in London. What with war veterans and occupational hazards—"

"Spare me the litany of statistics," snapped Grentham. "I'm not interested in numbers. I'm interested in information. Which is something I've gotten precious little of from you."

"Perhaps if I were not distracted with pointless meetings, I would have time to pursue my investigations more effectively." He paused. "By the by, what has the death to do with the Prince and his poisoner? Was it perchance the missing chef? How convenient if he were to have imbibed a surfeit of his own creations."

Grentham narrowed his eyes. "Don't play games with me."

"That would be foolhardy," replied the earl. "And I'm not a fool."

"So I have heard." Leaning back, the minister contemplated the stack of gold-stamped document cases arranged on his desk. The dark green grained leather mirrored the exact shade of his well-tailored coat. Both appeared nearly black in the subdued light. "The dead man is Gideon Kellton. Were you acquainted with him?"

"He was a director of the East India Company, was he not?" answered Saybrook.

"Yes."

"How was he killed?" inquired the earl. "Stabbed? Shot? Strangled?"

Grentham stiffened, his nose lifting slightly, like a bird dog catching a scent. "What makes you think he was murdered?"

A ghost of a smile flitted across the earl's face. "You would hardly be summoning me here to say that the fellow had died peacefully in his sleep."

"The cause of his death is not clear," said Grentham tightly, clearly unhappy at having to make the admission. "It's possible that it was a natural one. But certain things appear, shall we say . . . suspicious."

The earl lifted a brow. "Indeed? And is that the opinion of your medical experts? For I would imagine that you employ some very highly skilled men."

The comment drew an unblinking stare. "Unfortunately, the local physician who was summoned made a complete muck of matters. The body was moved, the clothing pulled in disarray, and the desk where he was sitting cleared of his work."

"A pity," murmured Saybrook. "I know of someone who is very good at discovering the secrets that lie beneath the skin. I am sure he would be happy to offer his services."

"Ah, yes, your erstwhile army comrade, Basil Henning. Who, interestingly enough, was a visitor at your town house this morning."

"Things must be dreadfully dull around here if a routine visit from the surgeon who treats my war wound draws the attention of your spies." Saybrook stood without the aid of his cane. "As you can see I am making great progress in my recovery."

Grentham ignored the barb. "How fortunate for you. Do try to make headway in other matters as well, Lord Saybrook. A clever man like you should not be finding the way so difficult."

"Patience is a virtue."

"Not for me." The minister rose and moved around his desk. "So save your platitudes for those dull-witted enough to believe that the meek shall inherit the earth. We both recognize a bald-faced lie when we see one."

"I defer to your greater experience with lies and deception."

"Oh, I seem to recall from our previous conversation that you and your family are not quite so virtuous as you wish to appear." The hazy gray light from the windows was just bright enough to catch the glimmer of malice in Grentham's gaze. "I trust you remember what we discussed."

"Every word." Saybrook's reply was almost lost in the sudden pelter of rain against the glass panes.

"Good. Then we understand each other." He dismissed the earl with a flick of his wrist. "I repeat, I am not a patient man."

16

From the chocolate notebooks of Dona Maria Castellano

By 1700, there were over two thousand chocolate houses open in London. They served as social clubs— for men, of course—and became known as places of political intrigue. I think Sandro would appreciate the fact that chocolate helped foment revolutionary ideas. Even as a young boy, he had very egalitarian views for a titled peer; I am proud of his principles, but I fear such they will lead him into trouble. . . .

Chocolate Whiskey Bundt Cake

1 cup unsweetened cocoa powder (not Dutch-processed),
plus 3 tablespoons for dusting pan
1½ cups brewed coffee
½ cup American whiskey
2 sticks unsalted butter, cut into 1-inch pieces
2 cups sugar
2 cups all-purpose flour
1¼ teaspoon baking soda
½ teaspoon salt
2 large eggs
1 teaspoon vanilla

1. Put oven rack in middle position and preheat oven to 325°F. Butter 3-quart (10-inch) Bundt pan well, then dust with 3 tablespoons cocoa powder, knocking out excess.
2. Heat coffee, whiskey, butter, and remaining cocoa powder in a 3-quart heavy saucepan over moderate heat, whisking, until butter is melted. Remove from heat, then add sugar and whisk until dissolved, about 1 minute. Transfer mixture to a large bowl and cool 5 minutes.
3. While chocolate mixture cools, whisk together flour, baking soda, and salt in a bowl. Whisk together eggs and vanilla in a small bowl, then whisk into cooled chocolate mixture until combined well. Add flour mixture and whisk until just combined (batter will be thin and bubbly). Pour batter into Bundt pan and bake until a wooden pick inserted in center comes out clean, 40 to 50 minutes.
4. Cool cake completely in pan on a rack, about 2 hours. Loosen cake from pan using tip of a dinner knife, then invert rack over pan and turn cake out onto rack.

The blaze of lights, brilliant in its fire ... the thrum of voices, edged with anticipation ... the feel of a costume, disguising her real self ...

Quelling a last little flutter of nerves, Arianna glided into the crowded ballroom, reminding herself of the ragtag theater in Barbados and how many times she had acted out a part in a play. This was just a more sumptuous stage, and the audience, despite their wealth and veneer of worldly sophistication, was just as willing to be deceived.

"You are looking deliciously lovely tonight, Lady Wolcott." Gavin bowed low over her hand. When he lifted his head, it was to reveal a wolfish smile.

"Good enough to eat?" she teased in a throaty murmur.

"Oh, I imagine the taste would be sublimely sweet." It was Concord who replied. He sidled closer, forcing his friend to step back, and took hold of her gloved palm. "Allow me to claim the first dance."

Gavin looked a little miffed but didn't protest.

"How can I resist such a charming invitation?" said Arianna with a coy flick of her fan.

He offered his arm, and led her onto the dance floor.

"Thank you for the flowers this morning, sir," she said, stepping just a touch closer than was proper. "How very kind of you."

"I regret that I was unable to be as attentive as I wished last night."

"Oh, you gentlemen and your boring matters of business." She made a little pout. "It's quite naughty of you to let it interfere with pleasure. But I shall allow you to make up for your neglect."

"I was hoping you would." His palm flattened on the small of her back, the slight friction raising an involuntary shiver. He smiled, interpreting her reaction as something other than loathing. "Tomorrow night we are having another party. Will you come?"

"Oh, yes," she replied, looking up through her lashes. "It's a pleasure to be part of such an interesting group."

"Just as it's a pleasure to discover someone who has an appetite for enjoying all that life has to offer," said Concord in a low whisper. "If you truly find our gatherings to your taste, we may invite you to become a member of an even more select group. A club, if you will. One that meets on occasion to partake of very special treats."

Arianna hid her excitement with a breathy laugh. "I assure you, I'm *very* interested."

"I thought you might be." The steps of the waltz drew them back among the other twirling couples, and for the rest of the melody they exchanged naught but light pleasantries. When the music ended, he bowed low over her hand. "Alas, I shall not be able to request another dance, Lady Wolcott, for I fear that another engagement demands my presence."

"I do hope you won't be distracted tomorrow," she murmured.

"I shall take care that no more unwanted interruptions occur."

Gavin's approach to claim the next set ended the exchange. Tapping her fan to Concord's shoulder, she flashed him a wink. "I shall hold you to your word, sir."

For the next hour, Arianna spun across the polished parquet, one partner blurring into another. Several of Concord's cronies were among them, as well as a number of gentlemen introduced to her by Mellon. She seemed to be treading a fine line between good and bad. *Light and dark.* Glancing around the glittering ballroom, Arianna reminded herself that she couldn't afford the slightest stumble.

A second look did not reveal Saybrook among the guests. He might be in one of the side rooms, she mused. Or he might have decided to change his plans. Regardless, he could find no fault with her actions this evening—she had performed her assigned duty of distraction.

Suddenly thirsty, she requested that her next partner, a captain in the Coldstream Guards, fetch a glass of punch in the short interlude between sets.

Her drink, however, was brought back by a different gentleman, who explained that the captain had been called away on a different duty.

"Oh?" Arianna eyed the stranger over the rim of the glass. A thin visage, tapering to a pointed chin, a straight nose, pointing to a pair of narrow lips—his face would have been unremarkable, save the intensity of his gunmetal-gray eyes. Something about them stirred a sense of unease.

Dropping her gaze, she asked, "I do hope it's nothing serious."

He responded with a razor-thin smile. "That remains to be seen, Lady Wolcott."

Perhaps it was just her imagination, but he seemed to be trying to frighten her. "Dear me, that sounds rather ominous," said Arianna lightly before pausing for a long sip of her drink. "Have we met, sir?" she challenged, deciding to match his slightly aggressive tone.

"I've not yet had the pleasure of a formal introduction, but having heard so much about you, madam, I couldn't resist the opportunity to make your acquaintance." His bow was barely more than a dip of his head. "I am Lord Grentham."

The announcement turned her insides to ice.

"Allow me to take the captain's place," he said as the musicians struck up the first notes of a waltz. It was more of an order than a request.

Somehow, she forced her lips to bend in a smile. There was nothing to do but brazen it out and slide into a second—or was it third?—skin.

I am not quite sure who I am anymore.

"But of course." Setting aside her glass, Arianna let him lead her out onto the dance floor. "Your name is familiar, sir—I must have heard it mentioned by Mr. Mellon. Are the two of you friends?"

"I am well acquainted with all of your relatives, including the Earl of Saybrook." Grentham spun them through the first turn. "Indeed, I am well acquainted with most everyone in London Society. Save for you."

"Alas, you won't find me very interesting, sir. I've lived far removed from the glitter and glamour of city life."

"On the contrary, Lady Wolcott. You fascinate me."

Fighting down a feeling of vertigo, Arianna moved through another twirl. *Steady, steady.* There was no reason to panic—she had been in slippery situations before.

"Then it seems you are easily amused, sir."

In another man, the rumble in his throat might have been mistaken for a laugh. "Ask anyone and you will be assured that I have no sense of humor."

"And why is that?" she asked.

"Because I am in charge of state security, Lady Wolcott, and as such, it is my duty to keep the country safe from those nefarious persons who would do it harm."

"I can see that is no laughing matter, sir."

Grentham subjected her to a piercing stare. Up close, his eyes appeared even more steely. *Sharp. Merciless.* They bore into her with unrelenting intensity.

"No, it is not. I take my responsibilities very seriously."

Arianna had long ago learned that any show of fear encouraged a predator to go for the jugular. Lifting her chin, she regarded him with a show of sangfroid. "Then I wonder why you choose to indulge in such frivolous activities as dancing, Lord Grentham. Especially with a provincial nobody."

"Oh, don't underestimate yourself, Lady Wolcott." His voice dropped a notch. "Be assured I don't."

She assumed an expression of polite puzzlement. "I confess, sir, I'm not sure that I follow your meaning."

A quick sidestep and intricate twirl seemed deliberately designed to throw her off balance. "And yet your footwork seems extraordinarily adroit," he remarked after she had come through the moves without missing a step.

"Dancing is a skill that all proper young ladies are expected to master."

The minister's gaze shifted for an instant, as if distracted by a movement across the crowded room.

"Along with a number of other feminine wiles," murmured Grentham.

"La, you appear to have a harsh opinion of the opposite sex, sir." Arianna batted her lashes, hoping her nonchalance didn't ring too false. Given his interest in her, the minister must be aware of her attraction to Concord and his crowd, so a bit of boldness was in character. "Is there nothing I can do to win your regard?"

His flash of teeth was clearly not meant to be a smile. "We shall see, Lady Wolcott, we shall see."

They danced through the next few figures in silence. Then, much to her relief, the music rose to a sweeping crescendo and came to a flourishing end.

"Thank you for such a delightful interlude," said the minister as he escorted her to the perimeter of the room.

An undertone of mockery gave an ominous edge to his words. "I enjoyed myself immensely."

Yes, I imagine that you did, thought Arianna.

He kept hold of her hand for just a fraction longer. "By the by, I won't find any record of a William Wolcott in Yorkshire, will I?"

"Of course you will," she replied without hesitation. "Why would I lie, sir?"

"I don't know, Lady Wolcott. But I intend to find out."

Inwardly shaken by the encounter, Arianna signaled to a passing footman for a glass of champagne. Being adrift in a sea of strangers only heightened her awareness of all the hidden shoals beneath the surface of London Society. The myriad faces, alight with . . .

Spotting the earl across the room, she suddenly veered away from the secluded spot behind the potted palms.

"Any shelter in a storm," she whispered under her breath. Saybrook was standing apart from the crowd with an elderly lady who, despite her advanced age, still possessed a regal beauty. It appeared that they were engaged in a private conversation.

Ah, but I am family, she thought wryly.

It would appear odd, too, if she did not pay her respects to him.

The earl looked up as she approached, his expression hovering somewhere between wariness and welcome. "You see, Aunt Constantina, I told you that our newly arrived relative would be anxious to make your acquaintance," he said dryly. "Lady Wolcott, I'm sure the dowager Marchioness of Sterling needs no introduction."

"None whatsoever," responded Arianna, picking up her cue. "It is, of course, a pleasure to finally meet you, Lady Sterling."

The dowager raised her quizzing glass to one eye, the thick lens magnifying its speculative gleam. After a long moment of scrutiny, she let the beribboned handle fall back against her bosom. "What side of the family are you from?" she inquired brusquely.

"Lady Wolcott's mother was a Peabody," interceded Saybrook smoothly.

"Hmmph." Another look, this one unaided by special optics. "I can't say that I see the resemblance."

"Such things are not always so apparent," replied the earl. Before his aunt could respond, he quickly changed the subject. "I see you have met Lord Percival Grentham, Lady Wolcott."

"Yes, and I cannot say that the experience is one I care to repeat."

"And no wonder." The dowager gave a small sniff. "These days I hear he is better known as '*Persecute*' Grentham. He was not, however, such an odious man in his youth. His mother would be greatly disappointed at what a stick in the mud he has become."

"Yes, but like most of London's citizens, she would be terrified to say it aloud, for fear of being hauled off to prison on charges of sedition," quipped the earl.

Repressing a shudder, Arianna tried not to recall his cold-blooded touch. "I admit, his manner was intimidating. I shall take care to avoid him in the future."

"A wise choice," murmured Saybrook. His gaze held hers for a moment, and for some reason, the fleeting connection helped settle her nerves. There was, she admitted, something to be said for not feeling utterly alone.

"Ha, let him try to breathe fire and brimstone at *me*, and he will end up with his own bum burned," remarked Lady Sterling.

Arianna ducked her head to hide a smile. Strange, but she felt an immediate kinship with the outspoken dowager. Which was ludicrous, considering that the only thing that had drawn them together was a web of lies.

"I don't doubt it," said the earl. "You can be quite a dragon when you so choose."

"Ungrateful boy." Lady Sterling rapped his shoulder with her fan. "You will have the poor gel more frightened of me than of Grentham."

Saybrook's jaw gave a tiny little tic, as if he were trying not to laugh. "I would guess that any relative of ours
is made of sterner stuff than that."

The dowager turned her attention to Arianna. "Ignore my nephew's teasings. He can be impossibly an-
noying at times." She cleared her throat. "Be that as it
may, he tells me you have only recently arrived in Town."

"Yes," she replied.

"Well, you must come pay me a visit if you wish any
advice for how to get along in Society. Sandro will tell
you that there is not a soul who knows more about the
ton and its secrets than I do."

Secrets. Keeping a smile pasted in place, Arianna acknowledged the invitation. "How very kind."

"Oh, pish." Lady Sterling waved a bejeweled hand.
"We are, after all, family, my dear, and family must look
out for each other."

For a fleeting instant, the cacophony of the crowded
ballroom was drowned out by a strange keening sound
in her ears. Like the weeping of the wind on a storm-
tossed night.

"May I get you more champagne, Lady Wolcott?"
asked the earl softly.

Arianna realized that she was gripping her glass so
tightly its stem was in danger of breaking in two. "No.
Thank you." All at once, the heat and noise seemed un-
bearable, but before she could excuse herself, Lady Sterling suddenly narrowed her gaze.

"Well, well, well. I see that Persecute isn't the only
odd guest here." The dowager's attention seemed riv-
eted on a spot to the right of the refreshment table.
"Hortense is such a high stickler. I am surprised that she
would invite Lady Spencer."

Sure enough, Arianna spotted her erstwhile employer deep in conversation with Gavin.

"Why do you say that?" inquired Saybrook. His tone
was deceptively casual, yet his body had become more
alert.

"To begin with, she is the Prince's current mistress,"

answered the dowager. "Or one of them. It's hard to keep a precise tally."

"If Lady Ravenell chose not to invite all the ladies who have slept with Prinny, the ballroom would be half empty," murmured the earl.

"True." Lady Sterling toyed with the ribbon of her quizzing glass. "Still, given the position that Hortense's husband holds at the Bank of England, I find it strange that she would overlook the other scandal."

Arianna noted the subtle sharpening of Saybrook's features. "What other scandal, Aunt Constantina?" he inquired softly.

"Oh, that unpleasant mess from the last century. Lady Spencer's maternal grandfather was Mr. George Carsall." The dowager waited expectantly for the earl to respond. When his only reaction was a raised brow, she heaved an impatient sigh. "For God's sake, don't they teach English history at Oxford anymore?"

He gave an apologetic shrug. "As you know, my interests lay in other studies."

"Well, much as I adore your chocolate creations, Sandro, all peers ought to pay attention to *that* particular subject in order to avoid repeating the mistakes of the past."

"I stand duly chastised," replied Saybrook. "Perhaps you would care to fill the hole in my knowledge?"

The dowager slanted another owlish squint at Lady Spencer. "My dear boy, Carsall was a governor of the Sword Blade Bank. Now, please don't tell me that you haven't heard of *them* and the South Sea Company, else I may have to resort to my smelling salts."

17

From the chocolate notebooks of Dona Maria Castellano

I've just found a wonderful colored botanical engraving of a cacao tree and fruit in one of the antiquarian bookshops. I shall have it framed for Sandro, as he will appreciate all the scientific nomenclature inscribed at the bottom. During his studies at Oxford, he was fascinated by Carolus Linnaeus, a Swedish scientist who in 1753 devised a system for classifying all living organisms. Each has a Latin name, and chocolate is called Theobroma cacao. How fitting that Theobroma means food of the gods. . . .

Chocolate Sambuca Crinkle Cookies

1¼ cups all-purpose flour
1 tablespoon baking powder
½ teaspoon salt
12 ounces fine-quality bittersweet chocolate (not unsweetened), chopped
½ stick unsalted butter
2 large eggs
½ cup walnuts, coarsely chopped
½ cup sambuca or other anise-flavored liqueur
2 tablespoons granulated sugar
1 cup confectioner's sugar

1. Preheat oven to 350°F.
2. Sift together flour, baking powder, and salt. Melt chocolate with butter in a metal bowl set over a saucepan of simmering water, stirring until smooth. Lightly whisk together eggs, walnuts, sambuca, and granulated sugar in another bowl. Stir in flour mixture and chocolate (dough will be thin). Chill, covered, until firm, about 2 hours.
3. Sift confectioner's sugar onto a plate. Roll heaping tablespoons of dough into balls and roll balls, as formed, in confectioner's sugar to generously coat. Arrange balls 2 inches apart on 2 lightly buttered baking sheets and bake in upper and lower thirds of oven, switching position of sheets halfway through baking, until puffed and cracked but centers are still a bit soft, 10 to 12 minutes total. Transfer to racks to cool.

❧

A rianna sucked in an audible breath.

"Bravo, gel," said the dowager. "You appear far more educated than my nephew on the history of financial scams and scandals."

"N-not really," she stammered.

"Even *I* have heard of the South Sea Bubble," said Saybrook.

"I should hope so." Lady Sterling grimaced. "Thank God that my brother—your grandfather—was convinced not to invest in their stock. Anyone with a grain of sense could see that the value of the company was built on thin air."

"And yet, a great many intelligent people were blinded by greed," observed the earl.

The dowager nodded. "Aye, greed is a powerful emotion."

"That it is," whispered Arianna.

"Even so brilliant a man as Sir Isaac Newton was caught up in the trading frenzy," added Saybrook. "It's said that he lost twenty thousand pounds, and later remarked, 'I can calculate the movement of the stars, but not the madness of men.' "

"Yes, well, no matter how often the lesson is taught, it doesn't seem to sink in," remarked Lady Sterling. "People have very large appetites and very small memories."

Arianna swallowed a bitter laugh. *Oh, how very true.*

"Thank you for the history lecture," said the earl.

"Don't be impertinent," scolded his aunt. Turning to Arianna, she gave a brusque wave. "Go dance with my great-nephew. My mouth is now dry and my feet are aching, so I wish to sit down and enjoy a cup of negus with my friends." Patting the snowy white plumes of her headdress into place, Lady Sterling marched off to join a group of matrons seated near the entrance to the card room.

Saybrook offered his arm. "Seeing as the waltz affords a modicum of privacy in which to talk, let us not waste the opportunity."

"I agree—the sooner we have a council of war, the better," murmured Arianna, once the lilting notes of the melody swept them into motion.

"Has something happened?" he asked quickly.

"Aside from having that watchdog Grentham sniffing around my skirts?" Expelling a harried sigh, she pushed aside her fears about abstract numbers to concentrate on a more real threat. "It is a good thing that plans are progressing quickly—at least on my end. The minister seems to suspect that I am not quite what I seem."

Saybrook's mouth thinned to a grim line. "It appears that he, like us, doesn't put much credence in coincidence. Apparently the timing of your arrival has set off alarm bells."

"Why is he so interested in your family?" she asked. "The comings and goings of various relatives shouldn't ordinarily attract much notice."

He ignored the question to pose one of his own. "How much do you know about your father's business dealings before he left England?"

"Why do you ask?"

He hesitated, moving with careful steps through a box turn before answering her. "I did a bit more digging into the past this afternoon. Your suggestion of illicit dealings involving military supplies reminded me of an old rumor I had heard—"

"But now we know that 'sword blade' refers to something else," she protested.

"Perhaps." His dark eyes turned more opaque. "Be that as it may, I have reason to think that your father's cleverness with numbers was used for more than playing cards."

Try as she might, Arianna couldn't keep a tiny skip out of her voice. "W-what do you mean?"

"My research has uncovered a business venture, one involving the supply of munitions to the Duke of Brunswick's army during the First Coalition campaign against the French revolutionaries. The duke was advancing on Paris and the French should have been no match for his veteran forces. However, at the Battle of Valmy, Brunswick was forced to retreat in the face of superior artillery fire."

She frowned. "I assure you, my father wasn't the least bit interested in politics or warfare."

Again the earl hesitated. "No, but he was very interested in money, wasn't he?"

Her throat grew painfully tight.

"There seem to have been some serious questions concerning the company's bookkeeping," he went on. "Nothing was proved, but in reading over the records of the case, I learned that one of the investigators thought that there appeared to be a complex and cleverly designed formula in place, one that allowed the partners to profit handsomely while leaving the British army short of cannon shells."

No, no, no! Would the lies of others forever haunt her life?

"Why are you telling me this?" she asked.

Saybrook's mouth thinned to a grim line. "Because

the names of the company's investors included not only Lord Concord and Lord Hamilton, but also Richard Hadley, the Earl of Morse."

Arianna felt her stomach begin to churn. Fear, trepidation, denial—a hot mix of emotion that burned like acid at her very core. And then suddenly all her pent-up anger surged upward rather than inward. "How dare you!" she whispered. "My father would never have betrayed or cheated his country. Never."

"We are often the last ones to see fault in the people we love," said the earl gently.

She saw a stirring of sympathy in the depths of his chocolate-dark gaze, which only goaded her to greater fury. Pity was the last thing on earth she wanted from him.

"You pompous prig," she hissed. "You just said yourself that there was no proof, yet you show no shame in repeating such scurrilous rumors. Oh, how easy it is to blacken the name of someone who isn't able to defend himself."

"Smile," he warned under his breath. "The other guests will get the wrong impression."

"On the contrary, we want them to think that I find your company odious," she said tightly.

"I know this must be hard for you," he murmured. "But if we don't explore every possibility, we shall never find the truth—"

"The truth? You don't care about the truth," she said bitterly. "This is simply a cerebral challenge for you. A distraction to draw you out of your own morbid musings. A body here, a scandal there—you may tell yourself how very, very smart you are when you piece it all together. As for what lives are ruined in the process, well, for a veteran officer, that's simply the casualties of war."

"Have a care about making your own unfair accusations, milady," responded the earl.

"What about the revelation we just learned from your great-aunt? That seems far more explosive information than some vague twenty-year-old charges against an obscure company," challenged Arianna. "Do you intend to pursue Lady Spencer as ruthlessly as you have my father?"

"Yes, you may be assured that I won't spare anyone."

Nor will I, she thought, as the whirling dervish blur of numbers in her head began to slow and form a more solid shape.

The music must have ended, for on looking up, Arianna saw that the earl was steering their steps for a secluded spot between the marble colonnading and a display of tall potted palms. Grateful for a moment of respite, she took shelter in the leafy shadows.

"I regret that my words caused you pain," began the earl after a moment of awkward silence.

"You must understand that my father was a dreamer, and in many ways naïve to the ways of the world," interrupted Arianna. "He was generous, and trusting—perhaps to a fault." The echo of a rich, baritone laugh danced unbidden across her consciousness. "If there is any truth to what you just told me, it would be because he was manipulated by his friends."

Innocent, innocent—his dying words reverberated in her head.

"In fact," she said slowly, "certain things are beginning to make more sense."

"What makes you say that?" asked Saybrook. Though bladelike shadows cut across his face, making his expression impossible to discern, his voice was sharp with skepticism.

Don't react, she warned herself. But the words, bitter as bile, had already escaped her lips. "Because he was *murdered*, sir. Stabbed in a dark alley in Kingston Harbor and left to bleed to death in the filth and garbage. He managed to crawl back to our tavern room, but . . ."

"I am sorry. I didn't know that."

Aware that she had already revealed far more than she meant to, Arianna remained silent.

Saybrook turned slightly, his big body shielding her

from the glittering lights and laughter. "I take it he told you who was responsible?"

"He said enough for me to figure it out on my own." She steadied herself with a deep breath. "My father swore on his deathbed that he was innocent of the cheating charge, and I believe him. As for any other—"

A rustling of the leaves warned that someone was approaching.

"Lady Wolcott?" said a tentative voice.

It was Ashmun.

"Ah, here you are." His hooded gaze lingered on the earl, and though the flickering light of the chandeliers did not quite penetrate the greenery, it caught the momentary pinch of a scowl. "Forgive me for intruding, but I believe we are slated for the next set, and I would be very disappointed to miss the pleasure of partnering you."

Despite her misgivings about the man, she was not unhappy over the interruption. "Oh, there is no need for apologies. The earl and I were merely discussing a relative. But reminiscing can wait. I would much rather dance."

"Excellent," said Ashmun.

Saybrook yielded his place without objection. After a perfunctory bow, he turned and walked off.

In the direction of Lady Spencer, noted Arianna out of the corner of her eye. Whatever else his faults, the earl was a man of his word.

"I don't mean to pry," said Ashmun. "But it appeared as if the two of you were engaged in a rather heated exchange. I do hope the earl wasn't upsetting you. He has the reputation of being . . . unstable."

"It was simply an old family matter," she replied brusquely. "There is no call for concern."

Ashmun didn't press, but even as the formations of the lively country gavotte drew them apart, she could sense that he was watching her like a hawk.

Silk swirled around her ankles, the paste jewel earbobs caressed her lobes, and for an instant she yearned to strip away the layers of lies, the practiced deceptions, the well-rehearsed lines, and flee from the past. Oh, to imagine that she might ever be free to be herself.

Whoever that was.

But as Lady Sterling had so wisely pointed out, there was no escaping history.

Another glass of champagne fortified her for the next set. And then another. Arianna was feeling a little light-headed when Gavin came out from the card room to claim his second dance with her.

"The Spanish Inquisitor seems to have shed his monk's robe for the evening," he remarked, eyeing the earl and Lady Spencer standing together in close conversation by the balcony doors.

"You mean Saybrook?" She made a pained face. "The man is a tedious bore. For propriety's sake, I had to take a turn around the dance floor with him, but then he insisted on subjecting me to a lecture on proper behavior for a lady."

"Boring indeed," remarked Gavin with a sardonic laugh.

"You can't begin to imagine. He thinks I'm too fast." Her palm slid suggestively against his shoulder. Leaning a little closer, she let her breath tease against his ear. "Do you?"

Beneath her touch, his muscles twitched. "I believe ladies should be able to . . . do as they please."

"Fay çe que vouldras," said Arianna, drawing out the French phrase slowly, like a strand of melting sugar.

"Precisely, Lady Wolcott." Up close, the predatory gleam in his eyes blazed bright as an open flame. "How very interesting that you would choose that exact phrase."

"Oh, I heard someone mention it recently," she said. "And thought it sounded . . . intriguing. French is such a *sensual* language, is it not?"

"Deliciously so," he answered. "It drips like melted butter from your tongue."

She tittered. "La, isn't the mention of body parts strictly forbidden in Polite Society, Sir Gavin?"

He glanced around the ballroom before locking his gaze with hers. "Among a select group of people, the rules don't apply."

"Even more intriguing," she whispered. She let a few more steps of the dance go by before adding, "Lord Concord mentioned a club. A very exclusive club. How does one apply?"

"One doesn't apply, Lady Wolcott. One is invited," responded Gavin. "But seeing as Concord is in charge of the membership, I am sure that your name will be high on the list."

"I do hope you will put in a good word for me."

"But of course." A series of tight twirls turned the ballroom into a kaleidoscope blur of colors. "I think you would fit in perfectly."

"So do I, sir." *So do I.*

18

From the chocolate notebooks of Dona Maria Castellano

I picked up several illustrated books on botany on my last shopping sojourn in Madrid, and now know there are three distinct types of cacao trees. Criollas are considered the "prince of cacao." They are very delicate and prone to disease, but produce the highest-quality beans. Forasteros are the most common variety, and although they are very hardy, they are the least flavorful. Trinitarios, named for the island of Trinidad, are a hybrid, and offer an excellent balance of taste and ease of cultivation. . . .

Mexican Chocolate Pudding

½ cup packed light brown sugar
¼ cup unsweetened cocoa powder
2½ tablespoons cornstarch
½ teaspoon cinnamon
⅛ teaspoon salt
2 cups plain unsweetened almond milk
1½ tablespoons unsalted butter, cut into bits
½ teaspoon pure vanilla extract

1. Mix together brown sugar, cocoa powder, cornstarch, cinnamon, and salt in a heavy medium

saucepan, then whisk in almond milk. Bring to a
boil over medium heat, stirring often, then boil,
whisking, 1 minute.
2. Remove from heat and whisk in butter and vanilla.
3. Chill in a bowl, surface covered with a piece of
buttered wax paper, until cold, at least 1½ hours.

❧

Fog floated through the chill night air, a sea of silver obscuring the rain-spattered cobblestones. The
shower had passed, but the mizzled moonlight was too
weak to penetrate the shadows separating the row of
town houses. Darkness hid any sign of movement along
the garden wall of Arianna's rented residence.

Saybrook slid his shoes over the damp grass, careful
to avoid any stray twigs that might make a sound. The
cloaked figure ahead of him was now only three steps
away . . . two steps . . .

Lunging forward, he caught his quarry by the shoulders. A half spin and hard jerk slammed the man up
against the mossy brick.

"Quiet!" he growled, whipping out a knife from his
coat and angling its edge beneath the upturned jaw.
"And don't move."

His prisoner held very still. "Are you going to slit my
throat?"

"That depends," said Saybrook. "What filthy game
are you playing, Ashmun? Answer me now, and I might
let your blood stay in your veins." The blade pressed
harder against the exposed flesh. "Why are you following Lady Wolcott?"

"Because . . ." Ashmun drew a ragged breath and
slowly lifted his chin. "Because I'm very concerned for
her safety."

"Explain yourself," ordered the earl.

"I'm afraid that she's gotten herself into deep trouble
with you, and the men you have introduced to her." His

gaze flicked down to the knife. "I might ask the same question of you, Lord Saybrook. Why are *you* following her?"

"What business is it of yours?" he demanded.

"I . . . I would rather not say," replied Ashmun.

The sharpened steel twitched, drawing a drop of blood. "I'm afraid I must insist."

The night was still, save for the rasp of their breathing. The ghostly puffs of vapor twisted and twined together against the blurred shades of black.

The earl waited, but Ashmun remained silent.

"I applaud your courage, if not your common sense." Saybrook eased back a touch. "If your motives are upright, you have nothing to fear from me."

Ashmun appeared uncertain. However, after a long moment he let out a soft sigh. "I suppose I really have little choice." His lips pursed into something between a grimace and a smile. "I am Lady Wolcott's godfather. Or rather, I am Lady Arianna Hadley's godfather. For she is, I am sure, the daughter of my good friend Richard Hadley, who was forced to flee to the West Indies some time ago."

Saybrook slowly lowered the knife. "She thought you looked familiar."

"Did she?" Ashmun looked puzzled. "I wonder how that could be? I was present at her christening, of course, but spent years abroad so did not see her again before her father left the country. And while I visited Jamaica to speak with Richard, I would have sworn that Arianna knew nothing of it. He and I took great pains to make sure that she wasn't aware of my visit."

"Lady Arianna has a knack of learning things that others might want to keep a secret." The earl thought for a moment. "It is odd, though, that she didn't recognize your name."

"Not necessarily. I was only the Honorable Mr. Josiah Becton at the time of her birth. I've since acceded to the title of Baron Ashmun."

"I see."

Ashmun pulled a rueful face. "Her father would have

been unhappy to hear that she spotted me. We were trying to protect her."

"She wouldn't thank you for it." Saybrook sheathed his blade. "Protect her from what?"

The baron fixed him with a searching stare. "Before I answer that, what is your interest in the lady?"

"I, too, am anxious to keep her out of harm's way," answered Saybrook. "I am not at liberty to say any more than that."

"But—"

A muffled crunch of leaves underfoot caused him to cut off his words.

Saybrook whipped around, the knife flashing out from inside his coat. The sound came again, from beneath the overhanging ivy, and then Arianna slipped out from the muddled shadows of the recessed gate in the garden wall.

"I thought I heard something," she murmured, eyeing the earl's weapon. Sliding a step closer, she saw that his other hand held a man pinned to the garden wall.

"And so you decided to come investigate?" Saybrook did not sound pleased. "Alone and unarmed?"

She revealed the small turn-off pocket pistol hidden beneath the folds of her India shawl. "I'm not quite so careless as you think." She thumbed the hammer back to the half-cocked position but kept the barrel aimed at the baron's head. "Once again, it seems you are following me, Lord Ashmun. Would you care to explain why? Or shall I be forced to reconsider using a more persuasive means of making you talk."

"I have the situation in hand, Lady Wolcott," said Saybrook. Lowering his voice, he added, "Go back inside. It is likely that someone is watching your house, and it would be prudent to give him nothing to report."

She took cover within the brick archway and then silently motioned for the men to follow her.

"Damnation," Arianna heard Saybrook swear softly. "We had better do as she asks, else she is capable of shooting *both* of us."

"A wise move, sir," she said as he and the baron ducked into the garden. "As you know, I'm unpredictable." A tug on the hasp clicked the lock shut. "Follow me. We'll be more comfortable inside, away from prying eyes."

Crossing the terrace, Arianna led the way through a set of glass-paned doors and halfway down the corridor to a small study.

"Help yourself to a drink," she said, indicating the decanters on the sideboard as she stirred the banked fire to life.

"May I pour you something?" asked the earl, measuring out a generous helping of brandy for both himself and Ashmun.

"Thank you, but no. I've imbibed enough for one evening."

Saybrook lifted a brow. "Dancing does work up a thirst."

"So, it would seem, does skulking through the dead of night," she replied. "Which raises the question of why you were lurking outside my town house."

"You mentioned your concern about Lord Ashmun. So I decided to have a look for myself."

Arianna had a feeling that there was more to the matter than met the eye, but put off confronting him for the moment. Instead, she turned to Ashmun.

"And what have you to say for yourself, sir? I think it's time you explained your interest in me."

The baron hesitated and cast a mute appeal at Saybrook.

"You do not need the earl's permission," snapped Arianna. "He is not my guardian." Her mouth tightened. "Or my protector."

The older man flushed, and then cleared his throat. "Very well. I've been following you because I believe you are the daughter of my very dear friend Richard Hadley."

She sat down rather heavily.

"*Are* you Arianna?" he asked. "You look exactly like

the miniature he showed me—the one he carried inside his watchcase."

For once, she couldn't quite slip out of her real skin. "I knew I had seen you before—somewhere other than here in London."

"I met with your father in Jamaica the day before his death." Ashmun pressed a hand to his brow. "I—I tried to find you the next day, after I learned of the attack. But you had already disappeared."

"I had no money to pay the landlord. And the barter he suggested was not a price I wished to pay for that hovel," she replied.

"I am so sorry, my dear."

She managed a careless shrug. "I wasn't your responsibility, sir."

"But you were." He regarded her sorrowfully. "You see, I am your godfather, and should have saved you from having to make such wretched choices." His hands knotted together in his lap. "Did your father never mention my existence?"

Oh, Papa—how many other secrets did you take to the grave?

Arianna slowly shook her head. "It appears that there was much he did not tell me."

"You were about to tell me earlier why you undertook a journey all the way from England to speak with Lord Morse," said Saybrook. "Please do so now, Ashmun. His daughter is anxious to learn everything there is to know about the circumstances surrounding his death."

"Before we get to that, I would like to be assured that you have a claim to her confidence," said Ashmun. He slanted a questioning look at Arianna. "Do you trust him?"

"You may speak freely," she replied, carefully evading a more specific answer.

Her response elicited a harried sigh. "Very well. But to be honest, my dear, I'm not sure that it serves any purpose to dredge up the past."

"I'm afraid that it does," answered Arianna. "Indeed, it may prove very important in solving a present problem."

The baron shifted uneasily in his chair. "Then I assume you wish to hear the truth, and not some rose-tinted version of it."

Truth. That cursed word again. It seemed to taunt her at every turn.

She signaled with a curt nod for him to go on.

After wetting his lips with a sip of brandy, Ashmun set his glass aside. "I need not tell you, Arianna, what a charming, fun-loving fellow your father was. But for the earl's sake, I will try to paint a quick sketch." He closed his eyes, taking a moment to frame his thoughts. "Richard had a magnetism that is hard to describe, an innate ability to convince you that black was white, even if the evidence to the contrary was right in front of your nose."

Saybrook stretched his legs out toward the hearth.

A wry smile tugged at Ashmun's mouth. "Now don't get me wrong—there was not a more loyal or generous friend in a pinch. But he also had a harder, sharper facet to his character."

Arianna stared at the freshly stirred coals, hot and cold points of ash and fire.

"You see, Richard took great delight in being just a little cleverer than the rest of us," Ashmun went on. "He was extraordinarily gifted in mathematics. And at times he used that talent to his advantage."

She quelled the urge to press her palms over her ears.

"You are sure that you want me to go on?" Ashmun's face was wreathed in concern.

"Yes," answered Arianna. *Was there really a choice?*

The earl rose and went to pour a fresh glass of brandy. He placed it in her hands before resuming his place by the fire. "If it makes your story any easier, Lady Arianna already has reason to suspect that her father may have been involved in some questionable business dealings."

Ashmun looked relieved. "Then what I have to say will not come as a complete shock." He puffed out his cheeks. "I do not know the specifics of the deal—it happened twenty years ago—but Richard had some sort of partnership with a group of gentlemen he knew from one of his gaming clubs. Concord, Ham—"

"Yes, I know the names by heart," interrupted Arianna.

"Then I shall not pain you by constantly repeating them," said Ashmun softly. "Suffice it to say, Richard had become their friend . . . he enjoyed the camaraderie of his fellow peers, and was flattered that a set of young, fast gentlemen courted his company. He found it easy to fit into the group."

Like a chameleon, thought Arianna. No wonder she found it so effortless to change her skin. If one simply shrugged off all questions of right or wrong when it suited one's purpose, the transformation was quite simple.

And apparently she had learned from a man who had mastered the art of amorality.

Looking up, she found the earl watching her intently, his dark eyes like daggers against her flesh.

"Yes, Papa enjoyed being the life of the party." She summoned a cool smile, though her insides were twisting in a painful knot. "The center of attention."

"Even when he had to cut corners to get there," murmured the earl.

"That is a good way of putting it, I suppose. Richard didn't see the harm in shaving a bit off the rules. I . . . but first, I should finish my story." Ashmun crooked a tiny grimace. "In any case, he recounted to me how he had created a complex mathematical billing model for a company that his friends had invested in, one that allowed him to manipulate the numbers. Don't ask me to explain it, but the formula created an extra profit for the company while shipping fewer goods than contracted for. So it proved extremely clever on both ends. And extremely lucrative for the investors. He was quite proud of himself for figuring it out."

"I assume he was rewarded for his brilliance," said Saybrook.

"Yes. A share in the partnership," answered Ashmun. "But for a man who was a genius with numbers, Richard seemed to have no concept of money. He spent freely . . . or, rather, flagrantly. While his wife was alive, she managed to control his wilder impulses. But after her death . . ." He lifted his shoulders. "God knows, I tried to counsel him on the dangers of . . . of . . ."

"Of cheating?" suggested Arianna. "Of consorting with criminals?"

"Your father saw things far more abstractly," replied Ashmun. "It is deucedly hard to explain, but Richard had great trouble seeing the connection between his actions and the consequences of them. He meant no harm—his calculations were simply an intellectual challenge, and he took boyish delight in solving them. It wasn't until later . . ."

Ashmun paused for a swallow of brandy. "But before I digress, let me finish with this part of the tale. To make a long story short, your father's cleverness went a touch too far, for you see, he couldn't help but add an extra equation that skimmed off a little extra for himself."

"In other words," said Saybrook, "he cheated the cheaters at their own game."

"Precisely," answered the baron. "It took them a year or so to discover it, and to be honest, I'm not quite sure how it came to light. Perhaps Richard admitted the joke one night when he was in his cups. That would be the sort of thing he would do—ha, ha, ha, no hard feelings, eh?"

"Ha, ha, ha," echoed Arianna.

"However, his friends did not find it amusing and so decided to take revenge. They, too, were very clever men. Ruthlessly so, as you have good reason to know, my dear."

"So they concocted the accusation of cheating at cards," murmured Arianna.

"Which forced Lord Morse to leave the country," finished Saybrook.

"Aye." Ashmun blotted his brow with his handkerchief and finished his brandy. "I believe that in the meantime, your father had constructed a few other ventures for them, and I suppose they felt they didn't need him anymore."

"And he couldn't very well reveal their wrongdoings," mused the earl. "For to do so would have ruined his own name as well."

"Correct. My understanding is that they gave him a sum to leave quietly. Richard was in financial straits at the time and, well, he really had no choice but to accept his punishment. To have been publicly branded a cheat at cards would have been a fate worse than death. He would have been ostracized from Society and all the convivial company he so craved. In Jamaica, at least, he could pretend that he was still part of that world."

The world of illusions?

"I can see that." Arianna lifted her glass and set the amber liquid into a slow, spinning swirl. "But what I don't understand is why they should want to have him murdered. They had taken their revenge—in spades, I might add. Papa's sun had long since sunk into an ocean of rum. He posed no threat to them." Her fingers tightened. "I am, of course, assuming that his death wasn't a random robbery. Having inherited a little of his knack for numbers, I would say the odds of that are virtually nil."

"Lady Arianna," began Saybrook.

"However," she said quickly, ignoring his interruption. "When I add two and two together, it becomes clear that you did not journey all the way to the West Indies simply to share a glass of planter's punch with an old friend."

"Unfortunately, your arithmetic is correct," said Ashmun with a doleful sigh. "I was never close with Richard's new set of friends. I was living in Scotland at the time of your father's first foray into partnership with them, else I would have tried to steer him away from any involvement. Even then, they had a reputation as being dangerous men to deal with. However, I have enough contacts within the world of commerce to have gotten wind of some disquieting information in the summer of

'05. I heard that one of the group—I am not sure who—
had approached a senior clerk at Richardson, Overend
and Company, which, by the by, specialized in handling
discount bills of exchange for a number of banks, both
here in England and abroad."

"What are bills of exchange?" asked Arianna.

"They are the grease that keeps the wheels of commerce turning." It was Saybrook who answered her
question. "They facilitate the exchange of money for
goods, especially over great distances or across borders."

Curious, she pressed for further information. "How
so?"

"Let us say the owner of a sugar plantation in Jamaica
sells his crop to a merchant in Liverpool. He may go to
a bank in Kingston and draw a bill of exchange against
the value of the shipment, which he verifies with a bill
of lading and a certificate of insurance stating the goods
are indemnified against loss. In other words, he is advanced the money for the sugar cane, minus certain fees
and interest, and the bank retains the bill of exchange,
which is redeemed when the merchant pays on delivery
of the sugar cane."

"I see," she said slowly.

"The Kingston bank may then resell the bill of exchange, or use it for collateral against other loans. The
rate of exchange is where profits can be made or lost.
It's a complex variable, which depends on distance, the
scarcity of goods, and a number of other factors." The
earl looked to Ashmun. "Isn't that right?"

"You appear well-informed on economics, Lord Saybrook."

"I've been doing some reading on the subject lately."
He slanted a quick glance at Arianna before asking,
"Samuel Gurney joined Richardson, Overend and Company in 1807, did he not? And controls the firm, which is
now known as Overend, Gurney and Company?"

"Yes," replied Ashmun. "The Gurneys are a well-
known Quaker family, with powerful connections in
banking circles."

Gurney. The name explained yet another bit of Kellton's disjointed rant.

But then Arianna reminded herself that for the moment it was only speculation.

"Theory is all very well, but let us get back to your story, Lord Ashmun," she prodded. However horrible, she needed to know the details. "I think we had better hear the rest of it."

"Very well," agreed Ashmun. "I received a letter from your father hinting that he had the promise of riches—and a return to England. It seemed to me that the only possibility was a new venture with his former partners."

She couldn't hold back an exasperated oath. "Bloody hell, you would think he had learned his lesson."

The baron's eyes flooded with sympathy. "He wanted so desperately to bring you home to England, my dear."

Yet another unrealistic dream. Genius could be a blessing or a curse.

"I sent him a long reply, trying to point out just such a thing," went on Ashmun. "However, the more I thought about it, the more I worried that he was desperate enough to do something that he would regret." A short exhale, hardly more than a chuff of air, emphasized the last word. "His missive made mention that a meeting to finalize the deal was set for sometime in the beginning of November. As I had some family estate affairs to settle in Jamaica myself, I decided to move up my trip in order to arrive in the West Indies before that date. I thought that I might be able to talk some sense into your father. As you know, we did meet. . . ." The baron shook his head. "In the past, he had always been willing to listen to reason."

"He had been drinking heavily for some years," said Arianna.

"I suppose that explains his error of judgment." Another mournful sigh. "As I suspected, his so-called friends wanted him to construct a mathematical model for manipulating bills of exchange. And Richard, being sure that they needed him, sought to drive a hard bargain. He wanted a higher share of the profits than his erstwhile partners were willing to offer. I think he considered it his due for the years in exile."

"You were there during the negotiations." It was more statement than question. "That is when I saw you."

"I was," corroborated the baron. "And I told him he was making a grave mistake. Not only did he ignore my advice, but as the talks were breaking down, he threatened to expose their scheme if they didn't agree to his demands. You see, this time, being as yet uninvolved, he had no reason to remain quiet. He was sure they couldn't afford to say no."

"What they couldn't afford was the chance of betrayal," observed Saybrook. "No matter how great his mathematical skills, he had broken a sacred rule among criminals—never grass on your cohorts."

How strange. She hadn't touched a drop of her drink, and yet Arianna felt that her head was swimming.

"Lady Arianna . . . Lady Arianna . . ."

With an effort, she shook off the sensation.

"May I get you some sherry?" asked Ashmun in some alarm.

"N-no, thank you." She stiffened her spine. "I'm simply . . . fatigued. Dancing and drinking until dawn is not a life to which I am accustomed."

Saybrook rose. "I think we have all had enough activity for the night."

"Indeed, indeed." Taking his cue, the baron levered up out of his chair. "I hope I have not make a mistake in being completely forthright with you, Arianna. I did not mean to cause you pain."

"It hurt far more not to know," she said softly.

Or did it? At the moment, Arianna felt totally numb. Her limbs must have moved by rote rather than command, for she found herself on her feet.

"Don't trouble yourself, Lady Arianna. I will see Ashmun out," said Saybrook, signaling her to stay by the hearth. "And then check that the back of the house is locked up."

"Before I go..." The baron hesitated. "I have answered all your questions, but I have a great many of my own."

Her silence only made him more determined. "I fear that you are in some sort of trouble, Arianna," he persisted. "Why else would you be hiding your identity? Why else would you be seeking the company of your father's erstwhile friends? At least now, I hope you understand that they are not men who would offer you any aid."

Coals crackled, emitting a hiss of smoke.

"Whatever coil you are in, I would like to help—"

"If you wish to be of service to Lady Arianna," interrupted Saybrook, "you will distance yourself from her, in order not to raise questions about why an old friend of Lord Morse is so interested in a young widow newly arrived in Town."

"That is all you will tell me?"

"Yes," answered the earl bluntly.

"Lord Saybrook is right, sir," she added. "However well-meaning, your attentions could be harmful."

"Then I shall, of course, do as you ask. No matter that I don't understand." Ashmun gave a courtly bow. "But please know that if anything changes, and you need my assistance, you have only to let me know."

"Thank you."

"It's the least I can do, seeing as I've failed you so miserably in the past." He blew out his cheeks. "If only I had been more persuasive."

If only, if only, if only.

"If only Papa had been more responsible," she countered. "However, weeping over what happened won't change anything."

"A wise philosophy, Lady Arianna," said the earl. "One should look to make the future free from the ghosts of the past."

Close to a quarter hour passed before Saybrook returned. "The locks are all secured. Is there anything else I can do for you before I take my leave?"

Arianna nodded abstractly, not really listening to what he was saying.

"Lady Arianna."

She looked up from her contemplation of the glowing embers. The candles on the sideboard had burned down low, leaving the room shrouded in shadows.

"Will you be all right on your own here tonight?" he asked, the gentleness of his voice rousing her from her stupor.

"Are you offering to come upstairs and keep me company, Lord Saybrook?" she said mockingly, hating herself for feeling so vulnerable.

The momentary change in his expression was too swift, too subtle to interpret. Or maybe she had merely imagined it. Her powers of observation were clearly not as sharp as she had thought.

"I was not under the impression that my company would be of any comfort," he replied slowly.

"I'm not looking for comfort," she retorted. "A distraction, perhaps. Nothing more."

"Ah. Well, I've enough distractions to suit me. So I think I shall decline any additional ones." A pause. "Assuming that was what you offered."

The rejection, however oblique, left her feeling even more fragile. Her whole life felt as if it had been built on a house of cards. Gaudy bits of pasteboard, colored with illusions and lies.

And a breath of air had just knocked it to flinders, leaving her with nothing to cling to.

I have myself. And yet, somehow that didn't seem like enough anymore.

But unwilling to expose how lost she was feeling, Arianna curled a cynical smile. "I don't blame you for not wanting to sleep with a slut. Bad blood clearly runs in my family, so you are right not to want to taint your exalted person."

His laugh held no mirth. "There are few in Society who don't consider me a mongrel because of my breeding. For me to denigrate you or your forebearers would be like the pot calling the kettle black."

"Then why won't you come to my bed?" blurted out Arianna. "Do you find me unattractive? Undesirable?"

His dark lashes hid his eyes. "It would be wrong to take advantage of your present emotions. I would rather not let you do something that you might regret in the morning."

"An honorable, incorruptible gentleman," she jeered. "I thought that species only existed in fairy tales."

Saybrook didn't react with any anger, which was what she was hoping for. "I do my best to live by certain principles," he said calmly.

"Why should any of us care about abstract principles?" she challenged. "What does it matter? One only ends up defeated, disillusioned."

"Only if you let yourself turn tail and run," said the earl.

Arianna sucked in her breath. "I see no reason to care anymore. Let Concord and his evil cronies do as they please. It no longer matters to me."

"I should think you would care about justice. It is an even more compelling reason to act than revenge."

"Unlike you, sir, I'm not idealistic," she retorted. "Far from it."

"Perhaps you will surprise yourself."

"How can you speak of justice? You heard the sordid facts—my father was guilty." Her throat constricted. "Guilty."

"Whatever his sins, he paid the price for them," answered Saybrook. "Don't you wish for the others to be called to account for their own misdeeds?"

"I . . ." Arianna was suddenly aware of the hot sting of salt against her lids. "I don't know," she said in a small voice.

"A show of feminine frailty?" His brow rose in a sardonic arch. "Of all the roles you've played, a weak, weepy female is by far the least convincing one."

Crack. The impact of her hand left an angry red imprint on his cheek.

He didn't so much as flinch. "Feeling sorry for yourself?"

"Yes!" she cried. "I bloody well am."

"So you want to give up? Crawl away and wallow in self-pity, leaving your father's murderers free to plot yet another sordid scam?"

She blinked.

"If that's what you wish, pack up your belongings and I will allow you to slip away to . . . wherever it is that you wish to go," he finished.

"Is that a challenge, Lord Saybrook?" muttered Arianna.

His mouth twitched. "Of a sort."

Walk away and forget about everything? The idea was tempting. After all, she didn't owe anything to anyone.

"Though it's understandable if you've lost your stomach for a fight," said the earl. "I did warn you that in a *mano a mano* duel of wills, you would not come out on top."

"Don't sheath your steel just yet, sir."

"Then come tomorrow, be ready for another round." Saybrook moved for the doorway, but paused with his hand on the latch. "By the by, in answer to your question earlier this evening, I was approaching your town house because I thought you might be interested in knowing that Lady Spencer is as rapacious in business as she is in pleasure." He turned slightly, setting his dark hair to dancing across his shoulders. "In addition to sleeping with Kellton, she was also making money from him, and in more ways than one."

He would have made an excellent actor—his sense of dramatic timing was superb.

"H-how do you know that?" she demanded.

"Armed with my aunt's revelation, I decided to pay a visit to her town house after leaving the ball," he replied.

"But your leg—"

"Like you, I can improvise, Lady Arianna." He

quirked a thin smile. "Your information about the hidden panel in her desk saved me a great deal of time. I was able to read through the packet of letters from Kellton before having to leave."

Click, click. The latch shifted slightly under his hand. "From what I could gather, she was involved in a business enterprise with Kellton, and was passing him some sort of valuable information." His smile had turned to a frown. "Though what that information was, I am not sure."

Arianna felt a twinge of guilt over keeping the folder of papers she had taken from the desk to herself. But until she was more certain of its meaning . . .

"We may never know," went on Saybrook. "In any case, it seems that Lady Spencer knew some details of the business that had Kellton worried. So he was paying her not only a cut of the profits, but a spot of blackmail to keep quiet."

He thought for a moment. "I am surprised that such a clever lady is careless enough to keep written evidence in her own home, even though it is well hidden. But I suppose we should count ourselves lucky, for it seems she hasn't yet noticed that anything has gone missing."

"The secret compartment is ingeniously designed, so she likely thinks there is little danger that a common thief would find it—or have any interest in mere papers," said Arianna. "It's easy to become overconfident—which leads to making mistakes."

"Very true. It's a good reminder that we must never let down our guard."

An oblique warning? She didn't need the earl's words to know how many slips she had made over the past several weeks.

She thought for a moment. "Perhaps you should have asked some further questions of Ashmun. He seems to know a good deal about the inner workings of English commerce."

"Yes—maybe *too* much."

"Oh, surely you don't think . . ."

"Let us just say that for now, I take his tale with a grain of salt," replied Saybrook. "And I would advise that you do, too. Think on it—he may sound sincere, but there could be a more sinister explanation for all the things he knows."

"Lies and betrayal," she whispered. "But of course, I've come to expect no less."

"Lies and betrayal." Saybrook shifted his stance. "You told me when we first met that you trusted no one. I hope you haven't had a change of heart."

"I don't have a heart, sir."

His face remained expressionless.

Arianna abruptly changed the subject. "How do you mean to pursue Lady Spencer? More and more, it appears she is intimately involved in whatever intrigue is going on."

"I've already taken the first steps. While you were dancing with Gavin, I was enjoying a champagne stroll along the balcony with her."

"I don't think you'll get very far," she said bluntly. "You are not her type."

"Some women find that a challenge."

"But she knows you are conducting the government investigation on the Prince's poisoning," pressed Arianna. "It would be dangerous to encourage your attentions."

"Danger is like a drug," replied the earl. A spark from the dying embers seemed to light a reddish gold gleam in his gaze. "It can bubble through your blood and reach down into the deepest, darkest recesses of your being, making you do wild things. Risky things."

"At times, you frighten me, Lord Saybrook," she said.

"At times I frighten myself." He withdrew a piece of paper from his pocket and dropped it on the sideboard. "One last thing—you missed a sheet of numbers when you were riffling the lady's desk. It looks like gibberish to me, but seeing as you mentioned tonight that you had inherited a little of your father's skill in mathematics, perhaps you can make some sense of it."

19

From the chocolate notebooks of Dona Maria Castellano

Sandro has sent me the most delightful chocolatiere that he found at Sotheby's Auction House. It is made of delicate cream-colored porcelain and is painted with a fanciful scene of the tropics. He thinks it is quite old, and in doing a bit of research on the subject, I found that this style of pot was invented in the late seventeenth century, and features a tall, thin shape and a lid with a small hole, designed to fit the handle of a molinillo....

Chocolate Peanut Toffee

4 sticks (1 pound) unsalted butter, cut into pieces
2 cups sugar
¼ teaspoon salt
4 cups whole cocktail peanuts, plus 1 cup chopped
(1 pound, 10 ounces)
7 to 8 ounces 70%-cacao bittersweet chocolate,
finely chopped

1. Butter baking pan and put on a heatproof surface.
2. Bring butter, sugar, and salt to a boil in a 4- to 5-quart heavy pot over medium-high heat, whisk-

ing until smooth, then boil, stirring occasionally, until mixture is deep golden and registers 300°F (hard-crack stage) on thermometer, 15 to 20 minutes.

3. Immediately stir in whole peanuts, then carefully pour hot toffee into center of baking pan. Spread with spatula, smoothing top, and let stand 1 minute, then immediately sprinkle chocolate on top. Let stand until chocolate is melted, 4 to 5 minutes, then spread over toffee with clean spatula. Sprinkle evenly with chopped peanuts, then freeze until chocolate is firm, about 30 minutes. Break into pieces.

❧

"I trust there is a damn good reason for dragging me out here." Saybrook turned up the collar of his coat to the cold, clammy breeze. "I had only a few hours of sleep last night and spent most of the day haring over the city, tracking down several leads."

His boot made a small sucking sound as the earl shifted his stance in the mud. "So if this proves to be a wild-goose chase, I shall not be pleased."

"No rest for the wicked, eh?" quipped Henning. He edged to the corner of the warehouse wall and peered into the gloom. Fog was drifting in from the inky waters of the East India docks, the thick swirls of vapor heavy with the grit of salt and soot. Rising up from the sea of silver, the rigging of the tall ships rocked back and forth against the scudding clouds, looking like a tangled web woven by some giant rum-drunk spider.

"You mean to say that you would rather be at Almack's than the Isle of Dogs?" added the surgeon.

"Not at all—dancing through the muck with you is far more fun that waltzing with an heiress," said the earl dryly.

"We must wait another five minutes," murmured Henning, after a quick look at his pocket watch. "Then move quickly. But based on what I heard from my friend, you won't be disappointed.

"You've more tentacles than an octopus, Baz. I hadn't realized that your reach extended to the merchant fleets."

"Illness and poverty are everywhere," replied the surgeon dourly. "People are anxious to repay my help as best they can." Hugging close to the shadows, he leaned his back to the wall. "The curare got me curious about recent shipments from the New World, so I asked around. And sure enough, a recently arrived sailor confided to my contact that his captain had been strangely secretive about the unloading of their cargo. A special crew of stevedores had been hired to work under the cover of darkness, rather than during the day. And the crew was paid off early, and replaced with a cadre of private guards. Tough-looking men who were strangers to the docks."

The earl gave a noncommittal grunt.

"We're in luck that there's no moon," murmured the surgeon over the low gurgle of the ebbing tide. "We turn left once we cross through the loading area. The warehouse we want is the third one on the south side."

"What about watchmen?" asked Saybrook.

"The one guarding that section has been asked to ignore any activity he might notice for the next hour. But we still must be careful not to be spotted by any of the other patrols." He pressed a finger to his lips and then signaled for the earl to follow.

Moving stealthily through the shadows, they traversed the narrow passageways.

"This is the one." Henning stopped by a recessed door set within the blackened brick. He felt along the iron bands reinforcing the rough-cut oak until his hands encountered the hasp and padlock. Metal rasped against metal for just a moment. "Quick, get inside."

He pulled the portal shut behind him. "Go ahead and light the lantern."

Saybrook struck a lucifer and set it to the wick. After

adjusting the metal shutters, he angled the beam around the cluttered room.

"This is the back office. The storage area is through there." Henning indicated another door. "My source says there aren't any important papers kept here, but if you wish, we can have a look. Our time, however, is limited. The watch changes in an hour, and we must be gone by then."

"Let's have a look at the cargo first," said the earl. "That is the reason we are here, isn't it?"

"Correct." Henning ventured a quick peek into the darkness, and then added, "Stop sounding so peeved, laddie. I had expected more gratitude for my cleverness."

"Sorry, but the only thing I'd give thanks for at the moment is a night of uninterrupted sleep." Saybrook ran a hand over his bristled jaw. "On second thought, I shall shower you with several cases of your favorite malt if this turns out to be worth the trip."

"I shall send my request to yer agent at Berry Brothers and Rudd first thing in the morning," shot back the surgeon. A grunt sounded as his boot hit upon a metal object. "Shine the light over here."

The oily glow pooled over a small chest. A padlock secured the hasp, but the earl drew a thin, flexible length of steel from his pocket and within moments the mechanism released with a soft *snick*.

"I see ye haven't lost yer touch from our times with the partisans."

"My skills are a bit rusty," said Saybrook. "But it's all beginning to come back to me." Throwing open the lid, he pulled out several burlap bags. "Dried leaves," he murmured, handing a sprig to Henning. A sniff was followed by a tentative nibble. "*Erythroxylum coca*."

"Aye," corroborated the surgeon after taking a taste. "A favorite stimulant of the ancient Aztec armies."

"As was chocolate," murmured the earl. He opened one of the canisters at the bottom of the chest, revealing a quantity of snow-white powder.

"Careful, laddie," warned Henning as the earl inhaled

a small pinch. "That's a potent drug, assuming it's what I think it is."

The earl passed him the container. After a tentative taste, the surgeon nodded. "Lumley and I did some experiments in his laboratory at Oxford, distilling the coca plant's essence." He refastened the lid and placed the powder back in the trunk. "When reduced to a crystallized form and ground into a fine powder, it has a powerful effect on the senses, stimulating a rush of energy and euphoria."

"You speak from experience?"

"A scientist must have empirical knowledge," replied Henning. "So aye, I tried it." He thought for a moment. "Interesting. I've heard rumors of a new elixir being offered within certain circles of the aristocracy. A special pleasure drug, an elixir called the Devil's Delight. It costs a fortune for a small vial, but there are many willing to pay the price."

"Interesting," echoed the earl. He dropped to his knees and began examining the contents of the canvas sack next to the chest. "Speaking of chocolate ... There are several bales of cacao beans here, and they appear to be rare *criollas* of the highest quality, rather than the common *trinitario* variety." There was a rustling as he edged the lantern along the planking. "Along with dried vanilla pods and what looks to be a half dozen crates of silver bullion."

Henning made a face. "An odd assortment. Granted, all the items are valuable, but it's not as if there is enough of any one thing to make the long voyage worthwhile." He picked his way along a line of assorted barrels and boxes, poking and prodding at the deeply shadowed shapes. Beyond the weak pool of light, the darkness was impenetrable. "Perhaps they are simply a sample. A taste to whet the appetite."

Wood scraped against wood as the earl shifted a stack of crates. "Did your contact say where the ship picked up this cargo?"

"There were three ports of call. Veracruz, Portobelo, and Cartagena."

"Which were all main points of embarkation for the old Spanish treasure fleets," mused Saybrook.

The surgeon ran his hand over a cloth sack, stirring up a swirl of spicy sweetness. "So, we have merchandise coming from the New World, all of it with the potential to be highly profitable."

"But none of it in enough quantity to justify the cost or hazards of a long journey," added the earl.

"Not yet, not yet. But I tell you, this new Devil's Delight is already turning an obscene profit. The canister we just found will go a long way to paying the expenses of the voyage."

Silence, save the sudden scurrying of a rat among the burlap bales.

Saybrook tucked the sprig of coca into his pocket and sat back on his haunches. "Who owns the ship?"

Henning cracked his knuckles. "I'm working on that."

"Well, spread your tentacles even wider, Baz. We need to know the names of those involved."

"The pieces of the puzzle seem to be coming together, eh?" mused the surgeon. "Kellton was murdered with curare, a New World poison, and here we've just discovered evidence of an enterprise worth killing for. Then we have Concord, whom we know to have been involved in dirty dealings in the past." He pursed his lips. "Like Lady Arianna's father, Kellton must have become a threat to the operation, and so they eliminated him."

"Perhaps. But I'm not as certain as you are." Dusting his hands, Saybrook rose and squeezed his way through the bales to another row of crates. "As of yet, the pieces are still too damn amorphous to show any pattern, or any way they interlock."

"Auch, we're getting close, laddie. I feel it in my bones," muttered Henning.

The earl swore as his knee banged up against a brass urn.

"And ye know damn well how my intuition saved our skin on several occasions in—"

A grunt cut short the surgeon's point.

"Well, well, well." Saybrook had dropped to a crouch and was shifting a burlap sack. "Come see what we have here, Baz."

Arianna set aside the book she had been reading and rose from her chair. From across the room, her bed beckoned, a sumptuous stretch of quilted satin and down-filled pillows that were whispering a Siren song.

Crash upon these gilded rocks and find oblivion in sleep.

"Tempting," she muttered. But instead she sought a spot by the bank of diamond-paned windows.

Think! she cajoled, forcing herself to review all the complex financial data she had been studying for the last few hours.

Her two footmen had been dispatched that morning, one to Hatchard's bookstore and one to Lady Sterling's residence, with orders to buy or borrow all books related to the South Sea Bubble. Despite her denial to the earl and his great-aunt, the name was painfully familiar. When drunk, her father had often extolled—albeit with a slur of envy—the cleverness of men who could create value out of thin air.

Value. Like most words, its definition seemed to depend on what tongue gave it voice.

A glance back at the stack of gold-stamped spines heightened the feeling that somewhere buried among all the mind-numbing array of facts and statistics lay some vital key to unlocking the current mystery.

"But what it is, I haven't a clue." Pressing her fingertips to her temples, Arianna paused and squeezed her eyes shut.

Mathematics was all about logic, order, precision. . . .

Perhaps she *did* have a clue. In any case, it was the only tangible thing she had to go on.

Fetching the paper that Saybrook had left, along with the documents taken from Lady Spencer's desk, Arianna spread them all out on her escritoire and smoothed out a fresh sheet of foolscap. *Patterns, my dear poppet.* Her father's brandy-warm laugh echoed through the deepest recesses of her head. *Numbers are supremely simple to understand if you know how to speak their language.*

"What are you trying to tell me?" she murmured, ordering the old and new papers from the folder into two neat piles. In between the piles she placed the single sheet of paper that the earl had discovered. It bore a list of numerical sequences, each line made up of three sets of pairs, separated by dashes.

"What is it that I am missing?"

The papers sat in taunting silence.

Taking up her pencil, she made yet another copy of the age-worn mathematical equations, then leaned back and studied the sequences.

Patterns, patterns, patterns. For all his weaknesses in seeing the repetitive themes in his own life, her father was a genius at understanding the core concepts of mathematics. Numbers, like letters, told a story, he always said.

Losing herself in the abstract challenge of making order out of chaos, Arianna tried not to think of the reality of what he had done. In some ways, perhaps a part of her vehemence for vengeance had stemmed from a fear that he was guilty of some crime. Perhaps a part of her secretly believed that such efforts could somehow atone for his wrongs.

A gust of wind rattled the window casement and a chill finger of air seemed to squeeze at her throat.

I've been as guilty as Papa of denials and delusions.

The pencil point dug into the paper, tearing a tiny rip.

"Damn." She was about to ball up the sheet in disgust when a certain section caught her eye. Leaning closer, she gave them a more careful study.

Patterns. Logic, repeated Arianna, giving yet another glance at the three sets of papers. What was the connection? They must be related—

Related.

Good God, how could she have overlooked the obvious until now? Seeing as Lady Spencer's grandfather was connected to the South Sea stock manipulation, it was logical to assume that the old papers in the folder were his. And if that were the case, the modern papers might be ...

Her heart began to thump a touch faster.

Sliding a fresh piece of paper across the polished wood, Arianna scribbled out a series of equations.

Excitement kicked up another notch.

Working a hunch, she gathered the books she had been reading and found the pages she needed for reference. Slowly, methodically, she worked through a progression of calculations.

Yes, yes, it was all beginning to add up. Page by page, she carefully compared the old documents with the new ones. After rechecking the numbers and copying the final results, she looked up, the first pale rays of dawn illuminating a small smile.

"Eureka."

"The South Sea Bubble?" Grentham set down his pen beside the silver coffee service on his desk and fixed the earl with a pointed stare. "Pray, explain to me why, when time is of the essence in solving the Prince's poisoning before our Eastern allies arrive, you interrupt my morning libation wishing to discuss a century-old scandal, Lord Saybrook." He carefully capped his inkwell. "Has the opium addled your brain?"

"If you wish to relieve me of my duties in this investigation, you are welcome to do so," replied the earl. "But somehow, I don't think you will."

The minister's eyes narrowed. "You keep making veiled threats."

"As do you."

Their gazes remained locked for several long moments before Grentham leaned back and tapped his fingertips together in a gesture that was smooth and soundless, despite the hint of impatience. "I am waiting for your explanation."

"I've reason to believe that the Prince was not poisoned because of a personal grudge," said Saybrook. "Nor do I think that the motive was purely political."

"Then what, in your expert opinion, is the motive?"

"I'm not yet prepared to say."

The tapping ceased.

In response, Saybrook took a piece of paper from his pocket and read over it before looking up. "I would like a look at some of the government files from December 1720, including the private notes of Mr. Robert Walpole's meetings with the Bank of England and the East India Company, along with the Parliamentary records concerning corruption charges against John Aislabie, Sir John Blunt, and the other directors of the South Sea Company." He paused for another glance at his list. "I also want access to the records on how the conversion of government debt to private stock was handled by the Sword Blade Bank."

"That material is highly confidential," said Grentham tightly. "Access is limited to a very small circle of ministers."

"Ah, but considering the power you wield in the government, I am sure you can arrange an exception, milord," answered Saybrook.

A tiny tic marred the smoothness of Grentham's jaw.

"There are several other dates that I'm interested in. I'll leave the list here." The paper dropped onto the desk. "I'll come by tomorrow, if I may."

The minister nodded.

Saybrook spun the head of his cane between his palms, and then rose. "Thank you." He made a half turn. "By the by, Lord Cockburn is a good friend of yours, is he not?"

Grentham had started to open a portfolio, but he suddenly went still as a statue. "Yes. He is."

"You must have enjoyed the shooting party at his estate this past August very much."

The leather case slid across the blotter as Grentham leaned forward. "Hunting is indeed my favorite sport."

"I rather guessed it was."

Easing back in his chair, the minister dismissed him

with a curt wave. "One week, Saybrook. If you haven't solved this case in one week, you won't be finding that word games come quite so easily to your tongue."

"Thank you for seeing me at such an early hour, Lady Sterling," said Arianna as a footman escorted her into the dowager's drawing room. "I apologize for the breach in proper etiquette."

The dowager waved off the words. "Oh, pish. Family are not expected to stand on ceremony." She patted a spot on the sofa. "Come sit beside me and help finish off Cook's breakfast scones. They are quite good."

Arianna dutifully accepted a pastry and a cup of tea, deciding to let the elderly lady finish her repast before peppering her with impertinent questions.

After several minutes of polite exchanges, the dowager set aside her empty plate. "Well?" she inquired.

"Excellent," murmured Arianna. "They have just the right amount of sweetness."

"So they do," replied Lady Sterling dryly. "However, I wasn't referring to the scones. I don't imagine you are here to discuss recipes."

"Much as the subject interests me, no." She had composed a carefully worded query during her carriage ride through Mayfair, and hoped that she had struck the right balance between asking enough without revealing too much. "Your nephew says that your knowledge of Society and all the intricacies of its inner workings is unrivaled."

A silvery brow rose a fraction, which Arianna took as a signal to proceed.

"So I was wondering . . . ," she continued. "Could you perchance suggest how I might arrange to see some certain business records?"

"Business records?" repeated the dowager. "What sort of business records?"

"Shipping records," replied Arianna.

A silence greeted the request. Then a cough. "You and Sandro ask the *oddest* questions."

As Lady Sterling lifted her quizzing glass, Arianna wondered whether she had made a mistake. It was a little unnerving to have a large pale eyeball subjecting her to such scrutiny. She felt as if her faults were magnified.

"By the by, what branch of the family did you say you were from?"

"I didn't," murmured Arianna.

The dowager took a moment to polish the glass lens, and then once again lifted it to her eye. "Perhaps you would care to clarify it now . . . cousin."

Arianna decided that honesty was best. "I think we both know there is no family connection."

"Hmmph."

She started to rise.

"Sit down, gel," commanded Lady Sterling. "And tell me precisely what it is you need." A twitch played at the corners of the dowager's lips. "At my age, I need a little excitement to spice up my life."

Arianna smiled in return. Fishing a list from her reticule, she handed it over. "I would like a list of ships arriving from South America at the West India docks on these dates," she explained. "Sorry, but I can't be overly specific about the ports of origin. My guess is that Veracruz, Portobelo, and Cartagena are the ones of most interest." She cleared her throat. "And it's important that I get them as soon as possible."

Lady Sterling took a moment to read over the request. "Lord Bevan is an old admirer, and he owes me a favor—a large one. Let me see what I can do."

"Please, you must be dis—"

"Discreet. Yes, yes, I know. Sandro said the same thing," interrupted the dowager. "It's dangerous, is it?"

Feeling a trifle guilty, Arianna nodded. "Yes, I'm afraid it is."

The twinkle in the dowager's eyes become even more pronounced. "Oh, piff. I can bloody well take care of myself. It's Sandro I worry about." She leaned in a little closer. "I trust you will help me keep an eye on him."

"I will do my best," promised Arianna. "Though His Lordship is not the easiest of men to manage."

"Somehow I think you are up to the challenge, gel." Lady Sterling rang the small silver bell on the tea table. "Shipping records, eh? Well, I had better hoist anchor and get ready to sail into action."

20

From the chocolate notebooks of Dona Maria Castellano

I must remember to tell Sandro that the exclusive gentlemen's club on St. James's Street to which he belongs was originally established to serve chocolate! An Italian named Francis White opened White's Chocolate House in 1693. These days, I have heard that the members prefer claret, brandy, or port— which may be why Sandro finds their company egregiously boring. . . .

Chocolate Espresso Spelt Cake

1½ sticks (¾ cup) unsalted butter, softened,
plus additional for pan
¾ cup unsweetened Dutch-processed cocoa powder,
plus additional for dusting pan and cake
1 cup boiling-hot water
1½ tablespoons instant espresso powder
1½ teaspoons vanilla
1 teaspoon baking soda
½ pound Medjool dates (12 to 14), pitted and coarsely
chopped (1½ cups)
2 cups spelt flour
2 teaspoons baking powder

¾ teaspoon salt
1 cup packed dark brown sugar
2 large eggs

1. Put oven rack in middle position and preheat oven to 350°F. Butter 9-inch springform pan, then lightly dust with cocoa powder, knocking out excess.
2. Stir together boiling-hot water, espresso powder, vanilla, and baking soda in a bowl, then add dates, mashing lightly with a fork. Soak until liquid cools to room temperature, about 10 minutes.
3. Whisk together spelt flour, cocoa powder, baking powder, and salt in another bowl. Beat together butter and brown sugar with an electric mixer at medium-high speed until pale and fluffy. Add eggs 1 at a time, beating until just combined. Beat in date mixture (batter will look curdled), then reduce speed to low and add flour mixture, mixing until just combined.
4. Spoon batter into springform pan, smoothing top, and bake until a wooden pick or skewer inserted into center comes out clean, about 50 minutes to 1 hour. Cool cake in pan on a rack 5 minutes, then remove side of pan and cool cake on rack. Serve cake warm or at room temperature.

～

Having exchanged her fancy silks and satins for threadbare cotton and moleskin, Arianna squeezed through a gap in the splintered planking and made her way down the dank alley. The earl's housekeeper had informed her that Saybrook had gone to Horse Guards for a meeting with Grentham, but was now likely at Mr. Henning's surgery.

Anxious to share what she had discovered in Lady Spencer's papers, she had decided to seek him out there, rather than return home and wait with ladylike restraint.

Despite the maze of byways and alleys, the directions proved easy enough to follow. The brick building housing Henning and his rooms stood out as slightly less shabby than its neighbors. Seeing the front entrance shut tight, Arianna went around to the side, where a primitive portico sheltered a door. The sign showed a scalpel crossed with a bone saw.

Crinkling her nose, she slipped inside, finding it difficult to draw a breath. The smell of blood, sweat, and fear seemed to ooze from the damp plaster walls, adding to the staleness of the air. It, too, felt heavy enough to cut with a knife.

The only light in the corridor came from the room ahead, where the door was ajar. She crept closer, loath to interrupt if Henning was in the midst of amputating a limb or dosing a man for the clap.

"I've not yet made up my mind about Lord Ashmun." It was Saybrook who was speaking. "So far I've uncovered nothing that indicates he is anything but what he says he is. However, his solicitous manner seems just a tad overdone."

Arianna hesitated, and then instead of announcing herself, she took up a position behind the oak planking.

"I hate te say it, but we can't afford te overlook something else, Sandro." Henning expelled an audible sigh. "Maybe yer lady is really the mastermind of the nefarious group we're chasing. And this fellow Ashmun is a cohort, whose sudden appearance is meant to throw you off the scent of the real trail."

"You think I'm being led by the nose?" Saybrook's voice was suddenly harder, colder than a moment before.

"Auch, ye wouldn't be the first man in history te fall for the wiles of a beautiful woman."

"She has the brains and the nerve to be heading a criminal consortium," conceded the earl. "As well as a grudge against Society. So perhaps you are right."

Arianna felt as if she had been kicked in the gut. "You really think me capable of *that*?" she demanded, stepping out from behind the door.

The earl turned around slowly. "Why shouldn't I?" he answered evenly. "You've told me more than once that you have no morals, no principles."

True. Arianna lifted her chin, willing the sharp, sour taste of disappointment to subside. *And I meant every word.*

Saybrook was watching her intently. "I've witnessed what a consummate actress you are," he went on. "You've an uncanny ability to be very convincing in whatever role you play."

"No doubt it's due to having trained for years at the knee of a master liar and blackguard cheat," she shot back.

His expression softened just a touch.

"No offense, Lady Arianna," apologized Henning. "We were merely looking at the problem from every possible angle."

"No offense?" She gave a brittle laugh. "Oh, none taken. I'm quite used to being thought of as a scheming slut."

The surgeon flushed.

"So why I bothered to care whether the two of you might be interested in another important clue is beyond me." Her work papers were now clutched in her fist and she shook them at Saybrook.

"What clue?" he asked quickly.

"Go to hell," snapped Arianna as she thrust them back into her coat pocket.

He folded his arms across his chest. "We apologized."

"No, *we* did not. Mr. Henning did."

"You wish one from me?"

Arianna looked away.

"If I truly thought you were involved in this, Lady Arianna, you would not still be waltzing through the ballrooms of Mayfair. At my expense, I might add."

She made a mock curtsey. "How reassuring to know I have your full and unqualified support, sir."

"Please sit down, Lady Arianna." Henning hastily pulled out one of the rickety chairs arranged around the small table. "We, too, have some interesting things to share."

"Just as long as you're not planning on using your scalpels or saws on me to extract information."

"Baz is a gentleman," remarked Saybrook. "I make no such claim."

"Then it's a good thing I don't consider myself a lady." Arianna took a seat and unfolded her notes. "You have to admit, at least I am not boring, like most of the demure young demoiselles of the *ton*."

"You are not boring," agreed Saybrook. His tone, however, gave no hint of whether he considered that a good or bad thing. His gaze flicked to her notes. "Now that we've settled personal concerns, might we get down to business?"

But of course—this was naught but a cerebral challenge for him.

Well, I, too, am capable of using my mind for more than lies and deception.

She hitched her chair a little closer. "I think I have figured out what's worth all the recent murder and mayhem." Paper crackled beneath her fingertips. "I believe that Lady Spencer is somehow involved in a conspiracy to establish a trading company based on the model of the South Sea Company."

The surgeon let out a low whistle but the earl appeared less impressed. "Why?" he demanded.

"Because along with taking the medallion and Kellton's letter from her desk, I also took this." She pulled the pasteboard folder from inside her jacket. "It's a set of mathematical equations—two sets, in fact, one old and one new."

Saybrook swore. Several times over. "I thought we went through the dangers of withholding information," he said through gritted teeth.

"We did. And I chose to ignore you." Arianna narrowed her eyes. "So, now you can either cut off my fingers with that disgusting-looking scalpel or you can hear me out."

"Listen to reason, laddie," murmured Henning.

"Bloody hell." The earl leaned back. "Go on."

"Your great-aunt's revelation that Lady Spencer's grandfather was involved in the South Sea Bubble got me to thinking." Arianna spread out the papers. "As I said, one set of documents looks quite old, so I started with them. First I gathered a number of books and read up on the history of the South Sea Company. Then I began to work through the mathematics. . . ."

Saybrook made a sound—more precisely a growl—but she ignored it.

"As you know, the Bubble revolved around the government partnering with a private company to divest itself of a ballooning national debt."

"Aye," muttered Henning.

"And on paper, the formulas work very well," she went on.

"Assuming, of course, that the company has real value, and is not just some empty shell made of polished lies and pretty promises," murmured the earl.

"Right." She traced over the first string of equations on the age-yellowed paper. "Once I worked through the numbers here, I started to see similar patterns to the things I had been reading about regarding the South Sea Bubble. I guessed that they were the confidential financial papers of Lady Spencer's grandfather, who, as you recall, was a director of the Sword Blade Bank."

"Which was the financial arm of the South Sea Company," added Saybrook, for Henning was beginning to look a bit bewildered.

"Correct, sir. So I decided to compare them to the set of newer documents that Lady Spencer had in the same folder. I ran a few projections, based on today's debt, factoring in inflation and a percentage of—"

"What?" interrupted Henning.

"Never mind. What we're really concerned with is the ratio of debt-equity swaps."

"What?" repeated the surgeon.

Arianna drummed her fingers against the table, trying to quell her impatience. To her, the concepts were simple, but she understood that many people did not find mathematics quite so easy to follow.

"Debt-equity swaps are designed to benefit both parties. In this case, the government paid a lower rate of interest on its debt, and the South Sea Company profited as its stock price rose—you see, a high profit-to-expense ratio makes the company worth more on paper." She looked up. "It can therefore issue more stock, which in turn generates more blunt for its partners."

The earl nodded for her to go on.

She paged through the modern papers and quickly explained what the complex mathematics meant. "So you see, the numbers mirror the same formulas used in the last century. And that can only mean one thing."

"What?" The surgeon appeared hopelessly confused.

Arianna glanced at Saybrook, wondering whether he grasped the significance of her calculations.

"What you mean is," said the earl slowly, "the scale and volume indicates that the deal can only be a very large one."

"That's right, sir. A very large one, and a very profitable one." She paused to pull out the sheet of numbers that the earl had found in Lady Spencer's desk on the night of their encounter with Lord Ashmun. "Bear with me while I go over one last thing. Based on what I discovered in the old and new documents—and something that Mr. Henning had said about dockyard mud—I had an idea of what these sequences might mean. So I visited your great-aunt this morning and asked her if, through her many connections in Society, she could get me copies of certain shipping records."

"And?" asked Saybrook.

"And sure enough, the sequences on this paper correspond to the dates when certain merchant ships arrived in London from the old Spanish Empire trading ports. Perhaps it's coincidence. But I doubt it. I think what we've uncovered is a new business venture—a New World trading company modeled on the financial scandal of the last century."

Arianna learned forward and propped her elbows on the table.

"Only bigger."

21

From the chocolate notebooks of Dona Maria Castellano

I know that it is not at all fashionable these days to speak well of the French, but there is no denying that despite all their faults, they have contributed greatly to the refinement of fine cuisine. So we must give credit to a Frenchman named Dubuisson, who invented a hand mill for grinding cacao in 1732. Having toiled for untold hours in the kitchen with mortar and pestle, I raise my cup in salute, and I am sure that Sandro will join me. Unlike many men of wealth and privilege, he has a very open mind. . . .

Mint Hot Chocolate

½ cup unsweetened cocoa powder
⅓ cup sugar
½ cup cold water
1 teaspoon vanilla
1 cup half-and-half
2½ cups milk
⅓ cup crème de menthe, or to taste
2 tablespoons crème de cacao, or to taste
whipped cream and shaved bittersweet chocolate
for garnish

1. In a heavy saucepan combine the cocoa powder, the sugar, the water, the vanilla, and a pinch of salt and heat the mixture over low heat, whisking, until the cocoa powder is dissolved and the mixture is a smooth paste.
2. Gradually add the half-and-half and the milk, both scalded, and simmer the hot chocolate, whisking, for 2 minutes. Stir in the crème de menthe and the crème de cacao. (For a frothy result, in a blender blend the hot chocolate in batches.)
3. Divide the hot chocolate among mugs and top it with the whipped cream and the chocolate. Makes about 4½ cups.

Henning opened his mouth to say something, but Saybrook signaled him to silence. He spoke instead. "How very clever of you to have figured this all out on your own."

Arianna drew in a sharp breath and narrowed her eyes. "Just what are you accusing me of, sir?"

"Of having a genius for mathematics which must rival that of your late father," he replied.

"I ..." She quickly composed herself, unwilling to show that the barb had hurt. "Yes, I've always had a knack for numbers. But I haven't ever used it for cheating...." Recalling several harbor towns in the Windward Islands, she shrugged. "Well, hardly ever."

The earl's brows rose ever so slightly.

"I'm *sharing* it with you, aren't I?" she retorted, nettled by the unspoken skepticism.

"A cunning criminal would," he answered. "I've not enough expertise to discern whether you've fiddled with the numbers. Or whether you're lying outright."

Their gazes locked.

"No," she responded. "You would have to take my word on it."

The floorboards groaned as Henning shifted in his chair.

"You have to admit," continued Saybrook, "it's rather hard to feel completely comfortable in trusting a person who keeps changing like a chameleon."

Arianna picked at a thread on her raveled sleeve.

"A master chef, a mathematical genius, a brilliant actress—have you any other hidden talents to reveal?"

"I can sail a schooner single-handedly and I'm rather good at picking locks." Lowering her lashes, she couldn't resist adding, "And, of course, I'm a dab hand at leading men around by the nose. But then, you know that."

The earl stretched out his legs and crossed one booted ankle over the other. "I would imagine that your father found your mathematical genius very . . . useful."

Oh, what a team we would make, poppet. With our brains and your beauty, we could be very rich, indeed!

Arianna looked away for an instant and fought to draw a ragged breath. "Yes. He would have been delighted to form a partnership."

"But?" The word was said softly.

"But it wasn't a life I wanted," she replied, then quickly added a laugh. "As you see, the one I have chosen is ever so much more respectable."

"I'm simply trying to gather information, Lady Arianna, not make any moral judgments," said Saybrook. "It would be helpful to know if you aided your father in constructing any business scams. That sort of information could be relevant."

"No," answered Arianna tightly. "I did not. When I was a little girl, my father hinted that we might . . . profit from my talents. But when I expressed my feelings on cheating, he never raised the subject again." She swallowed hard. "Though it must have cost him dear to hold his tongue. At the end, we were dancing on the razor's edge of poverty."

"Thank you." The earl carefully rearranged the folds of his coat. "Now, getting back to the numbers on the table—"

"You believe me?" blurted out Arianna.

"I didn't say that." The earl allowed a faint smile.

"But we are straying from the subject." A pause. "So it is your opinion that these equations indicate that the new company will seek a partnership with the government?"

The tension eased inside her. "Given the size of the sums involved, it's hard to imagine any other explanation."

"I possess no financial acumen, so what I've never understood is how did the South Sea Bubble expand to such mammoth proportions before it burst?" mused Henning.

"Having just read a great deal about it, I shall try to explain," responded Arianna. "The real turning point came in 1717, when the King admitted to Parliament that the country's finances were troubled and that the national debt needed to be reduced. In reply, the South Sea Company presented a proposal to raise its capital to twelve million pounds by selling a new offering of stock." She glanced down at the faded numbers. "Due to canny promotion by Sir John Blunt, the name of the South Sea Company was continually in the public eye. So, despite the fact that the company was earning virtually nothing from its South American trade, shares in the company were in great demand and the directors were eager to keep increasing the value of the company."

"And the public allowed the wool to be pulled over its eyes?" grunted Henning.

"Part of the frenzy was fanned by what was going on in France, Baz," pointed out the earl. "Your fellow Scotsman John Law had been invited to come in and revamp the entire banking system there, and as a result, the economy was booming. Emboldened by the success of his financial theories, Law established the Mississippi Company, a similar New World trading venture. Its stock was soaring, and the French—everyone from humble shopkeepers to princely lords—were growing rich on paper."

"The English watched and were jealous. Visions of unbounded wealth were now dancing like sugar plums in the heads of every man and woman. And the South

Sea Company saw a way to profit from the frenzy," said Arianna. "So in 1720, the directors presented a plan to the government that would virtually eliminate the national debt."

"They were not deterred by the expected failure of the Mississippi scheme, even though by then its flaws were beginning to show," added the earl. "The gentlemen of the South Sea Company and the Sword Blade Bank were arrogant enough to believe they could avoid the *faux pas* of the French and stretch their loans out forever without default."

Arianna nodded in agreement. "Sales of the company's shares on the stock exchange now reached fever point."

Neither man made a comment.

"Sir John Blunt took every opportunity to talk up the price of the stock. Free-trade agreements between England and Spain were said to be imminent, and with them the promise that New World gold and silver, along with countless other luxuries, would soon be pouring into the country in exchange for English cotton and woolen goods. In short, the South Sea Company would grow rich beyond imagination, and every one hundred pounds invested in its shares would produce huge dividends each year to investors."

Closing her eyes for a moment, Arianna tried not to think of her father and his desperate longing for easy money. "The Chancellor of the Exchequer, John Aislabie, championed the South Sea proposal, while a few voices of reason, led by Robert Walpole, warned of its danger. Indeed, the Earl of Cowper compared the bill to the Trojan Horse, saying that though the country welcomed it as a fabulous gift, it actually held the seeds of treachery and destruction within its core."

"Which, it turned out, was essentially true," said Saybrook.

A sudden gust of wind rattled the window glass.

"Er, correct me if I am wrong," ventured Henning. "But wasn't there some sort of law passed around the time of the South Sea Bubble prohibiting the creation of joint stock companies?" He pursed his lips. "The Royal Something-Or-Other Act."

"The Royal Exchange and London Assurance Corporation Act, passed in 1719," clarified Saybrook. "Which required that any new company wishing to establish itself as a joint stock venture needed to be incorporated by an act of Parliament or by Royal Charter."

"Why?" asked Arianna.

"Because on seeing how the South Sea Company parlayed naught but grandiose promises into actual money, a great many clever men began establishing companies and selling stock to a gullible public," explained the earl. "Some of the ventures included making a wheel for perpetual motion and transmuting quicksilver into a fine, malleable metal." He paused for a fraction. "And my favorite—carrying on an undertaking of great advantage, as yet undecided."

"You are joking," she said.

"Unfortunately not," replied Saybrook. "This scheme showed, more completely than any other, the utter madness of the people at the time. The gentleman who concocted the venture stated in his prospectus that the required capital was a half million pounds, to be raised by selling five thousand shares of one hundred pounds each. By paying a deposit of a mere two pounds per share, each subscriber would be entitled to one hundred pounds per annum per share. How this immense profit could be made, he did not condescend to say."

Henning snorted.

"The fellow did, however, promise that in one month the full details would be revealed, at which time the balance of the purchase price would be due. By three p.m. of the first day, he had sold one hundred shares—two thousand pounds in five hours. Deciding that was a decent profit, he fled to the Continent and was never heard of again."

"Is this Royal Exchange and Assurance Act still in effect?" asked Henning.

The earl nodded.

The surgeon made a face. "Then there seems little chance that our present-day conspirators can put their plan into action. I can't quite see Parliament agreeing to establish a private stock company, not with Napoleon once again marching east."

For a moment there was silence, and then . . .

"*PING*."

Both Arianna and Henning shot the earl a puzzled look.

"That," he announced, "is the sound of the penny dropping."

A long moment of silence greeted the statement.

Then Henning's jaw followed suit. "Good God, you think that may in some way explain why the Prince was poisoned?"

"When you look at it from that angle, it begins to make some sense," said the earl. "If Prinny dies, the Regency falls to his brother, the Duke of York."

"Who last year was embroiled in that sordid scandal over selling military commissions." Arianna smiled grimly. "No matter that it was his mistress who was likely the guilty party, someone seeking to buy influence would assume there was a good chance of success with York."

"All the King's sons are profligate wastrels," pointed out Henning. "Prinny is always in need of money, too."

Saybrook rocked back in his chair. "Seeing as Lady Spencer was his latest paramour, we can assume that she tried to coax a charter out of him, but was refused."

The surgeon made a face. "It's possible," he conceded. "But we have no proof, only conjecture."

"True," agreed the earl. "And yet the vague specters we chase are beginning to take on some flesh." Looking up at the ceiling, he pursed his lips in thought.

Arianna mulled over what she had heard. Was such a scheme possible? she wondered. What asset could a private company offer to make the risk of poisoning a royal worthwhile?

"Especially when we consider the shipping records obtained by Lady Arianna," added Saybrook.

She frowned. "How so?"

The earl's chair fell back down to earth. "Like you, Baz and I were busy last night. Acting on a tip from one of his friends, we visited the West India docks. The cargo of a certain ship had been off-loaded in unusual secrecy, so it seemed worth taking a look inside the warehouse."

"And was it?" she asked.

"Perhaps," answered the earl. "The goods were an interesting assortment—spices, cocoa, precious metals, a powerful narcotic. All goods that would generate a handsome profit if sold on a large scale. The curious thing was, none were in great enough quantity, save perhaps the narcotic, to have made the voyage worthwhile."

"They looked to be samples," added Henning.

Saybrook gave a small nod. "Perhaps," he repeated.

"I have a question," said Arianna, after considering the information for a moment. Her head was beginning to swim. "The original South Sea Company's targeted trading area was the Spanish colonies of the Americas, correct?"

"That's right," replied the earl. "Including Mexico and the large expanse of territory in what now is the United States."

"So we are talking about an area that is fabulously rich in natural resources." She frowned, unsure what it was that she was missing. "And yet the Bubble burst because the company and its stock was essentially worthless. They failed to make a penny of profit."

"The South Sea Company didn't collapse because the riches weren't there. It collapsed because it had no access." Saybrook's expression turned grim. "Regardless of the monopoly granted by the English government, the *Navío de Permiso*—the trading rights granted by the King of Spain—consisted of one ship per year. It was later increased to three, but that wasn't exactly going to generate an armada of profit."

"Lady Arianna raises an excellent point," mused

Henning aloud. "Why go to all the expense and risk of creating another South Sea Company—assuming she is right in her mathematical speculation—when Spain is our enemy? Napoleon's brother Joseph sits on the throne, so it seems rather absurd to think he would grant an English company access to the riches of Spain's New World colonies."

"Access," she repeated softly.

"Let us keep speculating for a moment . . ." Saybrook straightened slightly in his chair. "Imagine that Napoleon is successful this time in his march east, and forces the Russian tsar to make peace. Our Eastern allies will be forced to do the same. And so will England, for we cannot fight him alone."

Henning grunted. "Peace at last, which as far as I am concerned would be a bloody good thing."

"You are not alone in thinking that," said Saybrook. "Napoleon would also welcome an end to the unrelenting wars." He paused, as if suddenly distracted by some other thought. A spider crept across the wood and he watched it disappear into one of the cracks before continuing. "So I imagine that he would be enormously grateful to anyone who could help ensure that the forces opposing him did not forge a more united alliance."

Arianna blinked. "The poisoned chocolate—"

"Could kill two birds with one stone, so to speak," finished the earl. "Not only would it offer a better chance to obtain a royal charter, but it would also earn a reward from a grateful Napoleon, for the Prince Regent's death would throw our country—and our Eastern allies—into chaos."

"You think the conspirators behind this trading company have made a deal with the French?" asked Henning. "In return for weakening our government, and forcing a peace treaty, they have been promised a rich reward? But that would be . . . treason."

"It would also be a stroke of brilliance, and we know they are very, very clever. Think on it—if England makes peace, the Emperor would firmly control Spain and the rights to grant trading access to its New World colonies."

"Good God," whispered Arianna. "The conspirators do away Prinny to put his brother on the throne. They bribe York for a royal charter, which makes their company legitimate, and then they turn to France . . ." She paused. "It all begins to weave together."

"Out of speculative threads," reminded Henning. "It's a cloth fashioned out of pure conjecture."

"Indeed," agreed Saybrook. "But don't forget we have a very real new clue, which may help us stitch together the truth."

"What clue?" demanded Arianna.

"In addition to discovering the assortment of goods from the New World in the warehouse, we also found a waistcoat button wedged between the bales," answered Saybrook.

"A button?" She made a face. "How the devil is that going to help? There must be . . ." Running through a few quick mental calculations caused her frown to pinch tighter. "Suffice it to say, there must be millions of buttons in London."

"Not of this particular button. It has a distinctive design etched on it."

"I see." She studied his face for a moment before adding, "I take it by your supremely smug expression that you recognized the marking."

His mouth twitched at the corners. "Correct."

"Bloody hell, Sandro, why didn't you say so earlier?" growled Henning.

"I wanted to be absolutely certain, Baz," replied Saybrook. "As it turns out, the button belongs to the Marquess of Cockburn. He has them made up specially at a shop off Bond Street."

"It could have come from a servant's cast-off livery," pointed out Arianna, "or some such garment. No doubt the marquess has a large household, so there are any number of ways it could have ended up where you found it."

"I think not. This one is solid gold and the particular design is only for the earl's personal use," he said. "Indeed, I happened to overhear him showing it off to his friends at my club last week."

"You are sure?" pressed Henning. "We can't afford going off on a wild-goose chase."

"This bird is quite unmistakable." The earl took the button out of his pocket and held it up for them to see.

Arianna winced as the flash of gold suddenly sparked a jumbled memory. *A silk waistcoat, bright with fancy buttons. A watch chain hung with ornate fobs. Her father's laughter.* . . . But then, it was gone—so quickly that it must have been only a figment of her imagination.

"Is something wrong, Lady Arianna?" asked Saybrook.

"I was blinded by the reflection for just a moment," she murmured, rubbing at her eyes. "Please continue."

"As I was saying, the design is distinctive. It's a strutting cock, for the marquess fancies himself quite a ladies' man."

Henning cleared his throat and spit on the floor.

"What makes it even more interesting is that Cockburn is a high-ranking official in Whitehall—involved in the ministry of trade," went on Saybrook. "But that's not all." A pause. "His cousin was Major Crandall."

Henning emitted a low whistle.

"Grentham's top military attaché," said Arianna, feeling a chill skate down her spine.

"But it was Grentham who asked you to take charge of the investigation," pointed out Henning.

"Yes, me. A man by all accounts befuddled by opium," responded Saybrook. "Then he and Crandall all but painted a bull's-eye on the French chef's back."

"Clever," conceded the surgeon.

"Very," said Arianna. "I can see where having a so-called independent investigator go through the motions of tracking down the guilty party deflects any suspicion from the real villains."

"Yes, perhaps. And yet . . ." Saybrook's gaze held hers. "There is something that is bothering me about all of this." A pause. "Several things, in fact."

Something in his tone made her body tense.

"Concord is a clever man," he went on. "However, to me it feels like far too ambitious a plan for him to have put together."

"Well, in this case your feeling is wrong," she retorted. "Of course it's Concord." *Of course it's Concord,* she repeated to herself. "Remember, it was Concord who I overheard talking about sword blades and blunt."

"Was it?" asked Saybrook softly. "You were in the garden, and the voices were muffled. Maybe it was Kellton."

Loath to admit he might be right, Arianna remained stubbornly silent.

"Grentham and Cockburn have far more influence in the government," he mused. "Why would they be taking orders from Concord?"

"It's always smart for the head of a havey-cavey operation to appear less important than his minions," insisted Arianna. "Concord is more than clever—he is cunning. Which explains why he keeps his connections well hidden."

"She makes a good point, laddie," said Henning.

"Yes, well, I have some background in planning these sorts of things," she murmured.

The earl cleared his throat with a cough. *Or was it a laugh?*

Henning flashed a fleeting grin, but his expression quickly turned pensive. "If we are tossing out questions, I have a few of my own. How do Kellton and Lady Spencer fit in?"

"Kellton I can see, because of his trading experience with the East India Company," answered Saybrook. "Lady Spencer's involvement is a bit harder to figure out. She did, of course, provide the original South Sea documents, as well as easy access to the Prince. But we may be missing something else." He paused. "Or we may be entirely wrong in our assumptions."

"Auch, it's hard to know what to believe," groused Henning.

Saybrook didn't answer.

"It's not a matter of what any of us believe, Mr. Henning," interjected Arianna. "It's a matter of what we can prove." Her chair scraped back. "I've a party to attend tonight, where I intend to seduce a few more facts from Concord."

"Be on guard," said Saybrook rather sharply. "Never forget that he is likely a cold-blooded murderer."

"I, of all people, am acutely aware of that," she said.

"Good." His voice, however, was flat and devoid of feeling. "In the meantime, I shall call on Lady Spencer this afternoon and see what more I can learn."

"Bring her a box of chocolate," quipped Arianna. "Butter and sugar tend to melt her inhibitions."

"I had planned to," answered the earl brusquely. "And tomorrow I will be returning to Horse Guards, where Grentham has consented to allow me access to the confidential government dossiers on the South Sea Bubble."

"How did you manage that?" she asked.

"The minister and I are playing a little game of standing eyeball to eyeball, and seeing who will blink first."

"It's more like sticking your head into a lion's open jaws," muttered Henning. "And hoping that he doesn't snap them shut."

The earl ignored the comment. "I'll need to think more about Cockburn, too, but for now, Baz, see what more you can learn about the owners of the merchant ship."

"I'm meeting with Jem at the Crooked Cat as soon as we're finished here."

Arianna rose and stuffed the papers back into the folder. "Then what are we waiting for?"

*   *   *

Grentham picked up his penknife, and then set it down again.

"One ... two ..."

Before he reached "three," a knock announced the return of his secretary, who hurriedly flipped open a folder as he entered the office.

"The report just arrived, sir. An urchin was seen entering Henning's surgery. He wore the same hat and jacket as the boy who appeared at Lord Saybrook's town house, so our spy is of the opinion that it's the same person."

"I trust that he was smart enough to follow the imp?" growled Grentham.

The secretary shuffled his feet. "Yes, sir. But apparently the boy was a slippery little devil. Our man lost him...."

Grentham's eyes narrowed.

"In the vicinity of Lady Wolcott's residence. He swears that the boy must have taken refuge in one of the gardens."

The minister fingered the gold fobs hanging from his watch chain. "Bring me the file you've put together on the Widow Wolcott, along with the one on Lord Ashmun."

"Yes, milord."

"And have a new man assigned to the surveillance. One who is quick-witted and quick-footed enough to keep his quarry in sight." The fobs slid across the silk of his waistcoat. "Assign the current fellow to shoveling dung in the Horse Guards stables."

"Yes, milord."

"And Jenkins, do tell our operative that I expect him to stick to Lady Wolcott like a leech, understand? And tell him that his blood will be feeding the lice and bedbugs at Newgate if he fails."

Jenkins scuttled out the door, as if his own flesh were at risk.

"Wealthy widow, street urchin—what other roles are you playing, Lady Whoever-You-Are?" he said softly.

A sudden patter of rain hit against the windowpanes, momentarily blurring the troop of cavalry trotting across the parade ground.

"Not that it matters. For all your fancy footwork, you look to be heading exactly where I want you."

22

From the chocolate notebooks of Dona Maria Castellano

The British colonies in America came up with some interesting innovations. In 1765, Dr. James Baker and John Hannon of Massachusetts started one of the first chocolate enterprises to employ a machine. They used an old grist mill to grind the beans into chocolate liquor, and then pressed the paste into cakes to be dried for cocoa powder. Alas, poor Hannon was lost at sea while on a trip to the West Indies to buy beans, but Dr. Baker continued to produce high-quality chocolate. . . .

Mocha Mousse with Sichuan Peppercorns

¼ teaspoon Sichuan peppercorns
⅓ cup heavy cream
1½ teaspoons ground coffee beans
4 ounces 70%-cacao bittersweet chocolate, chopped
3 large egg whites
1 tablespoon sugar
whipped cream, for garnish

1. Grind peppercorns with mortar and pestle.

2. Bring cream, coffee, and pepper to a simmer in a small saucepan. Remove from heat and let steep, covered, 30 minutes. Strain liquid through a fine-mesh sieve into a bowl, pressing on solids.

3. Melt chocolate in a large bowl. Stir in cream. Cool slightly.

4. Beat egg whites with sugar using an electric mixer until they just hold stiff peaks. Fold into chocolate mixture gently but thoroughly.

5. Spoon mousse into glasses and chill at least 3 hours. Serve with lightly sweetened whipped cream.

The carriage lamp flickered as the wheels jolted over a rut in the road. Arianna braced herself against the squabs and peered out through the window. Darkness shrouded the surroundings, the moonless night made even more impenetrable by swirls of thick gray fog twisting through the tall hedgerows.

She could smell the river close by, but any water sounds were drowned out by the creak of the harness leather and the thud of the hooves.

How much farther? she wondered.

Her heartbeat kicked up a notch as she pressed a palm to the glass and wiped away the beads of moisture. The city lights had long receded, leaving naught but indistinct shapes of black against black shifting in the breeze. All she could see was her own taut reflection.

She must be getting close.

Concord's note explaining the sudden change of venue for this evening's party had said that the journey from Mayfair would take a little over an hour. Leaning back, Arianna closed her eyes and sought to steady her nerves. That her own personal vendetta had become entangled in a far bigger web of evil was still a little disorienting. In truth, she really shouldn't care very much anymore—her original motivations had, like so much else in her life, been based on lies. And yet, she found that she did care.

Could Saybrook be right? Could she actually believe in abstract notions like justice?

Arianna shook off the questions. She needed her head clear, her thoughts focused on the coming revelries.

Concord had added several lines below the directions, explaining that the arrival of a valuable shipment from abroad had sparked the idea of holding a special celebration—and that she was among the select few being invited to participate. An "initiation," he had called it. To see if the rest of the club would approve the offer of a full-fledged membership. Which, he assured her, would open the portal to every imaginable pleasure.

Fay çe que vouldras—Do as you please.

Her hands knotted together in a tight fist. And if embezzlement, treason, and murder were necessary to achieve one's desires, then so be it.

The thought of murder made her frown for an instant. Saybrook would likely be angry that she had set off without sending him word about the change in plans. But Concord's note had come late, and she had been in a rush to ready herself for the carriage ride to Wooburn Moor.

A special ceremony required a special venue. The directions had described an isolated manor house set by the river, well hidden from the main road. No other information had been given, save to say that it belonged to another club member.

Who?

The question recalled what she had read about Francis Dashwood, the original founder of the Hellfire Club, whose lands in High Wycombe were not far away. She wondered whether the rumors of secret caves cut into the soft chalky stone beneath the old Medmenham Abbey were true. Subterranean chambers of stygian darkness, where the devils could play at will.

"It doesn't matter whether Saybrook knows or not," she whispered aloud. "I've always looked out for myself."

A blaze of torchlight suddenly shone through the

misted panes. "Welcome." A masked figure stepped out of the fog to open the carriage door. Arianna didn't recognize the voice. Likely it was a servant, paid well to keep silent about what went on within the walls of the manor house up ahead.

"This way, madam." He led her along a gravel path and up a set of marble stairs. Taking hold of the brass knocker—a horned Satan with a monstrous erection—he rapped on the door and then retreated, leaving her standing alone in the gloom.

Several minutes ticked by before the iron-studded oak swung open.

"Ah, Lady W, I am delighted that you accepted the invitation." Concord was dressed in scarlet trousers and matching jacket, the rich fabric giving a reddish gleam to his overbright eyes and oiled hair. A musky scent oozed from the combed curls, a mixture of sandalwood and some exotic sweetness that made her want to gag.

Forcing a smile instead, she replied, "I wouldn't have missed the opportunity for the world."

He raised his glass in salute. It held a crystal clear liquid that he quaffed in one gulp. "To a memorable evening," he murmured. "Please help yourself to refreshments. I must have a word with the membership committee and our host about the coming ceremony. I shall join you shortly."

"Of course, sir." Arianna spotted Tipton and Gavin in one of the side alcoves. They were wearing white trousers and jackets, identical in cut to Concord's clothing.

"But pray," she added, "don't let them keep you too long."

Concord's gaze flicked to her cleavage. "Just a few matters of business, and then we may move on to pleasure, Lady Wolcott."

Arianna made her way to the far corner of the drawing room, where an array of drinks were set up on a gilded table festooned with bloodred candles. It was the one bright spot, aswirl with tongues of fire, licking up with silent laughter.

Insatiable, she thought, taking up a glass of burgundy wine. Men like Concord could never have enough.

The rest of the room was pooled in flickering shadows. She could dimly make out several other people standing together by the curtained windows, but the hooded robes they were wearing made it impossible to make out their identities. Whoever they were, they made no acknowledgment of her arrival.

Perhaps it was part of the ritual. She seemed to be the only one attired in evening finery. . . .

The soft swoosh of fabric suddenly intruded on her musings. Arianna felt a prickling of gooseflesh as a laugh sounded close to her ear.

"Nervous, my dear?" Lady Spencer was wearing a nun's habit, fashioned out of coal-black cloth. A half-moon of white hung over her shoulders, reflecting the fire-gold glow of the candles up to her face. Even without the highlights, her eyes looked unnaturally bright.

"Perhaps just a little," replied Arianna.

"It is only natural." Two points of red glittered in the center of her dilated pupils. "You are about to enter a whole new world."

"I—I am eager to experience a different life."

"Yes, you appear to have an appetite for pleasure."

Arianna answered with a little laugh.

"Speaking of which, your relative is a *very* delicious man." A cat-in-the-cream-pot smile twitched on Lady Spencer's lips as she drank deeply from a large fluted goblet. Her voice had an odd tempo to it—quick, yet strangely slurred. "That sour expression hides a feast of exotic flavors."

"Indeed?" murmured Arianna.

"Oh, yes, his kisses are quite divine." A wink hung for an instant on her kohl-rimmed lashes. "We had to put off a more intimate acquaintance for a bit longer, until he is fully healed. However, I am *quite* sure that his sword will prove magnificent when it's unsheathed."

Arianna took a small sip of her wine. "You don't say?" A discussion of Saybrook's sexual potential was the last thing she was looking for. Her concentration was all on Concord, and how she might coax some incriminating evidence out of him.

Lady Spencer did not take the hint and move away. "I confess, I am surprised you didn't grab him for yourself. Don't you find him attractive?"

How to answer? In her role as rapacious widow, eager for a taste of forbidden fruits, she must not stir any suspicions. "Oh, he has an undeniable physical allure. But there are . . . other complications. Family, you know."

"Yet you aren't closely related," probed Lady Spencer. "The connection is only by marriage."

"That is part of the problem." She lowered her voice to a confidential whisper, knowing how much her erstwhile employer loved knowing other people's secrets. "As the nominal head of the family, he wishes to manage my affairs, and I am heartily sick of having a man tell me what to do."

"I don't blame you," said Lady Spencer with a knowing nod. "We are, after all, much smarter than they are. But never fear, Lady Wolcott. You'll soon learn that it's laughably easy to wrap men around your finger."

Arianna looked up through her lashes. "I shall try to watch carefully and pick up a few tricks from you." Flattery was a sure way to stay in the lady's good graces. "Something tells me you have a wealth of experience in handling the opposite sex."

"Men are primitive creatures. Most of the time they think with their cocks and not their brains. So you must use that knowledge to your advantage." Lady Spencer took another thirsty gulp of her drink. "I like coaxing out their deepest, darkest secrets when their guard is down."

Whatever was in the glass, observed Arianna, it appeared to be loosening the lady's tongue. Her own senses sharpened. She, too, was experienced in using the same strategy. "I imagine you are very, very good at that."

"Oh, I am, I am." She sidled a little closer, her shoulder kissing up against Arianna. "Take Saybrook—I shall of course enjoy swiving the big, black devil. But I also intend to diddle some information out of him."

"Really?" drawled Arianna. "But he seems like such a bore."

A laugh gurgled in Lady Spencer's throat. "What if I told you he's in charge of a secret investigation for the government."

"No!" exclaimed Arianna, exaggerating her disbelief. "Impossible."

"Shhhh." Lady Spencer touched a finger to her lips. "Oh, I assure you it's true," she whispered. "It happened at my house. The Prince Regent took ill, and they think he was poisoned."

Arianna gasped.

"Yes, yes, take my word for it." Lady Spencer paused to fan herself. "Lud, is it warm in here?"

"Quite." Taking the lady's arm, she led her deeper into the alcove and opened one of the brass-framed windows. "Surely the earl doesn't suspect *you* of the crime," she whispered, quickly steering the conversation back to the Prince.

"He's been terribly closemouthed about the whole thing. But I shall soon be in a position to pump him for information."

Two could play at that game, thought Arianna. Leaning in a little closer, she whispered, "One could hardly blame you if you chose to poison the Prince in a fit of jealousy."

"Jealous of that fat turd?" Lady Spencer chuffed a laugh. "I was sleeping with him merely to coax him into using his influence for me."

"In what?" probed Arianna.

Lady Spencer turned her flushed face to the wafting of cool air. "A lady has to look out for herself."

"Oh, yes. Yes," she agreed eagerly. "But it isn't easy, is it?"

There was a moment of hesitation, and then came an answer. "I was hoping that Prinny, like his brother York, might be willing to indulge in a little bimble-bumble concerning a business matter. Things were going well, until the slimy little slug of a French chef went and ruined everything. I suspect . . ." Lady Spencer turned, and though her eyes were dangerously bright, there was still a sharpness beneath the glitter. "Perhaps we can help each other, Lady Wolcott. You know, use our feminine wiles to the benefit of us both."

"Oh, I should like that very much. How?"

"I could twist Saybrook into doing what you want." Lady Spencer hesitated for a fraction. "While you could do me a small favor. . . ."

"Gladly," said Arianna. "The men make all the rules in this world. But that doesn't mean we have to play by them."

The remark drew a throaty titter from Lady Spencer. "I think we are going to be *very* good friends. The thing is, can you keep a secret?"

Arianna crossed her heart.

"Good." Her voice dropped to a conspiratorial whisper. "This is all hush-hush, but I am involved in a business deal with Concord and several others that promises to be very profitable."

"What sort of deal?" asked Arianna quickly.

"Oh, some shipments involving military supplies," replied Lady Spencer. Her speech was growing more slurred. "I had lent one of the men—let us simply call him Mr. K—some important papers to help with the financial calculations, and when he returned them, he also included some documents I wasn't supposed to know about." A girlish wink. "You see, the Prince wasn't the only one I was sleeping with. In bed, I got Mr. K to admit that he was working on something bigger than the military deal, and if it all worked out, he would be able to cut Concord out of the new deal."

"What sort of deal?" urged Arianna.

"I don't know, but it looked important." Her smile returned. "And I could tell that Mr. K was very nervous that I had seen the papers, so I was making a little extra blunt from him for keeping quiet about it." She lowered her voice even more. "Concord has a nasty temper and tends to turn violent if he thinks he is being cheated."

Kellton was cheating Concord? Arianna gave an inward grimace. That didn't seem to make any sense. But given Lady Spencer's state of inebriation, perhaps she was getting things garbled. It seemed clear that she knew nothing about the New World trading company.

"How exceedingly clever of you," murmured Arianna. *Keep talking, keep talking,* she added silently. Saybrook needed to know *all* the details for his investigation, and she didn't want to disappoint him.

Lady Spencer nodded. "Yes! But unfortunately Mr. K succumbed to a fit of apoplexy. And now I fear that Concord suspects I knew about the deception and didn't tell him. So it's possible that as a way to get back at me, he bribed my chef to poison the Prince." She frowned. "Or he may have done it for a reason I don't yet know about."

Arianna thought for a moment. *Concord had been in the corridor near the kitchen on the night of the poisoning. But he hadn't been alone.* Damnation—if only she had been able to make out the other man's face in the swirl of shadows. Knowing his identity might help answer a number of questions.

Noting that Lady Spencer was watching her intently, she curled a cool smile. "Ah, I see what you mean. You would like me to see what dirt I can dig out of Concord."

"You *are* a sly little puss, aren't you?"

Arianna let out a little laugh. "I didn't become a rich widow by being a sweet, biddable little girl."

An answering cackle stirred the air. "Try to find out what his feelings are about me—men do like to talk in bed. And, by the by, try to find out where he's getting this Devil's Delight."

"The Devil's Delight?" repeated Arianna, pretending that she had never heard the name mentioned before.

Lady Spencer tapped her now empty glass. "It's a special drug that will bring in a fortune from rich men who crave new excitement. If we can learn who his partner is, and how they get their supplies, we could demand to be part of the deal." Her rouged lips curled up in a quick smile. "You would, of course, get a share of the profits. Do we have a agreement?"

"Oh, yes." How sublimely ironic that the request melded so well with her own intentions. "Be assured that you can count on me."

Lady Spencer's low titter was cut off by a loud laugh. Concord was fast approaching, his boots clicking a staccato tattoo over the polished wood floor.

Smiling, Arianna quickly turned to greet him with a flirtatious look. "La, I hear you've been sampling a stimulating new treat. Aren't you going to invite me to have a taste?"

"But of course." His eyes were dilated, and his whole body seemed to crackle with a strange sort of energy. "I was just coming to ask if you would like to join me in a special toast before the real festivities begin." He touched her arm, and she could feel the heat of him pulse against her skin.

Lady Spencer melted away into the shadows, but not before fluttering a last little wink.

"I would like nothing better!" Arianna didn't have to feign a note of anticipation. *At last, at last.* After all the years of battling for every hard-won step, things were beginning to move at a dizzying pace. No wonder she felt a little breathless.

Concord's grin stretched into a leer. "Then come with me."

"You suspected this," said Henning.

"Yes." Saybrook checked the priming of his pistol. "Put Lady Arianna in a position to do something that should strike terror into the heart of any mere mortal, and one can pretty much count on her setting off in a flash.

The surgeon blew out his cheeks.

"Your man is sure that her carriage was headed out of the city?" asked the earl.

"Aye, he trailed it until he was certain of the direction," answered Henning. "There's something else you should know, though. He's also positive that Lady Arianna was being followed by someone else."

"One of Grentham's spies, no doubt," replied Saybrook matter-of-factly. "I caught sight of a fellow when I was leaving your surgery."

"Well, your surveillance skills from the Peninsula seem as sharp as ever," said Henning. "And yet you seem awfully calm about it. Isn't the minister's interest in the lassie cause for alarm?"

Saybrook didn't look up from adjusting the flint. "There is no use speculating about Grentham's motives in this case. The man is a cipher. He could very well be the one who ordered her lured to Wooburn Moor, or he could have other reasons for keeping a close watch on her."

"By the by, how the devil did you know she was headed for Wooburn Moor?" demanded Henning. "Have you taken up reading tea leaves, or scrying the future in a crystal ball?"

"The answer is far more mundane. I visited Lady Spencer this afternoon, and in the process of becoming better acquainted with her, she invited me to attend the same party."

"You should have said yes. That way you could have kept a closer eye on Lady Arianna."

"I'm not sure she would welcome the scrutiny." Saybrook flicked a grain of gunpowder from the polished steel. "Besides, such a move might scare away our quarry. We've gone to a good deal of trouble to bring Concord sniffing around her skirts. It would be a pity to have all our efforts go for naught."

"Isn't that rather liked staking out a lamb to draw in a wolf," groused the surgeon.

"Ha—if he tries to take a bite, he'll break his teeth."

"The lady is remarkably capable," replied Henning. "But these men are ruthless murderers. I am surprised you aren't more worried."

"My feelings are irrelevant." The earl began loading the second weapon of his matched set. "There appears to be a dangerous conspiracy threatening to do great harm to the country. We have a duty to expose it, Baz, and see the miscreants arrested, no matter the risks involved."

"Sounds awfully cold-blooded to me."

"On the contrary, Lady Arianna would likely carve out my liver if I were to interfere in her quest to bring Concord and his coconspirators to justice. As you learned from Ashmun's revelations, she has personal reasons for wishing to see the men responsible for her father's death locked up in Newgate."

"I still don't like it," muttered the surgeon. "Ashmun—"

"Ashmun is no threat to her," said the earl.

"How do you know that? You weren't so certain at our last meeting."

"Because I paid him a visit after my tête-à-tête with Lady Spencer. As you know, I've experience in interrogating prisoners. I'm satisfied that he is telling the truth." His face was a mask of concentration as he methodically checked over the trigger mechanism. "Which means that, as I feared, Lady Arianna has been only partly right in her quest for revenge."

Henning pursed his lips. "What—"

"Never mind that now. I am taking what precautions I can, and will do my best to keep her safe." *Click, click.* The hammer cocked and released. "Speaking of which," went on Saybrook, "do you have your troops assembled?"

"Aye. I've four laddies from the First Royal Scots Foot Regiment waiting to come with us in your coach. In addition, a half dozen of my friends from the Royal Navy are traveling by boat to the estate. They will hide themselves and wait for our signal to show themselves."

"They will likely make better time on the water than the coach will over the rutted country roads," observed the earl. "Which is why I've decided to go on by horse-back while you and your foot soldiers follow in the coach. Lady Arianna has a head start, but I should be able to make up the time."

Henning made a face but didn't argue. "Yer leg will hold up?"

"I can ride to Hades and back if necessary." Say-brook tucked extra bullets and a flask of powder into his pocket. "I trust that your men are in fighting trim?"

"A few fingers and toes may be missing," admitted the surgeon. "But the men are still crack shots and handy with their fists. I'd pit them against any foe."

"Good." He slid the pistols into a well-worn cavalry saddle holster. "We may encounter no trouble. But if all hell breaks loose, I would like to believe that we can beat the devil at his own game."

Despite the sugar, the liquid was sharply sour, like dried lemons, and left Arianna's tongue feeling a bit numb.

"Odd," she murmured, regarding Concord over the rim of the glass.

"It's an acquired taste. But you will soon be craving more," he assured her. Smacking his lips, he quaffed the rest of his drink in one hungry swallow and then quickly poured a refill. "Come, let us drink to the Devil."

She drew in a mouthful before dissolving into a fit of giggles. Covering her lips with her glove, she muffled the sound. "Ooooh, it *tickles*."

He gave a wolfish grin, unaware that most of the liba-tion was now soaking into the delicate kidskin. "I can think of lots more ways to bring a tingle to your flesh, Lady Wolcott."

"You," she teased, "are a *very* naughty man."

His gaze turned lidded. "Guilty as charged." Placing a hand on her hip, Concord steered her to a long, low divan set near the hearth.

"Just how naughty?" she said archly, obediently taking a seat on the buttery soft leather. Bold striped pillows of black and gold accented the vivid shade of scarlet. Kicking off her slippers, she sunk her stocking-clad toes into the thick bearskin rug beneath her feet.

He merely smiled and moved away to latch the door shut.

The room, a private parlor located at the end of a long, winding corridor, reminded her of some of the fancier bordellos she had seen in her Caribbean travels. Gaudy colors, expensive decorations—her head was beginning to ache from all the gilding. Or maybe it was because of the drug. Despite all the little tricks learned in her tropical travels, she had been forced to drink more than she wished, in order not to stir his suspicions.

She tapped her nearly empty glass. "Lady Spencer says this is your own special elixir. I've never had anything like it."

"That's because it's something very new and very costly." Concord took a seat next to her, close enough that his thigh pressed against hers. *Twitch, twitch, twitch.* A strange current of heat was rippling through his muscles, making it hard for him to sit still.

Smoothing at her skirts, Arianna summoned her resolve. *I will sleep with Satan himself if it will bring justice for Papa.* The declaration, so forcefully asserted in another time and place, was harder to hold on to now, with the devil's hot breath tickling her cheek.

Concord had carried a slim crystal bottle of the elixir cradled in his arms from the drawing room. Holding it up to the sconce, he set the contents to turning in a slow whirl. "It's made from an exotic plant, brought all the way from South America."

Backlit by the flames, the tiny white flecks in the liquid swirled like snow. She widened her eyes. "Wherever did you find it?"

The elixir was spinning faster and faster and faster, a whirlpool of white. He watched, mesmerized for a moment, before emitting a low laugh. "Oh, I have my sources."

The Earl of Cockburn?

The name was on the tip of her tongue, but Arianna

caught herself. Recalling Saybrook's gruff growl only echoed the voice in her own head.

Be careful.

Concord surely considered himself cleverer than other men—she must turn that strength into a weakness.

"Oh, I see." Arianna deliberately added a shade of disappointment to her voice. "I thought Lady Spencer said that *you* had created it. But what she meant was that you merely purchased it from someone else."

A bit of smugness drained from his face. "Don't believe everything you hear from Lady Spencer." He sucked in a mouthful of his drink. "She may think she knows everything . . ." He reached out and ran a thumb along the line of her jaw. "But trust me, she is not quite as smart as she thinks."

Trust you? I should rather trust an asp.

His touch slithered down to the top of her bodice. "My partner and I will make a fortune off the Devil's Delight. There are plenty of wealthy men willing to pay any price for pleasure."

It took every ounce of her hard-won acting ability to repress a shudder. Up close, his fleshy good looks took on a grotesque twist—the dilated eyes, the lines of dissipation. . . .

Arianna gulped for air, hoping her reaction would be seen as desire and not disgust.

He smiled and smacked his lips. "You see, Lady Wolcott, everything I touch turns to gold."

Or blood.

She dropped her gaze to the hand hooked in her gown, and all she could see was his fingers dripping with her father's gore. Her pulse began to pound in her ears, and with it a whisper from the past.

Forgive me for being such a wretched parent. And for sinking you in such a sordid life.

Strange, but her father's dying words brought a sudden sense of calm. *Yes, I forgive you, Papa.* Perhaps bringing his murderer to justice was more about her own redemption than anything else.

The past could finally be buried, along with all the old sins.

Summoning a smile, she gave a feline stretch and reclined against the pillows, leaving his hand hovering in midair. "So, you have a Midas touch, milord?" she said. "How very intriguing. Pray, refill our glasses and then let us put your claim to the test."

"You won't be disappointed, m'dear."

Crystal clinked against crystal.

A splash of liquid sloshed over the leather. Oddly enough, though his gaze still held a dangerous glitter, the crackling energy of earlier seemed to have suddenly ebbed. His movements seemed mired in a heavy languidness.

She, too, was suddenly having trouble keeping her eyes open. "How . . . ," she began, but all her questions had turned terribly fuzzy.

"Drink," he urged.

Damn. All at once, his voice sounded very far away.

"Drink." His clammy hands were now on her throat.

As his face turned blurry, she was only dimly aware of the glass slipping from her fingers.

23

From the chocolate notebooks of Dona Maria Castellano

The Church figures into yet another bit of chocolate lore—although this time the situation takes on a far more sinister shade. It is said that Pope Clement XIV was murdered in 1774 by the Jesuits, who poisoned his cup of chocolate in retaliation for his persecution of the Order in earlier years. It is true that chocolate's rich flavor provides an excellent mask for lethal substances, so perhaps the story is true. . . .

Dulce de Leche and Nut Butter Truffles

4 ounces 60%-cacao bittersweet chocolate, finely chopped
2 tablespoons dulce de leche at room temperature
2 tablespoons well-stirred natural almond butter
or peanut butter

For coating

¼ to ½ cup unsweetened cocoa powder (preferably Dutch-processed)
2 ounces 60%-cacao bittersweet chocolate, finely chopped

1. Melt 4 ounces chocolate in a heatproof bowl set over a saucepan of barely simmering water, stirring occasionally until smooth. Remove bowl from heat and stir in dulce de leche and nut butter. Cool slightly, then roll level teaspoons of mixture into balls and place on a tray. Chill completely, about 30 minutes.

2. Sift cocoa powder into a medium baking pan or onto a tray. Melt 2 ounces chocolate in a shallow heatproof bowl set over a saucepan of barely simmering water, stirring occasionally until smooth. Remove pan from heat, leaving bowl over water. Dip truffles, 1 at a time, in chocolate, lifting out with a fork and letting excess drip off, then immediately transfer to cocoa, turning to coat. Let stand until coating is set, then shake off excess cocoa in a sieve. (Remaining cocoa can be sifted and returned to container.)

Darkness drifted in and out of her consciousness, shadows twining with shards of light.

What a bloody stupid fool I am.

After all the years of plotting and planning, to fail so miserably . . .

How very, very ironic that she, who had sworn not to repeat the mistakes of her father, had in the end proved less clever than Concord.

Recriminations were, she knew, a little late. Yet oddly enough, the sharpest pinch of regret was that she had let Saybrook down. He had been willing to risk his life for a higher purpose than personal vendetta. While she—

A light slap to her cheek jarred her eyes open.

"Lady Wolcott?"

"I . . ." She blinked, trying to clear the wooziness from her head.

"Let me help you sit up." Gavin was kneeling by the divan, his grip steadying her slumping shoulders. Prop-

ping her against the pillow, he brought a glass to her lips.
"Here, drink this."

She tried to pull away.

"It's just water," he assured her.

The liquid was blessedly cool and clean, washing the
sour taste from her mouth. "Thank you," she croaked.

"Don't try to speak quite yet," said Gavin. "You've
had a nasty shock."

"Concord . . .," she began, trying to clear the fog from
her head. The question died on her lips as she spotted
her nemesis sprawled on the floor.

"Won't be bothering you again." With a casual prod
of his boot, Gavin nudged the body faceup. A circle of
darker red was fast spreading over the scarlet jacket.
Centered in it was a dagger, sunk to the hilt in the baron's left breast.

"Or anyone else for that matter."

"I think he meant to kill me," she whispered.

"Actually, his intention was most likely just to rough
you up a bit," replied Gavin, touching a hand to his
pocket. He had changed out of his snowy white garb and
was now clad in a black coat and trousers. "Sex had an
extra edge for him when the women were frightened."

Fear—a primal, primitive emotion. Drawing a steadying breath, Arianna looked up to thank him again.

Only to find the snout of a pocket pistol hovering
inches from her forehead.

"It is *I* who you really need to fear," he said conversationally. "Get up, Lady Wolcott—or rather, Lady Arianna Hadley."

A fresh wave of dizziness washed over her.

"Get up!" The slap was a good deal harder than his
first one.

"How . . . why . . ." A myriad of questions tangled on
her tongue.

"You'll learn all that later." Gavin grasped her arm
and hauled her to her feet. "Move." Cold steel hit hard
against her temple. "And quickly, or I'll put a bullet
through your brain."

What brain? thought Arianna groggily. Still half dazed by the drug, she stumbled along unresistingly. A slave to her own obsession, she had been too stupid to see the truth.

"This way." Gavin unlatched a set of glass-paned doors and shoved her outside. A damp breeze ruffled through the dark foliage of an overgrown garden.

Gravel crunched underfoot as he hurried their steps away from the house.

"Where are you taking me?" asked Arianna, the chill and the sharp stabs of the stones helping to restore her wits. Up ahead in the shadows, she saw a team of horses harnessed to a covered carriage.

"To a cozy little spot where we won't be disturbed." His low laugh echoed the rumbled wash of the nearby river. "Don't worry, Lady Arianna. It's not far away."

Grentham let the draperies fall back in place and stepped away from the window. Half hidden by a grove of trees, the abandoned gamekeeper's cottage overlooked the ghostly ruins of Medmenham Abbey. "Has Lord Cockburn arrived?"

"Yes," assured the man who had just come in from the darkness. "He is waiting at the entrance of the caves."

"Excellent, excellent." The minister turned to the other two people in the room. "What of Lady Wolcott and Lord Saybrook?"

"The lady left London just after dusk, milord, and arrived at the Wooburn Moor according to schedule," replied the spy appointed to keeping her under surveillance.

"The earl followed shortly afterward, alone and on horseback," reported the other man. "His friend, the surgeon Henning, is coming by coach, along with four other former soldiers." A pause. "All cripples."

"Saybrook has considerable hubris, to face off against the unknown with such a paltry force." The spark of a flint scraping steel caught the slight upward curl of

Grentham's mouth. "But then, that doesn't really surprise me."

He lit a single candle and set it by the map on the table. Motioning for the three men to come closer, he then indicated the paper. "Martin, you and your group will keep watch on the London road here, while Finley, you are to station your forces by the Abbey ruins, in this part of the gardens."

Tap, tap. The minister punctuated his orders with a well-tended finger. "Beckham, you will come with me. Your weapons are loaded?"

One of the men nodded.

"A reminder to you others—stay well hidden. No one—*no one*—is to move unless I give the signal." Grentham drew on a pair of black gloves. "I've gone to a great deal of trouble to set this trap. So need I say that there will be hell to pay for anyone who cocks it up?"

Silence.

"Good. Then let us go take up our positions."

"Damnation," growled Saybrook. "You are sure that he called her Lady Arianna?"

"Aye, sor," answered the leader of Henning's sailors. "And he said the spot where they were going wasn't far away."

"Did you see which way the carriage was headed?"

The man flashed a gap-toothed grin. "Better 'n that, sor. I sent Davy te grab on to the back struts. He's a former maintops'l man, well used to hanging on te a shroud in gale-force winds. A few bumps won't shake 'im loose."

Saybrook glanced up at the sliver of moon. The crescent curve of light was almost imperceptible through the heavy scrim of clouds. "I'm not sure how that will help me find them in this ocean of darkness," he muttered. "Unless he has a lodestone in his pocket—one with a magnetic force powerful enough to guide me to their presence."

"No lodestone, sor," piped up one of the men, "but a

naval signal lantern, with a powerful beam that can be seen fer miles on a foggy night."

"Aye," added the leader. "And it's shuttered te make a pinpoint o' light, so the driver of the vehicle won't notice it."

"Well done," said Saybrook. "I've a good idea of where they are headed, but I can't afford to make a mistake. God knows, I've made enough already." A last lingering look at the manor house, whose rear façade rose like a spectral shadow from the deserted gardens, seemed to spur him to action. "One of you wait here for Henning to tell him of the change in plans. The rest of you row on to High Wycombe—is anyone familiar with Medmenham Abbey?"

"I am," volunteered one of the sailors. "I was raised in this area and know it well."

"Then you'll know about the entrance to Dashwood's caves."

The sailor nodded. "Devilish doing down there in years past, or so local rumor had it."

"I fear that the embers of evil may well have been stirred to fire again," replied the earl in a tight voice. "Flex your muscles, men, and make your boat fly." He turned to make his way to where his horse was tethered. "We haven't a moment to lose."

Arianna stumbled, her bare feet scraping over the rocky path. Pain lanced through her limbs as Gavin jerked her upright.

Oh, but pain is good, she thought, biting her lip to keep from crying out. It was helping to clear the last noxious vapors of the drug from her brain.

"Clumsy cow," snarled Gavin as she slipped again. His hold tightened on her arm as he shoved her forward. "Be careful. We can't have you breaking your lovely neck just yet."

"Why?" she rasped, tasting a trickle of blood.

Why hadn't he killed her along with Concord?

"You'll learn that soon enough."

They were halfway down a steep slope. Through the drifting mist, Arianna could just make out a faint rippling of moonlight on water. The sound of the current lapping over the rocks stirred a sudden swirl of memories from her island childhood. *Sun, surf, her father's warm laughter.*

Gavin yanked her back from her momentary reveries. "This way."

The path led to a courtyard framed by a high crumbling stone archway. Up ahead, the light of a single lantern pierced the gloom.

"You're late." The voice, a nasal drawl made shriller by a pinch of nervousness, was not one she recognized. "Was there any . . . complication?"

"None," replied Gavin with savage satisfaction. "The problem has been eliminated. What about you?"

"The samples have been moved, exactly as planned." As the man raised the light, an oily glow spilled over his features. His face was long and thin, with an air of aristocratic arrogance chiseled into the angled cheekbones and hawklike nose. A shock of silvery hair was swept straight back, accentuating a high forehead and bushy brows.

The picture of patrician refinement was ruined by a high-pitched cackle.

That laugh. All of a sudden, it came back to her in a gold-flecked flash. A long-ago memory of sitting curled in her father's lap, mesmerized by the gleam of shiny buttons as he and his friend "Cocky" talked late into the night.

"That's why our partnership works so well," went on Cockburn—for she was sure it must be him. "We both are extremely good at what we do." His laughter stilled. "So, this is Dickie's daughter?"

Arianna squinted against the glare of the beam. But before she could reply, Gavin pressed the pistol to the back of her neck. "Move inside, Lady Arianna."

It was then that she noticed a low, vaulted entrance cut into the hillside beneath the flinty Gothic archway.

A shove forced her inside.

Damp, dank air kissed her cheeks. She staggered and was suddenly, violently sick.

Cockburn jerked his perfectly polished Hessian boot away with fastidious quickness. "I told you that the combination of poppies and coca leaves was a dangerous mix."

"It was the only way to ensure that both of them would be sluggish enough not to raise any alarm," said Gavin. "A calculated risk, but not a great one. After all, it hardly mattered whether it would kill Concord. As for Lady Arianna . . ."

Wrinkling his nose, Cockburn thrust a handkerchief into her hand. "Here, clean your face."

Arianna was under no illusion that the gesture was an act of kindness. No doubt he didn't wish the sour smell of bile to follow them into the depths. She wiped her mouth with the soft linen, suddenly aware of a small patch of raised threads against her lips. *Embroidery?*

She offered the soiled square back to him, taking care to angle it into the lantern light. If there was any doubt as to his identity, the design did away with it. Though the stitching was cream on cream, she could just make out the image of a strutting cock.

He made a moue of disgust and waved it away. "Drop the damned thing and come along."

They walked on for what felt like an age—Arianna counted two hundred steps—before the tunnel narrowed and turned down to the left. The native chalk gave the walls an eerie, ghostly white glow. Roman numerals were carved into the stone at odd intervals, along with a series of grotesque heads.

"Dashwood called this the Robing Room," said Gavin. His voice was calm and complacent, as if he were giving a tour of Westminster Cathedral. "He had an Italian artist, Giuseppe Borgnis, help with the design."

So, she was at Medmenham, and the ruins aboveground were the old Cistercian abbey. She had guessed as much.

"The original club members would don their costumes here," he continued.

"Do you and your depraved friends follow suit?" asked Arianna, not bothering to disguise the contempt in her voice.

"Oh, we are not nearly as primitive these days," replied Gavin. "As you saw, we prefer a more comfortable setting for our debaucheries."

"May you all rot in hell," she whispered.

"Tut, tut, Lady Arianna," chided Cockburn. He turned, and a glint of gold shone from his waistcoat. "No need to be nasty. I am hoping we can all behave like civilized individuals."

Her impulse was to spit in his face. However, Arianna held herself in check. "Civilized?" she repeated. "Pray, how do you define the word, Lord Cockburn?"

He smiled. "Ah, so you remember me."

"We shall explain everything shortly," said Gavin curtly, before she could answer. "Come, let us keep moving."

They rounded a huge pillar, and after a short way emerged into a soaring circular chamber with several alcoves cut into the rock.

"This is the Banqueting Hall." Gavin smoothly resumed his explanations, and for the first time released his grip on her arm to point up at the ceiling. "See that hook? It is said that the Rosicrucian lamp from the first Hellfire Club meeting in the George and Vulture once hung there."

As if I give a fig for the sordid history of your satanic brethren.

A glance showed that Cockburn was watching her intently. "I fear you are boring Lady Arianna," he murmured.

"Yes, you are," she replied bluntly. "The Hellfire Club members seem to think their celebration of sexual perversion and mockery of morality is a mark of superior intellect." It wasn't very smart to bait one's captors, but the truth was, she knew she was going to die, so what did it matter? Concord at least had paid for his sins. "I think it's nothing more than infantile indulgence."

She heard Cockburn suck in his breath. And then let it out in a low laugh. "We think alike, Lady Arianna," he said softly. "I am not a member."

"They indulge in naught but childish games," agreed Gavin. He must have seen the skepticism on her face, for he went on to add, "It suited our purpose for me to join the Club, in order to keep a close eye on Concord, Kellton, and Lady Spencer. But while they played in the dark, so to speak, we turned their ignorance to our advantage."

For a brief moment, Arianna was overcome with confusion. Perhaps it was the residue of the narcotic, but she felt her dizziness return. The chalky walls seemed to press in and then recede.

"Why are you telling me this?" she asked haltingly. It was only one of the many questions now whirling like dervishes inside her head.

"Patience." The marquess smiled. "You will soon be enlightened."

His easy assurance heightened her confusion. She considered herself skilled at judging people and their motivations. But nothing was making any sense.

Gavin and Cockburn. She squeezed her eyes shut as their faces turned a bit fuzzy. *Concord, Kellton, and Lady Spencer.* The pieces of the puzzle no longer seemed to fit together as she and Saybrook had thought, yet try as she might, she could not discern a new pattern.

"You seem a trifle faint, Lady Arianna. Would you care for a sip of brandy?"

Her lids fluttered open in time for her to see Cockburn take a small silver flask from his pocket. *"No,"* she exclaimed, then hated herself for the half-hysterical squeak.

"It's untainted, I assure you." He uncorked it and took a swallow.

Arianna shook her head, unwilling to betray any further sign of weakness. She would not give them the satisfaction of seeing her fear.

Fear. Yes, she was afraid. Not that she had much to live for. Except for the chocolate recipes, she thought wryly, and perhaps . . .

Don't be a fool—the earl would not mourn her passing.

"This way." Gavin appeared impatient to continue their journey into the depths of the caverns.

The way sloped downward, and the rock beneath her bare toes turned damper. Shadows flickered wildly, and she was sure that she heard the echo of gurgling water somewhere deep in the darkness up ahead.

It felt as if she were trapped in the belly of the Beast.

"Watch your step—we are about to cross the Styx," warned Gavin. Sure enough, the lantern beam swung down to illuminate a small subterranean stream, its eddying waters black as coal. "Do take care. The bridge is narrow."

They crossed in silence, the still air growing more oppressive with every passing moment. Arianna felt her breathing turn shallow, half expecting fumes of sulfur and brimstone to flare up and fill her lungs.

"As you have seen, there are a number of catacombs down here," remarked Gavin. "Where a number of wicked things have happened in the past. That is, if the rumors can be believed."

A blade of light cut through the gloom, showing the entrance to another chamber. "Please, no ghost stories, Philip. Lady Arianna will think we are trying to frighten her." Cockburn came up beside her and took her hand. His touch was moist and cold, reminding her of a dead fish. "We are here, my dear. Let us sit down and make ourselves comfortable."

A wick flared to life, the fire-gold flame showing three straight-back chairs arranged around a small circular table in the center of the space. Several Turkey rugs lay scattered on the stone floor, but they did nothing to dispel the bone-deep chill.

"Please, have a seat, Lady Arianna," urged Cockburn with a courtly bow as Gavin circled the chamber, lighting the four oil lamps affixed to iron brackets on the wall.

The scene had an air of utter unreality to it—like some demented, demonic dream run amuck. For an instant, Arianna was tempted to turn and run. But reason quickly reasserted control. The odds of escaping through the labyrinth of dark tunnels were too high to calculate.

Might as well wait and see if Chance offered a better deal. Besides, she was curious. About a number of things.

"Cozy, isn't it?" said Gavin from within the spill of shadows.

The marquess shifted the lamp on the table and arranged the sheaf of papers into several neat piles. A plate of arrowroot biscuits and a pitcher filled with a clear liquid and lemon slices sat to one side. "You must be hungry and thirsty after your ordeal. Won't you refresh yourself before we begin?"

The absurdity of his pleasantries made her head start to ache again. "I would rather dispense with the charade of civilized behavior, Lord Cockburn. You must have a reason for bringing me here. What is it?"

He released a heavy sigh as he brushed a speck of chalk from his elegant claret-colored coat. "This does not have to be unpleasant, Lady Arianna."

And the Devil does not have to shrivel a man's soul. It all comes down to choices.

She clenched her jaw, refusing to reply with aught but a stony stare.

Gavin fished a rolled length of chamois from his coat pocket and dropped it on the table. The muffled chink of metal sounded as it thudded against the wood. "I told you that she would not—"

A sharp look from Cockburn warned him to silence. With a shrug, he retreated a step and folded his arms across his chest.

"Forgive my colleague." Cockburn sat and carefully pinched the pleats of his trousers into place, the very picture of gentlemanly refinement. "He forgets his manners at times."

Arianna quelled the urge to laugh at the absurdity.

"How to begin . . .," he said, fingering his smoothly shaven chin. "I knew your father quite well. A delightful man, and quite brilliant." A rustle of wool. "Though not without his faults."

"I'm aware of my father's personality," she replied. "Kindly get to the point."

"Very well." A pause. "The point is *you*, Lady Arianna."

Her eyes narrowed. "Why?"

The marquess folded his hands on the table. "We have a business proposition for you."

Business? The absurdity had now twisted into utter madness. "Wait—you still have not explained how you discovered my real identity."

Cockburn and Gavin exchanged a quick look.

It was Gavin who answered, his tone nonchalant. "I met with your father when I was passing through Jamaica shortly before his unfortunate death. He pointed you out to me from afar." A smile curled on his lips. "He was very proud of you, but very protective. He didn't wish for you to be exposed to his old friends."

How very like Papa, to think of shutting the barn door when the horses had long ago galloped away.

"So when I saw you in Lady Battell's ballroom, I recognized you immediately," continued Gavin. "And immediately thought that as a stroke of luck had brought us together, why not profit from it?"

"I have no idea what you mean," she replied.

"Oh, come, there is no reason to play coy with us," interjected Cockburn. "We worked with your father on a few deals in the past. Why not take his place, so to speak? We are putting together a business enterprise—a highly profitable one—that could make use of your talents." He settled himself more comfortably in his chair. "Mathematical geniuses are, as you undoubtedly know, scarce as hen's teeth. We had a perfect man for the job.

He did an impressive job on the preliminary papers. But alas, we recently learned that the ship bringing him from Denmark for the next round of work foundered in a Baltic storm.

"It was distressing news, for you see, timing is critical. Our foreign partner is demanding a further sample of how the numbers can be made to yield fabulous profits before making a final commitment, and it so happens that we promised him a special formula for how to shave an extra profit from the sale of every share of stock," continued Gavin. "The deal was in danger of falling through. Until I thought of you."

Her head began to swim. "*You* thought of me? From all that my father said, I—I always assumed that Concord, and his friend Hamilton, were behind all the business schemes."

"Concord and Hamilton?" Gavin gave a nasty laugh. "Neither had the brains nor the vision to be a real leader. Yes, they and your father did some deals together. But they were only small-scale swindles."

Arianna found herself longing for Saybrook's calming presence. Her hands were beginning to tremble with uncontrolled emotion. *Steady, steady.*

"So you see, my dear," said Cockburn, "we're offering you an extraordinary opportunity."

Clasping her fingers together in her lap, she squeezed out a terse reply. "I'm not interested."

"No?" Cockburn's genial smile faded. "Pray, why not?"

"Because I know what sort of deals my father was involved in, and I have no desire to repeat his mistakes in life." *I make enough of my own,* she added silently.

"We could make you a very rich lady," said Gavin.

"You are forgetting that I am already a rich widow."

"Are you?" he countered. "I don't think so. But whatever game you are playing with the *ton*, be assured that ours will make you far more blunt."

She watched the patterns of shadow and light dance

over the rough-hewn rock. "What makes you think that I have inherited my father's knack for numbers?"

"Because even before he left England, Richard used to wax poetic about how his little daughter was more of a genius than he was," answered Cockburn.

Her throat tightened, as if an unseen hand was gripping her flesh.

"A wizard," went on the marquess. "With a magical ability to make mathematics do her bidding."

Somehow she managed to keep her voice level. "If you knew my father as well as you claim, then you are aware that he often distorted the truth. He was, in a word, a liar. A charming one, to be sure, but a liar nonetheless."

Her words stirred a flicker of uncertainty in Cockburn's eyes.

Gavin, however, responded with a snarl. "It is *you* who are lying, Lady Arianna. Your family cook in Jamaica has regaled me with stories of you cleverness—"

"Philip," cautioned Cockburn.

She was suddenly tired of all the deceptions, weary of all the lies. What did it matter? For once, she would simply be herself. "Regardless of whether I possess my father's talents for mathematics, I will not use them to help you."

"Why, you haven't even heard our offer," said Cockburn.

"It's not the money, it's the principle," she said slowly, the statement surprising her as much as it did them. "What you are asking is . . . evil."

"Who do these financial manipulations really hurt?" asked Cockburn quickly.

Good God, he sounded as if he actually believed his own drivel.

"Yes, we will profit handsomely," said the marquess. "But so will a lot of other people."

Her mouth curled in contempt. "Ask that question of Concord."

Gavin shifted his stance. "Concord made the fatal

mistake of prying too deeply into our affairs. We had cut him into the business of distributing Devil's Delight because of his connections with the gaming hells in London, but he was greedy. He suspected we had bigger plans, and issued an ultimatum earlier today." He flicked his wrist, as if swatting at a fly. "In doing so, he became a liability and forced us to move more quickly than we would have liked."

"So we improvised," interjected Cockburn. "An ability that is the key to any successful endeavor."

"Concord was stupid," went on Gavin. "I had hoped that you would be smarter."

"What are you going to do? Stick a knife in my heart, too?"

His expression might well have been carved out of the surrounding stone for all the emotion that it showed. "It would be foolish on your part to let it come to that."

"Two bodies in one night?" she said. "Even you might have difficulty explaining that away."

"Not at all," he shot back. "Everyone saw you go off with Concord. I will simply claim that I saw you kill him and followed in pursuit as you fled the scene. That you put up a fight, forcing me to defend myself, won't be questioned."

True.

Her mouth went a little dry, but she managed to keep her voice level. "I won't help you. And there is nothing you can do to convince me otherwise."

"Nothing?" With a low laugh, Gavin slowly unrolled the chamois, revealing a set of slim steel scalpels.

In spite of her resolve, her heart kicked up and thudded against her ribs.

"We shall see about that."

24

From the chocolate notebooks of Dona Maria Castellano

What a pity that between the dangers of war and the achings of my old bones, travel is such a daunting endeavor for me to contemplate these days. I should very much like to visit Paris, where I hear that a physician by the name of Sulpice Debauve, who served as pharmacist to King Louis XVI, has just opened a shop at 4 Faubourg Saint-Germain that sells edible chocolate! I must write to Sandro right away and tell him about this marvelous idea. . . .

Mexican Turtle Chocolate Mink

*2 tablespoons unsalted butter, cut into pieces, plus additional for greasing ramekins
3 ounces bittersweet chocolate (not unsweetened), chopped
1 large egg, separated
pinch of salt
$1/8$ teaspoon ground cinnamon
1 tablespoon sugar
4 tablespoons cajeta (Mexican caramel)
4 tablespoons pecans, toasted and chopped*

1. Put oven rack in middle position and preheat oven to 350°F. Butter 2 oven-safe bowls or ramekins.

2. Melt butter and chocolate in heavy saucepan over very low heat, stirring until smooth. Remove from heat and cool, stirring occasionally, 5 minutes. Whisk in egg yolk, salt, and ground cinnamon until combined. Beat egg white in a bowl with an electric mixer at medium-high speed until it holds soft peaks. Gradually add sugar, and continue to beat until white just holds stiff, glossy peaks. Whisk one-fourth of white into chocolate mixture to lighten, then fold remaining white gently but thoroughly.

3. Divide batter between bowls or ramekins. Cover each bowl with small squares of foil and crimp foil tightly around rim. Place a baking dish in oven and pour hot water (easiest with a teakettle) into dish. Carefully place ramekins into baking dish. Make sure foil is above water. Bake until puddings are set, about 30 minutes. The desserts will be slightly gooey to the touch.

4. Transfer bowls to a rack and cool puddings, uncovered, about 1 hour. Just before serving, unmold puddings into serving bowls or onto a plate. First, unmold desserts by taking a knife and running it along the edge of the ramekin. Second, place ramekins into a bowl with hot water for about 15 seconds. Turn ramekin upside down and tap bottom. Top each pudding with 2 tablespoons of cajeta and 2 tablespoons of the pecans.

Edging around the abandoned curricle, Saybrook peered through the wisps of fog. There was no sign of light, no stir of movement on the footpath up ahead. And beyond the dark archway, the hillside stood deathly still, the vague shapes of stone and foliage cloaked in a silvery shroud of vapor.

"Davy?" he whispered.

Leaves rustled as a figure emerged from the nearby bushes. "Here, sor."

"Good work with the lantern," murmured the earl. "The beacon proved easy to spot from afar."

The sailor bobbed his head. "The gent took the lady up through them gardens. Another cove was waiting at the entrance te some sort of tunnel. I thought it best te come back here and wait te tell you, rather than follow them inside."

"The right choice." Saybrook gave another glance into the gloom. "Stay here and wait for Henning and the others to arrive. Then bring them along." He checked his pockets for the oilskin pouch of lucifers. While he dared not relight the lantern, the phosphorous matchsticks would provide an occasional flame. "Remind Henning to move quickly but quietly—we must take them by surprise."

In a quicksilver flash, a thin blade cut through the gloom.

"I spent some time in India several years ago," said Gavin. "An interesting culture." Back and forth, back and forth, the point teased through the air just inches from her nose. "They have honed the art of extracting information from their enemies to a fine art."

Arianna dropped her gaze to the floor, unwilling to let him see her fear. *That must be how he knew Kellton,* she thought, concentrating on collecting the facts to keep herself calm.

"Don't be a fool, Lady Arianna," urged Cockburn. "We just need you to work out a stock offering template to show to our partner." He picked up the closest pile of papers. "Why don't you have a look before making a decision you will likely regret? We will pay you very well for your work."

"And if I do, you will let me go free?" she asked.

"But of course," replied Cockburn smoothly. "As I said, we are civilized gentlemen. Violence is only a means of last resort."

"Oh, yes, how very, *very* civilized," said Arianna. *Strip away the fancy title and tailoring and all that would be left is dung in silk stockings.*

Gavin shot out a hand and seized her throat. "Mind your tongue, bitch, or I'll cut it out."

"Philip!" cried Cockburn.

The fingers slowly released.

"As you see, Lady Arianna, my partner is on edge. It would be best if you didn't trifle with us."

She sucked in a raw breath.

"She's just like her father," muttered Gavin. "Too bloody stubborn to see reason."

Oh, no. A sudden thought uncoiled like a serpent in her gut.

No, no, no.

"What do you mean?" she asked slowly.

"As we mentioned, we worked with Richard on a few enterprises before he left England," explained Cockburn.

"My father often mentioned Concord and Hamilton, but I don't recall him talking about you," she said, still fighting off the horrible suspicion that was slithering up from the pit of her stomach. "I wonder why?"

Gavin looked up from his blade. "Because generals don't mingle with their foot soldiers—unless there is the threat of mutiny in the ranks."

"Philip."

The warning came a split second too late. As Arianna watched Gavin's mouth twist into a bloodcurdling grin, she knew in her heart that Saybrook had guessed right—Concord and Hamilton were mere underlings. It was these two who were responsible for her father's murder.

The wind whistling through the shutters, the death rattle of her father's last breath . . .

All of a sudden, Arianna was no longer so resigned to death. She wanted very much to live.

Think, think. There had been times in the past when quick wits had been the key to her survival. *St. Vincent, Isla la Tortuga, Grenada . . .*

But here she was trapped deep underground with two ruthless men ... her only ally, the Earl of Saybrook, had no idea where she was. ...

How the devil was she going to dig herself out of this hole?

A faint whoosh, and a flare of weak light showed water up ahead. Saybrook noted the location of the bridge before the flame fizzled. The lucifers had allowed him to follow the trail of steps in the chalky dust, and while his supply was running low, he thought he could hear the sound of voices above the gurgling of the stream.

Easing a pistol from his pocket, he started forward.

"I told you she was going to be trouble." Gavin's blade swooshed in a lazy arc. "But don't worry. She will soon be begging to do the equations."

"I tried to warn you, Lady Arianna." Cockburn sighed and smoothed at the faultless folds of his cravat. "There really was no need for it to come to this."

"As I said, she's just like her father—willful, stubborn, and deaf to reason." Gavin touched the razored steel to Arianna's cheek and smiled darkly.

She didn't flinch.

The marquess turned away with a grunt of disgust. "I find the sight of blood *so* distasteful."

"While I, on the other hand, rather like the color crimson," answered Gavin. "What about you, Lady Arianna?"

Arianna ignored his question to ask one of her own. "You had my father killed, didn't you?"

"No, actually I didn't." His mouth stretched wider. "I did it myself."

Her pulse began to pound, the sudden rush of blood building to a deafening roar in her ears.

"So, what is your choice? Do you wish to be a fool and follow him to the grave?"

She held the air in her lungs, trying to bring her body under control. The array of blades was but a lunge away.

If she moved quickly, an upward thrust would slice through his liver. . . .

Saybrook would say there was more at stake than personal vengeance.

To hell with what the earl believed, she told herself. When had she cared for what anyone else thought?

And yet . . .

Gavin might die, and maybe Cockburn, if she were lucky enough to evade a bullet. But what about the other conspirators? The gentlemen of power and privilege who had betrayed principle for greed. For a plan of this magnitude, there had to be others involved. A better revenge would be to take them all down.

Her muscles unclenched and she slumped back in her chair.

Gavin saw the slight movement and sneered. "That is the first sign of sense from you yet, Lady Arianna. Thank God you did not try tears or pleas."

Their eyes locked.

"I have always thought that weeping or wailing is a waste of time," replied Arianna. Leaning back from the blade, she took several measured breaths. "What, exactly, is it that you want me to do?"

Leather scraped over stone as Cockburn pivoted on his heel and moved back to the table, his face once again wreathed in a smile. "I knew that you would see reason, once you had a moment to think about it."

"What choice do I have if I wish to live?" she countered. "The fact is, I've been forced to scrabble for my survival since I was a child. My father left me penniless and disgraced in Society, so it's not as if I owe his memory my blood." She shrugged. "I'm tired of fending for myself. A great deal of money would be welcome."

"What happened to your tender conscience?" said Gavin. He sounded a trifle disappointed at being deprived of his ghoulish games.

"I lied," she said coolly. "It was worth a try to bluff. I prefer to work alone. But I also believe in being pragmatic."

The answer didn't quite satisfy him. "Tell me, what were you doing with Concord?"

"Discussing business—and pleasure," replied Arianna. "I knew of him because of the connection with my father. I came to England six months ago, and as I'm not exactly welcome by the respectable members of my family, I decided to make myself known to him. He immediately saw the value of joining our talents." She gave an impatient wave. "But enough of the past. Tell me about your present plan."

"Yes," agreed Cockburn.

"And yet, Concord didn't look very amorous this evening," said Gavin slowly.

"He thought I was cheating on him in business," replied Arianna, quickly composing a lie. "I wasn't."

Like his exotic blades, Gavin's laugh had a nasty edge. "No, it was Kellton who was diddling him. They had partnered on a military contract, but it was a small deal. Kellton was going to pull out of it in several months after skimming off some of the advance money, and leave Concord in the lurch. Selling his services to us was far more profitable, and his expertise in shipping and bills of lading was useful to us in creating a model for false templates to be used on a far larger scale."

So that was the connection. Saybrook would find the information a key part to the puzzle of his own investigation, she thought.

Assuming, of course, that she lived to tell him about it.

Forcing her concentration back to the cat-and-mouse game with her captors, Arianna accepted the set of papers offered by Cockburn. "It's a moot point," she said, "seeing as Kellton had the bad luck to shuffle off his mortal coil in the middle of the deal."

"His Indian friends would call it bad *karma*." Gavin had backed off, but the scalpel was still in his hands, the sharpened steel tapping lightly against the pad of his thumb. "He panicked over a minor problem that occurred at Lady Spencer's residence, and was threatening to upset all our plans."

"Study the numbers, Lady Arianna," interjected Cockburn, who appeared eager to gloss over the topic of murder. *As if keeping his own hands lily white absolved him of any responsibility.* "Between the projected trade revenue and sale of company stock," he went on, "I assure you, our new venture will rival the East India Company."

She spread the first few pages out on the table and took a few moments to study the equations. To her grim satisfaction, it appeared that all her earlier conjectures were essentially correct.

"Profits are easy to put down on paper. But for me to work with these numbers, I need to have a clearer idea what you are actually doing." She paused, carefully choosing her next words. "Frankly, I can't conceive of any trading scheme that matches the scale of the East India Company."

"Perhaps it's because you have no imagination," answered Cockburn smugly.

She choked down a laugh.

"The Spanish colonies in the New World possess far grander riches than India," he went on. "There is Mexico, and a whole continent below it to exploit."

"Think of the ancient Aztec treasures brought back by the first Conquistadors." Gavin's eyes lit up. "Gold, silver, emeralds, spices. Not to speak of the potent coca leaf narcotic. And that's just the beginning."

"Yes, but the Spanish colonies are controlled by Spain," pointed out Arianna. "And Spain is controlled by France. Which in turn is ruled by Napoleon. Doesn't that present a slight problem for an English company?"

A smile blossomed on Cockburn's lips. "Not for us."

Gavin chuckled. *"Vivre l'emperor."*

Et voilà. With that simple French phrase, the whole puzzle fell neatly into place. Saybrook had been essentially right in his speculations. Granted, the people who made up the pieces were slightly different, but the overall picture was the same—a group of English aristocrats had conspired with the French to betray their country's interest for their own economic gain.

"Lady Spencer told me about the Prince Regent's poisoning," said Arianna slowly.

"Lady Spencer ought to confine her activities to the bedchamber. Else she is going to end up like the others," said Gavin darkly.

Arianna ignored him. "She thought it was Concord who bribed her chef. But it wasn't, was it?" The words came tumbling off her tongue as she sought to clarify one last bit of information. "It was *you* who poisoned the Prince. By throwing the government into turmoil, you hoped to ensure that the meeting of Eastern allies would fail, allowing Napoleon to conquer all of Europe and then force England to sue for peace."

"Clever girl," murmured Cockburn.

"There's just one thing that I can't quite figure out— how did Major Crandall tie in?" she asked. "Is Grentham involved in your group? If I am to be part of this, I would like to know who else is involved. It's all part of assessing the risk of a venture as well as its reward."

"Clever girl," echoed Gavin. A pause. "*Too* clever, in fact." With one hand, he slowly loosened the knot of his cravat. "Lady Spencer didn't know that Crandall was killed in her kitchen. Outside of a very select circle of Whitehall officials, only Lord Saybrook is privy to the knowledge of how the Major really died."

Arianna clenched her teeth, realizing her mistake a heartbeat too late.

"And if he shared it with you . . ."

I'm so sorry, Papa. I thought I was smarter than this.

Gavin tossed the length of linen to Cockburn. "Tie the she-bitch to the chair. I think it's time we cut through Lady Arianna's lies and extract the truth from her."

Not without a fight, you bastards, vowed Arianna.

She jerked up a knee, catching the marquess flush in the groin.

A yowl reverberated off the rocks as he dropped like a sack of stones.

Hurling herself sideways, she scrabbled to her feet from the overturned chair and darted for the dark opening of the passageway. Just a few quick steps and—

"Not so fast," snarled Gavin, snaring a handful of her hair. Pain sizzled through her scalp as he yanked her back and punched a fist to her temple.

The shadows began to spin and blur.

Still moaning, Cockburn crawled to his knees.

"Right the chair," ordered Gavin. He drew his pocket pistol from his coat and passed it over. "Use this to keep her under control."

"By God, I'll blow her brains out," gasped the marquess.

"No! Not yet," exclaimed Gavin.

Arianna felt herself shoved back against the wooden slats. Fear lanced through the fuzziness in her head. She knew she was going to die—and quite horribly. Sweat began to bead on her brow, and strangely enough, she could hear as well as feel the salty drops drip onto her lashes.

Click, click. The sound was unnaturally loud. Like metal against metal.

Clucking in impatience, Cockburn set the pistol down for a moment to finish knotting the linen looped around her chest and arms.

"First, we need to find out just how much the earl knows," finished Gavin.

A boot scuffed, sending a few pebbles skittering across the rough-hewn rocks.

"Then why don't you ask him yourself?"

Cockburn lunged for his weapon, but a blast erupted from the darkness, and an instant later a round of molten lead kicked it out of reach in an explosion of shards and sparks.

The marquess screamed and stared down in dazed

shock at the blood spurting up from the stump of a finger.

"Drop the knife, Gavin." Saybrook calmly jammed the still-smoking barrel into his pocket and took aim with his second pistol. "Blades make me very twitchy."

Gavin hesitated, and then lifted his hands in a gesture of surrender. "No need to get nervous." He moved a step closer to the table. "See, I'm just setting it down here."

"Are you hurt?" The earl's gaze flicked to Arianna . . .

In that split second, Gavin grabbed the lamp and hurled it at Saybrook's head.

The earl ducked and the glass shattered against the chalky walls, splashing hot oil and flames over his coat. A spark set off his weapon, the bullet ricocheting off the ceiling with a thunderous bang.

"Sandro!" cried Arianna, struggling to get free of her bonds. Gavin had snatched up the scalpel and hurtled a fallen chair. Plumes of silvery smoke spun through the slivers of wildly flickering light and shadow. "Watch out! He has a blade!"

The earl dodged the oncoming attack, moving with catlike quickness despite his lingering limp. A swing of the pistol butt smashed the nearest sconce as he danced away from the arcing steel.

Gavin slipped on the spattered oil, swearing a savage oath.

"Déjà vu," called Saybrook as he ducked low and pulled a knife from his boot. Patches of red-gold fire burned on his coat, painting him in a demonic glow. Sparks flared, catching the curve of his mouth.

Good God, was he actually grinning? Arianna blinked. That long-ago day of the kitchen duel he had looked like hell, while now—now he appeared a lithe, long-limbed Lucifer. An avenging dark angel.

"Watch out!" she cried again, seeing Gavin take up a jagged hunk of broken globe and fling it at the earl's face.

"Don't worry, sweeting." For an instant, a wink seemed to hang on his dark lashes, and then he whirled back with a deft sidestep, letting the missile fly harmlessly over his head. "I'll not need you to pull my cods out of the fire today."

Glass crunching under his boots, he angled away from the wall, forcing Gavin to retreat several steps. "Give it up. I'm not going to let you escape."

Sweat sheened Gavin's face and the glint in his eye reflected a rising panic. "Give it up? For what—Newgate and a date to dance the gallows jig?" The scalpel slashed through the air, a feint one way and then a quick cut that lanced to within an inch of the earl's chest. "I'll take my chances with a sodding cripple."

"It's your choice," said Saybrook, parrying the thrust. His own blade swooshed back and forth. "I daresay I'd do the same. A noose takes a long time to choke the life from a man."

With a snarled oath, Gavin suddenly pivoted and lashed out with a hard kick, desperation giving his attack added force. "The pistol, Charles, the pistol!" he screamed over his partner's mewling moans. "For God's sake, *shoot him!*"

As the earl's leg buckled, Cockburn started crawling across the floor.

Saybrook dropped to a knee, but as Gavin raised his weapon and cut an arcing downward slice, he caught the other man's wrist and gave a vicious twist.

A last frantic jerk and Arianna finally broke free of her bonds.

Too late? Too late?

The marquess was already reaching out for the weapon. . . .

Gulping for air, she dove for the table.

Struggling to break free, Gavin hammered a flurry of punches at Saybrook's face. The earl countered by smashing the hilt of his knife into Gavin's nose. Flailing and kicking, the two of them tumbled to the hard stone floor, tangled together in a bellicose blur of fists and steel.

Arianna dared not focus on their fight. Her fingers found the chamois and its bevy of lethal implements. *Thank God for the theatrical tricks and circus games needed to keep a restive pirate audience amused in her former life.* In one sweeping motion, she plucked up a slim two-edged blade, whipped around, and let it fly.

The point spun a quicksilver trail through the dancing dust motes and buried itself deep into bone and flesh.

Cockburn's hand spasmed, then went slack as he screamed and collapsed in a dead faint.

Arianna rushed to retrieve the pistol.

"Here, here, I'll take charge of that." Saybrook wiped a bloodied palm on his torn trousers. "Your hands are shaking so badly that I fear you might accidentally fire at *me*." He gently peeled away her fingers. "However unorthodox, we seem to make an effective team in fighting miscreants. Gavin is no longer a danger."

A lick of light caught the gleam of steel protruding from the dead man's throat.

She looked away. "Poetic justice, I suppose."

"Or divine retribution," said Saybrook with unholy satisfaction. "The deities do not like it when mere mortals play God."

Her lower lip was cut, and as she swallowed, the acrid taste of blood, salt, and grains of gunpowder stung her tongue.

"True," she whispered, and then was suddenly aware of another soft sound melding with her sigh. The slither of wool.

A wave of fury washed over her and for a moment she saw red—a deep, viscous bloodred.

Her kick hit flush on target, but bare toes didn't manage the desired wallop.

"Allow me." Saybrook drew back a booted foot. "Always aim for the jaw. It is a far more effective way to knock a man senseless."

Cockburn twitched as the muddy leather connected with a sickening thud, and then went very still.

Despite the swelling on her cheekbone, Arianna managed a lopsided smile. *"Gracias."*

"De nada," replied Saybrook with a soot-streaked grin. And then enfolded her in his arms.

25

From the chocolate notebooks of Dona Maria Castellano

I have mixed up a fresh pot of glue, and Luisa has wielded her scissors with great care, trimming the last batch of my recipes so that I may paste them into these pages. They shall fill the rest of this journal, for I have become quite loquacious in my old age and rambled on longer than I intended. Tomorrow, I shall start a new notebook, for there is still much I wish to record. . . .

Chocolate Chili Bread Pudding

1 tablespoon unsalted butter plus additional for
greasing ramekin
⅓ cup heavy cream
2 ounces fine-quality bittersweet chocolate (not unsweetened or extra-bitter), chopped
1½ teaspoons sugar
½ teaspoon vanilla
¼ teaspoon cinnamon
⅛ teaspoon cayenne
1 large egg, lightly beaten
¾ cup cubes (1/2 inch) firm white sandwich bread
(from about 2 slices)

1. Put oven rack in middle position and preheat oven to 350°F. Generously butter ramekin or 1 muffin cup.
2. Cook butter (1 tablespoon), cream, chocolate, sugar, vanilla, cinnamon, cayenne, and a pinch of salt in a 1- to 1½-quart heavy saucepan over low heat, stirring constantly, until chocolate is melted and mixture is smooth, 1 to 2 minutes. Remove from heat and whisk in egg until combined. Fold in bread cubes and let stand 5 minutes.
3. Fill an 8 ounce ramekin with bread mixture and bake until puffed and set around edge but still moist in center, 15 to 20 minutes. Cool 5 minutes before serving. Serves one.

The thump of approaching steps jarred her out of a dreamlike haze. She raised her cheek from Saybrook's shoulder and stepped back. "What—"

"Reinforcements," murmured the earl.

Before he could elaborate, Henning burst out of the darkened tunnel, brandishing a cavalry pistol. Behind him was a band of ragged men armed mostly with cudgels, though one or two naval cutlasses glinted in what light was left.

Skidding to a stop, the surgeon surveyed the chaos. "Hell and damnation. I promised the laddies that they would get to kick a few lordly arses, and here you have gone and spoiled all the fun."

"My profound apologies." said Saybrook dryly. "Next time I shall be more considerate of your men's tender sensibilities." He nodded at the ex-soldiers and sailors. "You can still lend a hand by carrying this corpse outside."

"What about that bilge rat?" asked one of the men, pointing to where Cockburn lay curled in the corner.

"Leave him for now," replied the earl. "Baz, perhaps you could tend to his scratches. We wouldn't want him to bleed to death before we hand him over to the authorities."

At that, Cockburn's whimpers grew louder.

The surgeon blew out a huff of disgust. "I'd rather cut off his *cojones*. But I suppose we ought to let justice take its proper course." He gave a curt wave at Gavin's lifeless form. "Haul the carcass away, laddies. And keep a close guard on things outside until we decide how te deal with this night's work."

"It was all Gavin ... he forced me ... I can explain ... ," began Cockburn.

Ignoring the appeal, Henning turned to Arianna. "What about you, lassie? Are ye hurt?"

She shook her head. "No. A few bumps is all." She chafed at her arms, feeling a chill seep through her skin now that the warmth of Saybrook's big body was gone. "And perhaps a slight headache from the Devil's Delight."

The surgeon brushed a callused fingertip to her cheek. "I've got some arnica salve in the carriage. It will keep the bruising down." To the earl he added, "I thought ye were going to keep her safe! Did ye stop fer a wee dram along the way?"

"Don't badger the earl," she murmured. "He was ..." *A storybook hero?* No, that made her sound like a sentimental schoolgirl. "He was ... quite efficient, especially considering his recent injury."

"Yes, well, we have chocolate to thank for a happy ending to this affair," quipped Saybrook. "I owe my restored strength to its potent healing properties."

Healing. For all her aches and bruises, Arianna realized that she felt remarkably free of pain.

"Help me! I'm dying." Cockburn's piteous whine interrupted their exchange.

"Ye deserve to," muttered the surgeon, reluctantly shuffling over to the marquess.

"I swear, it was all Gavin's idea," repeated Cockburn, as Henning began to tend to his injured hands.

"Indeed?" said Arianna. She imagined that Saybrook

would subject the dastard to a thorough interrogation, but first she had some questions of her own. "We've already figured out the basics of the stock scheme, and I now understand why Prinny was poisoned. But how did Major Crandall fit in? Why did he try to kill Lady Spencer's chef?"

"C-Crandall was my cousin." Cockburn groaned as Henning staunched the bleeding with strips of linen torn from Gavin's cravat. "He was recruited to keep us informed about state security activities."

"So it was he who told you about the upcoming secret meeting of allies?" asked the earl.

"Yes," answered Cockburn. "The timing seemed perfect, and he was supposed to ensure that the chef was blamed for the Prince's demise. But when you were called in to investigate, it was decided to eliminate the chef. You see, Gavin worried that the cursed fellow had spotted him sneaking into the kitchen."

Arianna thought back to the night, and the other shadowy figure she had seen with Concord in the corridor. "So Concord knew nothing about the poisoned chocolate?"

"No, nothing at all. We— That is, Gavin made up an excuse concerning the Devil's Delight narcotic in order to arrange for a clandestine meeting at Lady Spencer's town house. He claimed it was urgent business, but he didn't want Lady Spencer to know of the partnership, lest she demand a cut." Cockburn drew a deep breath. "As we told you, Concord was unaware of our plans for a New World trading company. He only became suspicious when Kellton panicked over Crandall's death and ended up revealing more about the scope of the business than he should have."

How ironic, thought Arianna. Once again, the echo of her father's laugh began to whisper in her head, along with the lines of his favorite poem. *The best laid plans of mice and men . . .*

"And Lady Spencer had no idea about any of this, either?" she asked.

"No. She was only involved with Concord and Kellton on a minor deal to supply cheap boots to the army at premium price. Her role was to persuade the Prince to award them the contract."

Saybrook shifted his stance, throwing his face deeper into shadow. "Kellton was brought in because of his experience with the East India Company, correct?"

"He was very clever with numbers and had a great deal of experience with drafting shipping records," confirmed Cockburn. "But more than that, his amorous relationship with Lady Spencer allowed him to gain access to certain important financial papers. Her grandfather was—"

"We know who he was," interrupted Arianna. "Just as we know his papers were key in helping you create your new company's calculations."

"How—," began Cockburn.

"Never mind that," said Saybrook brusquely. "I want to know more about Crandall. He was Grentham's lackey, so does that mean that the minister is one of your conspirators?"

"God, no. If Grentham has a weakness, it is not money." Cockburn grimaced. "Nor anything else that I could discern. I was delegated to judge whether he might be tempted to join our group, but in the end, I advised that it was too dangerous to try."

"So it was you, from your position in the Foreign Ministry, who made contact with the French?" pressed the earl.

"N-nobody in Europe is going to stop Napoleon," responded Cockburn evasively. "His new army is going to thrash the Eastern opposition. So it was in our country's best interest to engineer an end to this interminable conflict and sue for peace." His voice grew more wheedling. "Think of all the lives that would be saved."

"And what of my father?" asked Arianna softly. "Why did you and Gavin decide that he should die?

Cockburn wet his lips. "I swear, it wasn't my decision. I was quite fond of Richard—really I was. But he cost us a great deal of money by refusing a reasonable fee to handle the mathematics for a very lucrative deal with a Baltic supplier of naval supplies."

Her father's blood, calculated in buckets of pine tar and spruce spars.

"And then, he threatened to expose the arrangement. So, well . . ." Cockburn gave a beseeching lift of his shoulders. "I was an ocean away! Had I been there, I would have tried to use reason. But as you saw, Lady Arianna, Gavin could turn violent when crossed. If only Richard hadn't pushed him."

If only. Arianna couldn't find her voice. She looked away, only to catch a fleeting glance of Saybrook's lidded gaze darkening to the color of coal.

"Getting back to the present crimes, you must have a French contact here in London. Who is he—or she?" demanded Saybrook, darting a sidelong glance at her. "For I've learned not to underestimate the female intellect."

"I—I don't know, I swear! Gavin arranged it all. I only know his code name. *R-renard.*"

The fox.

"How very crafty of you," murmured Arianna. "Did you think a plea of ignorance would excuse your treason?"

"Gavin was just a lowly baronet, and had become obsessed with acquiring wealth and power above his station—he went too far! I couldn't stop him." Cockburn was babbling now, and appealing to the earl with a wave of his newly bandaged hands. "Surely you see that, Saybrook. He wasn't a true gentleman, not like us. God help me but I was as much a victim as anyone. I agreed to skim a few profits, not be party to murder. Once it began, I had no choice but to go along with his plans. You'll help me explain it all to the authorities, because . . . because . . ."

"Because of the bonds of blue blood?" suggested the earl. "The fraternity of titled families whose heritage stretches back centuries?"

"Yes. Precisely." Expelling a sigh of relief, Cockburn flashed a sweaty smile. "I knew you would understand."

"Ah, but you forget that I am a mongrel." Saybrook grimaced in disgust. "And you—you are a contemptible cur."

Cockburn's jaw went slack.

"Take him away, Baz. Before I succumb to the urge to kick his bloody teeth out through his arse."

The echo of the receding steps seemed to distort in the heavy air, for to Arianna, the thuds suddenly sounded like soft claps that were coming closer and closer.

"Bravo, Lord Saybrook." Grentham emerged from the gloom, his leather-clad hands coming together in mock applause. "Bravo. A most entertaining performance. Normally, I dislike it intensely when a crisis demands that I leave the comforts of my office and take charge of an actual mission. But I wouldn't have missed this one for the world."

Saybrook swung around with a scowl. "How edifying to know that I provided you with such amusement. Would you have enjoyed an extra laugh had the lady's throat been cut?"

"It was imperative to have Cockburn confess to his crimes," replied the minister. "By the by, you did an excellent job of drawing the details out of him. As I said, I much prefer to let my underlings mop up the muck, so it saved me a great deal of bother."

"Be grateful that I don't ram those supercilious words right back down you gullet," growled Saybrook. "You, too, have some explaining to do."

"Do I?" Grentham arched an imperious brow. "Actually, I don't answer to anyone. The Prime Minister has entrusted me with state security and doesn't much care how I get the job done."

"Officially speaking, you may be right." Saybrook flexed his bloody hands. "But at the moment I'm not in the mood for word games, Grentham. Why did you draw me into this mess?"

For a moment, it appeared to Arianna as if the minister wouldn't answer. Then, with a slight shrug, he said, "I suspected Crandall was spying on me, but hadn't yet figured out why. I needed someone outside my department to put pressure on him and his fellow conspirators. I had overheard your uncle mentioning your interest in chocolate. I knew of your war record, of course, and your intelligence work with Wellington's staff. So, seeing as chocolate was the agent used for the poisoning, I took a chance on bringing you in."

"Figuring you had nothing to lose," said the earl. "Whether I made a mull of it, or got myself killed, it didn't really matter."

"I did all I could to aid your investigations."

"Right—the dossier on Kellton." Saybrook frowned. "How long did you know about Lady Arianna?"

"That was, I confess, an unexpected twist. . . ."

Arianna felt his cold gaze flick to her.

"Not that it really matters who she is," added Grentham.

"Goddamn you," growled Saybrook. "If anything had happened—"

"Tut, tut, surely there wasn't any real danger. After all, you assured me on several occasions that you were quite capable of defending yourself." Grentham shot another faintly contemptuous look at Arianna. "And the females who are under your protection." The acrid air quivered with a deliberately drawn-out pause. "You seem quite fond of surrounding yourself with less than respectable ones."

A crystalline crackle broke the silence as Saybrook took several quick strides over the broken glass, bringing him nearly nose to nose with the minister. "Excuse us for a moment, Lady Arianna, while Lord Grentham and I step outside for a word in private."

After a slight hesitation, the minister followed him into the tunnel.

"Well?" drawled Grentham, his breath forming a pale puff of vapor against the netherworld shadows.

In answer, the earl seized him by the lapels and slammed him up against the rock wall. Chalk dust blossomed from the fissures, coating Grentham's well-tailored shoulders with a sprinkling of grit.

"Having done your dirty work for you, I'm anxious to go home and wash my hands of Whitehall and its sordid games. But before I do, let us get a few things straight. First of all, leave my family alone. Or do you wish to have your own peccadilloes made public?"

Grentham's nostrils flared. "Don't try to taunt me with vague threats, Saybrook. You heard Cockburn—I had no involvement in his filthy scheme."

"Perhaps not, but you, of all people, nursed a traitorous viper—several, in fact—at the very bosom of the government's highest ministries. At best, you will look like a bloody fool. At worst . . . well, I shall leave it to the newspapers to debate the possibilities. There is, after all, still the matter of an unknown French operative loose in London."

The earl's words wiped the last trace of smugness from Grentham's face.

"Second, I will not have Lady Arianna suffer for finding herself caught in this intrigue. Is that understood?"

"Let a murderer go free? Tsk, tsk, where is your noble sense of justice now?" Seeing Saybrook's jaw tighten, the minister added, "Oh, yes, I've figured that one out. Henning is a clever surgeon, but so is the fellow I employ for certain tasks."

"She has paid more than enough for her father's sins. If now she wishes to take her rightful place in Society, you will do nothing to stir up trouble for her."

"Trouble? Lady Arianna has created her own trouble." A note of malice had crept back into the minister's voice. "Even if I were to agree to your demands, she can hardly appear in London, claiming to be Richard Hadley's daughter. Not after parading around Mayfair these last few weeks as the Widow Wolcott."

The earl remained grimly silent.

"And be assured that no explanation of this affair will

ever be made public. It will be reported that Gavin perished in a carriage accident, fleeing after killing Concord in a drunken fight over gambling debts." The minister dusted a speck of chalk from his lapel. "And alas, Cockburn will suffer a hunting accident at his country house. A faulty cartridge, I believe. Yes, yes, it will explode his new rifle, taking off his hands and head."

"Plausible explanations," agreed the earl. "Assuming I agree to stay quiet. But if I don't . . ." Despite the murky spill of smoke and shadows, his low murmur carried clearly. "The blood in my veins may be less than blue, *amigo*, but I'm still the Earl of Saybrook."

It was Grentham's turn to remain mute.

"So, it seems to me that despite our personal antipathy, it's of mutual benefit to cooperate. In return for my silence, you will leave Lady Arianna alone."

"I am not in the habit of leaving stray pieces around that may come back to embarrass the government," answered Grentham slowly. "Or worse."

"Nonetheless, in this case you will allow me to arrange things as I see fit. You have my word that neither the government nor your own precious reputation for efficiency will suffer any consequences." Saybrook allowed a small pause. "Do we have a deal?"

"For now." Grentham took a candle from his pocket and struck a flint to the wick. "But be advised, I expect you to make this complication go away. Quickly."

The earl nodded grimly. "I'll take care of it."

"You had better, Lord Saybrook." The flame burned bright in the still air, a hot spot of color in the darkness. "For I shall be watching you very carefully from now on. And waiting for you to make a slip."

Closing her eyes, Arianna slumped back against the leather seat of the earl's carriage, undecided if the feeling pulsing through her body was exhaustion or elation. Henning had forced her to drink a bit of brandy, and in truth, the heat of the spirits was pleasantly pooled in her belly, and radiating out to her limbs. . . .

Or perhaps the warmth was coming from Saybrook. He had drawn close, and her head was tipped onto his shoulder.

"Feeling better?" he asked quietly.

"Mmmm. Yes. Thanks to you." She shifted. "How did you know where I had gone?"

"Lady Spencer," he answered. "I also stopped to have a chat with Ashmun, to make sure he was telling us the truth. And when it came out that Gavin was one of the most dangerous of your father's friends, I feared you might be in more trouble tonight than you bargained for."

"But Ashmun never mentioned Gavin in our meeting!" she exclaimed.

"You never gave him a chance." Saybrook let out a wry sigh. "If you recall, you cut him off when he began his warning, so he assumed you knew about Gavin, as well as Cockburn."

At the reminder of her impatience, and how many mistakes she had made, Arianna winced. "Lord, what a bloody fool I've been. You were right about Concord. If I hadn't been so blinded by my own assumptions, I might have listened to you . . . I might have remembered that Father had been friends with Cockburn. It only came back to me tonight."

"Don't be so hard on yourself," murmured Saybrook. "It is easy to look at others with a dispassionate eye. You saw me submerged in self-pity, and if you hadn't so kindly pointed out my faults, we never would have triumphed over these devils."

"Kindly?" A laugh slipped from her lips. "I'm surprised you didn't murder me on the spot."

"And lose your chocolate knowledge?" He tucked the carriage blanket over her lap. "Perish the thought."

She settled a little closer to him, savoring the woolly softness of his coat against her cheek. But a sudden lurch of the wheels jarred her from such momentary reveries. "You know, I feel guilty that Mr. Henning and his men must wait in the cold for another conveyance. They could have squeezed in—"

"Don't worry about Baz. He is extremely resourceful," said the earl. "With any luck, he and his ruffians will hijack Grentham's barouche. And then deposit it in the foulest stretch of the river once they reach London."

"You don't like Grentham."

"No," he answered tersely. "I don't."

It seemed a very visceral reaction, and Arianna wondered why. "Is there a reason?"

Ignoring the question, he shifted against the tufted leather. "Speaking of resourceful, Lady Arianna, we must decide on a strategy for the future, and quickly. The government will never admit to what really happened. The scandal would have dangerous repercussions both at home and abroad."

She straightened slightly.

"So that leaves you somewhere in Purgatory. Grentham has agreed not to arrest you for Crandall's demise. But he is also adamant that you cannot reappear in Society as Lady Arianna Hadley. It would provoke too many awkward questions."

And so I must leave England once again.

Arianna gave a halfhearted shrug. "I am used to being an exile."

"That is not fair," he growled.

"Life is often unfair." She watched a curl of smoke twist within the brass-framed glass of the carriage light. "Grentham is right. There really isn't any alternative."

"Actually, there is."

She suddenly felt very, very sleepy, and uninterested in talking about the future. "What?" she murmured, patting back a yawn.

Saybrook hesitated.

"I hope you aren't going to suggest that we do away with the minister. I've had quite enough shocks for one night."

"Have you?" The earl's voice had an oddly wry note to it. "Try to endure one more."

Arianna sat up a little straighter. He now had her full attention.

"What I propose is . . . marriage."

"Marriage," she repeated faintly, unsure if she had heard him correctly.

"It is an eminently practical solution," he went on. "A new name solves the conundrum of your past. I wed the wealthy widow and the tangle of your previous identities no longer matters. Richard Hadley's daughter disappeared long ago. Her existence is all but forgotten."

"You are not honor-bound to sacrifice your future for me, sir," said Arianna. "There are ballrooms full of rich, mannered young ladies who would eagerly accept the invitation to become the Countess of Saybrook."

"Perhaps, but as you have so kindly pointed out to me, they tend to be bland and boring. I find that's not to my taste." His gaze met hers. "You cannot deny that we have much in common. We are both outcasts of a sort. Unconventional individuals who share similar interests."

Damn the dark fringe of lashes, thought Arianna. The shadows hid his eyes.

"There is no reason why it can't work," he finished.

Unlike mathematics, emotions didn't always add up quite so neatly.

"I . . ."

"You don't have to answer right now," he said. "Think it over for the night."

"I . . . I shall."

A smile teased at the corners of his mouth. "Do keep in mind Dona Maria's diaries. They hold a promise that a future together could be sweet."

Arianna imagined the taste of fire-warmed butter and sugar melting with swirls of dark chocolate. Revenge had left naught but a bitter taste in her mouth.

Sweet.

The offer was awfully tempting. . . .

AUTHOR'S NOTE

Derivatives, debt-equity swaps, margin calls, stock crashes—our modern-day financial swindles and booms are nothing new. Both the South Sea Bubble and the Mississippi Bubble mentioned in *Sweet Revenge* are actual historical events that took place in the early part of the eighteenth century, and had grave economic repercussions for both England and France. I won't try to sum up the complex details here—for those of you interested in learning more, there are a number of excellent books on the subject, including *A Very English Deceit: The Secret History of the South Sea Bubble and the First Great Financial Scandal* by Malcolm Balen and *The First Crash: Lessons from the South Sea Bubble* by Richard Dale.

Though modeled on the original South Sea Company, my own New World Trading Company is pure fiction. But given current events in 1813, it could, with a bit of imagination, have been plausible. Despite his retreat from Russia during the previous winter, Napoleon still controlled most of Europe, including Spain. But under the leadership of Wellington, the British forces were making headway in the Peninsula, further threatening his aura of invincibility. As the Emperor rebuilt his army, and looked once again to conquer any opposition in Eastern Europe, he might well have granted trade concessions to anyone who could throw England—the lynchpin to a new alliance against him—into chaos. After all, he was notorious for passing out kingdoms and princely riches to his family and friends in reward for service to France.

And lastly, a morsel of history about chocolate! Some may take issue with seeing edible chocolate mentioned at this time in history. However, my research has turned up proof that chocolate was indeed served up in solid form. Sulpice Debauve, pharmacist to King Louis XVI, opened a chocolate shop on the Left Bank of Paris in 1800. By 1804, he had over sixty shops throughout France. Debauve & Gallais Chocolates still exists today, and though its bonbons are sinfully expensive, they are sinfully good. (Ah, the hardships of research!) You may visit their Web site at www.debauveandgallais.com.

I hope you have enjoyed the history behind *Sweet Revenge*. For more fun facts and arcane trivia, please visit my Web site at www.andreapenrose.com. I love to hear from my readers and can be contacted at andrea@andreapenrose.com.

Read on for a sneak peek of the next
Lady Arianna Regency Mystery
by Andrea Penrose
Coming from Obsidian in December 2011.

The book's binding was crafted out of dark fine-grained calfskin, its richly tooled embossings age-mellowed to the color of . . .

"Chocolate," murmured Arianna Hadley. Removing her gloves, which were still sticky from foraging through the food stalls at Covent Garden, she traced the delicate leaf design centered beneath the gilded title. "How lovely," she added, and then carefully opened the cover.

Dust motes danced up into the air, tiny sparkles of sunlight in the shadowed corner of the alcove. As she shifted a step closer to the diamond-paned window, the scrape of her sturdy half-boots on the Aubusson carpet momentarily disturbed the hush that hung over the ornate bookcases.

Her heel snagged, and to her dismay, she realized that a streak of mud—and something that looked suspiciously like squashed pumpkin—now marred the carpet's stately pattern.

Hell and damnation.

Arianna gave a guilty glance around, but the room appeared deserted. The only stirring was a small flutter of breeze wafting in through the casement. It teased over the polished oak, mingling the scents of beeswax, ink, paper and leather.

The smell of money.

A wry smile twitched on her lips as she turned her attention back to the book. Set discreetly within the marbled endpapers was a small slip of paper that noted the price. It was expensive—*very expensive*—as were every volume and manuscript offered for sale by Mssrs. Harvey & Watkins Rare Book Emporium.

But then, Arianna could now afford such luxuries.

She slowly turned the pages, savoring the feel of the creamy deckle-edged paper and the subtle colors of the illustrations. With her new husband's birthday fast approaching, she was looking for a special gift. And the intricate engravings of *Theobroma cacao* were, to her eye, exquisite.

"Chocolate," repeated Arianna, pausing to study the details of a *criolla* tree and its fruit. Her husband was, among other things, a serious scholar of botany, and *cacao*—or chocolate—was his particular field of expertise. The text was Spanish, and the date looked to be—

A sudden nudge from behind nearly knocked the book from her grasp.

"I beg your pardon." The deep voice was edged with a foreign accent.

Arianna turned, about to acknowledge the apology with a polite smile, when the man gave her another little shove.

"I beg your pardon, but that book is *mine*," he growled. "Hand it over at once."

Sliding back a step, she instinctively threw up a forearm to parry his grab. "I'm afraid you are mistaken, sir. It was lying on the display table, free for anyone to choose."

"I assure you, there is no mistake," he replied. "I must have it."

Turn over her treasure to a lout who thought to frighten her with physical force? Her pulse kicked up a notch, its hot surge thrumming angrily in her ears.

"Sorry but I saw it first."

Her husband had jestingly warned her that serious book collectors were an odd, obsessive lot, and this one in particular sounded slightly deranged. *Or demented.* But be that as it might, Arianna was not about to be intimidated by his bullying tactics.

"You will have to look around for something else, for I intend to purchase it," she added, and not just for spite—she had already decided that the engravings were the perfect present for her husband.

"You can't!" he exclaimed in a taut whisper.

Oh, but I can.

Closing the covers, Arianna drew the book close to her chest.

As the man edged closer, a blade of light cut across his pale face. Sweat was beaded on his forehead, and several drops hung on his russet lashes. "I tell you, that book is meant for *me*."

"Then you should have asked the clerk to put it aside." She gestured at the other volumes arrayed on the square of dark velvet. "Come, there is no need to squabble like savages. You have plenty of other lovely choices."

He snarled an obscenity.

"Be advised, sir, I know plenty of words worse than that," responded Arianna with a grim smile, and she added a very unladylike curse to prove it.

His eyes widened for an instant, then narrowed to a slitted stare. "Give me that book," he repeated. "Or you will be sorry."

His strike was quick—but not quick enough.

Her reactions honed by half a lifetime of fighting off drunks and pimps, Arianna caught his wrist and pivoted, twisting hard enough to draw a grunt of pain. "I wouldn't wager on that."

"Poxy slut." Breaking away, the man clenched a fist and threw a wild punch at her head.

She ducked under the blow and countered with a kick that buckled his knee. "True—if I were a real lady, I would be falling into a dead swoon." Her jab clipped him flush on the chin. "But as you see, I'm not. Not a lady, that is."

Staggered, the man fell against the display table, knocking several books to the floor. His curses were now coming in a language she didn't recognize, but the edge of panic was unmistakable.

What madness possessed him? It was only a book, albeit a lovely one.

Arianna glanced at the archway, intent on making a strategic retreat. The last thing she wanted to do was to ruffle the rarefied feathers of Mssrs. Harvey & Watkins by brawling among their rare books. Such a scene would only embarrass her husband, who, ye Gods, had suffered enough gossip on her account. . . .

Bloody hell. A glint of steel drew her eye back to her assailant.

His fumblings inside his coat revealed not only a book hidden in the waistband of his trousers but a slim-bladed knife.

"Try to use that on me, and you'll find your cods cut off," she warned softly.

He blinked, looking torn between anger and fear.

The sliver of silence was broken by the sound of hurried steps in the adjoining room. "Is someone in need of assistance?" called a shop clerk loudly.

Her assailant hesitated for an instant, then whirled and darted for the archway, bumping into the other man as they crossed paths.

Smoothing the wrinkles from his sleeve, the clerk frowned at Arianna. "This is *not* a place for assignations, Miss," he chided, looking down his long nose at her chipped straw bonnet and drab serge gown. As his gaze slid to the fallen books, he added a sharp sniff. "I must ask you to leave—immediately. We cater to a very dignified clientele, who expect an atmosphere of decorum when they visit us."

Ah, no good deed goes unpunished, thought Arianna sardonically. On her way home from the rough-and-tumble markets, she had stopped her carriage on impulse to browse through the fancy books. Better to have waited until she had swathed herself in silk and satin for the requisite morning calls in Mayfair.

"First of all, it is *Missus*," she corrected. "And second, I am quite aware of what sort of patrons frequent your shop."

The clerk winced at the word "shop."

"However, you might want to take a closer look at the so-called Quality you allow through your door," went on Arianna, assuming an air of icy hauteur. "That man was certainly no gentleman. He had a knife, and was probably cutting prints out of your precious volumes." Her husband had explained how some unscrupulous collectors sliced up rare books for the maps or prints, which were sold individually to art dealers for a much higher profit.

The clerk's look of disdain now pinched into one of horror.

"He also stole a book," she added. "I saw it hidden under his coat."

"B-but he has made several purchases recently, all properly paid for," protested the clerk. *Another glance, another sniff.* "You must be mistaken. By all appearances, he is a perfect gentleman, no matter that he is a foreigner."

"Well, he's not," shot back Arianna. "You may take my word for it."

His mouth thinned. "And who, might I ask, are *you*?"

"The Countess of Saybrook." Arianna held out the chocolate book. "Now, before you toss me out on my arse, kindly wrap that and write up a receipt. And do make it quick. My carriage is waiting, and the earl does not like for his prime cattle to take a chill."